Mike & Mary

Happy

Christmas

1987

Ninette de Valois

Ninette de Valois

■ IDEALIST WITHOUT ILLUSIONS ■

by

KATHRINE SORLEY WALKER

with contributions by

DAME NINETTE

Hamish Hamilton · London

Frontispiece: Ninette de Valois as the Tight Rope Walker in Douanes *(Vic-Wells Ballet 1935)*

HAMISH HAMILTON LTD

Penguin Books Ltd, 27 Wrights Lane, London W8 5TZ (Publishing & Editorial)
and Harmondsworth, Middlesex, England (Distribution & Warehouse)
Viking Penguin Inc., 40 West 23rd Street, New York, New York 10010, U.S.A.
Penguin Books Australia Ltd, Ringwood, Victoria, Australia
Penguin Books Canada Limited, 2801 John Street, Markham, Ontario,
Canada L3R 1B4
Penguin Books (N.Z.) Ltd, 182–190 Wairau Road, Auckland 10, New Zealand

First published in Great Britain 1987 by
Hamish Hamilton Ltd

British Library Cataloguing-in-Publication Data:
Walker, Kathrine Sorley
Ninette de Valois: an idealist without illusions.
1. De Valois, *Dame* Ninette   2. Dancers—
Biography
I. Title
792.8'092'4   GV1785.D4
ISBN 0-241-12386-0

Typeset in 11/13pt Sabon by Butler & Tanner
Printed and bound in Great Britain
by Butler & Tanner, Frome and London

Contents

Epilogue by Ninette de Valois

Acknowledgments

In preparing this book I have been helped by a great many people associated with Dame Ninette de Valois at various stages of her career. I wish it had been possible to talk to far more of them at length—everyone would have had a different contribution to make, a personal angle, an illuminating opinion. As it is I had to select a cross-section who could represent areas of her activity.

Those who have given me very substantial assistance are listed below, as well as organisations who have helped (through individuals). I would however especially like to thank Joan Lawson and Joy Newton who have been constantly available for consultation, and Gordon Anthony who went to great trouble to provide me with information and encouragement.

Special thanks also to Martin Lewis, for lending me his unpublished manuscript "The Chess behind Checkmate"; to Sarah C. Woodcock, for continued help over factual detail and pictures and for generously making available her own researches into the Diaghilev Ballet repertoire; to Janet Rowson Davis, for providing information from her own researches into televised ballet; to Beth Genne, who shared items of information from her parallel researches into de Valois' early dancing days; to George Dorris and Jack Anderson, who encouraged my initial research into de Valois' work at the Festival Theatre, Cambridge and the Abbey Theatre, Dublin for two articles in their journal, *Dance Chronicle* (New York) (Vol. 7 No. 4 and Vol. 8 Nos. 1 & 2); to Lorraine Abraham for designing the book with such imagination and skill, and to Craig Dodd for his handsome bookjacket.

I cannot thank Dame Ninette herself sufficiently for her time, patience, advice and support throughout the whole period of preparation.

People associated with de Valois in various capacities, in alphabetical order:

Beatrice Appleyard; Sir Frederick Ashton, OM, CH, CBE; Freda Bamford; Jean Bedells; Jonathan Burrows; Nesta Brooking; William Chappell; Kathleen Dillon; Richard Glasstone; Jill Gregory; the late Sir Robert Helpmann, CBE; the late Stanley Judson; Travis Kemp; Leo Kersley; the late Molly Lake; Sheila McCarthy; Dame Alicia Markova, DBE; Angus Morrison; Sara Payne; Ailne Phillips; Margaret Rawlings.

Other individuals who helped by introductions, lending material or giving advice were Jane Astafieva, Michael Bayston, Mary Clarke, David Drummond, Mrs Elsie Duncan-Jones, Philip Dyer, Margaret Gajewski, Dr Margaret Grimshaw, Alun Llewellyn, Sue Merrett, Sheridan Morley, Geraldine Morris, Janet Sinclair.

Organisations who helped were:

> The Cambridgeshire Collection (including access to a thesis by Bridget Joyce Utting on the Festival Theatre)
> The Theatre Museum, Victoria and Albert Museum, London
> The Archives of the Royal Academy of Dancing
> The Archives of Ballet Rambert
> The Archives of London Festival Ballet
> The Archives of the Royal Ballet School
> The Archives of the Vic-Wells Association
> The Dancing Times
> The Dance Collection, New York
> The Abbey Theatre, Dublin (The National Theatre Society)
> The Arts Theatre of Cambridge (especially Judy Messel who showed me round the Festival Theatre)
> The Royal Opera House, Covent Garden
> The Royal Society of Arts
> The British Council
> York University (Ontario) Dance Department
> The British Music-Hall Society
> The Newspaper Library, Colindale
> Westminster Library Archives Section
> Chelsea Library Archives Section
> Toronto Metropolitan Library
> Eastbourne Central Library

Portsmouth Central Library
Anglia Television Photographic Library
The Daily Telegraph Library
The London Ballet Circle
The Irish National Ballet
The National Portrait Gallery Photographic Department
The Times Photograph Library
The Illustrated London News Photograph Library
The City University newspaper files

The publishers and the authors wish to thank the photographers and organisations whose pictures appear in this book. They are listed by page number.

Frontispiece   *Gordon Anthony/Theatre Museum*
p. 2   *The Dancing Times*
p. 5   *The Dancing Times*
p. 7   *The Dancing Times*
p. 12   *The Dancing Times*
p. 15   *Hana/The Dancing Times*
p. 17   *The Sketch*
p. 18   *Bassano/National Portrait Gallery*
p. 21   *Theatre Museum*
p. 23   *Bassano/National Portrait Gallery*
p. 24   *Theatre Museum*
p. 28   *The Times*
p. 29   *Theatre Museum*
p. 31   *Hana/The Dancing Times*
p. 35   *The Royal Ballet School*
p. 39   *The Ball Room/Theatre Museum*
p. 42   *Sasha/Theatre Museum*
p. 43   *The Dancing Times*
p. 62   *The Dancing Times*
p. 67   *The Sketch/Theatre Museum*
p. 68   *The Sketch/Theatre Museum*
p. 72   *Cambridgeshire Collection. Cambridgeshire Libraries*
p. 76   *Scott and Wilkinson/Anglia Television*
p. 79   *Vaughan and Freeman/The Dancing Times*
p. 83   *Hana/The Dancing Times*
p. 89   *The Bystander/Theatre Museum*
p. 94   *Graphic Studios Dublin/The Dancing Times*
p. 103 *Sasha/Radio Times Hulton*
p. 105 *Radio Times Hulton*
p. 111 (top left) *J.W. Debenham/Theatre Museum*; *Arapoff/Theatre Museum*;
        (bottom left) (above) *Gordon Anthony/Theatre Museum*

Chapter I

"I remember I used to sit with the mask in my hands, and study it, put it on in front of the glass and find a flow of movement which didn't illustrate anything about me, but illustrated that mask—which again was illustrating the poet's words—which again was connecting a very special form of musical accompaniment—which again was touching on the very purified, simplified, abstract form of production. Now, can you imagine anything further in mood from that than *Coppélia*, which is the sort of thing I had been reared on and had to do? And this made me understand, this marvellous connection. I often used to think, oh, how sad it is that we don't realise, we don't bring all this side of theatre to the ballet ... "[1]

This is Ninette de Valois, talking to the Department of Dance at York University in Toronto in 1976, looking back to the time when she was at the Abbey Theatre in Dublin working with W. B. Yeats on his *Plays for Dancers*. It crystallises her entire attitude to the relationship between dancers and choreographers and the world of the theatre. For her they are integrated. Ballet and dance belong to the stage as do drama and opera; equally, they all belong to each other, separate facets of one diamond, complementary arts uniting in different ways to create living theatre, defined according to whichever element is dominant as drama, opera or ballet. From the beginning of her life she has recognised the interlocking nature of the performing arts, working, as dancer, choreographer, teacher, artistic director, writer and lecturer, to ensure that they continue to come together, to understand and appreciate each other, for the good of the theatre as a whole.

More than many artists of the ballet, de Valois' career has stretched across the whole spectrum of stage production. When the Vic-Wells

Jack and the Beanstalk *1914: NdV with Robert Roberty*

Ballet came into being, modestly, in 1931 she brought it a dowry of great value—experience of the complete range of work open to a performer at the time: ballet, plays, opera, music-hall, revue, musical comedy and pantomime. Young, gifted, energetic and purposeful, her world was the theatre, not merely the ballet.

Pantomime was her earliest major challenge. On Christmas Eve 1914, four months after the outbreak of World War I, an audience in London packed the Lyceum Theatre for the first night of another splendid example of that very special English tradition. The Lyceum panto-mimes, begun in 1910 by the owners of the house, Walter and Frederick Melville, were only rivalled in popularity by those at Drury Lane. The children and their parents, stepping down from carriages outside the portico and making their way into the welcoming gold and red plush auditorium, knew what to expect: a handsome principal boy with a good pair of legs, a pretty principal girl, a comic Simple Simon, a menacing Demon Mischief. They knew there would be a harlequinade with Clown and Pantaloon, and a magical transformation scene bring-ing all the stage machinery into play. They also knew, and for most of the little girls in frilled or accordion pleated silk frocks and satin hair ribbons it was their greatest delight, that before the interval there would be a Grand Fairyland Ballet.

In 1914 the *première danseuse* they gazed at, enraptured and envious, was a spirited 16-year-old with thick dark hair tumbling onto her shoulders. It was Ninette de Valois' debut in the adult world of London's West End, her first experience as part of a large professional company of seasoned artists in a complicated production.

She had auditioned successfully for the job in the late autumn. Rehearsals began three weeks before the opening, when everyone connected with the staging of the show dexterously took up familiar routines to assemble costumes and scenery, wigs and props, and the performers, from stars to the line-up of luscious ladies in the *corps de ballet*, applied themselves to the demands of *Jack and the Beanstalk*.

Speech in rhyming couplets, popular songs and custard-pie comedy all built up during the first half of the show to the richly detailed, imaginatively lit transformation scene, when a succession of gauzes gradually lifted to reveal enchanted worlds. In 1914 it was *The Clouds of Dreamland*, with a vision of the fabulous Hen with the Golden Egg and the magic harp which Jack would play to lull the giant into

3

sleep. Then dancing of various kinds took over. A golden-wigged and gorgeously dressed crowd of young women executed rather monotonous manoeuvres in high-heeled shoes, a beautiful backing for those with greater skills. There was a "speciality" number by the Lottie Stone Troupe and then scene and audience were ready for de Valois and Robert Roberty. "The end of the scene always found one standing in a golden chariot, or reposing on a cloud, or lying in a seashell"[2] and this time, as the tableau was programmed as "Sunrise", it was probably the cloud... ·

Mlle Rosa, who arranged the dances, had been in charge of the ballets for about five years. She herself had danced at the Alhambra Theatre and in pantomime, when she was a bewitching Columbine in a pair of tiny unblocked white satin French ballet shoes. In her day

> "we really did dance on the pointe; nowadays, with the help of *that* [a modern blocked shoe] anyone could shuffle on the toes. But how big and ugly it makes your feet!"[3]

De Valois was already known as a dancer. She had appeared with Lila Field's company, The Wonder Children. Her partner at the Lyceum, Roberty, was older and more celebrated. A Belgian in his early twenties, he had been dancing on the Continent since the age of five. The Sitter Out in *The Dancing Times* found him "hard to place".

> "He has so specialised in the pirouette—they call him in Paris 'the human top'—that he is almost a trick dancer. Though in serious ballet he would probably be found wanting, in pantomime or music hall turns no more attractive artist could be found."[4]

Roberty had appeared at the Folies-bergère, the Folies Marini, the Paris Opéra Comique and at Covent Garden in Raymond Roze's opera *Joan of Arc*. De Valois had seen him from the audience, spinning rapidly and accurately down a diagonal ramp at the Holborn Empire, a short, slight dancer with longish wavy hair and bare feet, a dancer whose stage presence was electric.

Twice daily performances of *Jack and the Beanstalk* continued for about ten weeks, always packed. Pantomime had its aficionados just as ballet has, people who saw it a number of times during a run and who went assiduously every year. De Valois quickly achieved a fan mail of letters and gifts, some treasured for ever. None of it turned her eminently well-balanced head, none of it inflated her sense of self-importance.

4

NdV, Doris Murray and group in The Children's Dream *(Lila Field's Wonder Children 1913)*

*   *   *

Edris Stannus—Ninette de Valois was a stage name decided on by her mother because of an historic family link with the French royal house—was Irish, born in the house of Baltiboys near Blessington, Co. Wicklow, on June 6 1898 and resident there for seven formative years. From then she grew up in England, at Walmer on the Kent coast. Her father was a lieutenant-colonel who achieved a DSO and death in 1916. Her mother, good-looking and clever, was before her marriage Lilith Graydon-Smith. She became a well-known collector of Waterford glass and a glassmaker herself—she is listed as contributing table glassware to the Queen's Dolls' House. Edris had an older sister, Thelma, and two younger brothers, Trevor and Gordon—better known as Gordon Anthony the photographer. She was always theatrically minded and in Walmer created marionette plays for her own home-made miniature stage, using cardboard cutouts operated by strings through their heads.

Family and childhood have been vividly recalled by de Valois herself in autobiographical writings, so we can move on rapidly to the beginning of 1913, when she led Lila Field's Wonder Children in *The Children's Dream* at the Kilburn Empire in London. She was fourteen. Her face and figure had a certain puppy plumpness but her beautiful expressive eyes and her liveliness and grace in movement marked her out as an extremely hopeful talent. The Sitter Out felt that "she gave promise of great things".[5] A month or two later he added a rider: "Now she is busy captivating the provinces."[6]

Eastbourne was one of the provincial towns to be captivated. In 1914 a reviewer there wrote:

> "In Ninette de Valois the company has a *première danseuse* of exceptional capabilities, and the young lady's various individual contributions were all presented with singular agility and grace."[7]

Looking back, de Valois has no high opinion of the technical standard she acquired from her early tuition. She went to dancing classes from the age of seven. When she was eleven and living in London she London she was sent four times a week to Mrs Wordsworth, the famous Society teacher, where she learned (as children did all over the English-speaking world) "fancy dancing". Mrs Wordsworth was not theatrical and increasingly Edris Stannus was drawn to the theatre. She was avidly watching the Diaghilev Ballet at Covent Garden and the Coliseum (theatres she came to know intimately in later life) and Pavlova at the Palace. She had already seen Adeline Genée at the Empire. Ballet, that extraordinary sorcery that enslaves so many of us, had her in thrall.

So when she was thirteen she began more serious dance training at the Lila Field Academy. Lila Field and her sister Bertha came to England from Germany. It was a time when stage schools for children were all the rage and she specialised in getting her pupils onto stages as early and frequently as possible. A promoter of her own ideas rather than a true woman of the theatre or teacher of acting and dancing, her activities were diversified into the areas of fashion and amateur aviation. She would be less remembered today if she had not, in 1911, staged a play, *The Goldfish*, in which her child actors included Noël Coward, Micheál MacLiammóir (under his real name of Alfred Whitmore) and June (Tripp).

De Valois, joining her school in 1912, was allotted to the "classical ballet" section and by the beginning of 1913 was principal dancer in productions. *The Children's Dream* came first, followed by *Roses Red*, which proved so successful that the Palladium Theatre management booked the Wonder Children for their London and provincial theatres for the next two years. The group was made up of about fourteen girls of diverse age and ability. The level of presentation was professional

NdV in The Swan Dance *(Lila Field's Wonder Children 1914)*

and the large audiences who patronised them were delighted at what they saw. Bertha Field, an excellent disciplinarian, was in charge, but there was no wardrobe mistress and there were no dressers. The children or their mothers were responsible for their make-up and costumes, for "packing and unpacking, mending, ironing and all necessary laundry work of these costumes, the care of shoes and tights".[8]

Performances started with a few short character dances. Then came a condensed version of *The Goldfish* followed by the *Russian Ballet*, a set of classical and *demi-caractère* dances in which, in quick succession, de Valois danced three solos—The Poppy Queen, The Moonlight and a Bird Dance—and two *pas de deux* with a girl partner. The programme ended with a Children's Revue, *Here We Are*, in which well-known theatre artists were impersonated. De Valois, featured as "The Great Pavlova", danced *The Swan Dance (The Dying Swan)*. According to her own recollection she had "laboriously noted this down myself from the upper circle of the Palace Theatre".[9]

It was all good family entertainment—"infinitely pleasing to both young and old".[10] This pressured activity, in which she danced "in every old pier theatre in England"[11] and travelled between them by train, helped to give de Valois stamina, a practical theatre education and, equally important, contact with a wide general audience. There were day trippers from London, there were people enjoying the traditional middle-class seaside holiday during the summer months, and there were the comfortably off who lived all the year round, sometimes for health reasons, at socially popular resorts. Engagements for the company were not limited to summer and they often paid return visits, as they did in 1914 to Eastbourne when they turned up in January, April and July.

Lila Field also arranged single performances at various London theatres. It always looked good in the provinces to say that they were from "the Queen's, Playhouse, Little, Royal Court, Ambassador's and Aldwych Theatres London" and had been "honoured by Royalty" (usually HRH the Princess Christian of Schleswig-Holstein). One of these performances, at the Ambassador's in July 1913, was given a good deal of space in *The Stage*:

> "Among the older girls and 'stars' were Ninette de Valois, a tall, nimble creature described grandiloquently as 'solo *danseuse* of Lila Field's Russian Ballet', and Marjorie Stevens, a graceful child, full of spirit and the joy of youth and labelled similarly '*première danseuse* of Lila Field's company'. Both showed talent that needed no such gratuitous testimonials."[12]

By April 1914 de Valois had a sufficient number of solos in her repertoire to give a small private recital. Friends and theatre contacts were invited along to her parents' house in Earl's Court Square where they had converted the large ground-floor room into a dance studio. The programme was made up of ten short dances, beginning with an Invocation (Chopin Waltz No. 7) and ending with a Brahms Russian Dance. There was considerable variety in the items. They were romantic, coquettish, or tragic and of course included *The Swan Dance*. This evening reinforced the Sitter Out's hopes for her:

> "This pretty child is really an artist and dances very well. She is quite simple and unaffected and is wrapped up in her art, which she loves. For so young a child her miming is good, gaiety, joy, coquetry and sorrow being in turn depicted on her expressive face..."[13]

The following August, on the outbreak of World War I, the Wonder Children (who included two of de Valois' cousins) were disbanded at

Leamington Spa. De Valois had no regrets. At sixteen she was ready to move on into the adult theatre and well aware of the shortcomings of the Lila Field set-up. As well as the Lyceum Theatre audition she had another important meeting in view, at the Empire Theatre where Edouard Espinosa had just been appointed *maître de ballet*.

Espinosa was initially dismayed at her idea of showing him *The Swan Dance*. "If anyone else comes here and does that I'll murder them!" Whatever she replaced it with, he liked her; but on hearing that she had the pantomime work lined up he said "You've got a wonderful job. What more do you want?" What she wanted was important—lessons. They agreed that he would take her as a pupil twice a week. It was a turning point, setting her on a proper professional road at last as a classical dancer. She herself knew, and had been told by those concerned with her development, that in spite of the success she had with audiences she badly needed technical improvement. The Sitter Out had made this point in print, in a pantomime notice obviously meant to advise her:

> "Some of her work is quite good; some, particularly in the *adage*, leaves room for improvement. But she is quite young and there is every encouragement for her future. I should like her to eschew all engagements for two years and just work, work, work, but as I suppose that is impossible she must not forget to work between times."[14]

One reason for weakness in the *adage* was that she was appearing for the first time on stage with a male partner. In *The Children's Dream* she had been offered an arm or shoulder by a girl about her own height who wore a short skirted and short sleeved tunic and tights, and she had danced her version of Pavlova's *Bacchanale* with another girl, Eileen Dennis (later her sister-in-law). This was of course carrying on a very solid tradition of "travesty" dancers prevalent in Paris and London during the late 19th century. Now, with Roberty, de Valois was involved in lifts and fish dives as well as supported pirouettes and balances.

The partnership with Roberty continued. After the pantomime ended they compiled a music-hall "Dance Scena" and launched it at the Oxford Music Hall, London, at the end of June. They went on to the Palladium with it for two weeks in July. Photographs show Roberty in shorts, with butterfly wings flapping from his arms, and de Valois in a Grecian dress, hair still shoulder length and free. *The Era* described their programme:

"Little Miss Maude first appears and gives a delightfully dainty and graceful solo, *Une Abeille*, and is followed by Miss Ninette de Valois, who is seen in *La Sylphe*, a particularly attractive and cleverly executed dance. Then came M. Roberty, whose sensational pirouetting called forth the loudest applause, and as a final contribution the gifted trio appeared in an artistic little ballet, most expressively mimed and danced, that brought down the house."[15]

After that de Valois was back on her own. Roberty took an engagement in *Theban Nights* at the Coliseum and de Valois appeared alone at Devonshire Park, Eastbourne. Roberty then returned to Belgium and served on the Western front with the Belgian Army, where he was badly wounded and gassed towards the end of the war.

De Valois continued to work very seriously with Espinosa. The Espinosa family, of great importance in British ballet history, arrived in London in 1889 when Edouard's father Leon was engaged to arrange crowd and mass movement for Henry Irving's production of *The Dead Heart* at the Lyceum. Edouard's dancing career had embraced every kind of theatre work from drama to vaudeville in Europe and the United States. His wide experience of Irving's company and in musical entertainment made him an appropriate teacher for de Valois, helping, even if only indirectly, to reinforce her instinctive belief in dancing as part of general theatre rather than some rarefied and separate art form. He began teaching in Holborn in September 1896 and by 1915 was settled in Woolborough House in Barnes.

De Valois went there three times a week for two private lessons and one class. His teaching specialised in good footwork, concentrating on *terre à terre* work such as *petite batterie* and pirouettes with very exact musicality and rhythm. As with many teachers, this reflected his own strong points as a dancer. When de Valois first went to him he insisted that she work in soft shoes for four months before resuming pointe shoes, correcting and eradicating the results of poor earlier training:

"His care of the feet, ankles and knees was superlative ... We were never allowed to go home in ordinary walking shoes; we had to wear laced or buttoned boots so as to support the ankles and keep them from swelling."[16]

Undoubtedly this basis for quick strong pointwork was responsible for the reputation she later built up in roles like Papillon in *Carnaval* or the *pas de trois* she created in Ashton's *Les Rendezvous*.

De Valois was again engaged for the Lyceum pantomime of 1915/16.

This year it was *Robinson Crusoe* and the ballet was *The Gems of the Ocean*. The Sitter Out was pleased with her: "During the past year her technique has improved under Espinosa and her personality 'broadened'."[17] The rest of 1916 was devoted to study and to that extension of study, teaching. Teaching others, and as a result having to analyse and think deeply about each detail of work, is a fruitful method of increasing one's own knowledge. She took pupils at her London studio and once a week spent the day in Eastbourne teaching classical dancing for a large and flourishing general dance school run by Miss Eleanor Ratcliffe. The third Lyceum pantomime, *Mother Goose*, began on December 23 and de Valois was listed as The Fairy of the Golden Valley. This time she was allowed to introduce a special dance taught her by Espinosa.

"The dance is a brilliant one yet well within the power of the dancer. It includes an *enchaînement* of *petite batterie*, some *adage* and the very showy finish consists of a series of *coupés, posés, attitudes en tournant*, about a dozen *fouettés ronds-de-jambe en tournant*, ending with the familiar *déboulés* ... I honestly think that in her we have a future English *première*. I should like to see her soon in a real little ballet as opposed to a divertissement, something in which she could show if she possesses the necessary dramatic powers without which no dancer can ever be really great."[18]

Almost the same pattern of work was followed in 1917: very few public appearances but regular tuition and teaching. In April Espinosa left for South Africa for what was initially intended to be a six-week visit; with travelling time added he reckoned he would be back on June 25. He left the school "in charge of Stephen Hall and Ninette de Valois, then my two most competent pupils",[19] but in the end he went on to Australia. The school was suspended and he did not return until 1920. De Valois began studying at home with a very fine teacher, Hilda Bewicke, a pupil of Pavlova's who had danced with Diaghilev.

From the beginning, 1918 gave signs of initiating a more solid stage in her career. The first engagements, admittedly, were merely at charity matinees, in both of which she was partnered by a well-known travesty dancer, Violet Curtis. The Sitter Out, an indefatigable recorder of her activities, was delighted:

"Her work has matured, her turns were sparkling and 'clean' and her arabesques beautifully 'soft' and well held. As regards her technique I

NdV aged seventeen

certainly regard her as one of the most promising of the new generation of dancers and trust that she will do her utmost to develop the corresponding dramatic power without which dancing is but a copperplate from a copybook."[20]

These performances may have led to the next, very different, event. Lady Constance Stewart-Richardson, a young socialite who specialised in barefoot free dance, took the Royal Court Theatre (a favourite venue for special performances) for a short season in June. She wanted a contrast to her own style in some solos from a classical dancer and these were supplied by de Valois. Lady Constance's part of the programme included a *pantomime dansante*, *Pan Laughs*. *The Era* quotes a synopsis all too typical of this kind of creation, about how

"a child of nature, only intent on the joy of life as expressed by dancing, is endeavouring to escape the unwelcome attentions of men".[21]

This piece reinforced the not very high opinion de Valois formed of what she terms "the barefoot ladies". The Sitter Out stressed the need for her to "turn her attention to real ballet".[22]

Opera however was her next experience. When Sir Thomas Beecham staged excerpts from operas with ballets in the Palladium music-hall bill in September, she had a three-week guest engagement: one week of *Faust*, one week of *Phoebus and Pan* and one of *Carmen*. There was a large company of seventy performers and *The Stage* commented:

"[it] will give lovers of ballet an opportunity to compare English methods with those of the Russians at another place"[23]

—the Diaghilev Ballet was at the Coliseum.

Phoebus and Pan was a dramatised production of Bach's secular cantata, *Der Streit zwischen Phoebus und Pan*, first given by Beecham in 1916. Costumes and sets were by Edmund Dulac and the interpolated ballet was arranged to music from one of Bach's French Suites. *Faust* and *Carmen* would turn up repeatedly in de Valois' life, at Covent Garden and at the Old Vic and Sadler's Wells, but the Palladium season was her initiation into working with opera singers and conductors, something she always found rewarding. In *Phoebus and Pan*, she composed her own solo—and greatly impressed Eugene Goossens, who was conducting. She had always invented dances, without thinking of herself as a choreographer or even knowing the word choreography. She was first conscious of it in 1917 when she asked Hilda Bewicke to look at "my new dances", and Bewicke, impressed, wanted to know who had "done the choreography for them".

In November 1918 came the Armistice and the end of World War I. On Boxing Day the last Lyceum pantomime in which she starred, *Cinderella*, got under way. Her role was Sunray, she was partnered by a celebrated Russian dancer, Alexander Goudin, and she remembers that for the first time she put up her hair. It was very much a comedians' pantomime, and this was an aspect of theatre she relished, treasuring memories of George Robey, Ella Shields, Nellie Wallace and other great music-hall artists. Watching them gave her an insight into the handling of the public, the control of an audience. Audible in the top galleries without mikes, they would take over a completely restless crowd and by sheer concentration quieten them down until you could hear a pin drop.

The fact that Diaghilev was at the Coliseum opened a new door for de Valois. Hilda Bewicke was arranging to rejoin the Russians and in the spring of 1919 took her along to a class being given by Enrico Cecchetti at Chandos Hall. Until then she had known the Russian Ballet only as an entranced member of the audience. Now she saw and met them on a working basis.

All great teachers make different contributions to their pupils, strengthening them in different ways: in footwork, pirouettes, line, *port de bras*, elevation, *ballon, pas de deux*, technically or inter- pretatively. Espinosa had given de Valois the qualities of the French school. Apart from the solid training for footwork, precision and turns, he had emphasised an analytical and logical approach to the theory of classical ballet. Now with Cecchetti were added the qualities of the Italian school, but the Italian school conditioned by Cecchetti's experi- ence of Russian ballet. De Valois has called him an artist-teacher as opposed to a pedagogue. "I learnt the meaning of symmetry, the hidden beauty of the studied detail, the harmony that can be achieved in movement, and the meaning of *port-de-bras*." In addition she was aware of his skill and understanding of mime, an area that she had so far not had the chance to develop but that appealed to her increasingly.

The rigorous and set routines of the Cecchetti classes however led, with her, to two years of "illuminating experience" which came to saturation point in the third year. She sums it up as a method "import- ant to study at some time in one's career but perhaps not sufficient on its own".[24] Further wide-ranging influences from teachers and choreographers were added to her own development as a dancer and

14

Cinderella *1918: NdV with Alexander Goudin*

composer of ballets and to her impressive future work as a teacher. It is too often forgotten that her continued contribution over many years as an inspiring teacher of other teachers, as well as of professional dancers, would have been of importance to ballet on its own, quite apart from her more spectacular achievements as founder-director and choreographer of the Royal Ballet.

In 1919, money had to be earned and experience gained in the commercial theatre, even as she worked assiduously with Cecchetti. In this sphere two men proved important. She had a theatrical agent, G. W. Robinson of Verts Concert Agency, who took a special interest in dancers. He had represented her from 1916, and in 1919 commented, in defending British talent: "Where can you find a more capable little dancer than Ninette de Valois, who certainly boasts French blood in her veins but is more Irish than anything else? ... She has done well indeed and will, I hope, go far in her profession."[25] He would have been impressed to know just how far she has gone.

The other man was Ernest C. Rolls, an impresario who presented musicals and revues regularly in the West End and on tour and who had seen her at the Lyceum. In January 1919 he was planning a topical revue, *Laughing Eyes*, of which he was part author, and engaged her as principal dancer at a very good salary. The fourteen scenes were called "twinkles" and Twinkle No. 7, *The Dope Fiend*, was the one in which de Valois appeared. In this she played an innocent lured into an opium den and given a cigarette which induced fantastic balletic dreams—balletic, because her contracts at the time always stipulated that she must wear ballet shoes and be allowed to dance on pointe. Her partner and choreographer was Fred A. Leslie, an Australian whom she remembers as a very nice man and a very good musical comedy dancer.

For the first part of the tour, which opened in Brighton in February, the *première danseuse* was Dithy Tarling from the Paris Opéra Comique—de Valois was still in *Cinderella* and only took over towards the end of March, taking over as well costumes which the French dancer had heavily drenched with perfume. *Laughing Eyes* was brought into the Kennington Theatre—a splendidly appointed and popular suburban house—on May 1 and was an instant hit. *The Stage* declared that it was

"quite one of the best of modern entertainments of a like character. The book sparkles with wit and epigram, the music is exceedingly

NdV in Laughing Eyes *1919*

NdV in 1920

tuneful and pleasing, with plenty of haunting melodies. The scenery is striking, with artistic novel features."[26]

It had all the essential ingredients for an enjoyable escapist evening. *The Tatler* stressed this. It was a pleasure because

"no one goes to a revue to think; all that he demands is that he shall not be bored and that he shall be compelled to laugh in spite of himself and in spite of the 6s. increase in the price of coal."[27]

The Graphic spoke of a "rollicking and enjoyable revue"[28] that was attracting a large and appreciative audience to Kennington and it was equally successful at the Strand Theatre when it reached the West End on June 17, running until mid-November.

A curious hint of de Valois' future had come that spring. Rolls, looking around for new ventures, became impressed with the possibilities of a forgotten North London theatre, Sadler's Wells in Islington. The previous January *The Era* had mentioned that it was up for sale as a warehouse, and posed the question, who will save it?[29] This elicited a letter from the British Empire Shakespeare Society to the effect that Sadler's Wells could become "a second Old Vic". All it needed was (1) enterprise (2) a love of Shakespeare and (3) cash.[30]

Rolls talked to de Valois early in 1919, saying he was thinking of acquiring a wonderful old theatre that was falling to pieces in a part of London that badly needed a theatre, and that he would ask her not only to be *première danseuse* there but to be in charge of the ballet. In April he purchased the freehold of the Wells[31] and was reported as saying that he intended to spend considerable sums on reconstruction and redecoration and would run it on popular lines, for drama, melodrama, Shakespeare and pantomime.

His great dream came apart. He overreached himself financially and was declared bankrupt. He had lost £12,000 on *Laughing Eyes*, in spite of its success; £16,000 on his next production *Oh! Julie!*; and £7,000 in respect of Sadler's Wells. In October 1921 he applied for a discharge from bankruptcy but did not again embark on theatre ownership. It would be another ten years before de Valois went into Sadler's Wells under Lilian Baylis' management—but fate certainly seemed determined that one way or another ballet at the Wells would be entrusted to her care.

In 1919 she was in great demand—she even refused an offer from Australia—and Rolls gave her permission to take up an important engagement as *première danseuse* in five operas at Covent Garden. An understudy replaced her in *Laughing Eyes* on the nights she appeared at the Royal Opera House.

This first postwar International Opera Season opened on May 12 and the next night, in *La Traviata*, de Valois stepped for the first time on to the famous stage. The opera was sung in Italian, with Ayres Borghi-Zerni as Violetta and Agostino Capuzzo as Alfredo, and was conducted by Leopold Mugnone. The ballet master for the season was François Ambrosiny from the Brussels Monnaie, and he taught de Valois dances he had already choreographed for the operas in Belgium. *Thaïs* followed on May 14, conducted by Beecham and sung by Louise Edvina. "An extremely lithe and graceful dancer, Mlle Ninette de Valois—English in spite of her name—made a big success in the scene outside Thais' house."[32] *Aida*, with Emmy Destinn, Kirkby Lunn and Ulisse Lappas, on May 28, was again conducted by Mugnone. *Louise* on June 6, with Edvina and Fernand Ansseau, had Albert Coates as conductor. The fifth opera in which de Valois appeared was the first production of Isidore de Lara's *Naïl* (July 18), conducted by Beecham and sung by Rosina Buckman, Frank Mullings and Percy Heming. The date was badly chosen, as it was the eve of Peace Day, and opinions on the quality of the opera were also not high.

In August *The Dancing Times* featured de Valois on the cover in *Laughing Eyes*, and wrote:

> "Ninette de Valois has won golden opportunities by reason of her work as *première danseuse* at Covent Garden. I believe the management were at one time a little dubious as to whether she could undertake the dancing in *Naïl*, Isidore de Lara's new opera, but after watching her magnificent display in *Aida* all doubts were set at rest. It is of course a great feather in her cap to have secured this very important engagement and as she has still many dancing years before her [she had turned twenty-one that June] she ought to do great things. In *Laughing Eyes*, Miss de Valois has shown that she possesses considerable mimetic powers and so every encouragement is given for some enterprising management to produce her in a proper *ballet d'action*."[33]

At the time *ballet d'action*, dramatic or *demi-caractère* ballet signified the peak of classical ballet. Not until the sensational vogue for Massine's symphonic ballets in the thirties were pure dancing works rated as highly. Not until after World War II were they to be considered rather more important in the Western world—and for this probably Balanchine and his disciples are largely instrumental.

NdV as leading dancer in Aida (Royal Opera House Covent Garden 1919)

From grand opera de Valois moved to musical comedy. In July 1920 she was once more engaged by Rolls, this time as leading dancer with Fred A. Leslie in *Oh! Julie!* at the Shaftesbury Theatre (a house destroyed in World War II). The dances came in the third act. They were arranged by Leslie, who gave her, she recalls, a stunning number ended by his sliding along a bar counter to her. At the dress rehearsal for the profession this had a great ovation and spoilt Ethel Levey's entrance, so that particular dance was excised from the show. This must have been disappointing—"but she was quite right, she was the star of the show after all" was de Valois' comment. The work was still fast and exciting and de Valois' fame reached the glossy magazines, with pictures in *The Sketch* and *The Tatler*. It was also the first time Ashton saw her, as a schoolboy theatregoer. The Sitter Out had reservations:

"It is difficult to describe her dance. It is partly operatic and partly eccentric. Nevertheless she is too good for this kind of work."[34]

Oh! Julie! failed to "take"—it ran only until mid-September. All the same it taught her yet another style of theatre work. Musical comedies were different in their technical and emotional demands from opera, pantomime and revue. She was learning to apply all that she had learnt from Espinosa and Cecchetti to the fast, flexible and varying demands of the commercial theatre.

She was also looking towards other spheres of activity. She wanted to run a group of her own and try her hand at dance arrangements, and she was encouraged to implement this ambition by Charles Gulliver, the managing director of a circuit of music-halls, the London Theatres of Variety. He liked to include dancing in his programmes and had a special friendship with the Hungarian-born dancer Derra de Moroda who was a regular folkdance recitalist. De Valois loved folkdancing, whether European or British—Morris Dance delighted her—and she studied with de Moroda, who arranged some dances for her. The idea of putting together a half-hour show for the Gulliver Halls appealed to her greatly. She had experience of the kind of thing from her appearances with Roberty in 1915 but she was more ambitious. She engaged a group of eight girls which included Margaret Craske who also acted as ballet mistress and Vivienne Bennett, later a well-known actress.

The girls loved it. Margaret Craske, long a much-admired teacher in New York, commented at the age of ninety:

NdV in Oh! Julie! *1920*

*NdV and her
dancers in
music-hall tour
1921; (above)
Vivienne Bennett,
Audrey Carlyon
and Vera Lyndall,
(right) NdV with
Serge Morosoff*

"Ninette de Valois took me into a small company which played the music halls. It was divine! That was absolutely the most wonderful audience in the world. If they didn't like you they threw things ... "[35]

De Valois also needed a male partner and came to terms, at an exorbitant weekly fee, with Serge Morosoff.

Morosoff was Moscow-trained, at the Imperial School of Ballet, and had come to London in 1914, appearing in musical comedy or music-hall programmes and arranging dances at various theatres. He taught at Delphine's Academy and because of his reputation for brilliant character work gave classes in classical, eccentric and character dancing. De Valois was not particularly impressed by his personality. She had much happier associations with Roberty and Goudin, but Morosoff was a useful partner and well-known on the halls. She rehearsed her little team in a programme largely made up of her own compositions, and they gave their first performance on October 26 1921 at the Camberwell Palace. *The Stage* covered it fully:

"Ninette de Valois, who has the support of Serge Morosoff and a British *corps de ballet*, had an enthusiastic reception on Monday evening when she presented an attractive divertissement admirably arranged and devised by herself and M. Morosoff. The ladies of the ballet contributed some of their finest dancing in the *pas de valse* item, the movements being notably precise and the groupings neatly done. Three of these ladies are also concerned in a delightful *pas de trois*, a cleverly arranged item given to one of Dorothy Foster's pleasant compositions. Of the work of the *première danseuse* one can speak in terms of high praise."[36]

Further weeks followed, with gaps, at the Holborn Empire and other suburban London theatres and they presented an excerpt from the programme at the annual Sunshine Matinee (a charity event in aid of blind babies) at the Queen's Theatre. For the last three weeks Morosoff was replaced—he was proving too expensive for her and a none-too-congenial associate—by a young New Zealand dancer, Jan Caryll. Caryll was a pupil of Astafieva's—de Valois saw him in class—and had also had some professional experience. He introduced a Trepak solo and danced the Czardas from *Coppélia* with de Valois.

The venture was an undoubted success—no one "threw things" at them—although Caryll in his memoirs comments

"Ninette's presentation was ahead of its time and the numbers sat rather uncomfortably within a typical music hall bill."[37]

Looking back, de Valois feels that although the scale was modest it was in fact the beginning of her career as a director-choreographer, one of the very first stirrings of British ballet. She was planning to build on this foundation when another, important, opportunity came her way.

October 1921, the month she launched her Gulliver Hall group, is celebrated in ballet history for a very different event—the premiere (on the 29th) of the Diaghilev Ballet's production of *The Sleeping Princess* at the Alhambra. This splendid staging, a connoisseur's joy and a commercial failure, had to close on February 4 1922, leaving Russian dancers in an unstable situation.

Leonide Massine, who had left Diaghilev in 1920, had come back to London towards the end of 1921 and now recruited a small company to appear in Britain. Led by himself and Lydia Lopokova, it included Lydia Sokolova, Thadee Slavinsky and Leon Woizikovsky, as well as de Valois.

De Valois owed her involvement not only to her ability but also to the contacts she made through her classes with Cecchetti. Lopokova in particular helped and encouraged her, even arranging for the younger dancer to share her private lessons, an invaluable experience. It was especially valid because as artists they had much in common. Both were primarily *demi-caractère* dancers with a tremendous sense of comedy: Lopokova had greater elevation and ballon, de Valois a sleeker elegance of style. Lopokova's temperament was ebullient, childlike, volatile; de Valois' Irish mental agility and flexibility were subject to great self-discipline and already considerable sophistication. All the same they enjoyed each other's company, appreciated each other's talents, and always remained in sympathy. They were bonded by a basic honesty and directness, a generosity of spirit and a delight in simple things, as well as their common devotion to ballet.

The Lopokova-Massine group went on tour in England and Scotland and then from April 3 were included in a twice-daily show at Covent Garden which combined ballet and film. This was a project promoted by Walter Wanger and Sidney Bernstein in partnership, intended to popularise cinema, and the movies shown included *Theodora* and a fine French film, *Atlantide*. The first week's stage programme offered a fairly routine suite of dances by Massine, *Fanatics of Pleasure*, as well as a divertissement. The item that got most publicity was Stravinsky's *Ragtime*. Stravinsky opposed the staging on the grounds that the music was not suitable for a ballet, only for a concert hall, but Massine circumvented this and composed a duet for himself and Lopokova that "parodied the grotesque attitudes of some of the modern dances to perfection".[38]

De Valois had a *pas seul*, *Cupidon*, as well as sharing in the various ensembles. She was also written up in *The Graphic* in an article on the theme that a "Russian dancer" had become a generic term, as many dancers in Russian ballet were of other nationalities, particularly Polish and English. The English contingent with Diaghilev included Sokolova (Hilda Munnings), Vera Savina (Clarke), Ursula Moreton, Dorothy Coxon and of course Anton Dolin (Patrick Healey-Kay).

The Massine-Lopokova programme was a stimulating new challenge for de Valois, more in the association it brought her with the dancers than in the material itself. These artists from the Russian Ballet had a different and much more elevated attitude to their art than anything she had come across in pantomime, opera-ballets, revues or musical comedies. They had high technical standards and vast experience in exacting and magnificent ballets by the most important choreographers of the time. Their grasp of *demi-caractère* was exceptional, their ability as actors equalled their ability as dancers. De Valois learned from them the effect of *demi-caractère* dance in choreography and the control of movement, the coordination of all physical elements in the service of chracterisation and narrative. There are films in existence of *The Good-humoured Ladies* as danced later by the de Basil Ballet that show this kind of performance, an integration of head, neck, arms, hands, legs and feet plus a lively command of facial expression, that produced results quite unlike anything that can be seen today. In *Come Dance with Me* de Valois instances "the intricate and often asymmetrical fusion of body movement with steps" in Massine's ballets, that led to an increased understanding of the control of movement.[39] She was ready, by virtue of her studies with Espinosa and Cecchetti, to gain much from the Russian ballet group of 1922/23 even if the standard of work tackled was not important.

They spent three more weeks at the Royal Opera House, with programme changes each week, and then moved to the Coliseum on June 19. Massine left after this engagement but in the October Lopokova re-formed the group to appear again at the Coliseum, this time in a new ballet called *The Masquerade*, to Mozart's *Serenade in G*. This was set in 18th-century Venice, with a lovers' rendezvous by gondola on an island in the lagoon. *The Era* spoke highly of it:

The Massine-Lopokova group (Royal Opera House Covent Garden 1922); (above) Fanatics of Pleasure: *group includes NdV, Lydia Lopokova and Leonide Massine (centre); (left) NdV in* Cupidon

"Lydia Lopokova with her talented company which includes Lydia Sokolova, Leon Woizikovsky, Thadee Slavinsky and Ninette de Valois, arouses the greatest enthusiasm with her beautifully presented one-act *ballet comique* ... a very beautiful medium for some of the most delightful dancing to be seen in town."[40]

It is significant that de Valois' name is now being naturally related to the ex-Diaghilev Ballet stars, something that could do an aspiring dancer nothing but good.

They were on the bill again at the Coliseum on October 23 when a new ballet was produced—*Les Elegantes* to Chopin. The featured dancers were Lopokova, Sokolova, de Valois and Slavinsky, and it had a typically simple theme—of a young man who has carelessly given three ladies a rendezvous at the same place and time. The third lady, Lopokova, ousts her rivals; but a shower of rain "turns the thoughts of all from their feelings to their clothes, and the two worsted beauties have, over their more successful rival, the great advantage of umbrellas ... "[41] This is the kind of balletic trifle that stands or falls by the skill with which it is presented.

NdV in You'd be Surprised *(Royal Opera House Covent Garden 1923)*

By January 1923 they were rejoined by Massine for a new engagement at Covent Garden. This was an ambitious revue, *You'd be Surprised*, which starred George Robey as well as the Russian ballet group. Subtitled a "jazzaganza", it opened to a good deal of publicity. Robey always rated highly—his fame, and his large salary, made excellent copy. But not even Robey could camouflage the weaknesses of the show. *The Graphic* reviewer declared "There is no pattern in the texture of *You'd be Surprised* ... It is a hotch-potch, not by any means of even quality";[42] while de Valois recalled it as "a loosely constructed entertainment presenting a collection of English and American revue stars".[43]

Massine's contribution hardly helped matters. It was a ballet, described later as *Togo or The Noble Savage*, with music by Milhaud and designs by Duncan Grant, in a scene titled *Wild Cat, Arizona*. Massine and Sokolova were Togo and his wife.

"It was so poor [wrote Sokolova] I can hardly remember anything about it. I know I was dressed in allover brown tights with a black wig, had an African make-up and did a war dance."[44]

De Valois, as their Negress Servant, "was dressed as a piccaninny, my face blackened, and with Slavinsky executed an intensely difficult duet dance".[45] *Togo* disappeared from *Wild Cat* within the month, improbably, but no doubt more enjoyably, replaced by a *Lezginka* from the previous year's divertissements. Then the Russian dancers were dispensed with altogether and de Valois, the only ballet survivor, continued with *Record Girl of Mine* and added a dance of her own choreography in a comedy scene, *Chicken à la King*, in which she was "assisted by six little chicks".

You'd be Surprised transferred to the Alhambra in April and de Valois stayed on as *première danseuse* in her two revue scenes. The show had its 175th performance on May 8 and continued until mid-June. She became increasingly bored with its trivial demands for three performances daily. Her lifeline was morning study with Nicholas Legat at his Hampstead studio.

Espinosa had provided her with insight into the French school of ballet, Cecchetti into the Italian. Legat added the Russian school. She was now taking "classes of perfection". Legat was his own pianist, explaining what he wanted from the piano stool. For de Valois he was a welcome and inspiring teacher and she profited from the "deep knowledge behind the elegant but apparently free and easy approach, highlighted by the everlastingly new and very beautiful *enchaînements* arranged from day to day".[46]

In July Lopokova reassembled her group at the Coliseum for a repeat of the popular *Masquerade* and followed this with a week of divertissements. The most exciting moment of de Valois' life to date was however approaching. The Diaghilev Ballet was once again in operation in France and Monte Carlo and looking for another young classical dancer. She was prepared and ready. Cecchetti spoke for her and Serge Grigoriev, Diaghilev's great regisseur, interviewed her in London. An offer was made and accepted, and in September 1923 she went to Paris to join the most stimulating and competitive company in the world.

Chapter II

De Valois has written a great deal in her three books about her life and work with the Diaghilev Ballet. She has presented, with her clear powers of observation and gift for literary description, all the major personalities of her new world—Diaghilev himself, Grigoriev, Bronislava Nijinska and the principal dancers who were her seniors or contemporaries. She has written about ballets and opera ballets performed. What must be filled in is the chronological unfolding of events.

In September 1923 the company were rehearsing in Paris at the Gaîté-Lyrique Theatre. For the first time de Valois had to learn a repertoire of wide-ranging ballets, from *Les Sylphides* to *Schéhérazade*, and according to herself she was a slow study. Life with the ballet was strenuous and enjoyable. She fitted in to the ranks of the dancers with the ease of a born cosmopolitan. The other newcomers that season were Alice Nikitina, Anton Dolin and Serge Lifar. Of the established artists she already knew Sokolova, Woizikovsky and Slavinsky; additionally there were Vera Nemchinova, Felia Dubrovska, Lubov Tchernicheva, Anatole Vilzak and Stanislas Idzikovsky.

From Paris they went on tour, appearing in Geneva, Lausanne, Berne and Antwerp before reaching Monte Carlo in November. From then until mid-April 1924 de Valois was part of a very particular world. The small principality with its famous Casino and its delightful winter climate, was a social rendezvous for the international well-to-do, and the charming theatre (familiar to later generations of ballet lovers from the film *The Red Shoes*) had a busy and closely integrated programme during winter and spring. Over five and a half months the Diaghilev Ballet appeared in operas, plays and twenty-five ballets—a considerably busier schedule than most dancers would accept nowadays.

The resident choreographer was Nijinska, a major new factor in de

Valois' ever-widening view of ballet. The Russian tradition which she had been learning with Legat was the basis of Nijinska's totally personal extensions and development of classical dance. Everyone who worked with her found her classes difficult but all those who seriously wanted to improve and stretch themselves as artists welcomed the challenges. A decade later Irina Baronova, when she created the intricate leading role of *Les Cent Baisers*, found the task rewarding. Ashton, from the time when he was a young dancer with the Ida Rubinstein Ballet and Nijinska was choreographer and ballet mistress, held her in the utmost admiration as a great creative artist. For de Valois in 1924 she was "a choreographer-teacher opening up my mind and strengthening my body".[1]

It was a happy trick of fate that brought together two remarkable women about whom some parallels can be drawn. Both were serious and gifted artists who would have creative, controlling careers in a sphere dominated by men. Both derived from strong national cultural traditions, in Poland and in Ireland, but had trained and developed outside their native countries. Both were interested in folkdance steps and patterns and in how the classical technique could be applied to modern music and in non-classical ways.

Nijinska, the elder by eight years, had been in close and sympathetic collaboration with her adored brother Vaslav while he choreographed his revolutionary ballets for Diaghilev. Even in latterday revivals the meticulously planned angular movement of his *L'Après-midi d'un faune* looks effective in contemporary terms and it is easy to believe that the lost ballets of *Jeux* and *Le Sacre du Printemps* were excitingly experimental. Writing of *Jeux*, Nijinska has said: "Everything in the choreography was new—free movements and positions of the body applied to classical ballet technique."[2] This proved to be her own gospel when she began practising the art herself.

As a choreographer Nijinska had a distinctly individual "voice" and outstanding artistic integrity. Her work was deeply considered, formidable in its musical understanding, adventurous in its personal language and at no point trivial in content. De Valois was eagerly responsive. When she assessed it, the qualities she chose to emphasise in Nijinska's choreography were its strength and clarity, its musicality, and its important contribution to the new academic classicism. In *The Choreographic Art*, Peggy van Praagh and Peter Brinson claim that Nijinska was the first classical choreographer to analyse expressionist movement in any profound sense. They cite Nemchinova's solo in *Les*

NdV: Rondeau in Les Biches *(Diaghilev Ballet 1924)*

Biches as an example of the union of new and old,

> "angular novel modern movements for the top of the body placed upon a foundation of classical leg movements, so that the styles were integrated in a single dancer".

In *Les Noces*, the dancers "moved in a strongly rhythmic manner, part geometrical and part architectural".[3]

There was a fruitful communication between the established Nijinska and the newly recruited young de Valois. Nijinska taught de Valois her version of the "Finger" Fairy variation and the Florestan *pas de trois* in *Aurora's Wedding*, in both of which the solid technical training she had applied herself to in England could be put to use in allegro or pizzicato dancing.

She danced in two new Nijinska productions, *Les Fâcheux* and *La Tentation de la bergère*; above all, and valuable from the point of view of the future, Nijinska selected her as the junior dancer on whom she could work out her own projected role of the Hostess in *Les Biches*, the ballet she was currently preparing. As we know now, this was an extraordinarily sophisticated and convoluted choreography, expressing a distinct personality of the period. The eccentric society lady with feather headdress and lengthy beads and cigarette holder dominates the house party by the force of her confident style of movement. The relation of her dances to the music is complete and they use the whole body—head, torso and limbs—with spectacular flexibility. *Epaulement* is of great importance, facial expressiveness vital and deep subtleties of sexual feeling contained in each step and gesture. There is a freely twenties air about its classical base. It is interesting to wonder what de Valois may have unconsciously contributed from her experience, for instance, of Fred A. Leslie's stage choreography in the opium den scene of *Laughing Eyes* or the fast eccentric dances in *Oh! Julie!*

De Valois did not at that time dance the Hostess although she was in the ensemble of girls, but her evenings with Nijinska and the two men, Woizikovsky and Nicolas Zverev, while Nijinska worked out the choreography of these leading roles, gave her an insight into ballet creation which undoubtedly had a profound influence in years to come. Already she was fascinated by this branch of work, determined to be herself a choreographer of substance, and this was an invaluable opportunity of watching a major creator on an important job.

Many characteristics of the Diaghilev Ballet were absorbed to future

advantage. The concept of unity, with composer, designer and choreographer each contributing vital elements to a production, appealed
to her greatly and would govern not only her own ballets but her
general policy in the Vic-Wells Ballet and its successors. Even at this
stage, in her early twenties, with only her experience of the tiny touring
group of 1921, she knew she wanted to build up a company of her
own, and she was alert, with the keen analytical intelligence native
to her, assessing the functions in the Diaghilev Ballet of regisseur,
conductor, choreographer, teacher and above all artistic director. She
was not uncritical and grasped instinctively what was appropriate to
her own future and what would not have relevance.

The way in which the Diaghilev Ballet was part of the European
artistic and cultural world was immensely relevant. London in the
1930s would reflect this state of affairs with a fascinating network
through which all the arts, performing and otherwise, were inter-
related. Then de Valois, as a major representative of British ballet
development, would enjoy close and regular communication with
leading figures in music, literature, painting and the stage, and through
this freemasonry each of the arts would benefit.

De Valois' first appearance in Monte Carlo came in a cross-section
of the repertoire. On the opening night, November 25, she was a
Polovtsian maiden in the *Dances from Prince Igor* and an Egyptian in
Cléopâtre, her earliest association as a dancer with the choreography
of Michel Fokine, whose genius she has always admired. *Petrushka*
and *Schéhérazade* were also performed, as well as the delicacies and
subtleties of *Les Sylphides* and *Carnaval*.

The belief at that time throughout the ballet world and until very
much later in the century was that Fokine was a master choreographer
and choreographic prophet. It was in fact true, however much his
reputation has been eclipsed by poor revivals and changes in fashion.
In 1914 he published, in a letter to *The Times* (London),[4] what
amounted to a manifesto about "the new Russian ballet", and his
tenets appealed strongly to many young dancers, including de Valois.
Where classical ballet was concerned, Fokine's innovative thinking
was the catalyst that altered everyone's conception of the art, radically
changed values and set other minds to work on totally new lines. His
"new ballet" broke every accepted convention and produced fresh and
fruitful principles for choreographic creation. Expressiveness was the
keyword. Each ballet was to be cast in a form suited to its specific
character—the field was thrown wide open, and the only criterion was

that its style should be appropriate to whatever period or place or emotion had been selected by the choreographer for treatment. Dancing and mime were to serve the action, mime being extended from traditional gesture language to acting "from head to foot". Groups and ensembles were to be equally integrated and, a vital point, dancing and mime should be allied on terms of complete equality with the other theatrical arts of music and scenic and costume design. Music of every kind was to be used with the only proviso that it should be "good and expressive". The designer should be equally free of restriction.

This charter of liberty was put into practical action by the Diaghilev Ballet and Fokine's famous works for the company underlined his points over and over again. By the twenties the equality and unity of the theatre arts were accepted by everyone, with a list of supreme collaborations, such as *Petrushka* (Stravinsky-Fokine-Benois) or *Les Noces* (Stravinsky-Nijinska-Gontcharova) to its credit. The amazing diversification of Fokine's output proved as much as anything how stimulating was his belief of suiting the style to the action. How far apart were the tenuously lyrical *Spectre de la rose*, the blazing melodrama of *Schéhérazade*, the tightly observed dramatic action of *Petrushka*, the pure romantic geometry of *Les Sylphides*, the witty charm of *Carnaval*! In the hands of a great choreographer the gospel of the "new ballet" produced magnificent free-ranging results.

Studying the Fokine ballets from the dancer's angle, de Valois became acutely aware not only of their own character but of what they implied for future choreographers—the possibility of development and depth they opened up for artists of her own generation who had choreographic ambitions. She had already worked with Massine, although only in inferior productions. He, like Nijinsky and Nijinska, reaped the benefit of Fokine's pioneering and she now discovered the riches of his creative imagination in ballets like *Le Tricorne*, *La Boutique fantasque* and *The Good-humoured Ladies*. She discovered too the extent to which *demi-caractère* dance and choreography could parallel the spoken play and—a lesson of prime importance for her own temperament and one that was not contained in the Fokine ballets—how every kind of comedy—wit, satire, caricature, plain fun and farce—could be brought to life by the ballet creator. All these Diaghilev Ballet productions confirmed her native conviction that ballet was as much a part of theatrical activity as drama and opera, operetta or musical comedy, and that the dancer as an interpretative performing artist was the equal of the actor or the singer.

De Valois' earliest solo roles came in the one-act divertissement from *The Sleeping Princess, Aurora's Wedding*, in which she danced the charming cameo of Red Riding Hood and the "Finger" variation. At that point, absorbed in contemporary choreography, she had little interest in the Petipa survivals, and this was reinforced by the revival of Acts II and III of *Le Lac des cygnes* for Vera Trefilova in December 1923, staged by Anatole Vilzak and Ludmilla Schollar with some additional choreography by Nijinska. Although de Valois considered Trefilova an outstanding classical dancer and an actress of great quality, she was not impressed by the ballet itself. It was not in good shape, much cut about and uncared for. But it had a delayed action impact that meant infinitely more to her afterwards, when it came to planning productions for the Vic-Wells Ballet, than it did at the time.

NdV as Red Riding Hood in Aurora's Wedding *(Diaghilev Ballet 1923)*

Travelling played a major part in the company's life and was a delight for de Valois, even when it involved train journeys like one she has described:

> "Leaving Barcelona one morning after a performance, at 3.30 a.m., we spent the rest of that day and the following night sitting up, eight to a second-class carriage. On the morning of the following day we arrived in Paris, to wander about for four hours, falling asleep in cafés. A further train was caught and another night spent under similar circumstances before The Hague was reached."[5]

However, years of war had meant confinement to Britain and she was open to the stimulus of foreign travel and the chances it afforded for pleasure and study. Barcelona was a city faithful over many years to

Russian ballet, first with Diaghilev and later with de Basil, and after performances she was introduced to all the Cuadro Flamenco companies in town. In Holland they performed at The Hague, Amsterdam and Rotterdam—she would look back to it all years later when the Sadler's Wells Ballet made its historic appearances and escape from Holland during World War II. Diaghilev returned to Paris in May 1924 for a season at the Théâtre des Champs-Elysées where in 1937 her great ballet *Checkmate* was to have its first performance.

Paris, always, was of the first importance to Diaghilev and the repertoire was tailored for a city of prime cultural standards. Holland had been shown the popular works, *Aurora's Wedding* and *Prince Igor*, *Les Sylphides* and *Schéhérazade*. Paris had the novelties, *Les Biches* and *La Tentation de la bergère*. A repeat of *Les Noces* (never frequently staged), *Les Fâcheux*, *Cimarosiana* and *Parade*, and the premiere of Nijinska's *Le Train bleu* in which Dolin was brought forward with a spectacular acrobatic leading role and de Valois danced a *pas de quatre* with Schollar, Zverev and Slavinsky.

Les Noces was a revelation to her. Exposed for the first time to its majestic simplicity and pulsating ensembles, she was enormously impressed. "We knew at that time no ballet that gave an artist a more intense emotional interest." She considered it "a rare and isolated instance of combined genius on the part of three people—Stravinsky, Nijinska and Gontcharova"[6]—and how accurately that sums up one's feelings today about this extraordinary ballet!

While the company danced in Paris, appearing also at various *soirées du gala*, Vaslav Nijinsky was brought by his wife Romola to visit a rehearsal—a strange and rather harrowing experience for the dancers. De Valois must have remembered his "patient, vacant, staring figure"[7] when she came to work on *The Rake's Progress*, even though Nijinsky's mental withdrawal seemed to her to have peace and serenity...

Like most dancers of the twenties and thirties, de Valois took the opportunity whilst in Paris of studying with the former Maryinsky prima ballerina Olga Preobrajenska, who nurtured so many marvellous talents. At this time she was teaching in a hall above the Olympia Theatre and her open classes were so large that it was difficult to profit very much from them. Private classes were essential for real help, and in the autumn of 1924 de Valois joined Dubrovska, Nikitina and Tatiana Chamié for some extra tuition.

Preo nicknamed de Valois "the Romanov"—a reference to a fancied resemblance to one of the Czar's daughters, and a compliment to her strong and refined facial bone structure, thick dark hair and magnificent eyes. Preobrajenska was especially good in developing solid balance with all that implies in the way of secure turns and coordinated body movement. She was also acute in diagnosis and help over physical trouble or defects—and no dancer is without something of that kind; de Valois had a weakness in her left side resulting from an attack of polio as a child—and could inculcate strength and stamina with a gain rather than a loss of expressive and emotional quality. A tour of Germany began in Munich on September 15 and was a special pleasure for de Valois, who responded to the cultural atmosphere and beautiful landscapes. They visited Leipzig and Berlin, Hamburg, Frankfurt and Cologne. It was the Germany of the Weimar Republic, struggling after defeat in war, before the ascendancy of Hitler and the resurgence of military aspirations. It was also the Germany of vital developments in modern dance, and the year in which Kurt Jooss was given his first job as "producer of movement" at the theatre in Münster. Already Mary Wigman was developing her dark and passionate art, having founded her Central Institute in Dresden in 1920. None of this came directly into de Valois' experience but it was all being talked about, new ideas were in the air and osmosis plays a recognised and powerful part in artistic influence.

Two and a half years elapsed between the failure of *The Sleeping Princess* and the Diaghilev Ballet's reappearance in England. Careful negotiations and the partial financial recovery brought about by his connection with Monte Carlo and seasons on the Continent eventually led to an engagement at the Coliseum in 1924. De Valois returned to London, not as *première danseuse* in grand opera or the delight of fans of Christmas pantomime, not as one of a select band of artists as she had been with Massine and Lopokova, but as a junior member of a large ballet company with a number of small soloist roles to perform. She did not however have the temperament that minded about such things. It was far more important to her that she should be working hard and learning a great deal in the best possible environment.

At the Coliseum the company gave ballets as part of twice-daily music-hall bills. They opened on November 24 with a matinee and the ballet was *Cimarosiana*, in which de Valois danced in a new *pas de quatre* by Nijinska with Nikitina, Lifar and Tcherkas. In the evening *Le Train bleu* was given its London premiere, a star vehicle for Dolin

NdV with Maikerska and Thadee Slavinsky in Narcisse *(Diaghilev Ballet 1923)*

NdV as Papillon in Carnaval *(Diaghilev Ballet 1923)*

on home ground, in which de Valois was one of the flappers (*poules*). Cyril Beaumont was not very impressed by the choreography: it had a "certain facile smartness, an atmosphere of the 'very latest thing', but as a whole I found it dull, even boring". Dolin, however, was the saviour of the occasion:

> "He danced like a man in ecstasy, like a man who suddenly felt possessed of a divine power of movement which raised him above mere mortals … All those complicated bounds, leaps, handstands and backbends were, in essence, stunts, if you like, but they were done with such grace and such apparent ease, that it was only when you began to examine them, that you realised how dangerous they were … "[8]

It was the early forerunner of the perilous acrobatic choreography of the seventies and eighties. It was also the aspect of Dolin's ability that de Valois would remember and draw on when she composed for him the role of Satan in *Job*.

Dolin was a lively, interesting, ambitious personality as well as a fine dancer. He and de Valois understood each other very well. From their first acquaintance she recognised the independent outlook that made it impossible for him to subject himself to discipline from ballet masters and directors, an outlook that conditioned his entire peripatetic career. They were intermittent colleagues during the twenties and thirties, dancing together at times, working as choreographer and leading dancer, amusing and irritating each other on many occasions. As early as 1934 Dolin was to give an after dinner speech about de Valois for a Dancers' Circle Dinner. He was ill and his notes were read by Philip Richardson, but their content and colour are typical:

> "Against the very few errors she has made are counterbalanced the magnificent work and the very definite triumphs she has achieved. Despite the small arguments there have been between us, about costumes, about lights and other, at the time, all-important details, I say to Miss de Valois 'continue with your leadership. You are at the wheel of your own boat. You have knowledge and you have sufficient capability to carry it through the storms…' "

Later in the speech he made a valid point, rarely put forward:

> "She has not reaped any great financial reward. Her work has been and still is long and arduous, far longer and more tiring than the office hours

44

of the average city typist, far more exacting and nerve-racking. Literally out of nothing, apart from a few loyal pupils and the enthusiasm, interest and belief of Miss Baylis, she has built and formed the first British ballet that has become recognised as an artistic enterprise."[9]

Dolin, sweepingly and typically, was completely disregarding Marie Rambert and the Ballet Club...

The most successful production of the Diaghilev Ballet season of 1924 at the Coliseum, ironically enough in view of the failure of *The Sleeping Princess,* was *Aurora's Wedding.* In this de Valois danced in the Nijinska *pas de trois* for Florestan and his sisters, accompanied by Nikitina or Danilova, Efimov or Zverev. It was Danilova's first season with the company. She had just joined them, with the other Soviet State artists Balanchine, Gevergeva and Efimov. She and Nikitina were de Valois' friends (and at times rivals) from the start.

The Coliseum engagement was a triumph. Beaumont reports how on the last night, January 10 1925, the audience cheered the ballet throughout its performance:

"It was not until an announcement was made from the stage to the effect that the company would return in May that the spectators consented to go home."[10]

A significant event took place while they were in London. One Sunday morning Balanchine's paces as a choreographer were tried out at Astafieva's studio in the King's Road, Chelsea. Diaghilev, Boris Kochno and Grigoriev watched a group of dancers, which included de Valois, in a trial composition. Recognising the importance of the moment, convinced of his outstanding talent, she was delighted when they returned to Monte Carlo to find him in charge of the opera ballets.

On the journey to Monaco she herself was in charge, in a different way, of fourteen-year-old Alicia Markova, Diaghilev's latest and youngest recruit. Markova was accompanied by her governess, but de Valois was needed, as an experienced traveller and fluent French speaker, to organise them on the journey to Paris and on to Monte Carlo. Once there, little Alicia led a protected life, working intensively with Cecchetti and his wife, watching the company rehearse and perform, and over-mothered by the governess, who even locked her up in their hotel room when she had to go out shopping. Then, in May 1926, when they had been left behind in Monte Carlo, the governess became seriously ill (and later died after a mental breakdown).

Markova had to travel alone to Paris to join the ballet where she was immediately handed over by Grigoriev to de Valois, who was no longer a company member but appearing as guest artist.

De Valois booked her in at her hotel and they really got to know each other. Markova admired greatly de Valois' elegance—at that time she was intensely interested in Paris fashions and wore very chic clothes and hats—and benefited too from a crash course from her in daily living—how to shop, how to order in restaurants, how to budget and generally look after herself—as well as informative tours to museums, galleries and theatres.[11]

The Monte Carlo season of 1924/25 was interrupted by a dancers' strike towards the end of January. De Valois recalls:

> "one ... participated in signed petitions, went on strike, and attended clandestine meetings in a deserted Monte Carlo bandstand with the best of them. What the main issue of the strike was about was not too clear; it really did not matter very much but it was all very exciting and curtailed rehearsals for a few days. That we lost goes without saying ... "

She admired the firm way Diaghilev and Grigoriev dealt with the problem and the fact that they did not show "any attempt or inclination to humiliate any of the prominent offenders once the matter ended". She learned that there had been no

> "absolute right or wrong on either side, only a stupid misunderstanding, perhaps handled at the beginning too hastily by the dancers and in an unnecessarily autocratic manner by the direction."[12]

Her statements are illuminating. The Irish independent in her character reacted to the excitement of being "agin the government" but her ability to see all sides of an argument evaluated cause and effect with clarity. Certainly her own record of directorship never included a similar situation.

The Monte Carlo season continued with ballets both at the Théâtre du Casino and in concert performances at the Nouvelle Salle de Musique (Salle Ganne), given twice weekly without scenery and with an orchestra composed of two pianos and a string quartet. De Valois added to her repertoire the swift fluttering solo of Papillon (*Carnaval*) and Dorotea in *The Good-humoured Ladies*. They were back in Spain in May with an exhausting schedule of four ballets a night. Programmes composed of *Petrushka, Les Sylphides, Carnaval* and *La Boutique fantasque* make great demands on a company. De Valois has often reiterated the need for young dancers to have "two tough years"— the hardening process that makes thorough professionals out of raw material—and she certainly had them herself with the Diaghilev Ballet. She was dancing in the *corps* in each ballet in the repertoire in addition to her soloist roles. In Spain she had a special bonus when she danced a coveted lead, the Favourite Slave in *Cléopâtre*—a role that contained the veil dance created by Karsavina.

Faithful to the promise of January, the London Coliseum once again housed the company in May 1925. The season began on the 18th with *Carnaval* in the afternoon and the addition in the evening of *Aurora's Wedding*. It was intended to open with *Les Biches* (*The House Party*) but Woizikovsky had a sprained ankle and it was postponed until the 25th. When it did appear it was inevitably a talking point. The sophisticated London public was not blind to the many implications of the relationships so brilliantly defined in dance by Nijinska. Beaumont wrote:

> "It was not a pleasant theme, and it was presented with an insight that could only be derived from an intimate knowledge of such occasions, but it was a genuine cross-section of a phase of contemporary life, a presentation rendered the more piquant by the very delicacy of its considerable imputations."[13]

The London season was interrupted by a short visit to Paris to the Gâité-Lyrique where Balanchine's *Le Chant du rossignol* was premiered. De Valois' contract came up for renewal at the end of July but she had no wish to renew it. She was restless, looking for new opportunities. She applied to the Pavlova Ballet, but back-pedalled on the application, inhibited from joining it by feelings of loyalty to Diaghilev. Her failure to acquire a personal knowledge of Pavlova and her repertoire has been a lasting regret—this was the one area in which she would have no direct experience. She has said she wanted "to get back to pure dancing for one year, prior to taking up teaching, as an aid to further study from the instructor's angle".[14] This idea of the time could only have been part of the truth. In 1925, when her main life's work was almost coming into view, her deepest ambition could not have been limited to teaching.

She made a graceful and friendly break with Diaghilev, so much so that she returned as guest artist both in 1926 and 1928. In 1926 she was with them in May when an uproar greeted the Paris premiere of Nijinska's *Romeo and Juliet*, for which Diaghilev had commissioned a score from the 20-year-old British composer Constant Lambert. The creation of this ballet was stormy. The music started life as *Adam and Eve*, with a scenario by the pianist Angus Morrison, but Diaghilev arbitrarily decided to stage it as *Romeo and Juliet*—a theme that was not as overworked in ballet as it now is—with designs by another young Englishman, Christopher Wood, recommended to Diaghilev by Picasso. Diaghilev then changed his mind on two important counts. The scenario would forsake the straight narrative of the drama and become a love story about dancers rehearsing *Romeo and Juliet*. The Wood designs were cancelled in favour of contributions from Max Ernst and Joan Miró.

Nijinska choreographed the work in Monte Carlo and left before Lambert arrived for the opening night on May 4. Lambert was outraged both at the abandonment of Wood's designs and at changes Diaghilev made in Nijinska's ballet. He was young, idealistic, passionate, and he launched himself into a row with Diaghilev without of course winning any concessions at all.

News of this drama was retailed to de Valois when she reached Paris, and brought Lambert to her notice very forcefully. The performance of *Romeo and Juliet* at the Théâtre Sarah Bernhardt elicited one of those bizarre, extrovert and vocal outbursts that punctuate Paris theatrical history. The surrealists Louis Aragon and André Breton incited a riot because their associates Ernst and Miró had betrayed their principles by working for the "capitalist" Diaghilev, and matters grew so noisy that the police were called in to restore calm. Lambert commented in a letter to his mother:

"If the protest against the scenery had been because it was bad I should have heartily sympathised but as the motive was a purely political one I was furious, particularly as the protest, being of an aural nature, merely spoilt the music and left the scenery untouched."[15]

De Valois' account of the evening is lively. She remembers

"gendarmes charging down the centre aisles hitting out right and left; gendarmes appearing at the rear of the boxes, and seizing protesting members of the avant-garde or the 'garde' no longer 'avant' (the argument was very complicated) by the back of their necks and dragging them forth into the cool night air . . ."[16]

A few nights later, when Sokolova was ill, she was called in to play the Nurse in a scene that Diaghilev had required Balanchine to choreograph and interpolate, and for which Lambert had refused to compose extra music. She danced her special variations in *Aurora's Wedding* (no one in the company had her outstanding command of pizzicato dancing) and appeared in *Les Noces* and *Les Biches* and in the premiere of a new Balanchine ballet, *La Pastorale*. This strained badly after novelty, involving a telegraph boy and his bicycle and a film company with their camera.

In June she was again a guest artist in London during Diaghilev's summer season at His Majesty's, as she was two years later. Her roles in 1926 included both Pasquina and Dorotea in *The Good-humoured Ladies* and when the company was in London and Turin in December she appeared as the Hostess in *Les Biches*. Her conception of this role was quite unlike Sokolova's—Gordon Anthony describes it as "not brash but typical of the genteel elegant manners of the *nouveaux riches*".[17]

Kaleidoscope

"Constantly changing group of bright objects" Concise Oxford Dictionary

Ninette de Valois

♪ Visions. Influences. They surge up from the floor of the mind until it is necessary to forget protocol, success, fame, and just spill the ensuing impressions strictly in relation as to how they have influenced the writer.

A vision of the porcelain princess—Dame Adeline Genée, the Danish ballerina—at the height of her career in London's Edwardian era. The scene is the famous Empire Theatre, a music hall in Leicester Square, London, that always presented a respectable one-act ballet as well as the conventional music hall caperings of those days. The porcelain princess surmounted it all. She was aloof and dignified, yet she resembled a study in delicately moulded, tastefully coloured china. Her technique was as impeccable as it was strong, and her outlook dedicated to the absolute purity of classicism.

Adeline Genée represented the true Danish School before changes and innovations were permitted. She danced to an audience profoundly ignorant of her severely disciplined background. She danced as she considered that she should dance, midst the smoke and noise of a music hall. This place was known for its famous "promenade" in the rear of the theatre, where the "Ladies of the Town" indulged in their own performance for the benefit of those not interested in the fare offered by the management to the general audience.

Adeline Genée's uncle was the *maître de ballet* and his wife her teacher and dedicated chaperone. She lived a secluded and very disciplined life. She created in England respect and interest in the classical ballet. Londoners took her to their hearts, and her original six weeks engagement was extended to ten years.

I was taken to see her dance for the first time when I was about

50

eleven years old. The Empire Ballet on that occasion was using the famous Covent Garden market as its theme and the backcloth was a painting of the old floral hall adjoining the Opera House.

My memory travels forward a few years to a vision of Anna Pavlova.

In London and the United States of America there are a legion of dancers who only started to dance after they had seen Pavlova.

Again her appearances in London were, for many years, in a London music hall—the Palace Theatre. But by then the music hall was fast becoming a family affair, and the first-class ones were beyond any form of reproach.

To see Pavlova dance was to place the memory of such an event in a state of splendid isolation—an experience that could not be repeated to the same degree with reference to any other artist. She danced with an extraordinary sense of dedication, coupled with an extroverted personality that she managed to wear as a crown of jewels. There were no actual highlights in her work, but she herself was one glowing highlight. Sometimes the intellectuals dismissed her with a condescending smile and a faint murmur of "banal". It mattered little. What mattered was Pavlova with her abandon, her frailty, her ecstasy, and her wonderful feet with their highly arched insteps, delicately wrought as a cast-iron piece of tracery.

She was, of course, a fanatic, and died in a state of exhaustion and weakness brought on through her own fanaticism, for she knew no rest and could not visualise any form of life except dancing. It has been said, and truthfully perhaps, that she did as much harm as she did good. Certainly her genius courted imitation, because genius gives the impression of simplicity and exaltation, and the result is imitation more often than inspiration.

Pavlova was no fool. She loved nature, travelling, art and the various dances of the countries that she visited. Once, passing through her Company's railway carriage when they were travelling through the Rockies, she came upon four girls playing cards. "What is that tree called?" she demanded of one of them. "I don't know, Madam," was the disinterested reply. Pavlova told her. Later she passed them again. They were still playing cards. "What is *that* tree called?" The girl once more expressed her ignorance. "Same one, idiot," was the terse reply.

It is as well to record here all that Pavlova's little company did in the twenties and thirties for English dancers. Hilda Butsova (in plain English Hilda Boot), Ruth French and Muriel Stuart were perhaps the three most prominent English members of her company—all principal

51

dancers of very real distinction and many years of faithful service.

In the very early thirties I have another vision of a singular figure. It is early morning in the classroom of young ballet students intent on learning to control their as yet uncontrolled limbs and bodies. One, with an extra colt-like quality, asserts herself with a graceful gaucherie. She is not in the least aware of her captivating wildness, only aware of the joy of movement. Her other quality? The symmetry that accompanies the perfect proportions of her physical make-up in general, a proportion that, in this case, later repeated itself in the mind's ultimate control of all movement.

"Who is," I asked, "the little girl on the left?" A little later it was necessary to come down to earth. "We must," I murmured, "do something about saving those feet." Something was also done about her name—for within a short period of time little Peggy Hookham was rechristened Margot Fonteyn.

She had all the studentship traits of the truly great to be. Some saw nothing in her, others, like the writer on that memorable morning, knew that a great star romped in our midst. Even in her character there were all the qualities and the defects to be found in budding greatness. Bouts of lethargy, carelessness, despondency and gaiety; then followed dedication, application and ultimate progress. This unsteady see-saw continued for some years. People never quite grasped her beauty, simply because she did not grasp it herself. I can recall seeing her one summer swimming in the South of France, covered, completely unabashed, in hideous mosquito bites. Her black hair streamed out behind her as she cut through the water and created for me a sudden picture of a beautiful skilful young seal.

She soon became the muse of England's leading choreographer— Frederick Ashton. The start was typical. After his very first rehearsal with her, he told me that he "was not at all sure ... " Meanwhile, his little muse went home to her mother and announced "I can't under- stand that man's choreography." But what a partnership later! A stream of Ashton works inspired by her. Life in the theatre is full of such experiences.

In the heart of the world's ballet scene, Fonteyn has perhaps taken over the vacancy left by Pavlova. They are not in any way, either as characters or dancers, the least alike. This is as it should be, and these two legendary figures will, no doubt, have their identities replaced one day by someone who will yet again have more to do with inspiration than imitation.

There suddenly fades the isolated impressions of individuals. The landscape swells, broadens and shows a distant fantastic horizon. I refer to the early Russian Ballet, an advent first thrust on us by the Russian Imperial Ballet, under the direction of Diaghilev, in its first London season at Drury Lane in 1909.

Gone overnight was the conception of Russian dancers as isolated performers. Here was something so exotic, so intoxicating and invigorating, that every London hostess's wardrobe and her drawing room went "à la Bakst" overnight.

In the midst of it all was that male wizard Diaghilev, and with him a host of Russian ballerinas led by Tamara Karsavina and the first great Russian male dancer Nijinsky. There were also *men*, men galore, whirling like dervishes, or hurling themselves about as war-like tartars, and all this crowned by one—Vaslav Nijinsky—who showed Western Europe the heights that a male classical dancer could reach—heights forgotten since the days of Vestris.

The discovery of "*Ballet Russe*" could be likened to landing on an outer space planet, and finding microscopic life in every crevice. Gone for good was the self-conscious dainty understatement; gone the plump lady disguised as a male partner; gone the distorted relics of early romanticism, the tinkly tunes of the old ballet scores—those obliging efforts written to satisfy the ballet master and more often the ballerina. The orchestra pit took over, fortified by the works of distinguished composers who were aware of their rights and demanded a proper hearing. Gone also, with a resounding landslide, were the efficient but complacent stage-sets for state operas and ballets, and in stepped the great painters of the era.

What a trilogy was presented by such music, such dancers and such painters. What a stepping-stone for the great choreographers, now to savour progress by following the lead of Diaghilev, who was bent on presenting, through Russia, the world of ballet in a new light and a new aim that demanded a hearing.

London perhaps took the advent of modern Russian Ballet more to its heart (and consequently subsequent influence) than many other countries in Europe. It had no subsidised old State Opera House to put in cold storage any progressive movement with the idea of its release at intervals in small doses. It is greatly to the credit of the Russian "Establishment" (or was it internal pressure?) that this could happen, and in all fairness there could not have been such a professionally staged ballet revolution without such a solid background

53

for the new form of creativity to break away from.

Once again in 1921 London was fortunate. It turned out that we were to see Diaghilev's only full length production of *The Sleeping Princess*, a yardstick for the Royal Ballet to measure things by when it later produced this work. It turned out to be the root of all our classical productions, mounted for us, along with all the others, by Nicholas Sergeyev who was responsible for the Diaghilev production.

Diaghilev, like Pavlova, favoured English dancers—in the early days it was Lydia Sokolova (alias Hilda Munnings). We forget that it was Diaghilev who, at the beginning of the young Balanchine era, gave us the first two English classical dancers of the middle twenties. They blazed their way to fame through the twenties, thirties, forties and early fifties. I speak of the then very youthful Anton Dolin and Alicia Markova. They spent the war in America, and the war in England lived on Helpmann and Fonteyn. Markova and Dolin returned to England to lead the newly formed London Festival Ballet—named (on the suggestion of Markova) after the newly built Festival Hall. Fonteyn and Helpmann entered the newly re-opened Royal Opera House.

A cold, damp and foggy November morning in London in the year 1925. Six unwilling younger members of the Diaghilev *corps* were ordered to report to a studio by 10.00 a.m., to aid in a choreographic composition by a young man from Leningrad. At noon precisely Diaghilev was to appear and to pass judgment on the result. For two hours, to the painful strains of the Funeral March from *Saul* (conjuring up for me pictures of royal demises), we were "choreographed". We soon forgot that Sunday was our one and only free day in England, we forgot the fog and the cheerless studio, we could only dedicate ourselves to the endearing young man who was grave yet humorous, demanding yet sympathetic—in other words the young George Balanchine. Diaghilev eventually entered the studio rather like an important customs official, accompanied by supporters to aid him in his suspect searchings . . . away we went to the Funeral March, and with smothered visions (on my part) of shiny Horse Guards in long black cloaks, veiled mourners, and silent crowds. We believed wholeheartedly in our present vision, and it was obvious that the over-aweing "customs officials" were well content. It was the beginning of the Balanchine era with the Russian Ballet, which was later to lead this choreographer towards the solving of the American ballet problems.

How do I see the creations of the Diaghilev Ballet in retrospect? They crowd in on my memory and I can only reflect on them subjectively, as a young dancer savouring the experiences of learning and executing them. I must admit to very strong musical influences. There is always the joy of the Dance of the Nurses in the Fair scene in *Petrushka*. I grew to love the music, the dance and the costume. Again the stirring finale of the dances from *Prince Igor*. Far removed from the two mentioned stands out Schumann's *Carnaval* with its romantic elegance, its tenderness and its subdued gaiety.

Time and again I have written and spoken of the effect of Nijinska's *Les Noces* on me. The strange and powerful score of Stravinsky's— mystical, ritualistic, the soul of Russia, was both felt and realised by all the dancers concerned. We became just dedicated parts of the whole—to dance in it was to forget the audience, for it required tremendous concentration, and that added to the exhilaration of the experience. It was always the same, no number of performances ever dimmed its musical and choreographic freshness, its challenge to one and all.

My solo roles in those Diaghilev days never unduly affected me. I suppose one was overcome; it was such an honour to have been chosen to execute them and this was followed by the inevitable attack of nerves. It was dancing in the great ensembles, the experience of being a part of such intricate patterns, that seemed to bring me within reach of the essence of the work. It all eventually started up dreams and ambitions that I did not know existed within me. A much treasured remark was made to me by Vera Nemchinova, who was a famous Russian Ballet ballerina of the 1920s. Many years had passed, then we met again after the Royal Ballet's triumphant opening at the old Metropolitan Opera House in New York in 1949. "Diaghilev gave us all something," she said, "but you took something from him." If I did, I took it when exulting in the many minor appearances that I made in his ballets, and in seeing the whole great machine at work day after day.

I was in many ways very fortunate to be with Diaghilev in the early twenties. His company was now orientated in Western Europe and its headquarters, for all the main performances and rehearsal periods, were either in Monte Carlo or Paris. Monte Carlo engaged the Diaghilev Ballet for nearly five months out of the year—from November to March. We shared performances with the Monte Carlo Opera Season, in other words a section of the Paris Opera Company.

Diaghilev was by now interested in the avant-garde of Paris, and also compelled to think more economically. It was the period of the Massine, Nijinska and Balanchine ballets with the works of Fokine, of course, still in the repertoire.

Monte Carlo at that time was alive with artists of fame and future fame. I can recall Ravel at rehearsal conducting one of his operas; Auric and Poulenc superintending their ballets. Stravinsky making a sudden descent on us. There was Alexandre Benois, a genial figure that I suspect Diaghilev was helping, giving him the work of designing certain opera productions. We all had to dance in the opera ballets, and I can remember wearing a lovely Benois costume that filled me with delight.

There stands out one great and inspiring figure—Picasso in his youth. At one time his wife had been a dancer in the company. They were frequently with us all, along with their small son. For years I possessed a precious snapshot that I took of the three of them on the steps of their modest hotel. Picasso could not believe that I was not French, and always said that I looked "more French than the French". I explained that this was a habit of the Huguenot-Irish, and I happened to be one of them.

Monte Carlo in that period was a dream world. The beaches were quiet and lovely to look at, they never appeared over-crowded. The little hotels were full of retired ex-army and navy officers with their wives.

The Monte Carlo season was followed by our annual visit to Spain, to Paris, Germany and lastly, London. Both in Paris and Monte Carlo were to be noticed the wandering ex-Grand Dukes and Duchesses from the old Czarist Russian days, living, as one member of the company said to me, "on their last row of pearls". We were haunted by a world of pre-revolution Russians, not only outside but inside the ballet, where we still had with us many members of the Imperial Ballet pre-war era.

Beyond the generous but unreliable help from his well-to-do admirers, Diaghilev was totally unsubsidised, and in comparison with what is happening these days, it seems impossible to believe. Extra money was made by glamorous appearances in big French houses at the height of the Paris season, dancing on elegant stages erected midst the trees on their expansive lawns; opening big Paris shops where the ground floor would be the auditorium, and the first balcony floor transformed into something representing a theatre's dress circle.

*   *   *

Well, what about the giddy public life of a dancer? Let us turn the penny over and see the other side, its cloistered private existence.

Days are spent in the seclusion of the rehearsal room, the canteen, the physiotherapy department. Evenings sweating through a heavy programme with the prospect of next morning's 10.30 a.m. class. What is the attraction? What does it feel like to put everything into the first half of your life and then in the late thirties or early forties take a further plunge in connection with a readjustment—the choice of a special line within your world of the ballet—or to try and adapt yourself to something totally divorced from it all? I wonder if it is really more devastating than that which often faces a late middle-aged business man? The readjustment of a dancer's life comes much earlier, and there is something to be said for the energy that still exists and is able to accept the challenge offered by change.

Whether through a life of discipline and dedication, or through the fact that at a very early age they decide on such a career, dancers do appear, in the end, to be extremely adaptable to change, and fit with ease and a sense of adventure into other branches of the theatre world—and even into entirely different occupations.

"I would rather take on the resettlement of a trained dancer than a member of any other profession," said an executive to me of a certain branch of the television world, "I find them quick and adaptable." I once asked a man, sent to talk to our dancers over executive matters, how he had got on? "Terrifying," he gasped. "I found myself confronted with a crowd of quick-witted monkeys."

They may be lively, witty, intelligent, but nevertheless there is an endearing yet exasperating streak of eternal youth about them. They do, on the whole, live in the present. But then I find that this is the artist's natural attitude; to think too far ahead with accent on future security can be dangerous. An artist is not a bank clerk, he is as much an adventurer as all athletes, explorers and members of the defence forces. There must be a slight line of division between the prosaic journeys of the average commuter and the artist's less clearly worked out path.

What is the ballet today? How fare its traditions? Oh, goosey goosey gander, where do you wander?

No real tradition in anything ever dies. It may get placed on a shelf or go into a temporary coma; it is though more likely to make a stealthy progress in a state of crafty subterfuge. One thing is certain, such old soldiers neither die nor do they fade away.

And so with the history of the ballet. There is the Italian, the French, the Danish and the Russian school (Russia the youngest, when it comes to strict protocol, in relation to the four traditionally established schools). There is also the Swedish, the Belgian, the Dutch, the American, the English and a host of others on the horizon throughout the world. Of course we all spring from the traditional four, and of course we must all return to these four roots from time to time—for they are our reference library.

Choreographically the picture is more complex, more individualistic than any form of pedagogy. It can, it fact, be agreed that in any period of time a few great creative influences are to be found at work in different directions at one and the same time. But "style" in the end can be recognised as the prerogative of every established whole, after the part may have bestowed its traditional and creative influence. "Style", the personal hallmark, emerges eventually regardless of the early imported seed, and so ensures that the offsprings and the saplings have it their own way, for they have been conceived and reared in their own soil, and the nature of the soil will have its say, and speak through them.

Chapter III

⟋⟍ Soon after leaving Diaghilev in 1925 de Valois was deep in plans for the opening of a studio in London. She had to renew old contacts and seek out influential new ones. She had to look for suitable premises.

The London of 1925 must be sketched in to understand the artistic climate in which she started her new career. It was seven years after the shocks and losses of World War I. That war was still present in people's minds, in the minds of the older generation who had seen so many sons killed in action, in the minds of those who had survived the horrors and had to build lives for themselves in a changed world, in the minds of those too young to have personal experience of war but who were now, as adults, the heirs of the peace.

Economically there were vast problems. It was a society in which demobbed officers had to turn to all manner of jobs to make a living, a hard world for those without money or influence, a bitter period for the working classes. For those who could afford it, however, there was every opportunity for an extravagant social round and many, in London especially, were determined to make the most of life through pleasure and gaiety and a certain amount of dissipation, but also through all forms of art. The cultural society in southern England was a remarkably closely knit community, a patchwork of friends, and friends of friends, who slipped in and out of each other's working lives with great dexterity, exchanging ideas and influences, as well as spouses and lovers, in a stimulating and exciting fashion. Looked at from the vantage point of history they appear to be performing a constantly changing and intricate quadrille.

In her years as a *première danseuse* de Valois had acquired many acquaintances in the theatre and these were now to stand her in good stead. An important contact was Philip Richardson, the tall, immensely elegant, indefatigable and perceptive editor of *The Dancing Times* who was always concerned about her career and ready to help in any way he could. The music critic Edwin Evans, who had been an adviser to Diaghilev and one of the contributors of ballet reviews to *The Dancing Times'* Sitter Out column, admired her as an artist and was to assist her greatly where music was concerned. Lopokova provided a stimulating friendship as well as an entrée into the Bloomsbury world. Dolin was an ally, freelancing in a zestful way as a dancer, appearing in music-hall bills with various partners and always quick to speak up for British ballet talent.

The ramifications of contacts and friendly relationships are impossible to disentangle. Introductions could come from more than one source and, as the twenties ended and the thirties moved on, it sometimes seemed as though everyone had common memories and mutual acquaintances. As the Vic-Wells Ballet developed, composers and designers began to be brought along to de Valois, some by way of Lambert and the Royal College of Music, some through William Chappell and the Chelsea School of Art.

London in 1925 was also full of dance teachers, many of them famous names, and studios, all busily turning out professional or semi-professional pupils and staging yearly or half-yearly shows of tap-dancing, song-and-dance numbers, national dance, Greek dance and that now curious term "operatic dancing"—at the time some stigma still attached to the term "ballet dancer", deriving from the kept ladies of the previous century. All these categories were reflected in the annual regional festival competitions and the Sunshine competitions, and shows were extensively covered in local papers or specialised magazines. Four organisations had been set up to promote good teaching standards in recognised systems: the Association of Operatic Dancing (later the Royal Academy of Dancing), the Imperial Society of Teachers of Dancing, the Cecchetti Society and Espinosa's British Ballet Organisation. De Valois was associated with them all.

She had no intention of competing with other teachers, although firm in her own views about teaching. Her underlying intention was to build up a ballet company. Here her main rival was Marie Rambert, who was just ahead—she had started teaching in London in 1920 and by 1925 had a small group of good students as well as the support of her playwright husband Ashley Dukes. Although de Valois, with her 1921 group, had preceded the Rambert Dancers to the stage, the continuity had been broken by her years with the Russian Ballet.

In considering this new phase of her life, it becomes obvious that de

Valois not only possessed the knowledge and experience of her dancing career. She had additional strengths: a capacity for working well—and very hard—with all types and levels of theatre artists and a marked ability for observing and analysing situations and individuals. She also had the undeniable asset of being a very beautiful and attractive young woman.

Her first step as an independent artist was to choreograph a short ballet for the December Sunshine Matinee. *The Art* (sometimes *Arts*) *of the Theatre* consisted of an entry, solos for five girls (Music, Painting, Dancing, Comedy and Tragedy) and a final ensemble. It was set to Ravel's *La Valse* and costumes and decorations were by Kathleen Dillon.

Kathleen Dillon, who married Angus Morrison, first met de Valois through classes with Cecchetti and Massine. She had been a leading child dancer with Margaret Morris and her group and also studied stage design with Margaret Morris' husband, the artist J. D. Fergusson, creating costumes for some of de Valois' early dance compositions.

The cast for *The Art of the Theatre* are all known names. Dorothy Coxon (Music) was with the Massine-Lopokova group at Covent Garden and the Coliseum and also with the Diaghilev Ballet. Molly Lake (Dancing) worked with the Pavlova Company and had first met de Valois at Mrs Wordsworth's classes when their waiting mothers became friends. Margaret Craske (Comedy), de Valois' ballet mistress in 1921, had appeared with the opera and ballet company of Ileana Leonidoff-Massera from Rome at Covent Garden in 1924. Ursula Moreton (Tragedy) was with the Diaghilev Ballet. De Valois herself danced Painting.

The Art of the Theatre was a worthy 'prentice piece. De Valois quotes Lopokova on it—"a bit of a highbrow muddle"—but other views were less dismissive. Sheila McCarthy, who later performed the Dancing solo, describes the action:

> "As 'Dancing', my work was flowing and wide—high *developpés, grands jetés en tournant* etc. 'Comedy' was angular, on bent knees, quick, with sharp head movements. It always reminded me of a small jester. 'Tragedy' was slow, lightly clenched fists, a suggestion of Greek movement, hands resting on her head." [1]

The range of style in this early work typifies de Valois' dance interests, her instinct for appropriate movement and theatrical contrast.

De Valois' studio, the Academy of Choregraphic Art, was opened

Opening of the Academy of Choregraphic Art 1926. (back) Vladimir Polunin, Anton Dolin, Edwin Evans, Margaret Craske, Elizabeth Polunin, Col. E. Cameron; (second row centre) Lydia Lopokova; (front) NdV, Ursula Moreton, Frances James, Marie Rambert

in March 1926, preceded by a short article she wrote on "The Future of the Ballet" for the February *Dancing Times*. This was a strong, thoughtful essay that set out quite a few of her basic tenets. She saw the "true aim" of modern ballet as "a serious practical effort to expand the possibilities of the art of dancing in harmony with the other arts of the theatre". Her dedication to the unity of the arts, confirmed by her experience with Diaghilev, was apparent:

> "Take the close relation of dancing to music through its rhythmical movements, and to painting through form and design. The dance cannot exist in its complete form without the direct cooperation of these two."

She saw dance in its relation to the theatre. "I dare to hope for and prophesy a revival of the more dramatic form of ballet." Already she was concerned with training first-rate dancers, advocating "a sound body technique of expressive movement" and "a wider and more sensitive mental outlook through general study".[2]

The new studio was carefully planned to implement these beliefs. Its curriculum had a thoroughly professional air. In her autobiography, Marie Rambert wrote:

"I thought the name of the school too grandiloquent but the prospectus impressed me very much. It showed great intelligence, immense knowledge of ballet and the theatre, as well as practical sense, and seemed to carry in it a promise of future great developments. It made me feel very small and useless. I seriously thought that I should send all my pupils to Ninette and close my school ..."[3]

She rallied however and the parallel but contrasted evolution of the Rambert and de Valois companies became the most fascinating and fruitful feature of British ballet history.

Many of the Academy students are known to ballet historians as the nucleus of the Vic-Wells Ballet; some have had lifelong connections with de Valois, others married and left the scene entirely after a very few years. They came to her from different sources and in different ways. Ailne Phillips was already a teenage leading dancer with her family company, the Carl Rosa Opera. Joy Newton was dancing Will o' the Wisp in *Where the Rainbow Ends* when she auditioned for de Valois around 1926. Freda Bamford was a drama student at the Old Vic, as were the sisters Rosalind and Sara Iden Payne; daughters of the theatre director Ben Iden Payne, they adopted the stage name of Patrick. Sheila McCarthy, who began dancing at the age of eight, had some celebrated teachers in London and Paris before reaching the Academy in 1927. Beatrice Appleyard, her mother and her Maidenhead dancing teacher picked the school by chance from an advertisement in *The Dancing Times*.

The premises at 6a Roland Gardens were on the ground floor with one room in the basement. There was a large hall with a door leading into an L-shaped room whose dividing doors could be made into two studios, and a further room served as dressing room. The studio was painted in lavender grey, with linoleum to match and in the bow window that looked on to the street there were Lloyd Loom armchairs upholstered in the same shade. The girls wore practice tunics of crêpe-de-chine, white for the juniors and a shade variously described as plum and petunia for the seniors, with flesh pink tights. Pointe shoes were bought from Raynes and made by Nicolini in Milan.

De Valois was an excellent (and strict) teacher. She emphasised Cecchetti in the syllabus because she had his personal certificate as her main teaching credential but she was never confined to one system, developing her own out of her diverse studies. Her method was a meld of the French, Italian and Russian schools plus modern-classical movement drawn from her work with Nijinska and Massine. She was always interested in Dalcroze eurythmics and their relationship of movement to music, although they were not directly taught at the Academy. She did include however, and it was an important part of the programme, "composition" classes comprising plastique dance movement based on geometric and sculptural foundations related to music, classes that provided a salutory counterbalance to the severity of classical dance training. Her classical classes laid great stress on thinking quickly—the *enchaînements* were many and rapid and had to be picked up at once.

Character dance she was always enthusiastic about and her character classes included the various Central European folk dances as well as those of the British Isles. She was advised by Derra de Moroda, in addition to her own experience with the Diaghilev Ballet where many works had a strong link with Russian or Polish peasant dances. She was in touch with Cecil Sharp House and the Morris Dance movement and about this time found that there was one Morris dance traditionally permitted to women. This she performed as a solo on a number of occasions. Historical and court dances she learnt, as fellow student Kathleen Dillon recalls, from Nellie Chaplin who had made a special study of "ancient dances and music" and arranged period dances for some of the plays staged by Nigel Playfair at the Lyric Theatre Hammersmith.

De Valois' early Academy prospectus, as well as listing both a music library and a reading library (Edwin Evans advised her on the former), includes a significant passage:

"With the growing realisation of the importance of the general knowledge a dancer should possess concerning the relation of the dance to the theatre as a whole, a special class has been arranged and will be held by Vladimir and Elizabeth Polunin. It will include
general knowledge in drawing and design
stage construction
scenic design
costume design
general knowledge of scene-painting
the correlation of scenery, costume and stage lighting
with movement and grouping."[4]

Vladimir Polunin had been the principal scene painter for the Diaghilev Ballet, realising for the theatre many of the great ballet designs commissioned by Diaghilev from outstanding artists, and had written a book *The Continental Method of Scene Painting*. His English wife Elizabeth was also a painter. They settled in England where Vladimir taught scene painting at the Slade. Later Kathleen Dillon gave theatre art classes at the Academy. She built six model theatres which she kept at the studio and with these demonstrated the principles of ballet design to help students gain a good understanding of sets and costumes in relation to dancers and their performances. From the beginning the girls were encouraged to create costumes for the dances they were taught. Classes in make-up were also given.

Another aspect of ballet performance was prominently featured—traditional mime. This conventional gesture language is often now considered too laboured and stilted, but in the hands of a master who marries it properly to musical phrasing and amplifies it by facial and bodily expression it is a splendid element of 18th and 19th century classical ballets. It only becomes tedious or ridiculous when it is used woodenly and without understanding or musicality. De Valois decided to take classes herself with a remarkable teacher, Francesca Zanfretta. An Italian born in Mantua, Zanfretta made her debut in Vienna and then came to London in 1880 to dance at the Empire Theatre. She was a superlative coach for mime and not only de Valois but Ursula Moreton gained greatly from her tuition. At Moreton's request, Sheila McCarthy wrote down what Zanfretta taught. This was handed on in its complex and fascinating detail to the Vic-Wells Ballet and its successor companies.

Two excellent pianists are remembered, Mrs Turner and Mrs Mackey. Mrs Turner was the more unforgettable in person—an eccentric character who wore a battered old hat on a shock of untidy grey hair and walked up the street in a black cloak "like a crow in flight."[5]

Once a month de Valois organised a Sunday evening recital to an invited audience, rather grand dinner-jacket affairs, when not only parents but other teachers, critics, up-and-coming musicians and artists, sat down to watch. Many of the divertissements featured at Cambridge or Dublin were first tried out there. Sometimes it worked the other way round, as with *Rout,* premiered at Cambridge and shown to London at one of these recitals. Beatrice Appleyard remembers it as

> "exciting to work on ... You had to count like mad, irregular phrases of 7, 9, 8, 5, hiccup and proceed in 6/8 temp for count of thirteen ..."[6]

This was certainly no ordinary school and Nadina Newhouse summed it up:

"The whole atmosphere of the studio was of a combined centre of the arts—dancing, music, art and drama (mime)."[7]

However, as with her companies in later years, de Valois could laugh with them as well as scold. What Joy Newton terms "a dotty fancy dress party" is remembered at which "everyone took off everyone else".[8]

The Academy prospectus mentioned that students could "cook light lunches" if they were there the whole day and many of them did. De Valois, a keen cook, taught them how to make omelettes. There was one crisis which Joy Newton recalls. They had been careless about not throwing out bits of food that were going bad, decaying tomatoes and so on. One morning they arrived for class and along the studio mantelpiece all these rotting items were spread. "The Prin" as they called her among themselves (from "Principal") said nothing at all, merely pointed to it with the stick she used in teaching. Never again did any girl fail to clear up properly . . .[9]

Still available as a freelance dancer, during the next few years de Valois appeared occasionally with Dolin in the commercial theatre. In the summer of 1926 he and Phyllis Bedells were touring in a programme due to come into the Coliseum in August. Bedells had to withdraw owing to an injury and de Valois replaced her and fulfilled the London season. Dolin was choreographer and planned the dances to include a suite of nursery rhyme items. They danced *Little Boy Blue,* based on two Elgar pieces, and *Jack and Jill.* The most striking dance was *Lacquer*—a Chinese-style masked duet set against a background of black curtains in which de Valois wore red silk and Dolin yellow.

The following May they were again together for a revue at His Majesty's. *White Birds,* presented by Lew Leslie, hoped to parallel the enormous success of the famous *Black Birds* but failed signally. The Dolin-de Valois number was as unoriginal as most of the other items— a Montmartre street scene, "Traffic in Souls"—but their performance lifted it out of the ordinary run. This time she was dancing in high heels, wearing a short sleeveless satin shift and tiny black cap, a picture of sexy sophisticated style. Their apache dance seems to have been the only successful moment of what *The Stage* described as an "ornate but stupendously dull and overloaded revue".[10] It made some money for her other projects, however, which her more serious activities rarely did.

*   *   *

NdV with Anton Dolin in Little Boy Blue *(London Coliseum 1926)*

NdV with Anton Dolin in White Birds *(His Majesty's 1927)*

De Valois had already begun her close association with the repertory theatre movement for which she would always remain an enthusiast. There are many levels on which repertory theatre operates, but in the twenties all the most stimulating and fruitful experiments and ideas appeared in a group of outstanding centres where productions were presented in repertory by a controlling individual, either an artistic director or a theatre manager. The names are readily recalled: J. B. Fagan and the Oxford Playhouse, Sir Nigel Playfair and the Lyric Hammersmith, Peter Godfrey and the Gate Theatre, William Armstrong and the Liverpool Playhouse, Barry Jackson and the Birmingham Rep, Terence Gray and the Festival Theatre Cambridge, Lilian Baylis and the Old Vic and Sadler's Wells.

In the summer of 1926, while the General Strike occupied the country's attention, de Valois put on a huge floppy hat—she was greatly admired by her girls throughout the twenties and thirties for the range and modishness of her hats—and went to see Lilian Baylis. Baylis and the Old Vic have been lavishly covered in books, memoirs and articles and need no elaboration. A formidable, eccentric, endearing and shrewd lady with a vast purpose and strong religious faith, the quality she brought to her management of the Vic-Wells meant that all encounters she had with theatre artists of the time were the stuff of history. Through her yea or nay to them she wrote a famous chapter in British theatrical development, to which the National Theatre, the Royal Ballet companies and the English National Opera daily testify.

She was not, in 1926, thinking in terms of such internationally known establishment organisations. She wanted a good sensible (and cheap) dancing teacher who could help her actors and drama students to move rather better on stage and use their hands properly, someone who could arrange dances in plays and operas. There were also office worker volunteers employed as extras—they badly needed movement tuition. She thought too that it would be nice to couple the rather short opera *Hansel and Gretel* to be given at Christmas with a curtain-raiser ballet on an expenses-only budget. Rather more at the back of her mind but none the less important was her ambition not only to acquire and reopen Sadler's Wells Theatre but to start a ballet company there. She had been head of a dancing school in the Rand, back in the 1890s, and her secretary Evelyn Williams recalls her saying after her interview with de Valois: "That's all right. Miss de Valois is going to run her school with the Vic and when we have Sadler's Wells she'll run a wholetime ballet company for us."[11]

De Valois had in fact written letters outlining a possible scheme for starting an English ballet company in a repertory theatre and sent one to Baylis and one to Barry Jackson. Jackson had refused. Baylis had asked her to come and discuss it.

Two women of genius sat face to face in cramped quarters backstage at the Old Vic. The older, with a clumsy body, a plain slightly twisted face, a lack of wide cultural knowledge but a total conviction about what she was doing and why she was doing it, was intent on achieving the greatest good for her theatre and audience for the smallest possible financial outlay. The younger, now twenty-eight, with a classical dancer's carriage and strikingly intelligent looks, was following an impulse of destiny and making instinctive decisions that would start her on a notable journey. What they shared, and this must have been an important factor, was limitless ambition for their particular dreams coupled with a down-to-earth attitude about building on limited practical foundations.

> [Baylis] "had my letter in her hand—and said that she thought it showed enthusiasm coupled with a practical mind. She thought I had had enough experience to know my job and that she liked my face—but had never heard of me professionally. She added that she had been told I was a good dancer—but did not consider that she had any proof, as yet, of my teaching ability, in fact I might be quite hopeless with her drama students."[12]

According to Evelyn Williams, Baylis had the gift of "knowing instinctively who was the right person for any special job"[13] and she was probably in no doubt by the end of the interview that the right person for ballet at the Vic-Wells theatres had walked into her life. However as a practical woman she went along to the Academy with her producer Andrew Leigh to watch de Valois give class and only then came to an agreement by which de Valois was to have a four-year contract from the beginning of the next season and be paid £1 a week for teaching the drama students and £2 for arranging dances in a Shakespeare production. De Valois managed to delegate the office workers and the opera dances to one of her Academy girls, Rosalind Patrick, working under her supervision and receiving a few shillings of her fee each time.

With the Old Vic settled, the Academy going well, de Valois was still hungry for work. Appropriately, another door was opened. In April 1926 her second cousin, Terence Gray, had in partnership acquired an old theatre just outside Cambridge.

Gray, who for a few years became a vital and controversial figure in British theatre, was born in 1895 in Felixstowe. He was doubly related to de Valois, with Stannus connections on both sides, but they had not grown up in any close association. They had met rarely, and were both deeply absorbed in their own pursuits. Gray had been schooled at Eton and at Magdalene College, Cambridge, before becoming an archaeologist. World War I intervened, when he served as an air mechanic, but after that he went to Egypt to dig—saying once that he was "one of the privileged few who had the distinction of being refused admission to the tomb of Tutankhamen by Howard Carter".[14] In Egypt he met Harold Ridge, a metallurgist in the service of the Egyptian Government who had also been an ardent small part actor at the Sheffield Repertory Theatre. Their mutual love of drama led them to plan an experimental house of their own. Excited by all the avant-garde ideas burgeoning in Europe for the staging and lighting of productions, they looked around for suitable premises and found the perfect place.

The house that was to be known as the Festival Theatre started life in 1808 as the Theatre Royal, Barnwell. It still stands today, just outside the city of Cambridge, in the Newmarket Road. Rebuilt in 1818 as a small compact horseshoe-circled proscenium theatre with a forestage and entrances from the audience side of the curtain, it operated until 1878, when the management went bankrupt. Until 1914 it was a mission hall, but when Gray and Ridge acquired it, it had for many years been dark.

The two young men in their thirties set to work with skill and vigour. Leaving the outer area untouched—corridors with fifteen box doors behind the main circles conjure up the early 19th century—they converted the rest to their own specifications. The acting area was split into three parts: a broad forestage with a fan-shaped flight of shallow steps curving down to the front of the stalls; a central revolve; and a raised and sliding backstage, which could be entered from below, in front of a 40-foot concrete cyclorama. De Valois, walking into the Olivier Theatre in London when it was new, recognised many of the features. Forty years earlier, the Festival Theatre had been a similar house in miniature.

The sections of the stage could be separated by curtains and the orchestra was under the forestage. Close communication with the audience was ensured by having two wide gangways through the stalls, used for stage entrances and exits. "It was difficult," wrote Norman

71

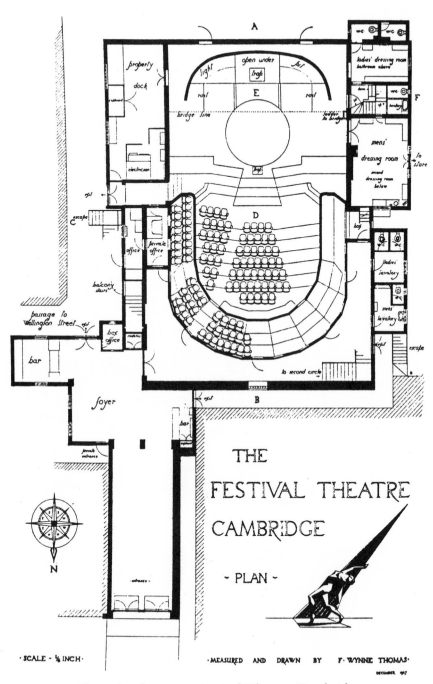

Plan of auditorium, Festival Theatre Cambridge

Marshall, "to find any definite point at which the stage ended and the auditorium began".[15] Additionally, the new theatre possessed the most advanced lighting system to be seen in Britain until the 1960s. Its prototype was worked out by Schwabe and Haseit and installed only a few months earlier in the Dresden Opera House.

Gray and Ridge were reacting against the theatre of realism and towards the theatre of imagination and illusion, the theatre of Edward Gordon Craig and Adolphe Appia, of W. B. Yeats' poetry, of Central European expressionist techniques. Their concept of production included the use of dance and dance movement, mime and masks, and Gray realised that de Valois was the perfect choice to bring these elements into action. In spite of her strict classical dance training she had been subjected to many freer influences and had eagerly responded to them. Gray's enthusiasm for dance drama—he was already writing his own—and de Valois' growing interest in the use of dance movement in dramatic productions made them ideal collaborators. Needing a choreographic director for his Festival Theatre, he enlisted her cooperation.

Terence Gray may well have been unaware of the extraordinary capacity of his new choreographic director. He himself was an original and iconoclastic thinker, whose keen and thorough interest was applied to plays ancient and modern, to production, design and lighting—and peripherally to *haute cuisine* and good wine. He was brimming over with ideas, enchanted with his advanced stage and lighting possibilities, absorbed in his splendid new toy; and he was wise enough to recruit an excellent play director in Herbert Prentice who had founded the Sheffield Repertory Company two years previously.

Gray's first, very special, production at the Festival Theatre was *The Oresteia of Aeschylus* (November 22 1926) in a translation by Professor R. C. Trevelyan. Prentice directed, supervised by Gray; music was composed by Donald Tovey and Gordon Jacob and conducted by Dennis Arundell; the chorus was produced by de Valois. An unknown young actor, Maurice Evans, was the Orestes and Torin Thatcher the Aigisthus. Miriam Lewis was Klytemnestra, Rita Daniel the Elektra, Marion Prentice the Cassandra. Hedley Briggs led the chorus.

De Valois had to work closely with the text of Trevelyan's translation—he attended rehearsals to check on correct words and emphasis from his point of view—and devise movement that would illustrate and complement speech for a masked group of six girls from her Academy surrounding the chorus leader.

The opening night was triumphant. Next day the *Cambridge Daily News* wrote of the wonderful wit of the producer and the revelation of the lighting effects,

> "a good deal supplied from the auditorium so that the lighting in the audience is the same as that for the stage. Consequently the atmosphere and spirit of the production is carried all over the house."

The use of spotlight and cyclorama was effective as was the beautiful colour blending in the lighting of the last scene. Where the chorus was concerned they were particularly impressed:

> "Theirs was work which could easily have been made ridiculous by under-rehearsal but every action was perfect, every gesture just sufficient and well-timed, and the many pictures they formed were artistically conceived and splendidly carried out."[16]

The *Cambridge Review* was slightly less enthusiastic:

> "Her most successful groupings were two of the Furies at the end of the second scene of *The Eumenides*, but her management of the Trojan bondwomen produced many striking effects. In the *Agamemnon* she had little scope. Two criticisms may be offered. Firstly, there was a certain monotony in the 'swimming' movement of the Furies as also in the rhythmical swaying of Cassandra; excellent ideas were robbed of some of their effectiveness by repetition. Secondly, it is impossible for an audience, however willing, to lose sight of past associations. Gestures therefore that suggest the toothache should be avoided and the chorus should not, as they run stooping, be allowed to raise their hands as though to keep their masks from falling off . . ."[17]

Norman Marshall, in retrospect, was solidly appreciative:

> "There are three separate choruses in the play, the chorus of Argive Elders, the chorus of Trojan Bondwomen and the chorus of Furies. Both the opportunities and the difficulties for the choreographer were immense. What Ninette de Valois achieved reduced one's memories of all other Greek choruses one had ever seen to a series of pretty posturings by comparison."

He also spoke of "the strength, the depth of feeling, the originality and dramatic force" that characterised her work.[18]

De Valois was now commuting between Cambridge and London, where her energies were divided between the Academy and the Old

Vic, "sometimes stretched out in a third-class carriage on the milk train after a first night, so as to get to my school early in the morning". English milk trains trebled the length of a journey but at least they operated overnight. At Cambridge new productions went on every ten days or so but not all required the services of a choreographer. She had a weekly commitment to the Old Vic for the actors' lessons, where her classes included Elizabeth Allan, Heather Angel and Esmond Knight, whose natural ability as a dancer gave her tremendous pleasure. He possessed "quite the most remarkable jump that I have ever seen".[19]

Her first choreography for the Vic had been seen on September 27 in Andrew Leigh's production of *A Midsummer Night's Dream*. Leigh was resistant. He didn't want dancers, he didn't like dancers, and he hoped to kill the whole idea of using them. In the *Dream* de Valois combined drama and dance students. Cobweb, Peaseblossom, Moth and Mustardseed used two of each, and seven drama girls danced in the fairy ensemble. Pre-dating the *Oresteia,* it was the first drama production in which she was involved as choreographer and she was out to learn as much as possible about spoken acting and direction. *The Tempest* followed, and her work was briefly mentioned in *The Stage* which praised "the arrangement of the dances by Ninette de Valois in the well-staged masque and banquet".[20] Critical notice of choreography or dance arrangements was rare indeed from drama or music reviewers. The Christmas show was a children's play, *Christmas Eve,* by Rose Fyleman, a popular writer of children's verse and stories.

The next significant Cambridge date came in January 1927, when Norman Marshall directed W. B. Yeats' play, *On Baile's Strand*. Gray had carefully chosen this Cuchulain play, written in 1904, as he considered it a fine and subtle piece, dealing with an engrossing theme— the confrontation between the politician King Conchubar and the warrior Cuchulain, a conflict that could be interpreted on many levels. He gave it a superb setting of pillars, doorways and steps, creating by shaded blue and green lighting on the cyclorama an impression of sea and mist. The overall costume tones of black, white and grey against the cyclorama were magnificently evocative of ancient dramas. De Valois staged the rituals demanded by the text and choreographed the roles of the symbolic characters of the Fool and the Blindman (Hedley Briggs and Walter Meyjes). She echoed the stylised angularity of their masks (designed by Briggs) in similarly striking gestures and relationships of movement. Masks had not been used in the original Dublin staging, but Yeats recommended them for later production.

On Baile's Strand *(Festival Theatre Cambridge 1927)*

Briggs, who was associated with de Valois in ballet as well as at Cambridge, was not yet twenty, but had already spent five years with the Birmingham Rep as actor and assistant stage manager. His work in Cambridge over the next few years is cherished in recollection by many members of the audience.

The evening finished with a selection of de Valois' choreography collectively called *Dance Cameos*. *The Arts of the Theatre* was the opening ballet, but this time without a design credit. The programme note said

> "No attempt has been made to create atmosphere by means of masks or carefully designed costumes. Movement, sound and colour alone are utilised."[21]

De Valois was presenting dance composition without camouflage. She included another Ravel piece, *Beauty and the Beast,* and three solos, one of which she danced. This was *A Daughter of Eve,* to the Coquette movement from Arensky's *Silhouette*. The costume had a fluffy, white, calf-length skirt, a peasant apron, and a bonnet with coloured ribbons. This became an immensely popular item, a *demi-caractère* miniature of a flirtatious young woman in silent dialogue with an unseen young man. At the end she offered him an apple, was refused, and then sat on the forestage steps and bit into the fruit. With a provocative smile, she left it on stage as she walked away.

The substance of the *Dance Cameo* programme came at the end with the first performance of *Rout*. Set to music by Arthur Bliss, *Rout* opened with a dancer-actress, Vivienne Bennett (who had been with de Valois' 1921 group) reciting a poem by Ernst Toller in a translation by Ashley Dukes. The movement began during the poem and continued as the music started.

Bliss originally designed the score for a musical party given in December 1920 by Baroness Catherine d'Erlanger. In it he was experimenting with the use of the singing voice purely as an instrument without the literary content introduced by words. The singer for whom it was composed, Grace Lovat Fraser, writes:

"There were to be ... only meaningless syllables chosen for their colour values and percussive or soft impact. Lyric passages were to be vocalised on the syllable Ah. When the work was finished I was wildly excited for it bristled with difficulties and gave the singer the most wonderful opportunity for pure musicianship. It was scored for voice, flute, clarinet, bassoon, bass, harp and glockenspiel. We spent hours fitting the right syllables to the voice part and when we had done this it was called *Rout,* not in the sense of a defeat but its other meaning of a jollification."[22]

The score was heard a number of times during the next few years including a performance as an interlude to a programme by the Diaghilev Ballet arranged for a larger group of musicians, when perhaps de Valois made its acquaintance.

At Cambridge *Rout* was scored for two pianos and danced by de Valois and five of her girls wearing the simple plum-coloured tunics of the Academy (Joy Newton remembers that "they called us the Purple Virgins"[23]), tights and soft shoes. Some photographs of later performances show longer but equally plain costumes. The choreography incorporated the elements of expressionist movement in its use of the body to depict the sombre or exultant emotions of grief, oppression, defiance and rebellion. It was a group work, building up its effects architecturally or geometrically. When it was seen in London a year later, *The Dancing Times* was greatly impressed. The Sitter Out commented that de Valois was

"an honest enquirer into the possibilities of the dance as a mode of interpreting modern thought ... A clever attempt was made to portray in a dance built up of decorative groupings and 'futuristic' movement, frequently of a contrapuntal nature, the 'revolt' of modern youth against the conventions of an older generation."[24]

On that occasion Bliss and Malcolm Sargent were the pianists with young Joy Newton page-turning their music.

The Cambridge critics in 1927 were not particularly well disposed towards *Rout*. The *Daily News* chose to see it as a

> "fiery outburst against the age of jazz ... There was an inclination towards blatancy but whether that was intended in order to suggest the vulgarity of the jazz age we cannot say."[25]

The *Cambridge Review* felt it "quite failed to give any impression of revolutionary youth".[26] Norman Marshall describes it as "a harsh, angry, rather pretentious work in which the dancers seemed to have been deliberately and ruthlessly drained of individuality".[27] The stimulating undergraduate journal *Granta* however was enthusiastic:

> "A most exciting 'cameo' called *Rout* ... Miss Vivienne Bennett spoke the prologue with magnificent ferocity—a poem of Ernst Toller about revolutionary youth—and the ballet which followed was the triumph of the evening. It was German idealism—that is American 'pep' which has somehow lost its vulgarity and become real—and the audience applauded until it was tired."[28]

Almost concurrently with *Rout* de Valois staged a ballet for Phyllis Bedells and Anton Dolin. These two great dancers were once again planning a programme for a provincial tour that would finish at the London Coliseum. *Movement,* with music by Leighton Lucas and black-and-white designs by Phyllis Dolton, was planned for the two principals and a group of four girls, with pointwork this time but still employing the modern groupings and steps that could lead *The Dancing Times* to caption a picture of it as "a curious ballet".

> "To a casual observer there is too great a cleavage from the old methods and too much suggestion of—is it *The House Party?* Some of the positions and movements are frankly ugly and meaningless but anything new like this is difficult to appreciate unless one can understand exactly what ideas are running through the choreographer's mind and what she is aiming at. Miss de Valois has had an intimate association for some years with the older choreographers of the Russian Ballet but she is a lady with ideas of her own and would never produce on certain lines 'just because the Russians did' unless she most thoroughly believed in it herself. That she is sincere in her work I am confident and sincere work is always worthy of most careful consideration no matter how much one may disagree with it."[29]

Rout *(Academy of Choregraphic Art 1927); (left to right) Frances James, Ursula Moreton, Joy Newton, Rosalind Patrick, Freda Bamford, Anne Coventry, Marie Nielson and Beatrice Appleyard*

This is the tone of a man who is offered a work he dislikes by an artist he admires. It is also additional evidence that de Valois as a choreographer at this time was experimental and avant-garde rather than classical and traditional.

An interesting assignment came her way in April 1927. The Forum Theatre Guild asked Robert Atkins to direct a Yiddish play, *The Dybbuk,* which had been an enormous success in a Hebrew version produced by the Habimah Players in Moscow—a remarkable drama based on ancient legends of possession by the souls of the dead. It was a story of a poor student, Channon (Ernest Milton) and his love for Leah (Jean Forbes-Robertson) whose father intends her to marry a rich man. Channon dies, but returns as a Dybbuk to disrupt the wedding. The tragedy turns on the struggle between the Dybbuk and an exorcist for Leah's soul. The 1927 production at the Royalty Theatre was the first in English and de Valois' contribution was a beggars' dance to Hassidic music performed in the shadow of the synagogue. Atkins was a cooperative director although he thought de Valois was far too severe with the artists; she, on the other hand, thought him far too lenient ...

In May she staged another dance programme in Cambridge. This time she did not appear herself but produced some ensemble pieces for the girls. Ailne Phillips remembers taking part and finding the theatre very easy to dance in, with a warm and responsive audience.[30] Joy Newton recalls it as having a specific and attractive smell—"lightly spicy, slightly musty, very distinctive".[31] There must also have been enticing aromas emanating from the kitchen and dining room. Gray's delight in food and wine meant that refreshments had been featured from the beginning—"special delicacies and wines obtained direct from Bordeaux will be available at very reasonable prices". This soon led to a small roof garden bar (a novelty) and a celebrated grill room (with black tablecloths) serving gourmet food and wine, with its menu printed in the programme and changing from day to day. A typical Thursday in 1929 offered "*cuisses de grenouilles au beurre, navarin d'agneau, cerises au kirsch*" and suggested as a liqueur a new kümmel which "has the most exquisite round and full flavour". It also had "a super saturation of sugar crystallised on the bottle. Finish the bottle and have it broken; the crystals in coffee give it a subtle lacing."[32]

The divertissements in this second dance programme included *Rhythm* (Beethoven), a non-classical piece using what would now be termed floorwork. The six girls never completely rose from the stage and the rhythms were reflected by arms, heads and torsos. *Poissons d'or* (Debussy), for four girls, also made considerable use of the floor as well as of darting, wriggling movements caught in a spotlight. Hedley Briggs appeared in a *pas de trois*, *Nautical Nonsense* (Bach) in which, according to *Granta*, he "knocked 'em all with his airy impudence".[33] *The Legend of the Aspen Tree* was based on the tradition that the aspen leaves shiver because Christ's cross was made of aspen wood. It was set to an arrangement of Hebridean songs as collected by Marjory Kennedy-Fraser and at one point the cast sang wordlessly to the music. They wore masks, which they found easy and lightweight, and the tree was created choreographically by dancers depicting the swaying of the branches and the quivering of leaves.

The evening's plays included Yeats' *The Player Queen*. Yeats was in Cambridge for the Saturday matinee and welcomed the chance of meeting de Valois. He had heard from Gordon Bottomley of the excellence of her work in *On Baile's Strand*. De Valois has described the encounter:

"It is the year 1927 and I am sitting in the dark vestibule of the Festival Theatre in Cambridge. I am listening to a rich Irish voice that seems to intone a request that I should come to Dublin and produce for the Abbey Theatre ... The mind of Yeats was made up: he would have a small school of ballet at the Abbey and I would send over a teacher. I would visit Dublin every three months and produce his *Plays for Dancers* and perform in them myself: thus, he said, the poetic drama of Ireland would live again and take its rightful place in the nation's own theatre."[34]

What Irishwoman could have refused such an appeal? She accepted the offer, arranging for Vivienne Bennett to open the Dublin school. Later Sara Patrick would run it under de Valois' supervision.

Yeats was envisaging a resurgence of an old dream. In 1913 Ezra Pound had introduced him to Japanese No plays in the versions translated by Ernest Fenollosa, and Yeats had begun writing his own *Plays for Dancers*. The first of these to be performed, *At the Hawk's Well*, was given in the drawing room of Lady Cunard's house in London in April 1916. The dancer was Michio Ito, a twenty-three-year-old Japanese who had never been associated with No but had trained at the Mizuki Dancing School in Tokyo before spending three years at the Dalcroze School in Paris. He adapted Oriental forms of movement to European modern dance, producing an expressive and rhythmical personal style. Michio Ito however left for New York, bringing the staging of Yeats' plays to an abrupt end. As Yeats wrote:

"Perhaps I shall turn to something else now that our Japanese dancer Itow (sic), whose minute intensity of movement in the dance of the Hawk so well suited our small room and private art, has been hired by a New York theatre, or perhaps I shall find another dancer."[35]

Now, ten years later, he found one in de Valois.

Terence Gray planned to stage Wilde's *Salome* in October 1927. The dance of the veils was to be composed by de Valois who would also choreograph a dance drama devised by Gray himself for the same programme. In his book *Dance-Drama: Experiments in the Art of the Theatre*,[36] Gray not only expressed his views on the use of dance in the theatre, but printed six examples he had written. These comprised dialogue and detailed instructions about staging, lighting, expressive movement, the points where dance should take over and what kind of dancing it should be. None was staged as a play but he now hoped de Valois would set one of them, *The Scorpions of Ysit*, as a ballet.

The public performance of *Salome* however was banned in England and *The Scorpions of Ysit* was temporarily abandoned. Instead, two other plays were presented along with three solos by de Valois, which were unnamed in the programme. They included the best remembered of all her single dances, *Pride*, a flaunting and effective composition on pointe to Scriabin's *Caresse dansé* for which she wore a striking green and blue costume and headdress. There was a Russian dance learnt from Derra de Moroda which she enjoyed performing. The remaining dance may have been *A Daughter of Eve* or the charming Boccherini *Serenade*, fast, flirtatious, based on travelling turns, small jumps and mandoline-playing hand and arm movements. The *Cambridge Review* was delighted to have de Valois on her own:

> "Miss de Valois is most effective where her powers of mime are given greatest scope ... The emotions of the dancer appear not only in the gestures of the dance but even more clearly in the subtle changes of expression which perhaps can only be realised in a small theatre."[37]

This was a splendid answer to The Sitter Out's fear in 1918 that she was purely an excellent technician rather than a dramatic artist. The repertoire of the Diaghilev Ballet had awakened and intensified her latent mimetic powers, especially in comedy.

A quartet of plays for the Old Vic required dance arrangements from de Valois during the autumn and winter. First came an extra-mural event—the Vic, greatly to Baylis' grief, had to cease functioning temporarily while the builders were at work. De Valois writes:

> "I have a vivid picture of her despair when she was ordered to close the Vic for six months for very necessary repairs: 'The Lord has let me down—I always thought he would see that this theatre was left alone—at least until Sadler's Wells was built ...'"[38]

The Lord however provided a home from home at Nigel Playfair's Lyric Theatre Hammersmith where Sybil Thorndike and Lewis Casson led the company in productions of *The Taming of the Shrew, The Merchant of Venice* and *Much Ado About Nothing,* all directed by Andrew Leigh. De Valois choreographed dances in the first and last of these. Then, in February 1928, back at the Vic, came *Romeo and Juliet* starring Jean Forbes-Robertson (the Leah of *The Dybbuk*). De Valois was enchanted by her—"she was young, and so beautiful, and with so much promise".[39] She was also leading lady in *The Two Noble Kinsmen* for which de Valois created a wedding masque.

NdV in Pride *(1927)*

Dublin was now added to de Valois' journeys (and she also taught once a week at the famous girls' school Heathfield at Ascot). Yeats implemented his intention of arranging for a ballet school to be started at the Abbey Theatre—not without some disapproval from regular patrons of the Abbey—and this began towards the end of 1927. Pupils and teachers worked in premises behind the theatre: one small studio with a tiny dressing room and washing facilities. The curriculum was on similar lines to that of the Academy in London.

For the opening performance on January 30 1928, a pilot event to make people aware of the school's existence and purpose, de Valois relied principally on her own dancers from London although a few local students were included. They shared the bill for a week with a play, setting a pattern for all future dance performances. De Valois choreographed a new work, *Venetian Suite,* with music by Respighi and designs by Kathleen Dillon. The plot recalled Lopokova's *Les Elegantes* in its setting, showing the reactions of a Romantic Lady, a Sophisticated Lady and two Unsophisticated Ladies when they receive identical love letters sent as a joke by a young Minstrel. De Valois danced *Pride,* sitting down in her hotel bedroom in Dublin to stitch an extra piece of material to the front of the cutaway costume to satisfy Irish notions of propriety.

This first public occasion was kindly received. The *Irish Independent* reviewer wrote:

> "What lent a special and particular interest to the programme was the remarkable series of ballets by Ninette de Valois and her pupils. This proved to be in fact an experience far and away beyond what many people anticipated ... What amazed one most was the extraordinary intelligence and supreme grace with which every movement was apparently spontaneously developed."[40]

By April it was possible to stage a slightly more ambitious evening with fewer dancers ferried over from London and as a finale de Valois choreographed *Rituelle de feu* (Falla) for herself as the Maiden and an ensemble of girls as Sun Worshippers. This was a stylised, rhythmic, architecturally constructed composition. Costumes were loose sleeveless ankle-length gowns and short dark veils in reddish hues for the group while de Valois had a similar dress in white with a narrow headband.

At Cambridge that February Gray produced an imaginative *Richard III* in which de Valois collaborated, staging the scene of Richard's dreams before Bosworth as a ballet of shadows. Richard's face was spotlit, and the understage lighting flooded the visions so that

"the seemingly endless procession of their gyrating figures, their gaunt arms outstretched in an appeal for vengeance, set monstrous purple shadows looming over the cyclorama".[41]

De Valois was now closely attuned to the mood of Gray's productions and able to contribute as much or as little as was needed to complete the total effect in classic or poetic plays. Her keen, inborn love and enthusiasm for poetry, later expressed in poems of her own, made her a distinguished collaborator in this field. She had raised to a fine art the amplification and illustration of words by movement, using the rhythms of music, speech or chanting to give it choreographic form. The actors, selected by Gray for their ability to further his theatrical aims, had been trained by her in mime and gesture and were well able to supplement the dancers she brought from London. Where dances were appropriate, as in *The Shoemaker's Holiday* for example, she provided them; elsewhere she devised eloquent and imaginative groupings and controlled motion.

At this time she struck Norman Marshall as earnest, abrupt and dictatorial—her sense of humour seems to have been obscured, as far as Cambridge was concerned, by a serious purposefulness and a brusque manner. Hindsight makes him admit that she was probably more apprehensive and insecure than she ever allowed herself to appear.[42] Stretched physically to considerable limits, she had four tough and demanding areas of work, all dependent on her ability to direct and control many different kinds of people. At the Academy she was principal and administrator, responsible for the training and development of her girls; at the Old Vic and at Cambridge she had to deal with actors and directors, convincing them of the importance of the contribution she could make to their training or to their productions; at the Abbey she had to supervise the running of a school and persuade everyone concerned with the theatre as well as its public of the validity of Yeats' belief in her. Heavy responsibilities everywhere—and peripherally she had views to present and contributions to make to the Cecchetti Society and the Association of Operatic Dancing. Moreover, above and beyond directional work she was a performing and creative artist. As a leading dancer she could not neglect classwork, as a choreographer she was at the beginning, flexing inventive muscle, exercising, strengthening and all the time developing her special talents.

In 1927 she was never long enough in one place to relax as part of a group or company, to get to know people with whom she was working in any familiarity or companionship. Norman Marshall remembers:

> "At rehearsals her way of dashing about the stage, scolding, goading and exhorting, was so reminiscent of a hockey practice that the company nicknamed her the Games Mistress. One of the actors who had a habit of getting out of position remarked that at any moment he expected her to blow a whistle, admonish him for being offside again, and send him off the field."[43]

In May the Festival Theatre staged Gordon Bottomley's verse drama *The Riding to Lithend*. Bottomley is an overlooked, largely forgotten poet who was born at Keighley, Yorkshire, in 1874. He was a pioneer in a revival of English verse drama soon after the turn of the century, and *Lithend* was written in 1909. Its basis was an Icelandic saga about an ambitious and bloodthirsty woman urging on her husband to seek death in war. De Valois' contribution lay principally in the treatment of three beggar women who prophesied tragedy, characters who might well have seemed ridiculous if not sensitively handled. Again she worked closely with a lighting plan. Each woman was highlighted in turn as she spoke and moved, while, throughout, the enlarged shadows of all three shifted on the cyclorama. Their dancing was linked to the rhythms of their speech.

Gray's lively and impertinent humour was often on show in productions and in a merry staging of *The Birds of Aristophanes* as a modern musical comedy in June—a Paris adaptation by Bernard Zimmer with music by Auric—he amused his audience with all kinds of production tricks. The gods descended by rope from gallery to stalls and Jupiter threw thunderbolts into the auditorium as music hall artistes threw favours. De Valois reflected each type of bird, its action and behaviour (Hedley Briggs was the Peacock) in cleverly satirical style and then went on to working out the movement in one of the best remembered and most controversial of Gray's productions, the all black and white *As You Like It*. This presented Orlando looking like a pantomime principal boy in thigh boots, Rosalind as a Boy Scout and Celia as a Girl Guide. In spite of such eccentricities the *Cambridge Daily News* felt it was an inspired interpretation of the play, marked by an imaginative quality of "harmonious integrity".[44]

That year, 1928, de Valois was again *première danseuse* at Covent

Garden in the opera season that opened on April 30 with *Rheingold.* She appeared on the second night, in *Armide,* sung by Frieda Leider and Walter Widdop and conducted by Robert Heger. Ambrosiny was ballet master and her other assignments were in *Samson and Delilah, Louise, Carmen* and *Aida.* Half a dozen young men danced in the opera ballets, two of whom, Ashton and Chappell, would be close associates in years to come. Chappell has a clear memory of her looking exquisite in a blonde wig and a floating Grecian tunic, standing at the rosin box in the wings talking to them—considering their possibilities, he feels, as members of her future ballet company.[45] For her part she remembers with delight their high spirits and inventive fun during performances. Ambrosiny saved himself some trouble over the *corps de ballet* by encouraging them to improvise and they took full advantage of this.

In September she crossed to Dublin for another ballet programme. This time Arthur Hamilton, a young Belfast dancer, created the lead in *The Faun* to a score by an Irish musician, Harold R. White. White had entered a competition held to find music suitable for an Irish ballet and made an attractive winning arrangement of old Irish airs. There is considerable confusion over a similarity of titles, as a later and different de Valois work, *The Picnic,* was afterwards called *The Faun.* Photographs of the Irish one show a link with Nijinsky's ballet in that the Faun is perched on a rock and there are six barefoot girls in Grecian dresses led by de Valois. There was also however a group of small elves wearing the conventional tunics and headdresses of children's fancy-dress costumes of the period. The choreography was not conceived in terms of Nijinsky's angular images and staccato motion but used the more curved and plastique linked lines and softer groupings characteristic of de Valois in lyrical mood. Local appreciation for her in Dublin is evidenced by a review in the *Irish Statesman:*

"After a year's work at the Abbey, she has produced a group of Irish dancers whose work is a revelation of beauty and she has opened out a new field to Irish musicians ... In *The Faun,* Mr White's music joined Miss de Valois' imaginative invention and Miss Patrick's designs in a pure evocation of moonlight and elvish life amongst the trees and rocks. Patches of moonlight took shape and danced, combining incessantly in new forms and withdrawing again into still patterns of singular and suggestive beauty."[46]

De Valois now felt that the Academy in London was ready to show its work. *Rout*, given a studio performance the previous January after its try-out in Cambridge, had been well received. Now she took the Royal Court Theatre for three matinees beginning November 26 with an augmented company that included Molly Lake and Stanley Judson in "Ballets for the Repertory Theatre". She lost £200 but did what she hoped to do—attracted serious appraisement from critics and public. The Sitter Out went to the heart of the matter.

> "Miss de Valois is essentially a choreographer who thinks ... [she has] a modernity that has sound technique behind it."

He described her use of form and design "which might be likened to a phrase of music in so much as it has its opening, its climax and its cadence".[47]

The programme included *Rout*, *Scène Venitienne* (*Venetian Suite*) and a new *Scène de ballet* to music by Gluck, while *The Scorpions of Ysit* (already shown at an Academy Sunday recital) was at last given its public premiere.

This "Egyptian fantasy dance", as Gray termed it, was demonstrably the idea of an Egyptologist. Who else would conceive of a comedy "taken from a story of the Goddess Ysit, found on the Metternich stela"? It concerned the visit of Ysit, guarded by her seven scorpions, to the houses of marshwomen in the Nile Delta. One woman refuses her entry, one admits her. The scorpions sting to death the child of the first woman in revenge, but Ysit brings him back to life before going on her way. Gray lays down in his directions certain indications about mime and movement:

> "Her movements betoken weariness ... [The woman] assumes the correct attitude of reverence for those in the presence of gods and kings, back bent and hands before face to shield the eyes from the blinding radiance of the Deity ..."

There is also a detailed description, easily translatable into a dance passage, of the activities of the scorpions when they decide to kill the baby.[48] Gray was fascinated by the concept of dance in Ancient Egypt, writing articles on the subject for *The Dancing Times*.

The Scorpions of Ysit had music by Elsie Hamilton—"and very dull music, too, though possibly clever", commented the Sitter Out. He did not like the work except for the remarkable choreography for the scorpions but he acknowledged that

NdV as Beauty in Beauty and the Beast *(1928)*

"the intense sincerity of it all sent me away with the memory of the ballet predominating over all else that I had seen during the afternoon."[49]

The programme made its mark. Francis Toye, in a BBC radio broadcast, found it extremely interesting and original:

"We have heard a great deal lately about schemes for starting English ballet and so on, and I must say that enterprises like this one are most encouraging in that respect."[50]

Dance arrangements at the Old Vic continued. De Valois worked on dances for *Love's Labour Lost* in June and in December came an extraordinary premiere—*Adam's Opera* by Clemence Dane, an ambitious mixture that fell between almost every stool. Directed by Andrew Leigh, it had music by Richard Addinsell. In her preface to the printed version, Clemence Dane wrote:

"The play is nothing but a fairytale: an attempt to answer the questions which every child asks—'What happens when the Sleeping Beauty wakes up?' and again 'What happens to the man who wakes her?'"[51]

But of course it tried to be much more than that. It was linked with World War I and the new society that emerged in the 1920s, and it dealt with all kinds of symbolic situations and hidden meanings. Adele Dixon and John Laurie played the leading roles and a full complement of Old Vic actors and singers filled in a huge cast list.

A more significant event for de Valois came on December 13. Baylis now implemented the idea mooted when they first met of having a ballet as a curtain raiser for the opera *Hansel and Gretel,* and de Valois choreographed Mozart's *Les Petits Riens* for the occasion. Watteau-esque designs were created, scenery by Doria Paston from the Festival Theatre Cambridge and costumes by Owen Smyth, the Old Vic's resident designer, and musically the work began a notable association. De Valois needed someone to arrange and orchestrate the score and one of her girls, Marie Nielson, suggested Constant Lambert, the young composer de Valois remembered from the Diaghilev *Romeo and Juliet*.

For once, too, in those early days, she was able to work with male dancers as well as with her girls. Stanley Judson, who had taken classes with her although he had already danced professionally with Pavlova's company, was Corydon to her own coquettish Rosalind, and Hedley

Briggs had the role of Tircis. It was a light and stylish love story with Ursula Moreton as the slighted but spirited rival.

Terence Gray returned to Greek drama in February 1929 with *The Prometheus of Aeschylus*, the first time the play had been seen in England either in Greek or in translation. As with the *Oresteia*, de Valois produced a small chorus with a leader (Vivienne Bennett) emphasising significant moments through expressive gesture. The principal actors declaimed their speeches from behind immense carved and painted wood figures, and only the masked chorus, the character of Io, and the messengers of Zeus were of human size and moved freely about the stage. Many of the images and groups were influenced by Epstein's sculpture and de Valois has termed the style in which she worked on these Greek dramas abstract expressionism. Her understanding and appreciation of sculpture, painting and stage design, like her knowledge of music, were steadily increasing.

Another play, this time a comedy, came in April with *Beggar on Horseback* by George Kaufman and Marc Connelly, in which de Valois choreographed the trial scene as a ballet, and in May a staging of Toller's *Masses and Man* was followed by *Les Petits Riens*, which the *Cambridge Daily News* greatly enjoyed:

> "After the nervous strain imposed by Toller's play it was a pleasure ... to find relaxation in the lighthearted ballet produced by Miss Ninette de Valois ... a very blithe piece of choreographic comedy ..."[52]

Between these performances de Valois whipped over to Dublin for a week to support Sara Patrick, now in charge of the Abbey School, in another programme of ballet. A *pas de deux, Jack and Jill*, probably contained ideas used by her three years later as part of the Elgar *Nursery Suite*. Sara Patrick was also by now contributing choreography and a competent team of senior dancers had emerged. For the *Irish Independent* critic the evening was notable for *Rout*. He wrote of

> "the imaginative power and inspiration of Ninette de Valois' interpretation of Ernst Toller's poem of resurgent youth ... The poem—a challenge to jazz and decadence—breathes the very spirit of revolution. With beautiful lighting effects and artistic costumes ... it seemed to promise a new age."[53]

The second Old Vic ballet production came in May with *The Picnic*, set to Vaughan Williams' *Charterhouse Suite* with designs by Hedley

Briggs. This was a work that never quite settled down, either in title or cast list, and constitutes a charming example of the trivial tangles into which the ballet historian constantly finds himself plunged. At its premiere, the leading male role danced by Harold Turner was called The Satyr, and the leading female role, danced by Ursula Moreton, The Nymph. Molly Lake was Phoebe, Judson was Colin and the ensemble was termed either Dryads or Phoebe's Friends. Nine months later, at Cambridge, it was given as *The Satyr*, danced by Judson and de Valois as The Satyr and The Dryad, but with only four Nymphs and no sign of Phoebe or Colin. At special performances in London in March and July 1930 it was *The Picnic* again, with a full cast, but with Phoebe's Friends described as Peasants. However at Bournemouth in December it was called *The Faun* (no connection with the Irish *Faun* of 1928). Briggs and Moreton danced as The Faun and The Nymph with four supporting (female) Satyrs and no Phoebe or Colin. Obviously there was a fuller and an abridged version going the rounds and nobody could make up his mind as to nomenclature. The theme remained the same—one of villagers on a midnight picnic. Their quarrels disturbed the denizens of a wood who revenged themselves by frightening off the human beings. M. E. Perugini found it:

"original in conception, clearcut and sound in its choreography and danced with purity of technique, joyous verve and sense of classic style by a well balanced and brilliant cast."[54]

In June 1929 at Cambridge the play was Dekker's *The Shoemaker's Holiday,* with dances and choreographed movement by de Valois, in which Hedley Briggs had an ideal role as Firk. Slight, light and equally expressive in comedy or tragedy, Briggs was well described by the *Cambridge Review:*

"His characteristic virtue was partly an exact feeling for the moment to stop, having done enough to leave the audience wanting much more, the art of creating the impression that you have a lot more tricks in the bag ..."[55]

Gray could not, as he wished to do, beat the ban over public performance of Oscar Wilde's *Salome*—he had a running battle with the Censor's office about which he kept his audiences informed in many witty ways—but he could and did present one private performance in his theatre in June 1929. The stage was ideal for his production, allowing activity on different levels with a wide downstage area for Salome's dance. Columns and staircases were coated with aluminium paint to give the effect of shining silver, and imaginative lighting in greens and reds pointed climaxes in the drama. De Valois was concerned only with the role of Salome, taken by Vivienne Bennett. Briggs choreographed the rest of the movement.

Salome marked the end of Gray's first connection with the Cambridge Festival Theatre. He handed over to Anmer Hall for the following eighteen months, resuming the directorship at the beginning of 1931. De Valois' commitment to Cambridge was therefore lessened—fortunately, perhaps, as her work elsewhere had become steadily more demanding.

August 1929 brought de Valois' first collaboration in Dublin in a ballet play by Yeats. In February 1928 Yeats wrote to Lady Gregory from Cannes, where he was living for his health, that he had dictated "a vigorous prose version of *The Only Jealousy of Emer* arranged for stage dancing" which he had titled *Fighting the Waves*.[56] The theme was the rescue of Cuchulain from the goddess Fand by the self-sacrificing devotion of his wife Emer.

As with *At the Hawk's Well*, the earlier play was written for private performance but it was given a public staging in Amsterdam in 1922 by Albert van Dalsum. Yeats then rewrote it with the Abbey Theatre in mind, adapting it for de Valois, who never undertook a speaking role. The speeches for the Woman of the Sidhe (Fand) were changed to dances and *Fighting the Waves* was produced by Lennox Robinson, with music by George Antheil. Hedley Briggs danced the Ghost of Cuchulain and half a dozen girls from the ballet school created the effect of the waves.

It was a controversial experiment, particularly where the music was concerned. Antheil, a young avant-garde American composer, was introduced to Yeats by Ezra Pound. He used dissonance and non-musical instruments for sound effects and his score for *Fighting the Waves* was strident and tuneless. According to some reports, at the first rehearsal the orchestra involuntarily stopped after the first few bars apologising for having, as they thought, got the parts mixed up. Antheil himself was satisfied. In *Bad Boy of Music*, he speaks of it as being "true Irish music" and recalls Yeats sitting with him in a Paris cafe and giving him tips about ancient Irish music, singing old Irish melodies "in a rather cracked voice" out of which he built his score.[57]

Fighting the Waves *(Abbey Theatre Dublin 1929); (above) NdV as Fand, Hedley Briggs as the Ghost of Cuchulain, Michael Dolan as Cuchulain, Merial Moore as Emer; (below) Hedley Briggs as the Ghost of Cuchulain with dancers from the Academy of Choregraphic Art*

One Irishman totally disagreed with him. An avid Dublin theatre-goer, Joseph Holloway, wrote in his diaries:

"I met F. J. McCormick and Eileen Crowe as I came out of the Abbey at 11 o'clock after the ballet *Fighting the Waves* and Mac said to me 'I see you have survived it. Oh, what noise!' It is the first time I ever heard Stevenson sing that I didn't enjoy his lovely clear carrying voice. Oh, the harsh discordant notes he had to sing! . . . At the piano, Dr Larchet conducted and couldn't extract head or tail out of the score."[58]

A more expert estimate, from a reviewer in *The Spectator*, was very different:

"The music, with its cunning ripples of wave on the crest of wave and its lightnings and thunderings, was the most wonderful thing of the sort ever heard at the Abbey."

This reviewer gave a vivid and detailed account of the action:

"In the first passage before a curtain of huge tumbling seas, six green-veiled figures represented the flowing waters; and against these strove, in a dance that moved through and through their ranks, the figure of the hero Cuchulain, blade in hand. These unwearying rhythms prevail against his failing strength and at last he sinks, the proud white mask thrown back in agony, as they rise . . ."

The play then began, showing the death scene of Cuchulain and the emergence of his wraith:

"Fand, the sea-god's daughter [de Valois], a wild, metallic creature of frantically rapid gestures, whirls noisily in and dances before the wraith. The hero's ghost, starting up, pursues her in new desire."

Cuchulain's wife Emer then makes her sacrifice, renouncing his love, and the spirit returns to the dead body:

"The sea curtain closes on the scene, and now Fand is seen, her lightning movements changed to the slow, dead motions of despair; and this is her dance of sorrow among the waves."[59]

Like the music, the masks caused differences of opinion. These are of special interest because the use of masks in plays and dances was widespread at the time. They were of many different kinds, whole-headed, face only, brow and eyes. Those Hildo Krop had devised (originally for the Amsterdam production), enclosed the head, so that it was out of proportion to the body. Writing in the *Irish Independent*, one critic described them as making the performers look like "a collection of battered nursery dolls who had by some strange freak begun to discuss life and love and death". By the end, however, he found he had forgotten the masks and was able to appreciate the action and the play.[60] The one de Valois wore was less exaggerated. Yeats calls her "a strange, noble, unforgettable figure".[61]

It is interesting to find that this leading Irish critic had such reservations about masked players—Dublin was lagging behind Cambridge, where Terence Gray had educated his public to accept and enjoy the convention—and also that he dealt with the dance element on a different level from the rest of the production. In common with most critics of the period he could analyse drama and music in depth but only comment very generally on dance. The best he could do over de Valois' contribution to *Fighting the Waves* was

"The dance of Cuchulain fighting the waves which serves as a prologue and Fand's concluding dance of despair were delightfully decorative . . ."[62]

Diaghilev died in August 1929 and very soon a group of people in London began to put time and thought into the matter of building up ballet on their home ground. One of the moving spirits was Philip Richardson of *The Dancing Times;* another was Arnold Haskell, a man who followed personalities that captured his admiration rather than artistic movements but lent enormous enthusiasm and vitality to the promotion and publicising of ballet. A third was Edwin Evans. Additionally there were two great dancers from the Diaghilev Ballet, Tamara Karsavina and Lydia Lopokova, who had married Englishmen and settled in London. Lopokova was at that period the more active, backed by her husband John Maynard Keynes and the power of the Bloomsbury Group.

De Valois had a key role to play in this burgeoning activity. She was already writing short articles and in April 1929 she spoke (possibly her first talk, an art of which she became a complete mistress) at a Liverpool Dancers' Circle meeting. She was therefore one of some 25 dancers, musicians and artists invited by Richardson and Haskell in the autumn of 1929 to an informal dinner at the Moulin d'Or in Romilly Street to discuss the possibility of starting a performing ballet society on the lines of the Stage Society. This lively and valuable drama organisation, founded in 1900, regularly gave Sunday evening performances of stimulating and experimental plays from all over the world. Pirandello and O'Neill, Toller and Giraudoux, Cocteau or Odets, all and more turned up in production, along with British playwrights of similar ideas if not of similar stature.

That night at the Moulin d'Or the hosts and their guests laid the foundation for what they determined to call the Camargo Society after the 18th-century ballerina Marie-Anne Cupis de Camargo, an innovator in her time. They went on to organise a firm structure with M. Montagu-Nathan as honorary secretary and, from the end of the first season, Keynes as honorary treasurer. Their aims were to produce original ballets before a subscription audience at a West End theatre four times every year, giving each time a Sunday evening performance with a Monday afternoon repeat. They intended to engage the best dancers in London and work out first class collaborations of composers, painters and choreographers for each new production.

Three advisory committees were set up. De Valois served on the one for dancing (she has termed it a "large, slightly woolly-minded committee");[63] the others were for decor and music. It took almost a year to plan and bring to fruition the first programme. If the dancing committee was stellar, including Karsavina, Lopokova, Markova, Dolin as well as de Valois and Rambert, the music committee could not have been more eminent. The names are worth citing, as almost all are represented by scores in the early British ballet repertoire: alphabetically, they were Arnold Bax, Lennox Berkeley, Lord Berners, Arthur Bliss, Gustav Holst, Herbert Howells, Constant Lambert, Malcolm Sargent and Ralph Vaughan Williams.

The subscribers' list contains influential people of the time in the arts. Culled at random, it reveals Augustus John, Edwin Lutyens, Ottoline Morrell, Osbert Sitwell, the Nevinsons, Oswald Stoll and Lytton Strachey. Quite apart from the fact that de Valois was enthusiastic about its purpose, the Camargo Society was an ideal assembly point of people who could give practical support to her own ballet company as years went by.

De Valois was invited by Adeline Genée, President of the Association of Operatic Dancing, to create a ballet for a special performance at the Gaiety Theatre in July 1929. *Hommage aux belles viennoises* was set to music by Schubert and De Valois' enduring interest in folkdance came into play, almost for the first time. The ballet began with a Tyrolese Schuhplattl trio for two girls and a man, so popular that it was often given as a divertissement. There were then a *pas de quatre* and a *pas de huit* for girls and a mazurka duet danced by de Valois and Judson.

The Tyrolese trio was in a programme at Cambridge in February 1930—a programme with no substantial new item but one that arouses initial curiosity. This was a *pas de trois* (music Poulenc) called *The Rake's Progress*. De Valois however recalls that it was a little comedy number about two girls flirtatiously impeding the work of a gardener's boy with a rake—nothing at all to do with Hogarth and her 1935 masterpiece. These divertissement compositions of de Valois in the early years, quite apart from her ballets, are significant for the music she chose, in which Diaghilev's interest in contemporary composers is clearly reflected. Poulenc, Debussy, Milhaud, Ravel, Falla are featured, as are Bliss, Vaughan Williams and Elgar. Other composers used are Gordon Jacob, Gavin Gordon, Hugh Bradford and Geoffrey Toye. Edwin Evans was one of her guiding influences over music and in January 1930 she supported him with a dance demonstration in a lecture he gave to the Faculty of Arts on "Music and the Ballet".

In March she brought together the scattered strands of her repertory theatre activity in a remarkable matinee at the Lyric Theatre, Hammersmith. The programme began with a dance drama by Gordon Bottomley, *So Fair a Satrap (Laodice and Danae)* staged by the Cambridge Festival Theatre company although never shown at their own theatre. Beatrix Lehmann had the principal role of Laodice, the rejected and revengeful wife of King Antiochus of Syria, but half the cast were de Valois' girls. Then the Academy of Choregraphic Art danced *Les Petits Riens* and *The Picnic* and the afternoon ended with Yeats' *Fighting the Waves* with the Abbey Theatre company from Dublin. This time de Valois only lost £60 and felt that Yeats' reputation accounted for the greater success.

Chapter IV

~ Much of de Valois' time and energy was now occupied by prep-
arations for the opening of Sadler's Wells Theatre. There were visits
to the stripped-down old house with Lilian Baylis and Sir Reginald
Rowe, the Acting Governor of the Old Vic, who played a vital part in
the re-birth of the Wells. She must almost have held her breath as
events took the course she had hoped for from the beginning, moving
towards the establishment of a small ballet company and school in
Islington. As always when a cherished private ambition has to be
guided towards fulfilment, there must have been diplomatically steered
conversations, the right word at the right time in the right ear, the
unobtrusive manipulation of influential decisions. De Valois, among
her many remarkable characteristics, not only mixed idealism and
practicality but retained a firm core of intention beneath the feminine
and Irish charm and seeming impulsiveness.

Over the Wells she achieved exactly what she wanted. It was
arranged that she sell the lease of her Roland Gardens studio and
transfer the school (now called the Vic-Wells Ballet School) to Rosebery
Avenue. She acquired a small flat in Taviton Street, Bloomsbury, fitted
out to her liking (Nesta Brooking remembers with delight that the
chairs were painted scarlet). She kept on the Heathfield School connection to tide her over until she came on the payroll of the new theatre
in September 1930:

> "I was virtually self-sold to the one institution for which during nearly
> five years I had worked with this one end in view. It was like coming
> to the end of a very long tunnel with the sure knowledge that the new
> countryside was not entirely unfamiliar."[1]

The Camargo Society gave its first performance on October 19 at the Cambridge Theatre London. De Valois both danced and choreographed for it. The dancing came in Nicholas Legat's *Variations and Coda* (Glinka) in which she and Dolin took the leading roles. Her own ballet for the evening was *Danse sacrée et danse profane*.

In February 1929 she had composed a duet, *Danse profane*, for herself and Hedley Briggs for a programme of dancing given with the *Prometheus* at the Festival Theatre Cambridge. Now she used the whole Debussy score for two groups of girls, each with a principal. Ursula Moreton led the *Danse sacrée*, Sheila McCarthy the *Danse profane*. Briggs designed it, using pale pink and black to great effect. The sacred ladies wore draped pink skirts with parti-coloured sleeveless bodices and Hellenic pink and silver headdresses; the profane ladies, in black long-sleeved, short skirted tunics, were half masked in silver. The choreographic concept included crescent-shaped symmetrical groupings, with head-above-head structural patterns.

H. S. Sibthorp, a balletgoer of the time, in an unpublished manuscript lodged in the Theatre Museum, London, described it as memorable for

"its sensitive underlining of musical nuances and its skilful use of light and colour as an emphasis to movement; almost a forerunner of Massine's symphonic experiments. The use of solistes as chorus leaders somewhat in the Central European style faintly foreshadowed the second movement of *Choreartium*. She sank her dancers into the music, leaving them to sway in its current ..."[2]

Hansel and Gretel was again in the Old Vic repertoire that Christmas, given with a new curtain raiser by de Valois, *Suite of Dances*, to Bach arranged by Eugene Goossens. This was another but very different divertissement ballet, opening with an Allemande, followed by a *pas de trois* for girls (Air on the G string) and a Menuet danced by McCarthy and Bamford. A solo Gavotte was created by Harold Turner, de Valois danced a solo Bourrée, and they came together in a Sarabande *pas de deux* before a final ensemble Gigue. A delightful and popular work, it survived for some time in the Vic-Wells repertoire. De Valois had now exercised her choreographic ability in an assortment of dance forms: modern (Central European) in *Rout*; folkdance (*Hommage aux belles viennoises*); historical dance (*Suite of Dances*); classical and *demi-caractère*. Following Fokine's lead she had used pointwork only where she felt it appropriate, for instance in her *Pride* solo.

After Christmas 1930, almost as a pilot for the new regime to be so soon inaugurated at Sadler's Wells, a small ballet company appeared at the Bournemouth Pavilion for three performances as The Vic-Sadler's Wells Opera Ballet. De Valois and Moreton were the featured principal women, Turner and Briggs the men. The Bach *Suite* was given, as well as the Vaughan Williams' *Faun* and a number of divertissements. The programme was greatly appreciated:

"Miss de Valois and her talented company revealed artistry, deportment and vivacity of a very high order. The ensemble was perfect in its precision and the individual numbers were marked for their brilliance and clever execution . . ."[3]

Sadler's Wells Theatre was reopened by Lilian Baylis on January 6 1931. From then plays, operas and ballets were given at both the Old Vic and Sadler's Wells in repertory, involving constant commuting for everybody from south to north of the Thames. The Wells presented many and varied problems, both for staging performances and attracting audiences. Even today, when it has been an accepted part of the theatrical scene for over fifty years, it frequently struggles for life and takes every persuasive modern publicity and marketing technique to capture attention. In 1931 advertising was minimal, word of mouth and press reviews were all that could be relied on. The first took time, and even the stage journals like *The Era* and *The Stage* only rarely covered events in what was basically a suburban theatre. Unpopular productions had to be swiftly jettisoned for financial reasons and a surprising number of rare operas were shown for no more than three performances.

From the opening of the Wells, de Valois took over the dance arrangements for the operas—in fact it was with opera that her work at the theatre began. Her appearance as a dancer at Covent Garden made her very well aware of the problems and possibilities of ballet in opera, an art form very different from ballets and dance works with a life and purpose of their own. The relationship of dances, dance scena or ballets to the operas in which they take place has many facets. Some of course are optional extras, to be included or not as suits the opera producer or company; others are much more closely integrated. In both cases however their style and content is dictated by the opera production and not variable in accordance with the choreographer's decision. Lilian Moore has put it concisely:

"While [the choreographer] does invent the actual steps and patterns of the dances, these must always be in harmony with the general stage picture and with the period and style of the opera as a whole. Occasionally even historical authenticity must be sacrificed to this end."[4]

There are examples of every kind of way in which choreography can be applied to opera in de Valois' work at Sadler's Wells—her assignments were indeed a mixed bunch. For *Carmen*, she composed a Spanish ensemble for herself and half a dozen girls. The piece was long enough and attractive enough to be excised and presented separately as a divertissement. Other operas included *Maritana* and *The Lily of Killarney* as well as *The Marriage of Figaro* and *The Magic Flute*, *Tannhaüser*, *Aida* and *Il Trovatore*, and Gounod's *Faust*. The pace of production necessary at the Old Vic and Sadler's Wells—the operas that season were all given at both theatres, usually premiered at the Vic—meant rapid composition and apart from *Carmen* the only substantial choreography came in *Aida* and *Faust*, with both of which she was already familiar.

Aida is always a considerable task for a choreographer. The first of the incidental dances comes in Act I, as a temple ritual and a prayer for Radames' victory. Its purpose is to heighten the mood of religious fervour. Then in Act II comes the splendid triumph spectacle that remains most in memory. The music is exultant and entirely suited to dance arrangement but there are practical limitations on a choreo-eographer depending on the opera director's conception of the stage picture. The entire chorus is on stage as well as Pharaoh and his court and the procession of captives. Inevitably the amount of dancing area is hardly large enough to contain choreography of real exuberance and spaciousness.

In the *Faust scène de ballet*, de Valois' chosen partner was Frederick Ashton. Ashton's career has been thoroughly chronicled by David Vaughan.[5] By 1931 he had danced with Rambert and Ida Rubinstein, and had choreographed ballets for Rambert's Ballet Club and for the Camargo Society. When *Rout* was given by the Camargo, in January 1931, it included five male dancers—Ashton, Chappell, Briggs, Jack Spurgeon and Ivor Beddoes—and Ashton apparently had trouble adapting to the emphatically rhythmic choreography, emphasised at times by the performers' foot-stamping. *Faust* gave him different problems—those of partnering de Valois—but she was already thinking of

NdV as leading dancer in Carmen *(Vic-Wells Opera 1931)*

him more in terms of a choreographer than a cavalier. Looking ahead, she knew that as time went on she would need various elements for developing her little ballet group into a strong and important company. Another choreographer besides herself, a prima ballerina and *premier danseur*, an able musical director and conductor. From what she had seen of his work Ashton seemed to her the best choice as choreographer.

For the January Camargo evening she choreographed *Cephalus and Procris* (music Grétry, designs Chappell) for Markova and Turner, a stylish comedy about marital infidelity. Cephalus betrays his wife Procris, whom he really loves, with Aurora and in his absence Procris succumbs to the charms of a rich merchant. When they recognise their mutual inconstancy, husband and wife are reconciled.

Sibthorp writes:

"It is a pity that subsequent works with like subjects have possessed so little of its simplicity and lightheartedness ... The choreography was sophisticated yet strictly classical, and that exactly suited the half mocking and half serious telling of the story. The scenery and costumes revealed Chappell's mastery of the art of making bricks with very little straw ..."[6]

This was an art that was vital for all ballet designers to practise in the thirties, when money was acutely short, with no help from government or local council grants nor from industrial patronage. Of course expectations were also different, and neither artists nor audiences thought in terms of getting into the red over expensive costumes and sets. The cheapest possible materials were used, and in a less trades-union-dominated world underpaid volunteers spent long hours on practical work over the staging of a show. The results might be delicately or robustly imaginative, they might be tasteless or even dowdy, but they usually reflected the enthusiastic vitality with which they were achieved.

The neo-classical quality of de Valois' choreography for *Cephalus and Procris* emphasises her versatility of style as a ballet creator. Here the subject, and the presence of a ballerina of pure classical ability, dictated the type of dance vocabulary she used. For one critic, Leslie Rees of *The Era*, this ballet improved on acquaintance. He reviewed it first in November 1931 when it was given with the opera *Dido and Aeneas* at Sadler's Wells. Lopokova, Judson and de Valois

Rehearsal at Sadler's Wells Theatre 1931; (left to right) Sheila McCarthy, Freda Bamford, Nadina Newhouse, Doreen Adams, Beatrice Appleyard, Phyllis Worthington, Ursula Moreton, Marjorie Stewart, Joy Newton, NdV

> "performed the dance with classic formalism touched with the neatest humour. It was a lovely thing with a thread of narrative to give meaning to the movements while not important enough to absorb attention from the ballet proper ... The whole piece had the severe and beautiful outline which was lacking from the opera."[7]

Some days later, reviewing it again, he called it

> "a gossamer flux of story which grows more irresistible to the eye and ear each time I see it ... Ninette is not only a dancer of superb craft and grace; she is also a creative artist materialising rare conceptions of beauty on this stage. All the dances in this programme are of her composing. They show an imagination and a grasp of significant gesture and the beauty of form in motion which cannot be too highly valued by lovers of the ballet."[8]

Terence Gray returned to the Festival Theatre at the beginning of 1931. He opened in January with a pantomime, *Aladdin*—as the *Cambridge Daily News* wrote, "Gray has taught Cambridge to expect from him anything except the obvious"—[9] for which de Valois arranged a Grand Fairy Ballet and a Ballet of the Jewels. In February she went to Dublin to dance, and staged a mime ballet *Fedelma*. This was to a score by William Alwyn, a flautist and teacher at the Royal Academy of Music who established himself in composition with a piano concerto in 1930. In later life, when he became well-known for concert music and film scores, he considered all his work prior to 1939 as immature and *Fedelma* is forgotten. The ballet's theme was an Irish equivalent of *The Sleeping Beauty*. The sleeping Fedelma was guarded by a hag with long poisoned fingernails, which were triumphantly cut off by the King of Ireland's son with one sweep of his sword. He then wakened Fedelma and carried her off as his bride.

At Cambridge the plays included *Henry VIII*, *The Insect Play*, *The Festival Revue* and *The Antigone of Sophocles*. One of the interested regular playgoers there, Alistair Cooke, was that year editor of *Granta* and also wrote in *Theatre Arts Monthly* (New York) about Gray and his dramatic experiments. He analysed the staging of *Henry VIII*, in which "all the court entrances were danced, so that there was a preliminary visual cartoon of character and mood for each person in the play". He went on:

"As a convention, the ballet technique stylises situation, helps to crystallise the producer's talent, and here maintained a surprising and moving contrast between hilarity and pathos."

He found the technique particularly convincing when used in the *Antigone*:

"One felt, for the first time in performance, that the chorus had a clearly appreciated function, that by rigidly patterning the correct response to each moral situation they monopolised the ethical elements, which in modern productions of Greek tragedy are too often sentimentally diffused throughout the play."[10]

In the April programme of the Camargo Society, de Valois staged her most important ballet to date—*La Création du monde*, to the score Darius Milhaud had composed for Jean Borlin and the Ballets Suédois in 1923. Borlin and Milhaud, fascinated by African dance and music, had looked at the myth of the Creation from an African Negro standpoint. Out of chaos emerged three gods—Ngama, Medere and K'kva—who gradually called into being plants, animals and mankind. The music was linked to jazz and blues rhythms and melodies, utilising an unusual selection of wind, string and percussion instruments. De Valois followed the original concept of a primitive African drama, and Edward Wolfe's designs included black body make-up and impressive masks. The notion of a physical mass in rhythmic labour bringing forth life has been used by so many choreographers in the years between that it is perhaps not easy to appreciate de Valois' vision in this work.

Beaumont stresses it as

"a work of originality ... much more than the stringing together of a series of movements to fit a given rhythm ... a successful attempt to use the dance as an art form to convey the impression of a primitive people seeking to express a lofty aim."[11]

The Borlin ballet had run into strong criticism in Paris because the avant-garde music and designs had not been echoed in equally advanced choreographic ideas. Borlin had remained within the framework of classical dance, but de Valois, using and developing the kind of dance techniques she had first exploited in *Rout*, was very much in touch with the music's intentions.

On May 5 1931 history was made at the Old Vic with the first full evening of ballet. The programme had enough substance to declare the de Valois' dancers a company at last. Twenty-six dancers were involved—de Valois and twenty-one girls plus four male guest artists: Dolin, Judson, Beddoes and Leslie French.

The opening ballet was *Les Petits Riens*, followed by *Danse sacrée et danse profane*, *Hommage aux belles viennoises*, and a new work, *The Jackdaw and the Pigeons*. The Faun (*Picnic*), the *Faust scène de ballet* and the Bach *Suite de danses* completed the evening.

Reactions to *The Jackdaw and the Pigeons*, which had a specially composed score by the Canadian composer Hugh Bradford and was based on the Aesop fable, were widely varied. Richard Jennings talked of surviving "the stale prancings and pantomimic trivialities"[12] but Sibthorp, in retrospect, terms it

"the first real Vic-Wells ballet, in the sense that music, choreography and decor—all unpretentious but perfectly apt and successful—were created in collaboration ... [De Valois'] choreography, pointed to Hugh Bradford's melodious if slightly staccato score, had most of the qualities of wit, elegance and raillery which have distinguished the greater part of her subsequent output. Chappell decorated it in tones of black, silver grey, pink and lemon yellow that moved against a giant watering can and giant sprawling flowers. It would scarcely bear reviving, but it *was* a complete ballet."[13]

De Valois' performance in the leading role was highly praised in *The Stage*:

"Ninette de Valois again distinguished herself greatly by her expressively mimed and danced, genuinely pathetic assumption of the too daring Jackdaw who, forsaking the company of his four black brethren, dons some blue breast plumage and thus for a time is admitted to the society of the five blue and white pigeons. But finally he betrays himself and is cast out, and as his old comrades refuse to take him back the poor bird expires, seemingly of a broken heart. This beautiful little ballet should assuredly be seen again."[14]

Critics of today would inevitably look for moral attitudes and inner significance in all this. Here indeed is a tale of an outsider trying to break in, of the individual against cruel society; but this was 1931 and de Valois was not concerned with such matters. She and her collaborators were simply using ballet to tell a well-known story with humour and pathos.

Later in May Peter Godfrey of the Gate Theatre Club, always closely in touch with Gray, decided to stage Wilde's *Salome*, again with Salome's dance choreographed by de Valois. This time it was for the strikingly beautiful young Margaret Rawlings—someone who, like Esmond Knight, de Valois felt could have made a career as a dancer. Incidental music was by Lambert, nine movements for clarinet, trumpet, cello and percussion, which he conducted; John Armstrong contributed splendid designs. By the end of the year the censorship ban was lifted and the Cambridge Festival Theatre was able to present public performances with Beatrix Lehmann as Salome.

Mixed notices greeted the Gate production. *The Stage* was happy about it:

"The dance was performed with grace, skill and as decorously as the circumstances allowed by the exiguously attired Miss Margaret Rawlings ... (she) made that erotic young creature pass from almost childlike naivete and seeming innocence to apparently sadistic fury in the rhapsodic kissing of the lips of the butchered Prophet ..."[15]

Richard Jennings felt very differently. He had wanted Salome (for some unspecified reason) to be "a faraway figure of purity"—

"and this she seemed to become for a moment when Miss Rawlings, after dancing in a 'daily dozen' or Swedish abdominal manner behind veils, annexed one of them to cover nudity and with a garland of rosebuds appeared suddenly as Perdita or Miranda, an English maiden strayed into that bad Syrian company."[16]

*   *   *

Meanwhile a remarkable project had been occupying de Valois' thoughts. Its origins go back to 1927. In June that year Dr Geoffrey Keynes, an authority on William Blake, wrote to Diaghilev:

"Je vais envoyer le livre de gravure de William Blake dont ma belle-soeur Lydia Lopokova vous a parlé. Sous ce pli se trouve aussi une esquisse d'un ballet tiré des mêmes gravures. Le centenaire de sa mort a lieu en 1927. Mme Raverat [Gwen Raverat] (graveur en bois) a preparé pour un theâtre miniature des dessins pour la mise en scène et des figures costumées, que je serai enchanté de vous montrer."[17]

Diaghilev, fortunately, was not interested. It seems unlikely that the depth and grandeur of the concept that was taking shape would have been as well served by a Diaghilev Ballet production at this period as it was to be by the Camargo Society.

Keynes had in fact brilliantly distilled for the theatre the essence, not of the biblical Book of Job but of Blake's own Vision of the Book of Job which has been described as "the account of a man's inward struggle and triumph, the conflict between his indwelling Good and Evil powers".[18] His scenario combined narrative, dramatic contrast and resolution in powerfully economical terms.

Dr Ralph Vaughan Williams was approached to compose the score. Staging, after Diaghilev's refusal, seemed unlikely, so thinking only of concert performance he orchestrated it for eighty instruments, finished it early in 1930 and conducted it for the first time in October at the Norfolk and Norwich Triennial Music Festival. Frank Howes dissects the musical origins.[19] He establishes that the "bony skeleton" of the score is that of the suite but based on early dances—Pavan and Galliard with Sarabande and Minuet. Vaughan Williams fused these together into a personal and marvellously majestic contemporary score, making use of a wide variety of orchestral colour to mark the different elements in the story. His synopsis varied slightly from that of Keynes, and he

Job (*Camargo Society 1931*) (*top left*) *The Downfall of Satan; (bottom left) Anton Dolin as Satan with War, Pestilence and Famine; (above) Robert Helpmann as Satan (Sadler's Wells Ballet 1943)*

firmly defined the piece as "a masque for dancing", a phrase always afterwards employed.

When it was suggested that de Valois should be the choreographer Vaughan Williams and she met. He was reluctant to give permission, feeling his music could only be staged by a dedicated amateur folkdance group. His stipulation about avoiding "toe-dancing" however did not even require compromise—de Valois had no intention of using pointes in her choreography and was far too much in tune with the whole conception to introduce any jarring step drawn from classical ballet.

For anyone familiar with it, this magnificent work sums up de Valois' mastery of every trend of the time in dance. The eloquent, expressive groupings and gestures of Job and his family relate to her use of movement in Greek drama. Masked and expressionist dance is effectively employed by the Comforters, by the powerful scene where Satan drives on War, Pestilence and Famine as a three-in-hand team of horses, and by the pyramidal ensemble of white hands emerging from black-hooded figures that part to reveal Satan in power. Lyrical feeling and curving fluent line are brought in from plastique movement, while English folkdance yields steps and patterns to evoke the pastoral happiness of Job's children. For Elihu, representative of the good, she turns to classical dance and for Satan she evolves a vibrant personal idiom out of classical and ethnic sources. All are combined with the utmost confidence and control, proving that she was in no way a disciple of any one school or style but a choreographer who could select at will from the whole range of social and theatrical dance.

The Camargo Society production (July 8 1931) opened with Gwen Raverat's tableau of Job and his family in their peaceful country surroundings. The splendid drop curtain of The Ancient of Days striking the first circle of the Earth was only added a year later. The action was then divided into eight scenes.

It began with the sons and daughters of Job engaged in a tranquil dance reflecting their pastoral happiness. Satan, desiring to disturb such contentment, appeals to the Godhead (Job's Spiritual Self), seated at the top of a broad flight of steps on which move the winged figures of the Children of God, to allow him to tempt Job into rebellion by plague and peril. Given permission, Satan dances in triumph, an athletic warrior dance featuring dramatic backbends, strong jumps and pulsating rhythms. Its climax comes when he ascends the stairs and climbs onto the throne of God.

Job's tragedies begin. His children are destroyed. Satan summons

Job *(Sadler's Wells Ballet 1948); (left to right) Franklin White, Henry Legerton, Paul Reymond, David Davenport, Jean Bedells*

up the masked figures of War, Pestilence and Famine, and they are followed by messengers who bring the news of loss to Job and his patient wife. Three hypocritical and accusing Comforters add to his troubles, and when he calls on God the opening heavens show him only Satan enthroned.

Elihu, Son of the Morning, appears and reproves Job for his bitterness. Job confesses his sin and is rewarded by a vision of the Godhead in glory, by the overthrow of Satan and the return of his children and his prosperity.

In *Job* de Valois worked with a larger cast than ever before—the largest, apart from *Don Quixote*, of her career. Her response to her three collaborators was close and complete, on the literary, visual and musical levels, and her application of human presence and movement was unerringly devised. As a choreographer she has always had a remarkable instinct, and courage, for determining when to use dance and when to allow pose and tableau to create an effect—a talent more usual in Oriental than in Western dance drama. She has an exact eye for the abilities of the artists she uses and a clear judgment over theatrical impact. Examples of all these qualities exist in *Job*.

Job, his wife and the Godhead are static and reticent creations but in no way weak. The eye is drawn to them unfailingly at key moments, by a significant gesture or by the deployment of other figures on stage. The focal element is of course Satan and here she had perfect material in Dolin. This role, with its one astonishing solo, is strong, arrogant, superhuman; and she set against it a dance of tranquilly controlled attitudes and courtly grace for Elihu that matched well with Judson's blond good looks. Four contrasted trios pointed the narrative: Job's daughters, womanly and compassionate; War, Pestilence and Famine, grimly masked and terrifying in their angularity and menace; the three sad young men whose mourning dance brings news of death; and the witty, sardonic mimed lamentations of the insincere Comforters. Again, she contrasts the fluent and tender intertwining patterns of the children on earth with the celestial ecstasy of the children of God and the Sons of the Morning, endlessly moving on the stairs of heaven.

Job was generally recognised by critics in 1931 as a powerful and unforgettable creation. Frank Howes sums up one unique aspect of it:

"What the dance does is to give movement to Blake's drawings, to add temporal rhythm to graphical design, to absorb and be absorbed by the music, which has itself the double inspiration of Blake and the Bible."[20]

The Times found it "that rare thing, a completely satisfying synthesis of the arts".[21] De Valois herself felt that it was too large and ambitious a work "to produce really successfully in this country at present" but went on to state forcefully an article of belief that would always have relevance where dramatic ballet was concerned:

"I often hear it accused of not being a ballet. Let those dance critics try to cast it with anything but really skilled dancers. A production requiring such dancers *is* a ballet, although it may not use one movement of an everyday class lesson."[22]

Richard Jennings, a great admirer of Blake, wrote interestingly:

"Job is a little sacrificed, having little to do but turn his head and look on while his family obediently posture in prosperity or in grief. Mrs Job, too—she passed her days in a somnolent or placid trance. But their tranquillity was an effective contrast to the redheaded, claw-handed Satan of Mr Anton Dolin, a whirlwind in the pastoral atmosphere, and to the hypocritical gestures of the three false Comforters."

As a humorous coda to his notice he recorded

"a comic after-ballet which took place in response to the audience's enthusiasm. Dr Vaughan Williams ... colliding in a *pas de deux* with Mr Dolin, the Angels exhibiting the sewn sides of unlighted wings, and Miss Ninette de Valois, to whom we owe the production, skipping capriciously in and out of the pleased company".[23]

A notice that recognises *Job*'s quality came in 1934 from Richard Capell, always a perceptive critic:

"This is a masterpiece. Ballets containing even one little idea have been rare in the last sixteen years. Many have had no idea at all. The idea of *Job* is grand, and it is carried out with daring and nobility. Indeed a unique work—a ballet that attains to the sublime! No one else had even thought of such a thing. Only two of the ballets of these later days could have excited anything but scorn in Diaghilev—*Job* and *The Green Table*—and of the two *Job* is in all ways the greater."[24]

Job was a substantial part of the Vic-Wells repertoire for many years although not many performances were totalled each year. When the company went to Covent Garden, a revival was planned for May 1948 and at this point de Valois took an important decision—to have the whole re-designed. She consulted the original initiator of the work,

Geoffrey Keynes, and John Piper, who had designed Ashton's *The Quest* for the company in 1943, was commissioned to take on the difficult assignment, with magnificent results. Even those who, like myself, had warm memories of the Raverat-Blake designs, could respond to the majestic translations of Blake produced by Piper as setting and costumes. They were lit with tremendous skill by Michael Benthall, an eminent young theatre director who staged notable productions of drama and opera before becoming artistic director of the Old Vic Drama Company.

Richard Buckle wrote of Piper "treating Blake's themes in his individual way and imparting to them his own special atmosphere or 'weather'" and went on

> "Benthall's lighting increases immeasurably both the beauty of the settings and the impact of the drama. When Satan is on God's throne, Benthall makes it shine like a poisonous amethyst, and his sunset glow matches the serenity of the final music."

The music was splendidly conducted by Sir Adrian Boult. Buckle writes:

> "For the way Miss de Valois has matched with movement the vision of the composer, of William Blake who saw God's face at the window, and of that bearded, forgotten thinker among the hills of Israel, no praise can be too high."[25]

Job was not a work to repeat frequently or to throw haphazardly into the repertoire with inferior casting but it is sad that it has been allowed to lapse so completely. De Valois feels that it is not now suited to a theatre but has said that she would like it to be performed in St Paul's Cathedral ...

Job opened the ballet season of September 1932 at the Vic and for the same evening Ashton staged his first work for the company. *Regatta* was a comedy trifle with a score by Gavin Gordon in which de Valois danced the role of a Foreign Visitor. Her own choreography that winter included dances in *Dido and Aeneas* and two new ballets, *Fête Polonaise* and *The Jew in the Bush*.

With *Fête Polonaise* she returned to the divertissement ballet, a form always popular with audiences. This time she used music by Glinka, and it was a joint production with the Camargo Society who staged it within the week at the Savoy Theatre. Opening with a Polish ensemble, it continued into a *pas de six* led by two women soloists which Beaumont found the most interesting composition, as it was "based on the four corners of the stage and the diagonals connecting them".[26] There was then a variation for the ballerina, guest artist Phyllis Bedells, a mazurka for four couples, a solo for the *premier danseur* (Judson) and a *pas de deux*. The first costumes and sets, by Owen Smyth, were later replaced by the ones the Camargo commissioned from Edmund Dulac of a handsome stylised ballroom with a balcony opening onto a night sky, and costumes of white, rose, pale greys and powder blues.

The Jew in the Bush was something of an oddity. It was a character comedy based on a tale by the Brothers Grimm, with Ashton in the leading role and Judson as the youth who plays the fiddle to make the Jew dance. To read, the story is a nasty little anti-Semitic episode but the ballet was not concerned with such matters. It was without malice or racial content, concentrating entirely on the compulsive dancing not only of the Jew but of other characters—king, queen and executioner. It was also, unfortunately, without much choreographic interest. Gordon Jacob had composed the music in 1923, offering it to Diaghilev as a project that did not appeal to him.

By now de Valois had been faced with a change-over at the Abbey Theatre. Sara Patrick wanted to leave, so de Valois approached Nesta Brooking, recommended to her by Margaret Craske, to see if she would take over the ballet school and also form a more substantial little company in Dublin. Nesta had danced with the Carl Rosa Opera ballet and was interested in teaching but not to the exclusion of performance. She also wanted to do some choreography. Classically she was Cecchetti orientated, but shared with de Valois an enthusiasm for the freer styles of modern dance.[27]

In August 1931 Nesta remembers visiting de Valois in Taviton Street and then going out to a local ABC cafe to discuss Dublin over a pot of tea. Nesta was to work for three months with de Valois at Sadler's Wells, taking classes with her, assimilating her methods, teaching the office workers, and learning the dances de Valois wanted her to stage in Dublin. She was immediately delighted with the inventiveness of the classes and found de Valois a strong and striking person to work with. She was taught the dances initially to beats with the music being introduced at a later stage, and set off for Dublin—a new city to her— in early November.

Her contract with the Abbey was similar to Sara Patrick's—£5 a week for forty-four weeks' work, £2.10.0 a week for eight weeks' vacation, and an extra £2.10.0 for any week in which she performed on stage. Her initial fare was paid, and a couple of settling-down nights in the best hotel in Dublin were a present from de Valois. Sara Patrick then found her digs in Lower Baggot Street.

She found that she had about twenty full-time students, but there were also flourishing evening classes—on Tuesday and Thursday for business girls and on Wednesday and Friday for "business men". Apparently they had very reasonable attendances by the men. They also had a splendid pianist in Julia Gray. Students tended to be careless over hours and slipshod over dress, and saints' day holidays made inroads on each term, but they were otherwise keen workers. Mothers were as much a problem as anywhere else, but de Valois' advice was to take no notice of their outbursts, and she was invariably supportive if they made difficulties.

She came over herself once in three months, staying for about ten days and taking an individual interest in the pupils, assessing capabilities and potential, and understanding their temperaments and problems. Nesta remembers her as a young woman very much in a hurry but never too rushed to consider and help on the human aspects of the job. She was in touch with every branch of her work, in London, Cambridge or Dublin, writing innumerable short practical letters (where nowadays one would phone), for the most part undated or part dated, about day to day matters like arrivals and departures, programme notes and performances. Answers would be begged for "by return of post", "as quickly as possible", "at once"—there is an overall impression that there was not a moment to waste. So much had to be done, so full a life had to be lived. Every letter to Dublin, however rushed, seemed to conclude "Give the girls my love and tell them they must work hard . . ."

Nesta was immediately involved in an important programme, attended by the Governor General and his lady. This contained the first performance of Yeats' *The Dreaming of the Bones*, choreographed by de Valois to music by Dr J. F. Larchet, the Abbey's musical director, whom de Valois remembers as an exceedingly interesting and intelligent man.

In this dance drama Yeats was dealing with the belief that the dead dream back to the events of their life. A young fugitive from the Easter Rising of 1916 (the play had been written contemporaneously with that event) encounters, while wandering on the hills of Clare, the spirits of the 12th-century lovers Diarmuid and Dervorgilla. Diarmuid, when banished from Leinster because he had eloped with a married woman, committed the grave sin of bringing in the English under Strongbow to help him regain his kingdom. The Yeats' play is about the ghosts' plea for forgiveness from the young man as representative of Ireland, a plea that is refused. In the programme Yeats declared that once again he had written it for private house performance before very small audiences, without scenery or lighting effects. Everything was to be suggested by the acting, singing and dancing. As in Japanese or Chinese theatre, certain movement conventions were used: "a movement round the stage to the accompaniment of drum and flute represents a mountain climbed".[28] The poignant climactic dance for the lovers who must continue in purgatory was entrusted to Nesta Brooking and John Stevenson.

The Irish Times found this play "a thing of beauty, which one would never weary of seeing"[29] and Joseph Holloway felt it was a complete success—something of a triumph, as he was not an enthusiast for ballet. He had been pleased the previous April when the Dublin Gate Theatre's *Dublin Review* included a ballet to Debussy, *Le Chèvre indiscrète*, about which he wrote:

"MacLiammóir in some of his gestures and poses hit off Ninette de Valois' method of dancing very aptly and well, just the right amount of emphasis."[30]

The year 1932 in London began for de Valois with a small and sadly shortlived ballet for Markova and Judson, *Narcisse and Echo*. It was set to Bliss' Rhapsody for strings and two voices and was Markova's first appearance at the Wells. She recalls it as a very modern ballet.[31] Chappell's set, in black and white, used three levels. The action opened with Echo on the highest level with her attendant maidens below her and Narcisse lying on stage gazing into a pool created—and this was at the time unusual—by lighting effects. Echo's dancing was barefoot and largely in profile, and in retrospect Markova feels that the choreography had links with Central European Dance. De Valois was obviously employing the style she had already exercised in *Rout*, in *La Création du monde* and in parts of *Job*.

De Valois herself was dancing regularly at this time and a delightful role came her way in March when Rupert Doone choreographed *The Enchanted Grove*. Doone is an interesting figure in the dance theatre of the time but never settled down with any ballet company as dancer-choreographer. De Valois recalls him as very gifted, an exciting but difficult artist, temperamentally impossible to work with. He had run away from home at the age of 16 to train as a dancer with Astafieva and then embarked on a widely varied career. Geraldine Morris, in an article in *The Dancing Times*,[32] mentions affiliations of brief duration with most of the great dance names of the epoch. He worked with Massine in London and joined the Ida Rubinstein Ballet in Paris.

As early as 1924 de Valois danced in a ballet he composed (of which nothing is remembered) at the Playhouse Theatre. She knew of his work later when he arranged dances at the Festival Theatre Cambridge in 1930 and for Nigel Playfair, and she met him also through the Bloomsbury group and the Camargo Society.

The Enchanted Grove was set to Ravel's *Le Tombeau de Couperin* and had gorgeous baroque designs by Duncan Grant. It concerned an open-air party at the court of Louis XIV, entertained by strolling players disguised as an Oriental courtesan and her attendants. This was de Valois' role and one she loved dancing. Everyone who saw it remembers especially her entrance, on a white stage horse flanked by two strikingly costumed and quarrelsome warrior lovers, and how she dismounted and walked downstage on pointe with crisp, coquettish steps and flutterings of a fan.

> "Doone has understood this admirable dancer, and has exploited all her wonderful purity of line. She completely dominates the stage and when she appears the ballet takes on form and is held together."[33]

Haskell, who wrote this, did not think highly of the choreography although he did not go as far as P. W. Manchester's uncompromising description—"a ghastly bit of Rococo Chinoiserie which was mercifully dropped fairly swiftly."[34]

De Valois contributed choreography that January to an unusual and successful West End revue, *Bow Bells*, at the London Hippodrome. Devised and produced by John Murray Anderson, this starred Robert Hale and his daughter Binnie. De Valois' ballet was a scene of Victorian flirtations in a park on a rainy day. Rather than her own work, she recalls Harriet Hoctor's celebrated turn—still to be seen in the film *Shall We Dance?*—of crossing the stage in *bourrées* on pointe with an exaggerated backbend.

In March at Sadler's Wells de Valois staged Elgar's *Nursery Suite*.

Elgar had sent this score initially to Dolin because he had so much enjoyed his *Little Boy Blue*. Dolin, having no inclination to do it himself, passed it on to de Valois, who liked the idea.

Apart from its own merits, the ballet was excellent publicity for the Wells. The music was dedicated to the two little princesses, Elizabeth and Margaret Rose, and they were taken to see a performance by their mother, the then Duchess of York, with consequent photographs in the press. *The Era*'s review was unintentionally prophetic in its headline, "The Royal Ballet at Sadler's Wells", but royal at this juncture merely meant the Royals' presence there. The critic described it as a

"quaintly humorous affair ... Anton Dolin as Georgie-Porgie was priceless but Little Bo-Peep etc. all arrived to delight with their coquettish or perky humour an audience which had clearly not forgotten the existence of these heroes of juvenilia."[35]

The Times also enjoyed it:

"The touch is light, always pretty, sometimes amusing and the spirit of Elgar's whimsical music is well caught."[36]

The ballet opened with the Georgie-Porgie scene, followed by a solo for Little Bo-Peep. The Three Bears led in to duets for Snow White and Rose Red, and Jack and Jill, with another, less technically demanding solo for the Little Match Girl. A *pas de quatre* for girls and a classical *pas de deux* and variations for Markova and Dolin as the Prince and Princess completed the work.

In June 1932 the Camargo Society embarked on an ambitious four-week season at the Savoy Theatre, putting together programmes from all their most successful ballets and including Act II of *Le Lac des cygnes* and an historic production of *Giselle* in which Olga Spessivtseva danced with Dolin as Albrecht. For one performance, de Valois played Giselle's mother Berthe. Her own new work for the season was *The Origin of Design* with a Handel score arranged and conducted by Beecham. The scenario for this was from the original of Carlo Blasis, contained in his *Code of Terpsichore*, and concerned the legend that the young Dibutade was inspired by Love to draw a likeness of her absent lover Polydore. "The sight of these simple lines supplied to mankind the idea of the admirable art of painting." The drawing is then presented and dedicated to Apollo and the Muses. The designs by Chappell for the two scenes were "faithful renderings" of designs by Inigo Jones—scene 1 for an unidentified woodland and scene 2 a palace designed for Ben Jonson's 1611 Masque of Oberon.[37] The choreography was very stylish, very classical and danced by Lopokova, Dolin and Markova.

A British Trade and Arts Fair was about to be held in Copenhagen and Adeline Genée, as Chairman of the Anglo-Danish Society, asked de Valois to organise a programme of ballets, mainly drawn from the Camargo Society and the Vic-Wells Ballet, to be staged at the Royal Theatre, Copenhagen, and represent Great Britain. The final choice of productions was a complete cross-section of work from Fokine's *Les Sylphides* danced by an all-British cast to de Valois' *Création du monde*. Four performances were given by what was termed "The English Ballet Company", between September 24 and 28, with no two evenings alike. Geoffrey Toye and Constant Lambert conducted and royal galas were attended by the King and Queen of Denmark and the Prince of Wales.

The Danes had a hard time adjusting to de Valois' experimental choreography—they were then firmly conditioned to Bournonville with no disturbing outside influences. According to *Dagens Nyheder*, *Job*

"utterly failed to please Danish taste ... the musical setting by Vaughan Williams was melodious, at times full of character, but often more banal."[38]

Politiken was engrossed by the novelty of a ballet on a religious theme and commented

"This remarkable work was carried through with a solemnity which should be acknowledged even by the *Kristeligt Dagblad* (*Christian Daily News*) ... If the English Ballet initiate a school, we may perhaps in time live to see *Skatten i Lerkar* (a religious play written by Danish clergymen) as ballet."[39]

Dagens Nyheder was obviously intrigued by *Création du monde*:

"In a reddish gleam of light which spread over the twilight scene, one saw three godlike gigantic figures on the lines of Meunier's bronze statues. Before their feet lay some large shapeless bundles, and out of these wriggled, little by little and with slow movements, brown half-naked people ... It was a modern symbolical ballet, which was more curious than beautiful. Each of the grotesque groupings was effective, and there was in a way harmony in the midst of discord."[40]

De Valois' divertissement ballets *Hommage aux belles viennoises* and *Fête Polonaise* appealed far more to the Danish critics, and she herself was greatly admired as a dancer. *Pride* was termed coquettish, amusing and exultant.

It was the first time ever that an English ballet company had gone abroad and the success of the venture was of great importance for the future backing and reputation of the Vic-Wells Ballet. Reporting a Faculty of Arts dinner in October for members of the company, Leslie Rees elaborated the theme that English Ballet "had arrived". He instanced the Camargo Society season, the hopes of another in 1933, and the high level of dancing, music and design represented. The Vic-Wells Ballet was providing regular public presentations of ballet and by the end of 1932 would have a repertoire of twenty ballets, while Marie Rambert's Ballet Club was giving Thursday and Saturday performances for its members for the greater part of the year.[41]

As well as directing, choreographing and teaching, de Valois was still a prima ballerina of her own company. Her repertoire included the leads of *Fête Polonaise*, *The Origin of Design*, *The Lord of Burleigh*, *Nursery Suite* and *Cephalus and Procris*, and she danced *Le Spectre de la rose* with Dolin—one of the few instances of her involvement in a romantic and lyrical ballet. Sympathetic as she was to Fokine's choreography, her musicality, sense of period and fine *port de bras* allowed her to give a very acceptable performance. She also created the lead in her new ballet, *Douanes*.

This was a witty *demi-caractère* work to a score composed by Geoffrey Toye, set in 1859 at "The Customs House at St Maritime, France". The programme note, perhaps written by the choreographer, declared with tongue-in-cheek blandness, "The plot of the ballet is extremely simple and follows the lines of the ordinary scenes which take place daily in customs houses."[42] The central situation was the fleeting flirtation of the man from Thomas Cook (Dolin) with a celebrated Tightrope Dancer (de Valois) whose elderly husband eventually had to pay up for smuggled cigars, but the detail was filled in with Massinesque thoroughness. Gendarmes, porters, passengers of all types and ages and a Passport Officer, surrounded the principals and the lively finale was couched in the terms of an English country dance.

Sibthorp delighted in de Valois' performance—"The role gave scope as did few others for her gift of gaminerie and slightly malicious raillery"—but did not think it a one-role ballet. Both music and dancing created "deft character studies", and the vigorous and often ingenious ensembles were highly entertaining. He found the original designs by Hedley Briggs caught "exactly the right mood of fantastic improvisation" (in photographs they look totally eccentric and over-elaborate) and that the Sophie Fedorovitch scheme in 1935 was more modern but rather too reticent.[43]

Fedorovitch—a name to conjure with in the realm of pure, unclut-tered settings and costumes for ballet—had her first assignment for the company in November 1932 with an entirely revised production of *The Scorpions of Ysit*. She had designed Ashton's first ballet, *A Tragedy of Fashion*, for Rambert in 1926; de Valois' admiration for her was immense. In an obituary she wrote:

> "Her understanding of ballet design was the outcome of a selfless imposition of study. She had a real knowledge of movement and of the significance of the dancer's lineal expression. She was never known to permit a line or a curve of her design to interfere with or confuse the clarity of the choreography. Her efforts were ceaseless in their search for creative unity."[44]

For *Scorpions* she designed palm trees against a neutral background, and for lovely Beatrice Appleyard as the Goddess Ysit a flowing sleeveless white gown with a round banded collar and a handsome Cleopatra-style headdress with a scorpion motif. Elsie Hamilton's unpopular music was abandoned in favour of a score by Gavin Gordon. Neither contribution however salvaged the ballet—it remained too awkward a proposition for the general repertoire. As P. W. Manchester points out:

> "Nobody ever knew whether it was meant to be funny or not. Pre-sumably the death of a baby through being bitten by scorpions was not intended to amuse, but the antics of the scorpions as they tossed the baby from one to the other and finally sat on it were not calculated to do anything but raise a laugh."[45]

It was indeed meant to be funny but there was no appreciation in the ballet theatre of the time for black comedy.

Choral ballet, in its different way, also left the Vic-Wells public confused and in spite of some critical praise the next production, *The Birthday of Oberon*, failed to establish itself. It was a project of Lambert's—he had been musical director and a compelling force for

The Scorpions of Ysit *(Vic-Wells Ballet 1932) Beatrice Appleyard as
the Goddess Ysit, Ursula Moreton as the First Marsh Woman*

good since September 1931. He had a lifelong affection for Purcell but this was the first time he arranged a Purcell score for ballet. It used the Masque of the Seasons from *The Fairy Queen* with additional music from the same work. Thirty dancers and an opera chorus of forty meant a large production.

The ballet began with a series of simple rural dances, reflecting the character of 17th century masque, before embarking on the seriously balletic Dances of the Seasons. *The Dancing Times* thought it one of the most successful and interesting ballets produced by the company[46] but without the audience's support it proved too large and expensive a production to keep in the repertoire.

De Valois was not only practising choreography at this period but writing and lecturing about it, and looking ahead to the training of future choreographers. In 1929, when she had stood in for Marie Rambert at the Dancers' Circle meeting at Liverpool, she chose to speak on "Dancing and its relation to the theatre". Drawing on her own experience, she considered the possibility of dancers and choreographers becoming more widely used in dramatic repertory theatres, and how dancers should keep in touch with modern trends in world theatre. She went on to talk of modern experimental dance and contemporary innovations in ballet, as seen in the most recent Diaghilev Ballet productions such as Massine's *Le Pas d'acier*, and she appealed for classical dancers to take the broadest view of dancing. *The Dancing Times* quoted her summing up: "She begged them all not to become slaves to that technique of classical ballet but to use it as the basis of any other dancing that might be required."[47]

Now in 1932 she spoke on "The Modern Ballet" during the Association of Operatic Dancing's Special Week in July.[48] She opened with a broadside:

> "The dance of today must keep pace with the theatre of today and be prepared to go in for the same experiments. Ballet is not an isolated art, consisting merely of technical display and virtuosity."

She spoke of Traditional Choreography (e.g. the ballets of Petipa) and Romantic Choreography (e.g. *Giselle*). Fokine carried the Romantic ballet into a second stage under Diaghilev. Massine represented early Expressionism and Nijinska produced ballets in which emotions were expressed by architectural means of grouping, line and design. She talked of Meyerhold and the theatre of constructivism. In her association with Terence Gray's theatre, and Peter Godfrey's Gate Theatre, she had of course been in close contact with the so-called "abstract" theatre practised by Meyerhold in Soviet Russia, the equation of actors—the human elements—with all other facets of the production of a play.

In 1933 she extended her arguments in a series of articles in *The Dancing Times*[49] dealing with various aspects of modern choreography and its elements: dance and dancers, music, decor and costume, theatrical presentation. Her experience and inclination led her always to consider ballet as a theatre art—not necessarily dealing with any dramatic narrative of course—and she reinforced this with the challenging view that "the true history of choreography is just the history of the theatre influencing another of its important arts". She placed no confining limitations on choreography, considering it to have in every way as much freedom of expression as painting, music, sculpture or drama. Choreographers should "remain true to their intuitive impulses". They should however put "constant study" into the realisation. Her own way of working was reflected in her analysis of a choreographer's methods: familiarity with the music, a discussion with the designer as to the pictorial mood, and then the composition of choreography with the dancers. Her collaboration with Terence Gray led her to emphasise the role of lighting—"the importance of the join between dances, scenes etc. and the length of certain light plots are points to sit and visualise in solitude for many hours". An illuminating reference also covers the "invisible link" between dances and scenes that created "the rhythm of ballet production", and she suggests that after the basic choreography has been set a choreographer should go through the work and make sure that there is a smooth overlapping of action from one section to another.

Where modern music was concerned, she recommended choreographers to work out a system of counting according to the phrasing of the music so that dancers could work on ballets initially by building up what she described as a mental picture of the music which would then be developed into aural appreciation when they heard it played by an orchestra. The aural appreciation of course was of paramount importance:

"Only by listening can the light and shade of music penetrate, and tone is as much a part of the ultimate musical picture as the phrasing and technical points one analyses at the beginning."

NdV as Swanilda in Coppélia *(Vic-Wells Ballet 1933)*

Chapter V

～ Planning a repertoire for the Vic-Wells Ballet was one of the major new responsibilities in de Valois' life and here she deserted the Diaghilev pattern to produce a distinctive one of her own. From the beginning she was aware of the need for her dancers to gain experience in traditional ballets and had intended to take the pioneer step of staging English productions of full-length works that in fact she had never seen herself—*Casse-noisette* and the entire *Le Lac des cygnes*— as well as those she knew from the audience—*The Sleeping Princess*, *Coppélia* and *Giselle*.

She began with the two-act *Coppélia* in 1933, choosing the Russian derived version rather than the one made familiar to London by Alexander Genée at the Empire Theatre, and asking Nicholas Sergeyev to stage it. Sergeyev, who produced the Camargo *Giselle* from his notated records of Maryinsky Theatre ballets, had left Russia in 1918. Formerly regisseur at the Maryinsky, he brought with him an invaluable collection of these notebooks and had reconstructed *The Sleeping Princess* for Diaghilev in 1921. For *Coppélia*, Lopokova acted as consultant and interpreter and, as guest artist, danced the role of Swanilda, an enchanting interpretation. Judson was a vigorous boyish Franz and Hedley Briggs a fine Dr Coppélius.

De Valois herself danced the leading peasant girl on the first night and then took over Swanilda after two performances. It was a role for which she was ideally suited. Her technical strength and precision was enlarged by her exceptional mimetic ability and flair for comedy. The *Morning Post* critic wrote:

"Her performance was characterised by superlative neatness and elegance but it was in her miming that she particularly excelled. In the second act especially she reflected to perfection every idea and fancy passing through the heroine's brain. Not only her face but all the movements of her body seemed to be called into play."[1]

The Era declared that she was

"something of a sensation as Swanilda. Her grace and charm; her precision and sense of rhythm; and her gaiety and perfect miming, went to the creation of a very fine performance."[2]

Her brother Gordon Anthony has written of her gorgeous sense of humour and finesse and calls her one of the best pizzicato dancers of her day—a judgment that is supported by everyone who saw her. He recalls her Swanilda as having "phenomenal speed and precision of footwork with an almost saucy gaiety";[3] while Michael Bayston says "For me all Swanildas have a long way to go before they blot out memories of the style and piquance of de Valois and the glamour of Danilova."[4] It was the only traditional lead she danced with her company but it was obviously a performance to treasure.

Choreography in two Russian operas for the Vic-Wells gave de Valois pleasure that year—*The Snow Maiden* in April and *Tsar Saltan* in October. Both were London premieres and gave considerable scope for dancing. *The Snow Maiden* involved a team of tumblers and an extensive ballet for Flowers and Birds separately characterised and including some charming solos. She also set dances for six of her own company for the successful Nigel Playfair production of *The Fantasticks* at the Lyric Hammersmith.

Whether she realised it or not, she was nearing the end of her diversified choreographing and performing activities. From mid-1934, with the exception of the Old Vic *Midsummer Night's Dream* in 1937, she had to devote her total energy to the mainstream of her work with the Vic-Wells Ballet, its successors and offshoots. In July 1933 however she embarked on an important visit to Dublin. Yeats' first play for a dancer had been *At the Hawk's Well* and now it was revived for de Valois. It was about the young Cuchulain but had no basis in legend. Yeats was applying to him a situation popular in No drama, in which a hero has a significant meeting with a god at some sacred place. There are many holy wells in Celtic tradition and the figure of a hawk-god or goddess as a guardian is a recognisable symbol of divine power that contains an element of danger to mortal man.

De Valois fitted, and wore, Michio Ito's striking costume designed by Edmund Dulac in 1916: a black hooded cloak which was thrown off to reveal a black and white feather-patterned gown over scarlet tights. The fitted cap and make-up gave the impression of a beaked predatory bird. She devised new dances in which she expressed the character's emotional content in stylised form and "the dance progressed from an evocation of brooding power through suggestive seduction to the violent ecstasy of a wild bird". Andrew Parkin describes the scene.

The play began with the unfolding of a cloth (as in No or Kathakali) and with singing. Then the cloth was folded, the musicians could be seen sitting by their instruments (drum, gong and zither) and the audience became aware of the Guardian of the Well crouching beside a blue cloth:

> "Because the dance allures Cuchulain away from the well it must in part be erotic and tempting. But it begins with fear ... the dance choreographs the invasion and possession of a human imagination and body by a spirit, in this case the hawk god. This choreography of mediumship begins with the shivering of the Guardian. Her shuddering, her rising to strike a first pose, the shedding of her cloak to reveal the masklike face and the stylised hawk costume, amount to a *coup de théâtre*."[5]

In the same programme de Valois staged two other dance plays. The more important, *Bluebeard*, was a 'ballet poem' by Mary Davenport O'Neill, set to music by Dr Larchet. The *Irish Independent* discussed this score in some detail. By means of *leit motif*, Larchet made the music cohesive and coherent, and suggested very delicately the various details of the story—the familiar fairytale. The production itself was

> "an elaboration of the existing form of ballet, since it includes as well as gesture and dance, declamation and free recitation".

The story was transmuted into a psychological commentary in the form of a poem, a melange of fantasy and reality. It did not seem however to achieve a balanced meld of the various performing elements:

> "There are so many periods of inactivity that the dance as such recedes into the background and we find ourselves fascinated by the distinctive art of Joseph O'Neill in his admirable vocal declamation; the expressive narration of Ria Mooney as Sister Ann or the enchanting beauty of the concealed vocal quartet."[6]

It was effectively designed and lit. One of the ballet school students, Victor Wynburne, had the title role with de Valois as the Seventh Wife. Dancers were cast as the ghosts of the previous wives and other roles were taken by actors and singers.

The third work of that evening was *The Drinking Horn*, book and music by Arthur Duff and choreography by de Valois. It was performed entirely by students. As it had a curiously similar theme to the much more significant *Hawk's Well*—that of young lovers and a knight who stood guard over a sacred well—it was oddly juxtaposed in the same programme. The music was described by the *Irish Independent* as being full of colour and modern in feeling.

Terence Gray came to the end of his activities in Cambridge in June 1933 with a production of Rostand's *Chantecler*. Seven years had passed since he planned the first Festival Theatre season. There had been talks about development by means of a closer association with J. B. Fagan of the Oxford Playhouse and Peter Godfrey of the London Gate Theatre, the establishment of a larger London house (a site was actually acquired in Covent Garden at 43 King Street) for them to share, and a regular exchange of productions, but the consequences of the Depression made the project collapse.

It did not affect de Valois. As she had no time to spare, she had ceased her connection with the theatre at the end of 1931. The years of Gray's dominance had been exciting ones for Cambridge, uneven artistically but, like firework shows, alternating dud rockets with magnificent set-pieces and blazing brilliance. Their effect is hard to estimate, but the stimulus of experimental productions, in particular with Greek and Shakespearean drama, and the advanced concepts of lighting, was felt throughout the English theatre.

Gray's keen interest in dance drama and in the use of dance movement and choreography in play production was not of course unique among theatre men of the time in Europe but he did much for the cause in Great Britain. Influence spreads widely and is not dependent on continuity of activity. People who worked at the Festival Theatre or who regularly formed part of his audiences, often in their impressionable undergraduate years, owed much in later life to his concept and daring.

British ballet owes him a debt. De Valois' association with him and his theatre was an important stage in her artistic development and both consciously and unconsciously affected her policies and outlook as a director and choreographer.

The last ballet de Valois staged for the Vic-Wells Ballet in 1933 was *The Wise and Foolish Virgins*. This had a score by Kurt Atterberg, a Swedish composer who won an important prize awarded in 1928 by the Columbia Graphophone Company for a symphony to mark Schubert's centenary. Atterberg was a controversial figure in the musical world and never very popular. The score for the de Valois ballet derived once again from the Ballets Suédois—Jean Borlin commissioned it for his ballet *Les Vierges folles* in 1920.

De Valois' production made little mark. *The Era* wrote:

"the pert, sparrow-like humour which is characteristic of Miss de Valois' choreography made it a thing of pretty and continuous charm."[7]

Sibthorp thought it "elegant to a degree" and "a shade too sophisticated, even tongue-in-cheek, for its theme"[8]—in 1933 the Bible was still considered very seriously by the majority of people in Britain. Chappell's designs were boldly medieval, with the wise virgins in tall pointed headdresses and the foolish ones in the coiffed, short-veiled type reminiscent of Mistress Quickly. Judson was the Bridegroom and Markova had an unexpectedly sprightly role as the Bride.

In November the Vic-Wells Opera staged a production of Gluck's *Orpheus* directed by Sumner Austin and conducted by Geoffrey Toye for which de Valois created a substantial amount of choreography. She performed a solo during the overture and arranged dances for the Mourning Women, for the Furies, for the Blessed Spirits, and a general ensemble in Act III. She would return to *Orpheus* at a later date.

December brought Ashton's second ballet for the company, one that still delights audiences wherever it is seen—*Les Rendezvous*. Technically clever and intricate, youthfully joyous in mood, it was particularly notable for the delectable variations he composed for Markova and for the sharply light-hearted *pas de trois* created by de Valois, Judson and Robert Helpmann.

Helpmann, a young Australian, joined the company early in 1933, appearing first in the *corps de ballet* of *Coppélia*. He had learnt dancing from an early age in Adelaide and was associated as a student with the Pavlova Ballet in Australasia. His father considered him too young to travel overseas with Pavlova and for the next few years Helpmann was engaged in Australia as a principal dancer in musicals. His arrival in England and introduction to de Valois was primarily due to Margaret Rawlings who had seen his work while on tour in Australia and felt confident of his potential.

De Valois too perceived the possibilities whenever he arrived at Sadler's Wells for an interview. It was a meeting of major importance. Helpmann's outstanding gifts as a versatile dramatic dancer and his magnetic stage personality were invaluable to the developing company, while his excellence as a partner and *danseur noble*, first with Markova and then in a classic collaboration with the young Fonteyn, maintained the standard of the traditional works. Helpmann's first major assignment came as Satan in *Job* in the opening performance of the autumn season of 1933, and following Dolin's notable creation was by no means easy. They were totally different artistically and at that time Helpmann could not equal Dolin's athleticism and confidence. His performance gained over the years until de Valois herself could say

> "Physically Dolin was the perfect replica of the Blake drawings. But it was Helpmann who caught the spirit of Blake, and the true outline, both plastically and musically, of the choreography in the eyes of the choreographer."[9]

De Valois began to plan her next ballet, *The Haunted Ballroom*, to give Helpmann his first created lead, but meanwhile she arranged for three important revivals. Fokine's *Carnaval* was inaugurated with the role of Harlequin brilliantly danced by Idzikovsky, while New Year's Day 1934 saw a landmark production of *Giselle*. On an evening of thick fog in Islington, the audience entered a magic world with the twenty-three-year-old Markova's marvellous dancing, her unique ethereal lightness in the second act. Dolin too, great and unselfish partner, contributed to an exceptional event. Helpmann was an effective Hilarion and de Valois danced the peasant *pas de deux* with Judson.

At the end of the month *Casse-noisette* (*The Nutcracker*) was revived—at that time a rarity outside Russia. Sergeyev's staging (with help from Lopokova) was straightforward: the first act party, with a child Clara, an old man Drosselmayer and the duets for the mechanical dolls; a snowflake ensemble without a Snow Fairy; and a divertissement in the Kingdom of Sweets when the Sugar Plum Fairy and the Nutcracker Prince (Markova and Judson) appeared for the first time to dance their *grand pas de deux* and variations. The other numbers were limited to the Espagnole *pas de deux*, the Danse Arabe (with Elsa Lanchester as the lady), the Chinoise for two men, a Russian solo (Bouffon), the Danse des Mirlitons for five girls and the ensemble of Fairies. It was an agreeable if not very exciting production that drew its strength from Markova's exquisite Sugar Plum Fairy.

Meanwhile de Valois had a fascinating extra-curricular task, the last time she would be associated with a West End drama production. This was to weave a pattern of dance through a handsome staging of Carl Zuckmayer's very free adaptation of the classic Indian play *Vasantasena*. Under the title of *The Golden Toy*, it reopened the London Coliseum as a theatre after its use as a cinema.

Ambition was the name of the game—it planned to give the public every form of entertainment, comedy, tragedy, dancing, singing and spectacle. There were lifts on either side of the proscenium which brought soloists in front of the arch to sing while the three sections of the stage revolved. Each section could revolve eccentrically and separately, and in either direction.

The play was directed by Ludwig Berger, with music by Schumann. The principal dramatic roles were taken by Peggy Ashcroft, Ion Swinley and Wilfrid Lawson, with Nellie Wallace and Lupino Lane in character parts. De Valois, who greatly admired Nellie Wallace as a comedian, remembers with pleasure that Nellie thought she had come for an audition as a feed. "I'll have that girl" Nellie said as de Valois walked across the stage on her own choreographic business, "the funniest face I've seen in years." The leading dancer of a very large company was Wendy Toye, and de Valois had never before had to arrange so much dancing in a play. She was working on all three revolves plus a precariously high performing catwalk incorporated into the set, over which the dancers had to move.

The story is a fairy tale. It concerns Vasantasena, a temple dancing girl, menaced by the powerful Prince Samsthanaka and loved by an apparently poor widower, Karudatta. The lovers attempt to flee but are caught, Vasantasena disappears, and Karudatta is accused of her murder and put on trial. Meanwhile, a precious golden toy-cart belonging to him has been stolen from his house. Karudatta is condemned to death, but two things save him: Vasantasena returns, having escaped from Prince Samsthanaka, and the thieving barber owns up to the theft of the toy and restores it. It proves Karudatta to be the rightful Prince and Samsthanaka an imposter.

The complexities and grandeur of the staging however were the point of the whole production. It elicited extremes of opinion. W. A. Darlington found it "a really beautiful show which builds up finely to its last and most impressive scene" and spoke of a tremendous welcome from the audience. His proviso against the likelihood of its running long depended on the dearth of good comic material and on the music.

This he felt was

"not insistent enough ... There are too few songs, and those there are, are sung not by the characters in the play but by two singers who are accomplished but extraneous."[10]

The Times critic obviously found it all rather exhausting. To begin with, the spectacle charmed him:

"A pearl grey city gleams with mysterious grandeur against a sky of lapis lazuli; momentarily the stage darkens and we are in a street with the snarling sinister Prince whipping his slaves into a frenzied pursuit of a girl whose beauty has attracted him; the peace of the romantic widower's house is ours at the price of another brief darkness; and from the elegance of his home we pass to the house in which the heroine earns a shameful living. It seethes with picturesque life, with maidens whirling and twirling in the frenzy of a native dance, and when the scene has served its purpose it gives place without effort to the next."

His problem lay in the fact that "all these good actors are given no opportunity to act".[11] There was unanimity over the lack of a proper use of actors and comics. Leslie Rees blamed the book. The dialogue "did not in any sense confirm the visual triumphs of the evening". It was "unfair to the audience and to Nellie Wallace and Lupino Lane— the former has scarcely a single line which is in itself funny".[12] Edwin Evans, writing as music critic and commenting on the musical structure, dissected its composition:

"The greater part of it is used as incidental to action or as the foundation of ballets—in which association it is interesting to note how well it suits Miss Ninette de Valois' clever, fantastic choreography. Portions of the symphonies are used in this way and there is a particularly effective scene based on the Manfred overture. Great use is made also of the piano music and since chamber music is under suspicion of being 'highbrow', it is amusing to find it so well received in this adapted form. Many people whom wild horses would not draw to a classical concert will applaud—let us hope for months to come—the music they would hear there. And this has all been done with a kind of affectionate reverence for Schumann."[13]

De Valois' choreography included dances for bayadères, for apparitions, for pastrycooks, and for ladies of the harem. Her influence was omnipresent, in the fluent and inventive stage movement, the delightful

The Haunted Ballroom *(Vic-Wells Ballet 1934); (left to right) William Chappell, Beatrice Appleyard, Alicia Markova, Robert Helpmann, Ursula Moreton*

comedy scenes in the kitchen or the striking ensemble of umbrellas in the rain, in the lyrical quality of the blue grotto where the lovers met and ran into tragedy, and Karudatta was beckoned from all sides of the stage by fantasy visions of Vasantasena; and she was responsible not only for Wendy Toye's varied dances—in one she wore a hoop with arms on her back to give an impression of a four-armed goddess figure—but for the convincing illusion that Peggy Ashcroft was able to create of being a dancing girl. In the *corps de ballet* was a young and beautiful dancer appearing under her own name of June Bear. She joined the Vic-Wells Ballet soon after, with an anagrammatic name change to Brae. "I can't have performing bears in the company," de Valois had declared . . .[14]

The Haunted Ballroom was given its premiere on April 3. A Gothick tale of a doomed man danced to death by ghosts in his own ballroom, this was excellent theatre, with a fluently choreographed and atmospheric central section flanked by strongly mimed and extremely economical scenes as prologue and epilogue. Geoffrey Toye composed the score, very tuneful and romantic with an easily assimilable waltz dominating the rhythms. Much was owed, too, to the three women—Sophia and Margaret Harris and Elizabeth Montgomery—who designed as "Motley", the creators of exquisite sets and costumes in tones of grey, white and black with touches of ruby red.

Markova had the principal ballerina role, brilliantly suited by the drifting ethereal dancing of the supernatural agents of doom, the wraithlike counterparts of the guests in ballgowns who appeared in the prologue. William Chappell, always a fine and sensitive dancer, gave a strong and sinister performance as the Stranger Player who controls the action. Helpmann, whose qualities of graceful movement and impeccable *port de bras* were exceptionally well captured in the choreography, displayed for the first time the mimetic subtlety and authority that would be cherished by connoisseurs of great acting.

It was the first time de Valois tackled a highly emotional and impassioned theme. So far she had staged witty and sophisticated works, strong modern-movement works, and the stylised and restrained drama of *Job*. In *The Haunted Ballroom*, where she had a full-blooded theatrical theme and a leading dancer capable of responding to the demands of a lyrical and passionate situation, her choreography adapted in style with immense conviction to produce a modern-classical ballet in an expressionistic staging.

The Haunted Ballroom was popular with wartime audiences in a 1942 revival and in 1947 was adopted by Sadler's Wells Theatre Ballet, where it lasted for ten years. Then in 1965 it had a sudden, unexpected revival by London Festival Ballet, who were scheduled to go on a tour to South America. Their repertoire had no specifically "British" character and the British Council suggested, and financially supported, a production of *The Haunted Ballroom* to introduce that element.

The main difficulty was remembering it, at a time before notated scores could be produced on demand. G. B. L. Wilson jotted down an impression of rehearsals:

"It was a surprise to find some middle-aged women occupying the floor. They were running about in short bursts, with knit brows and hands clasped over their heads, and appeared lost to the world ... Festival Ballet were mounting *The Haunted Ballroom* and Dame Ninette called in her old Sadler's Wells dancers to help her ..."[15]

They got it all together in the end and it was given first in Cardiff. The local press described de Valois at rehearsal:

"she continually interrupted from the wings with advice, cajoling, commanding, helping, suggesting—all with the patient pursuit of perfection that has made her so loved and respected by dancers throughout the world ... 'Of course it is a period piece,' she said, 'it is no good trying to change its mood. Times have changed, and you can like it as it is, or not ...' "[16]

Critics who went to see it on the whole didn't. A. V. Coton wrote:

"Significant impact is made through the strong square-cut mime and the unique de Valois-style of harsh dramatic dancing ... A special performing ability is necessary to make it vivid and believable, an ability which this present company seem to lack even allowing for the unevennesses of a first performance. Decor and costumes are very heavy-handed copies of Motley's originals and the lighting as well as the stage action needs more clarification ... Much should be worked upon to give this ballet something of the sweep and slickness it once showed ..."[17]

Most of the other notices were written by Clive Barnes, at that time contributing to a multiplicity of journals:

"Unfortunately much of the ballet nowadays looks dated. The choreography for Alicia is full of character but the dances for the ghosts, and even those given Treginnis himself, are dull and conventional. On the other hand it is a highly professional ballet, it has two very efficient star roles, a remarkably effective decor by Motley and some of the most popular British ballet music ever composed."[18]

Oleg Kerensky, confessing himself "a romantic, a sentimentalist and even perhaps a square", welcomed it even while he admitted that:

"People who think that ballet stories should always be Freudian, nuclear or in some other way 'with it' and that ballet music must at least be by Stravinsky or preferably be electronic or *musique concrète*, are unlikely to have much time for *The Haunted Ballroom* ..."[19]

Festival Ballet gave it an unlucky thirteen performances in all, showing it in Buenos Aires, Montevideo, Santiago, São Paulo and Rio de Janeiro before letting it slide out of their repertoire.

One television production was tried, in February 1958, when Christian Simpson produced it with dancers from the Royal Ballet touring company. It would be interesting to see what an imaginative director would make of it now, in the days of colour and increased technical sophistication.

Immediately on the heels of *The Haunted Ballroom* de Valois turned to chamber ballet of the Rambert style. It was her first and only production for Marie Rambert's company.

Rivals to some extent, de Valois and Rambert nevertheless had an admiration for each other as well as an understanding of each other's aims and problems. In the long run they were to prove complementary in their achievements but this was not the intention of either of them. De Valois, paying generous tribute to Rambert at a thanksgiving service after her death, remembered one of their early encounters when Rambert begged her to accept the single vacancy with the Diaghilev Ballet. When they were both retired from their famous directorships— Rambert was ten years de Valois' senior—they had leisure to make friends and did so.

In 1934 the situation was different but they were all the same closely linked. They served on the same advisory committee for dancing with the Camargo Society and artists moved from one company to the other—with de Valois on the whole drawing considerably more from Rambert than the other way round. As de Valois points out in an essay written in 1975, the Mercury Theatre was too small to provide proper salaries for its artists. "The aims and the training of the Mercury dancers were the aims and training that we [the Vic-Wells Ballet] were looking for." So dancers from Rambert, as well as the choreographer Ashton, contributed valuably to the development of the Vic-Wells Ballet while dancers from the Wells very occasionally appeared at the Mercury.

De Valois writes:

"Everybody loved the Mercury Theatre. In spite of its smallness, its atmosphere for me was not far removed from that of the Festival Theatre Cambridge and the Abbey Theatre Dublin. There was dedication; there was the love of the development of the theatre for itself; there was always a stream of dancers, actors and actresses ready to offer their services."[20]

Certainly the policy of the Rambert company was akin to de Valois' own: the conception, derived from Diaghilev, of the one-act ballet that whatever its scale should unite choreography, music and design in a unified whole. Rambert was freer, mainly because her scale was small and her activities backed by subscribing supporters rather than the management of the Old Vic and Sadler's Wells, to try out as many novice choreographers as she could find. De Valois' budget, which she did not herself control, restricted her vigorously to a certain number of dancers and ballets and choreographers. She had to make decisions that were governed by this factor, decisions that might be unpopular at the time and severely questioned by people later who did not fully understand the period context. An example of this concerns Antony Tudor who appeared as a dancer with the Vic-Wells Ballet. Already choreographing for Rambert, he deserved the chance to do so for the larger company; but there was only money available for one more artist and the overriding need was for a strong virtuoso dancer. Harold Turner rather than Tudor had to be offered the engagement. De Valois, explaining this to Tudor, advised him to join a large professional company with a mixed repertoire including Fokine, Massine and Balanchine works—the de Basil Ballet was the one she had in mind—to get experience in that way for a couple of years and then come back to her. Tudor said, "How do I know you would take me then?" to which she replied, "You have only my word . . ."

In May 1934 the ballet de Valois created for the Rambert dancers was to a scenario worked out by Ashley Dukes. He appealed to her lasting appreciation of painting by linking the pictures of Manet and the Paris of Toulouse-Lautrec in *Bar aux Folies-bergère*. Lambert suggested Chabrier (*Dix petites pièces pour piano*)—Chabrier, a friend of Manet's, had bought the original painting—and de Valois produced, very quickly, a taut, trim and witty work.

Lodged in Ballet Rambert's archives is the notebook in which she outlined the action.[21] It was found after Dame Marie Rambert's death in a cupboard at her home in Notting Hill Gate—a typical Temple Bar looseleaf book of the thirties, such as most students bought, on which Rambert had clipped a handwritten note:

"Ninette de Valois' script for 'Bar aux Folies-bergère' in 1934. Will be valuable one day"

As with writers or composers, choreographers have distinctly personal methods of recording their works. De Valois' notebook is an aide-memoire for herself rather than a performing record in the modern sense. It takes for granted that the technical sequences of dancing are stored in the dancers' memory, as was the custom of the time, in addition to the mimetic expressiveness and characterisation of the

Bar aux Folies-bergère *(Ballet Club 1934); (left to right) Frederick Ashton, Ann Gee, Walter Gore, Pearl Argyle, Alicia Markova, William Chappell, Tamara Svetlova, Mary Skeaping, John Reynolds*

various roles. There are only one or two indications of actual steps.

The action is divided into bars—for example, the opening, when the curtain goes up (as it eventually comes down) on Chappell's brilliantly recreated tableau of the Manet picture, is designated "Bars 1–9: holds picture". She then notes in the margin the musical cue, e.g. "1. Mélancolie", and describes action, entrances and exits on the main part of the double spread page. Simple signs denote characters: ○ = Barmaid; + = Waiter; ◇ = Principal Grisette, and so on. In the programme the roles are given other names. Barmaid (Pearl Argyle) becomes La Fille au bar; Waiter (Frederick Ashton), Valentin, garçon; Principal Grisette (Markova), La Goulue.

"Mélancolie" introduces the two Habitués. "Tourbillon.2" brings on the Waiter, the Grisettes and includes the Can-Can. In the "Idylle.3", with the note "the last seven bars of the Mauresque are played", the Old Gentleman enters through the audience. The "Menuet Pompeux.4" is the setting for La Goulue's solo, and there is a sketch for this in the notebook with indications of the floor pattern.

The story was nothing—the unrequited love of the Barmaid for Valentin who goes off with La Goulue; the evocation of place and character was everything. As *The Morning Post* declared, when Ballet Rambert staged it a few months later at the Duchess Theatre in London's West End:

> "Those who have already seen Ninette de Valois' *Bar aux Folies-bergère* had better go and see it again. It wears extremely well and may not unjustly be regarded as a little classic in the *ballet intime* style. It has emotion, wit and humour and it is charming to look upon."[22]

Markova was dancing at Sadler's Wells as well as at the Mercury while *Bar* was in creation, and most Saturdays after morning classes at the Wells de Valois took her to lunch in Soho before going to see a film. En route one day they went along the prostitutes' beat in Lisle Street. De Valois delightedly pointed out to her the kind of provocative, hand-on-hip mincing walk she wanted for La Goulue, to be transposed from high heels to pointe shoes ... Achieving it widened Markova's range. Dolin quotes a letter he had from his mother:

> "You just won't know Alicia when you see her. She has developed an extraordinary sense of humour, like a singer who has suddenly given evidence of feeling in her voice. Her roguish impertinence as the coquettish star of the can-can girls is a superb piece of effrontery, which makes the audience rock with laughter."[23]

      *   *   *

The Abbey Theatre, affected by financial shortages, decided to cut down on the ballet school. Nesta Brooking moved back to London and de Valois' regime came to an end. She wrote to Nesta:

> "Give all the girls my love and tell them how sorry I am that the Abbey can't afford to continue. Tell them I appreciate the good will and loyalty they have shown me during the last year."[24]

Except for the distinguished work she had done as choreographer and dancer in the Yeats' dance dramas, the fruits of her efforts for Ireland were not spectacular. Apart from Jill Gregory, soloist with Sadler's Wells Ballet and later ballet mistress to the Royal Ballet at Covent Garden, and Toni Repetto, who made a career in British ballet, none of the students became professional dancers. A solid body of teachers emerged, however. Muriel Kelly and Cepta Cullen, Doreen Cuthbert and Thelma Murphy, all ran schools in Dublin. Arthur Hamilton became principal of a highly successful dancing academy in

Belfast and did a good deal of choreography locally. One assignment reminiscent of the de Valois days was when he choreographed movement and groupings to the rhythm of the words in a production of Gordon Bottomley's verse drama *Culbin Sands*.

One production was left for de Valois to collaborate on in Dublin. Yeats had written a dance drama especially for her which he called *The King of the Great Clock Tower*. The theme had little to do with a king—it was the Queen who was the dominant element, descending from the tower to take a wandering stranger as her lover, an act that led to his death. Her climactic dance came after his beheading. Music was composed by Arthur Duff and Lennox Robinson, of course, directed, as he had the earlier plays. This was a man for whom she had the greatest respect and affection—"a long, quiet, untidy-looking eagle, peering at us from the gloom of the Abbey stalls with his glasses reflecting shafts of light".[25]

The King of the Great Clock Tower was produced in July 1934. Yeats wrote to Olivia Shakespear:

"It [the play] has proved most effective—it was magnificently acted and danced. It is more original than I thought it, for when I looked up *Salome* I found that Wilde's dancer never danced with the head in her hands ... My dance is a long expression of horror and fascination. She first bows before the head (it is on a seat) then in her dance lays it on the ground and dances before it, then holds it in her hands ..."[26]

A feeling of guilt at the stylised form of the costume designs possessed him where de Valois was concerned and he inscribed her copy of the play:

To Ninette de Valois
asking pardon for covering
her expressive face with a mask[27]

But what he had done from the first had been to reveal to her the dancer's ability to use masks as an additional method of physical expression. The masks she wore, as Fand or as the Queen of the Great Clock Tower—the masks she held in her hands in the dressing room and moulded mentally into the link between poetry, music and dance—freed rather than shackled her inspiration as a performer:

"I was certainly behind a mask, but able to dance in complete unison with what was covering my face, and both the mask and the dance sprang from the vision of one of the world's greatest poets."[28]

144

NdV at Sadler's Wells

145

The whole question of facial expressiveness is one of great delicacy and anyone who analyses and compares the acting and mime of great actor dancers with that of their less gifted fellows discovers that the deepest emotional communication is made without grimaces, without wide-open mouths, distorted features and staring eyes but by the subtlest and most economical of expressions projected from within by powerful feeling. This was the level on which de Valois was operating in the Yeats' dramas.

The King of the Great Clock Tower was presented in the same bill as Yeats' *The Resurrection*, but the anticipated detailed notices never appeared in the Irish press. A newspaper strike intervened, from July to October. *The Irish Independent*, catching up with a Stage Survey, found it difficult to follow Yeats "into the realm of abstruse poetry and metaphysical speculation" but thought the plays powerful and stimulating:

"They have form and beauty, balance and harmony, and the curious style of production with its studied formalism and clever use of music and masks greatly increases their absorbing interest."[29]

They were not alone in finding the text difficult. De Valois has put on record:

"Down had come the curtain with a smack of despondency on the last rehearsal of *The King of the Great Clock Tower*. The gloom of the theatre was cut off and also those two whispering figures [Yeats and Lennox Robinson]. I arose from my throne and removed my mask, behind which I had sunk for an hour, lulled to peace by the voice of that great actor Peter McCormick [F. J. McCormick]. Within the folds of his costume of the heroic age, he looked at me, sighed and shook himself like a dog. 'Well, may the spirit of Mr Yeats be with us tonight, and may it spread itself a bit and give a clue to the audience as to what it all is that we be talkin' about ...'"[30]

For literary critics *The King of the Great Clock Tower* was eclipsed by a subsequent reworking of the same theme, *A Full Moon in March*, but by the time Yeats completed this de Valois was no longer able to spend time in Dublin. She told him in 1934 that her duties at Sadler's Wells would not allow this.

" 'And who,' he said, gazing elsewhere as usual, 'will do my *Plays for Dancers*?' "[31]

Yeats, with his long and closely packed working life, his poetry, plays and metaphysical writings, is a magnet to the literary researcher and commentator, the kind of genius about whom each new generation feels it has fresh and revolutionary insight. Books about him proliferate, studies of every aspect of his thought and work, and because of this de Valois has been constantly asked about her association with him. Often it amuses her. Arriving to lecture at a celebrated women's college in the States without time to prepare, she started with Yeats and devoted her whole talk to him. The Principal thanked her profusely— "you've just given us material for our entire first semester's work" ... In Sligo in August 1969 she was asked to speak at a Yeats International Summer School run by the Yeats Society, and found that two thirds of her audience were Americans. Joan Lawson, who was there, recalls the baffled expressions on their faces and the delight of local people when she made her opening remarks in a broad Irish brogue ...[32] The probing and discussion of the significance and symbolism of his writings is something with which she is not entirely in sympathy. The possessor of a poetic gift herself (and with a similar talent I can appreciate her attitude), she comments:

"A great poet sings to us from his heart, and how his heart arrives at all the wonderment that it finds is a matter of vision; it has more strength left alone, left wrapped in its own mystery, and he would mean us to absorb the ultimate with the accent on a sublime and contented acceptance of any one of his sequence of words ..."[33]

Acceptance is what she recalls as essential in assessing the productions of the *Plays for Dancers*:

"You had to allow yourself to be absorbed into the whole, never to exist as an isolated part, only as a part of the whole ... In the end there was a fusion; you felt your body and your emotions take part in the spirit of the general production."[34]

From this unity that existed at the Abbey Theatre between performers, director, musicians and designers, writers and the specialised and receptive audience, de Valois must have drawn strength to deal with all her other responsibilities across the Irish Sea.

The Opera Ballet

Ninette de Valois

ダ. This was once an exhilarating influence on me. How well I
remember my temporary withdrawal from the commercial theatre in
the summer of 1919 (and again in 1928) to the magic world of the
Covent Garden Opera season. In the year 1919 it was something so
very far removed from my theatre life of that time; an introduction to
the workings of "The Establishment" collected from all parts of
Europe—austere, autocratic, unrelenting in its approach to perfection,
but so stimulating that its awesome effect was to take you back in
theatre history and make you aware of Opera House traditions and
their mysterious values. It was a new world to me yet I was sensitively
aware of its great age . . .

It is 1919 and I am standing outside the Opera House looking at one
of its posters announcing the cast for a certain opera. It contains a
column of distinguished names including the great Melba—and then
"*première danseuse* Ninette de Valois"—the same billing and the same
placing as all the great preceding artists. I thought that I would faint
there and then—what right had I to be "billed" in the same way as
the great Melba? Living in my world of the commercial theatre I was
used to my name being printed a little bigger than so-and-so, a little
smaller than someone else, and equal with another performer—a very
sensitive proceeding that you had to toughen yourself to accept.

At "The Garden" in 1919 I came under the highly efficient old ballet
master from the Brussels Opera House—Ambrosiny. Again he was
there in 1928, and I was drilled in his accumulation of solo roles
through the years of his choreographic opera-ballet work in Brussels.

I grew, at that time, to love opera and I also worked with the Sir
Thomas Beecham Opera Company, but only as a guest artist for certain
productions. I can remember the young Eugene Goossens conducting
one ballet in which I had choreographed my own variation. He asked

to meet me and was highly complimentary over the way I had "interpreted the music". I departed slightly dazed over such a reading of—what seemed to me—a simple, straightforward solo. I think that it was one of my first choreographic efforts—I could not face the "assistance" of the ballet mistress!

But I had not finished with my opera ballet experiences. It all returned to me in Monte Carlo—actually sandwiched between my 1919 and 1928 Covent Garden engagements.

In Monte Carlo we had to dance—when members of the Diaghilev Company—as members of the opera ballet during the French Opera season held every year at the Monaco Theatre in the very early spring. Nijinska and the young Balanchine were responsible for the choreography of a fairly stiff onslaught of opera ballets. I remember Nijinska giving us all a lecture when the greater number of the artists grumbled about such work imposed on them, for they were busy working on new productions for the Diaghilev season that was to follow. Nijinska informed us that a lot of opera ballet work was "important" and I recollect that she and Balanchine did some interesting choreography for us. She arranged the vision solo for me in *Thais*—a role that I had already danced at the Garden in 1919. It was Balanchine though, in his *pas de trois* for Danilova, Dubrovska and myself in another opera , who left me swooning in the dressing room, and solemnly assuring everyone that he was "a genius".

By the time I reached the Old Vic and later the Wells my enthusiasm for opera ballet rapidly evaporated. Small stages, tiny casts, poorly designed costumes etc., made it all very depressing and unrewarding for the choreographer; of course it did not help that I was busy embarking on a ballet company, to challenge a right of place *vis-à-vis* the opera. But nevertheless my past opera ballet experience influenced Lilian Baylis at our initial interview. ("You seem to have had more experience than all these others, dear" was her comment as she went through the other applications with me sitting in anxious anticipation in front of her.)

There were, naturally, at both the Old Vic and Sadler's Wells some interesting opera ballet productions for me to tackle. The whole of the *Faust* ballet was always included. (This was notable for me as Frederick Ashton was engaged to dance a *pas de deux* with me—a short time before he joined the Company.) I greatly enjoyed choreographing and helping in the general production of the Russian opera *The Snow Maiden* daringly produced at Sadler's Wells. (Geoffrey Toye considered the whole thing so crazy for the Wells to attempt that he refused to conduct it.) We had a great deal of interesting Russian "exile" help in its construction—I found the experience as fascinating as it was informative and I loved the opera. Again there was the big Purcell *Dido & Aeneas* production, in which apart from a great deal of dancing I had to produce the chorus entrances and exits. It was a little reminiscent of a Greek chorus in structure. The Vic-Wells chorus were enthusiastic and helpful. A crowd production on such a scale demands discipline on the part of the choreographer and strict attention to the demands of the production in general. You would also be faced with requests from stage and conductor to bestow close attention on the necessary "sight line", or rather visual contact between singers and conductor, easily upset when so much movement was in partnership with the singing. This opera was a very real success, and one in which the ballet played an important role.

As time passed the ballet grew; slowly but surely it demanded its recognition on equal terms with the opera. History was to repeat itself, this duality, already the case abroad, would at last reach England.

With the reopening of Covent Garden a drastic and historical situation arose. Owing to the decision of an equality of performances of opera and ballet I asked that we had a small separate opera ballet—particularly as the Opera did not wish to include any of the big opera ballets. Roland Petit—who was then still at the Paris Opera—said I had "made history" by succeeding in this all-important separation. At that time the Paris Opera had no division and his rehearsals, he told me, were continually broken up by a demand for a certain number of dancers to attend an opera ballet stage call.

In Ivor Guest's interesting book *Le Ballet de l'Opéra de Paris* there is an important and painstaking breakdown listed of divertissement suites from the large scale opera ballet repertoire of nearly two centuries' work. I would like to see some of our choreographers study these works. (It was at Monte Carlo that the Paris Opera staged, if I remember rightly, three different *Faust* operas and there were some quite lengthy divertissement ballets in them.)

It is true, of course, that at the time the opera demanded of the composers the inclusion of some ballet music as the ballet was so popular. The reluctant composers did not always give of their best in this particular direction! I cannot help feeling that even some of their poorer efforts would, however, be of better service than the unnecessary musical torture of today chosen to accompany what amounts to, choreographically, a simple divertissement ... May some of it come back, properly presented and controlled, and allow the ballet to do for the opera what the latter does for us in our choral works. Opera companies are in a position to present choral works, and it would be good to see this enterprise continue, for those presented by the Royal Ballet (three works by MacMillan) have all been a success.

The opera and the ballet were born together. It would be sad to see this all-important alliance parted forever. For the sake of choreographic composition, long may they share the burden of great opera houses everywhere. The Ballet, as a part of the opera world and originally known as opera ballet, has its own title under which it has the right to be reviewed instead of suffering from the ambiguous title of "Dance". Perhaps one day people will want to describe opera as "Song"...

Why do I write so much about opera ballet? It taught me a great deal; the give and take between dancer, producer, choreographer and conductor. I feel that opera ballet work is good for aspiring choreographers—even the ensuing disillusionments! To see your little ensemble smothered by corpulent singers in the background and to realise that the conductor has it all his own way—time after time.

Scene of the Play

Ninette de Valois

✍ My experience in play production assistance had some stimulating moments: Yeats' *Plays for Dancers* at the Abbey Theatre Dublin; the many and varied plays produced at the Festival Theatre Cambridge during the twenties; the Old Vic during the same period of time. It all left me with a wide sense of how much the theatre demands, has a right to demand and an equal right for unstinted collaboration, however far it might be removed from the world of the classical ballet production.

What are to be recalled as my most exciting, exacting and rewarding experiences? The Abbey Theatre Dublin with Yeats' *Plays for Dancers*—strongly influenced originally by the No Players. (I saw these players, some years ago, at Sadler's Wells and felt again the same strange remote influence that ran through *Plays for Dancers*.) Although in such productions every conventional balletic movement had to take a back seat, its actual background influence was ever present with me—bestowing an overwhelming sense of help, with an understanding and professionalism alerted to grasp and serve the present situation.

At the Festival Theatre Cambridge, the highlight of my choreographic work was the production of the chorus work in the *Oresteia*. I recollect the study of the strophes and anti-strophes, so painstakingly read to me by the translator—Professor R. C. Trevelyan. Those were days to remember, time spent with wisdom at my side, an experience that was not an everyday occurrence.

The Old Vic kept me busy for the three years prior to the opening of Sadler's Wells; the latter enticement was held up to me until I felt like an alerted donkey chasing the ever-out-of-reach carrot! I helped with Shakespearian play productions and operas, and gave weekly classes to drama students and young actors and actresses. There is one constant, recurring memory. I never see any production of the ballet *Romeo and Juliet* without recalling the magic of Jean Forbes-Robertson's debut in the play. I can still visualise her in ... "My only love sprung from my only hate ..." For me no dancer, nor any choreographer, has caught the spirit of the above line as that young actress did.

One of the most interesting, exacting and complex producers that I ever worked under was Tyrone Guthrie, when he became director of the Sadler's Wells Theatre upon the death of Lilian Baylis. He worked through the late thirties, the war and for a short period afterwards before he left for the States. In the very beginning he was dedicated to a rather alarming theory—he saw the venture working as a whole. By that he meant an intermingling of drama, opera and ballet on the stage at one and the same moment. His was a very intelligent and alert mind (I will never forget his superb production of a modern dressed *Hamlet*), nevertheless I was worried, because I felt that, of the three graces that he wished to intermingle, ballet had his smallest interest for his knowledge in this direction was not very much developed. I did several productions with him; I found him stimulating, very professional, but we had no real rapport. He was serious to a humourless point. I can remember in some gloomy provincial wartime town he asked me, in the midst of incredible turmoil—"What are your *aims*, Ninette?" "To get to the end of the war intact ..." I snapped back. He obviously found my reply unenlightened and uninspired and failed to notice that was exactly what I meant it to be! Nevertheless he was a big man in the English theatre world, full of serious purpose. He met with great success in the States, where he eventually went after the war.

There was also, among many productions outside the Wells, a third very special and lively experience in the world of musical comedy— the production of *The Golden Toy* by Ludwig Berger at the London Coliseum. I had a wonderful time under the direction of this German producer. (He informed someone that I "always sat on the beat".) The Coliseum had to have in this production three turning stages. In one big scene I had to produce three different crowd ensembles on the three separate stages—all three were turning at the same time and all, of course, to the accompaniment of the same piece of music! But there were many exciting little ballets in this production. I recollect that it was among the crowd of young dancers engaged I found June Brae and once again encountered Wendy Toye.

I have already spoken of the opera world in relation to movement and now I propose briefly to sum up my general reaction to working with both opera and drama.

Opera restrictions and discipline are not unlike the world of ballet; both are subjected to the domination of (a) music, (b) conductor, (c) producer or choreographer, (d) chorus master or ballet master and repetiteurs.

There is a freedom of approach in the play. A crowd scene (with the exception of a Greek chorus) working in such a world has a tendency to become a free for all, instead of what is demanded of an opera or ballet. The licence permitted by the producers, in straight plays where I have assisted, was embarrassingly obliging to the performers. Rarely did the pattern of an exit, an entrance or movement on the stage conform strictly to the original. Equally rarely did the ensuing changed outcome worry the producer.

I have been given to understand that I was known in the drama world as "the games mistress"; this was due to a demand on my part that any entrance, exit or general stage movement, when once set, was set for good. One, of course, learnt to appreciate a certain freedom of outlook in an acting role, just as one recognised the natural gestures of the dancer led up to a certain limited liberty of movement, as a form of natural self-expression. But from the producer's angle, the approach to an opera chorus and a play crowd are miles apart.

Is my attitude towards drama players justified? It is, I know, shared by other choreographers. Yet perhaps the word "attitude" does not present a strictly true picture of any particular case under review. We must remember the actor takes his book of words home to study and memorise in private; it is when they, the actors, are sometimes almost "word perfect" that the producer comes on the scene. Does a dancer take fully written choreology home with him to study the steps, and then attend a choreographer's production call when *he*, the dancer, is almost "step perfect"? This we know is not the case; if it were, it might well be possible to see a similar display of independence on the part of a dancer when confronted by the choreographer.

It is an important fact, though, that after a few years of performances, choreographers are often faced with a disturbing distortion of their original choreography ... These are sidelights on two sides of the theatre world—will they ever find the solution in some ensemble thinking?

Another influence on my development in the play producing world was Peter Godfrey. He worked at the Festival Theatre and later at the little Gate Theatre, built under the railway arches just outside Charing Cross Station. I helped in the staging of *Salome* there with the well-known actress, Margaret Rawlings, in the leading role. She was a born dancer. I will never forget Peter Godfrey's production of *Martine* in this little theatre, it was quite perfect and deeply moving. He was a sensitive and intelligent producer. The *Martine* production later in the West End did not touch Peter Godfrey's effort.

Lastly I would speak of Norman Marshall. He was Terence Gray's right hand during those years at the Cambridge Festival Theatre . . . a born critic of the theatre scene in general, his knowledge of play production and ballet were equally developed. I learnt a lot from him—both from the point of view of agreement and disagreement. His book *The Other Theatre*, devoted to the work of the repertory movement in the twenties and thirties all over England, makes wonderful reading today, when most of the aims portrayed in it have become a part of the general theatre scene all over this country. I speak of a loyal friend and a stern critic of all and everything that I did. Praise from him was a satisfactory experience.

My reminiscences of these operas, plays and musicals are dwelt on to show how professionally helpful, in one's development and experience, they can all prove to be. As an example Frederick Ashton did much work in his early days in the commercial theatre. I cannot help feeling that the young choreographers of today need some such experience. They form themselves—immediately after their training years—(a very great weakness of the Contemporary Dance in general) into "groups", producing and choreographing their own little shows—which are more than often subsidised. Why? Why not subsidise establishments everywhere to engage these young people individually to adapt themselves to the theatre as a whole? I am, of course, talking about those who cannot get a job in some established ballet or contemporary company. Those who can do that have no right to be encouraged in any other direction until they have submitted themselves to such an experience. But those that are left unemployed should be able to seek institutions that are specially subsidised to employ such people, individually, for a period of time. This should be a priority use of the taxpayers' money until the situation is steadier and more professionally developed than it is today. But this is another *book*; particularly after the involved scholastic statements issued about "progress" in the theatre. The English theatre has a rather lovable amateur touch about it. It tends to develop through ponderous thinking produced on paper. Yet the answer is basically so simple ...

All these articles about other sides of the theatre, and what I learnt in such forms of collaboration, must have one point firmly stated. I did no such work until I had been a professional dancer in the theatre world for some 15 years. I had professionally danced at the Covent Garden Opera House, the Diaghilev Ballet, numerous West End productions—not to mention pantomimes and music halls ... But my choreographic efforts were left to be developed when the opportunity would be born ... I always feel that the long life of *Checkmate* and *The Rake's Progress* owes a great deal to the above experiences; time and again today I see a young choreographer lacking background theatre experience in production—and I speak of young choreoeographers whose talents are greater than mine ever were.

Of course I must remember what it meant to work with Diaghilev's great choreographers, and to realise afterwards that the great state theatres that they all sprang from had offered them, from the beginning, a kaleidoscopic view of the wide range of experience found in a true state theatre. I think it was this that I was trying to establish inside myself, before embarking on the development of a national ballet.

Thus the games mistress emerged from an orgy of learning—or shall we say a prolonged glance at the other side of the penny?

Chapter VI

⚬⚭ Before the middle of 1934 de Valois' career had fallen into two parts. The first comprised her early work as a dancer, the second expanded her experience into choreography, enlarged her already considerable knowledge of general theatre by her work in the repertory theatres and saw the beginning of her influence as teacher and director. Until the opening of the Wells and her commitment to the establishment there of a ballet company, her life might have moved in a number of directions; but once the opportunity was offered to consolidate and build up an English ballet on the firm base of the Vic-Wells organisation, other choices must have seemed almost non-existent. The ensuing years were to see other distinct phases: the later thirties at the Wells, the years of World War II, the early and later period at Covent Garden and the formation of Sadler's Wells Theatre Ballet, her work with the Royal Ballet School and with the Turkish State Ballet.

All these demands meant that her outstanding talent as a movement collaborator with drama directors and opera producers had to be sacrificed to other activities, sadly indeed for British theatre. She continued to exercise her now greatly underestimated ability as a creator of ballets but unfortunately with decreasing frequency. The eminence she attained as founder-director of the Royal Ballet and as a dominant force in world dance was not achieved without the stifling of a unique gift for choreographic creation.

The Vic-Wells season beginning in October 1934 is an excellent point at which to look at the organisation at Sadler's Wells. The company was now approaching the form that carried it through the years to the Royal Opera House. It was not large but it was settling into character as a team of de Valois artists—*de Valois* artists because in spite of the

157

emphasis on the long traditional ballets and historical values she was the controlling centre of policy and activity, the moulder of their talents and careers.

She was very conscious of the need for a second resident choreographer and gave this constant serious thought. She knew she was fortunate in acquiring Lambert as musical director and artistic adviser. Where the dancers were concerned, Markova was undisputedly preeminent and had agreed to stay for one further year. De Valois still danced, and Ruth French, a fine and experienced soloist, added strength to the top echelon. Helpmann, at twenty-five, was *premier danseur* and Markova's partner. Judson had left but Harold Turner, a lively virtuoso technician, was soon to exchange guest status for company membership, share top billing with Helpmann and create the right kind of stimulating rivalry with him that audiences love and artists profit from. There were extremely able all-round *danseurs* in Chappell and Walter Gore. The second line of women included Moreton, Appleyard, Ailne Phillips and Hermione Darnborough.

As always de Valois was looking further ahead. She had a school and was bringing on a fine group of girls in Pamela May, Elizabeth Miller, June Brae and the dancer destined for future fame, Margot Fonteyn. Among the boys were Michael Somes, Richard Ellis and Alan Carter. In June 1934 she launched a special plan for "A Vic-Wells Junior Ballet", an interesting scheme aimed at fostering talent and cementing relationships with the best independent schools and teachers in the country. Each participating school would contribute £10 a year for two years and for this one or possibly two of its pupils would gain a scholarship to the Vic-Wells School and receive theatrical training. A dozen schools responded and sent students along to be polished for professional careers. Among them from the Cone School was a charming little girl later known as Julia Farron.

The Vic-Wells Ballet repertoire was now strong in long traditional works. *Giselle, Coppélia* and *Casse-noisette* were well established and in November 1934 *Le Lac des cygnes* "in its entirety" (a once-popular phrase) was staged for the first time in England. How can any young balletgoers now imagine a world in which *Swan Lake* and *The Nutcracker* were rare and unfamiliar!

It was of course for Markova that *Lac* was produced, allowing her to add one of the greatest ballerina roles, the dual one of Odette-Odile, to Giselle and the Sugar Plum Fairy. De Valois was always very conscious of what was due to a classical dancer of Markova's calibre and made a deliberate effort to provide the right opportunities. She also intended that her young dancers should be firmly experienced in classical traditions which she was certain they needed as a basis on which neo-classical and *demi-caractère* ballets could stand.

Markova's Odette was already known and admired from the familiar Act II; it was the Odile that astonished and delighted everyone. P. W. Manchester recalls the occasion:

"Her *petits tours* were exquisitely finished, her *échappés* from the front to the back of the stage were effortlessly perfect. Only those wretched thirty-two *fouettés* were open to question. They were performed travelling instead of *sur place* ... but apart from this it was impossible to find a flaw. Her poise and control were so absolute that she seemed hardly to need the support of her partner. Helpmann, who partnered impeccably through three strenuous acts, thoroughly deserved the ovation he had the opportunity of winning when he sailed round the stage in a series of *grands jetés* which displayed an elevation of which he had never previously been suspected ..."[1]

The evening was perhaps rather too big a task for the rest of the company, although it all went well enough. Hugh Stevenson's designs were uneven—it was a larger assignment than he had ever had and the budget was small. Lambert arranged the score, achieving, as he always did with the traditional ballets, a tight and satisfying flow of theatrical development full of contrast and colour.

New ballets by Ashton and de Valois were regularly produced to keep up audience interest, and de Valois' contribution this season was another Borlin-derived ballet, *The Jar*.

Alfredo Casella composed the score in 1924 for the Ballets Suédois and de Valois' action followed the original pattern. The story came from Pirandello—a comic tale of an enormous jar belonging to a Sicilian farmer and a tinker who climbed inside to mend it and could not get out. A slight romantic interest rested in the farmer's beautiful daughter. Chappell gave it delightful designs in clear and charming picture-book lines and colours and the company found it plenty of fun to perform.

Sibthorp enjoyed it enough to write fairly fully about it. It had

"a breathless, clamorous score matched by a choreography into which Ninette de Valois had infused something of the spontaneity of a Sicilian country dance ... despite much bustle and an occasional shrillness in movement and sound there were some passages of quiet, contemplative beauty—the scene of the serenade, for instance, and Nela's charming, graceful, typically de Valois *pas seul*."

He found it "richer and subtler in characterisation than any previous de Valois ballet".

"Gore's Tinker, with its air of resigned surprise, was a whole, rounded study and Helpmann revealed a new burlesque side to his talent as the irascible Don Lollo."[2]

De Valois was responding with delight to the various possibilities of her dancers and stretching them happily in various directions. Helpmann in particular was rewarding material, a true theatre artist who revelled in every kind of challenge.

De Valois' position at the Wells was unlike any she had held before. In Cambridge, as visiting choreographer and occasional dancer, she had no permanent day-by-day contact with directors and actors. She was a specialist called in where necessary and disappearing back to London as soon as a production had been staged. In Dublin she had a dual character—as overall supervisor of the school, which was primarily in the charge of its own principal; and as a choreographer and dancer in the close union characteristic of the Yeats' plays. At Sadler's Wells however her work was of a more diverse, more integrated and at the same time more isolated nature. She was artistic director. She was principal, and a teacher, of the school. She was choreographer. She was a principal dancer. Each of these functions carries a different relationship to other artists.

As one talks of a President's men, so one must think of an artistic director's team of collaborators—and at every point in later years de Valois has gone out of her way to give credit to her team in the 1930s. Most important was Lambert. Not only was he a guide on music for the company but a man of wide cultural contacts, interests and knowledge who could provide stimulating advice, comment or debate whenever she needed them. He was many-faceted, opinionative, versatile and utterly devoted to ballet. De Valois has termed him

"the greatest ballet conductor and adviser that this country has had ... there is no one to equal him in that all-round knowledge and intellectual understanding demanded of this eclectic side of the theatre world..."[3]

Equally vital, as a superb choreographer, was Frederick Ashton.

Knowing her need, de Valois had carefully considered her options. She was well aware of both the experience and the ambitions of the eligible few, and by 1935 she decided that Ashton was her man. Devoted to classical ballet, he had already shown skill and ingenuity in dance composition. The diversity of professional assignments he had undertaken, both in England and America, had given him an understanding of the theatre, an ability to cooperate with directors and colleagues, and a disciplined approach that she totally respected. She recognised his potential and the fact that his creations would provide the contrast and balance to her own that would extend and strengthen her dancers.

Ashton joined the company for the September 1935 season and from the first created ballets rich in dance invention, fresh in mood, springing out of their musical scores and celebrating the specific talents of individual dancers. He was a priceless acquisition to the repertoire, enabling it to balance *Les Rendezvous* against *Job, Apparitions* against *The Rake's Progress, A Wedding Bouquet* against *Checkmate, The Wanderer* against *The Prospect Before Us*—providing food for every balletgoer's taste and using to the full the range and ability of artists.

He discovered of course, as did everyone who worked at the Wells, that life with de Valois was far from calm. The Russian ballet companies always outstripped their English counterparts in terms of passionate rivalry, emotional crises and maternal tantrums, but de Valois' unpredictable, mercurial moods ensured that no one ever really knew where they were from one hour to the next. Ashton had been involved in constant rows with Rambert, and in a true frying-pan-and-fire situation had moved over to constant rows with de Valois—rows of different content and character, but equally frequent. They would break off on a high note of disagreement. After some time he would ask her over for a cup of tea and they would re-establish relations by enjoying "a good giggle", something they both loved. She was quite capable, next day, of a complete volte-face, having seen the situation in a different light.[4]

She was certainly always conscious of his unique qualities as a choreographer. In summing him up, she cited one of the rarest:

"He has a remarkable sympathy with and understanding of any artist's particular individuality. He 'presents' his young dancers in such a way that the balance between the whole and the part is fused with a skill that amounts to genius ... Let all of us study Ashton's work from this angle—his complete sense of proportion betwen role and artist..."[5]

Certain elements are traceable throughout the characters of de Valois' colleagues. They were flexible, versatile, indefatigable workers, theatrically professional, and always liable, as she was, to see the funny side of things. The combination of Lambert, Helpmann and Ashton ensured that solemnity never got the upper hand. All the same, however much she enjoyed and treasured their company, however much they were all members of a partnership, she was in the final analysis as much alone as any other commanding officer.

Ideas for de Valois' ballets did not stem from herself. Usually suggestions came from composers or from Lambert, and this was the case in her next project, *The Rake's Progress*.

Gavin Gordon had known Lambert from the Royal College of Music, where he was a pupil of Vaughan Williams. He was another example of the wide-ranging artists of the period, being an actor, a bass singer, and a producer as well as a composer. In 1934, while at work on his score for *The Rake's Progress*, he was acting in plays at the New Theatre and the Ambassador's. His previous contributions to the Vic-Wells Ballet were *Regatta* and the second score for *The Scorpions of Ysit*.

The notion of basing a ballet on Hogarth's paintings of 1733/34 may have originated with Cyril Beaumont. At any rate, he first proposed the subject to Ashton, and possibly Beaumont's enthusiasm for it excited Gavin Gordon who settled down to write music for a scenario that reduced the number of episodes in the moral tale. This he also offered to Ashton who felt it was not for him. De Valois however was immediately attracted to it. She set to work, continuing even through illness and surgery, visualising for the stage the narrative and characters in conjunction with Gordon's intensely theatrical and well-judged music. With the acceptance of a design commission by Rex Whistler, a notable British collaboration was completed.

The seminal dramatic impulse of *The Rake's Progress* comes directly from Hogarth. It is not an imaginative projection from one tableau, like *Bar aux Folies-bergère*, nor is it a conjunction of pictorial tableaux and written story as in *Job*. The tale itself, in full life and vigour, is a deliberate creation of the painter with a clear and sturdy histrionic content. Sometimes termed "novels in paint", the Harlot's and Rake's Progresses were perhaps more correctly "plays in paint". As David Bindman puts it:

The Rake's Progress *(Vic-Wells Ballet 1935); (left to right) Claude*
Newman, Leslie Edwards, Maurice Brooke, Alicia Markova, Walter
Gore

163

"Like most plays of the period they have fully worked-out plots, dramatic confrontations and changes of scene, serious and tragic elements juxtaposed and a high degree of topicality."[6]

In Sir John Soane's extraordinarily diversified and crowded museum in Lincoln's Inn Fields, it is possible to study the eight smallish pictures in sequence. They are:

No.1 The Young Heir taking possession. Tom Rakewell has inherited a fortune on his miserly father's death. Lawyer and tailor are present and Tom is trying to compensate an irate mother with money for the seduction of her daughter, Sarah Young.

No.2 The Rake's Levee. Tom is now a man of fashion and at his levee he is giving audience to suitors and instructors—dancing and fencing masters, hopeful operatic composers, a jockey, a hornblower and a bravo.

No.3 The Tavern Scene. Tom is the central figure in notoriously lewd company.

No.4 Arrested for Debt. On his way to the Court of St James's, Tom is arrested by the Sheriff's officers. Sarah Young, the Betrayed Girl, pays his debts from her savings.

No.5 Marriage. Tom is marrying an elderly woman for her money. In the background Sarah Young and her child are being hustled out of the church.

No.6 In a Gaming-House. A crowded scene, in which Tom is seen with discarded wig in despair over his losses.

No.7 In the Debtors' Prison. Tom, on his way to madness from his debauches, is harassed by his wife while Sarah Young collapses in grief.

No.8 Bedlam. Mourned over by Sarah Young, watched with amusement by a society visitor and surrounded by other madmen—a king, a bishop, a violinist and a man with a rope—Tom dies.

Each of these paintings is rich in significant and symbolic detail. Analysis yields a remarkable list of clues that throw light on the successive scenes, easily overlooked unless pointed out, and fully understandable only through expert guidance on topical allusions of the time. Many of these were preserved in the *Notebooks of George Vertue*, a contemporary engraver.[7] Certain people and milieux can be confidently named—the setting of the Orgy is the Rose Tavern in Covent Garden and of the Marriage the Church of St Mary-le-bone.

This wealth of information available to the scenarist of the ballet has been brilliantly selected and telescoped. It opens with the Levee, introducing not only the Rake (never called Tom Rakewell), the Dancing Master, the Fencing Master, the Hornblower, the Jockey and the Bravo, but from the first picture the Tailor, the Betrayed Girl and her harridan mother. For each de Valois sketched character and intentions with the apt economy that is one of her most impressive choreographic qualities. She produced apposite dance movement, keeping faithfully to the period style and finding in each a touch of moral caricature. Scene 2 is the Orgy, prefaced by curtain action—a resort much loved by Ashton as well as by de Valois, not always successful but in this case a perfect means, perfectly used, of carrying forward the story. Here, between scenes 1 and 2, the Dancing Master, a fastidious, pernickety gentleman, reflects outrage as he watches bawds and a little black serving maid with a flagon of wine avidly scurrying towards the tavern.

The Orgy itself is scaled down from the painting to a brilliantly evocative group: five clearly differentiated Ladies of the Town, the Rake and his Friend, the Ballad-singer (a marvellously cheerful slut) with her two Street Musicians, the ripe and ribald Dancer, and the little servant. A tumbled box bed on the backcloth, general disarray of dress, a drunken blurring of movement, conjure up the context, while dance and crowd management are infinitely skilful in suggesting licence and profligate behaviour. So, without any of the explicit indications of corruption and obscenity that Hogarth includes for a knowledgeable contemporary public, the spirit of the scene is captured. It is a riotous, uninhibited episode choreographed with the utmost vigour and humour. Each whore is an individual whose role is couched in distinctive, convincing terms. The black servant girl longs to be part of it, the Dancer, performing on a large pewter plate, tilts up her skirts and doffs her red stockings with abandon for the Rake's delectation. Drink flows and the Rake climbs unsteadily onto the table to fling handfuls of money on the floor.

This is the point where the mood of the action entirely changes.

Comedy ends and grim drama takes over. Helpmann always made this entirely clear in the brief space of the closing moments. Collapsed in a chair among the carousing women, he turned head and shoulders away from them with a look of despair, of haunted anxiety, that foreshadowed the debacle of the gaming house.

Curtain action once more, after scene 2, constitutes scene 3, and the background is always Rex Whistler's magnificent dropcloth of an 18th century London street with church, houses, statue, and cobbles holding puddles of rain water. This time it represents the Arrest for Debt. Three creditors accost the Rake, already showing signs of dissipation, and he is only saved by the intervention of the Betrayed Girl with her little bag of savings.

The ballet omits the marriage of convenience. Instead, scene 4 is the gaming house. Again, it is shorn of the detail of the painting and concentrates effectively on a low-lit baize table and a confrontation between the Rake and a small group of menacing, predatory gamblers including the Friend. The Rake is already a broken man, well on the way to prison and Bedlam.

The gaol is not, however, given a full scene. On stage, a gaol and a madhouse would overlap too much in content, the one ruining the effectiveness of the other. So, in an imaginative extension of thought, the Rake's imprisonment is represented by a long and sensitive solo for the Betrayed Girl as she waits outside the gates, patiently stitching on an embroidery frame.

She waits in vain. The Rake goes on from prison to the madhouse. His companions there, faithfully to Hogarth, imagine that they are kings or prelates or violin players, while additionally one is a card player, and one a sailor. All are expressionless and absorbed in their own thoughts. A "Gentleman with a Rope" is the most violent, breaking into a despairing dance and beating the ground with the rope. The Rake, still aware of his disaster but mentally and physically wrecked, has spells of rebellion, apathy and terror.

Three fashionable women with fans come in on a sightseeing visit and the pathetic madmen huddle together. The Betrayed Girl follows, crystallising in a touching solo the qualities of love, fidelity and grief in the face of tragedy. All she can do in the end is to hold the Rake's hand, giving him a brief moment of peace before a horrifying death.

Both theatrically and choreographically de Valois coordinates the entire action magnificently. The brilliance with which she establishes the dynamics of the narrative belongs on the highest level of stage

direction; all the experience gained in the "straight" theatre is unerringly applied. Very rarely indeed is a choreographer disciplined enough
or courageous enough to present the minimum necessary in movement
or dance to create character and situation—to give a perceptive audience exactly the right pointers so that their imaginations can "body
forth" the rest. It is dismaying to think how nowadays, in the age of full
evening ballets of uneven quality and areas of tedium, a choreographer
would treat *The Rake's Progress*; the crowd scenes, the spelt-out
detail of each of the eight stages, the endless duets and the emotional
wallowing that would ensue. This would be popular, probably, but
what de Valois has given us is a master work.

She is flawless in her decisions about when to use extended sections of
dance, when to restrict it, and when to create her effects by expressionist
movement. The game of cards, for example, is superb in its hair-trigger
timing, its use of chairs to heighten the tension, its significantly angled
glances and its dramatic asides by the Rake to the audience. The levee,
the orgy and the madhouse are meticulously orchestrated, each strand
cleverly woven into the overall pattern. Variations or cumulations of
pace are ably manipulated. Solo dance, on the other hand, is employed
at exactly the right moments, when it can prove most telling. The
Betrayed Girl's sad resignation and yearning appears in the sewing
dance—significantly she is the only woman with pointwork—and her
other solo, in the last scene, creates the contrast of sanity and the better
qualities of normal emotion as opposed to the tragic degradation of
self-destruction. The mannered elegance of the era is remembered in
the Dancing Master's role, and the varied aspects of madness are
vividly differentiated—the turned-in hobbling walk of the sailor, the
ungainly hopping of the violinist, the puzzled circling of the card
player, the man with the rope's wild, almost visionary fluency, and the
Rake's staccato and angular agony. Characterisation, down to the
tiniest role, is rich. Although all come together in a stylised framework,
each part is singular and interesting and its creation is a cooperative
inspiration from composer, choreographer, designer, make-up artist
and dancer.

Each of the three contributing creators took Hogarth's early-18th
century as their point of departure. Each modified it acceptably to
theatrical demands and the state of their specific arts in the mid-1930s.

As a dramatic score, Gavin Gordon's music could not be bettered.
It is consistently interesting without surpassing its partners of dance
and design. It is tailored to suit each scene and each character, linking

with remarkable ease and fluency the comic and serious elements, varying pace and colour with sensitivity. Insufficient praise has been given to the astonishing craftsmanship with which he defines the rumbustious gallop of the orgy, the whiplash ruthlessness of the gaming house, the tender entr'acte for the Betrayed Girl and, above all perhaps, the interwoven threads and themes of the madhouse. Music critics patronise it, pointing out that it cannot stand alone as a concert suite, but this is irrelevant where ballet music is concerned. The criterion must be that it should enhance the theatre experience and this, without question, is the case with the score of *Rake*.

Equally faultless are Rex Whistler's designs. In 1935 he had done more book illustration than theatre design but he never fell into the trap of confusing the two. His stage work had the strength and selectivity essential for theatrical effectiveness. Before *The Rake's Progress* his theatre credits included settings for a Covent Garden *Fidelio*, costumes for Rodney Acland's play *Ballerina* and for a Stratford-on-Avon *Tempest*. *Rake* involved him in a study of Hogarth and the necessity for eliminating elements while preserving overall faithfulness. He had to produce costumes that would complement the choreographic movement and sets that would immediately declare the purpose of scenes. In each of the major episodes, de Valois allows an infinitesimal pause when the curtain rises for a tableau to establish itself in the audience's mind before she swings it into action, and for these the collaboration between Whistler and de Valois (and the lighting designer) is both close and cunning, over geometrical and colour values, in the initial groupings.

As inevitably happens with a ballet so constantly performed modifications to the designs have occurred over the years. It is worth glancing at the kind of costume differences visible in *Rake* between 1935 and the present day. They are most clearly seen in the costume for the Betrayed Girl. In 1935 Markova wore an ankle-length black skirt, a crimson sateen bodice, long white frills on the short sleeves, a long narrow white apron, a wide waistlength white fichu and a plain white cap set forward on her head with short white streamers. Black pointe shoes succeeded pink ones quite quickly and the skirt was also slightly shortened. In 1942, however, Fonteyn's black skirt was just below the knee, the apron was small, the fichu replaced by separated white strips from shoulder to waist on the front of the bodice and the cap was considerably more modish—frilled and ribboned and set at the back of the head. These differences suggested a subtle change in

168

character, a rather less modest and self-effacing "betrayed" young woman.

An analysis of the dance content of de Valois' choreography must emphasise the integrated conjunction of styles. One of her firm tenets has always been that the classically trained ballet dancer is capable of all other kinds of movement, and although *Rake*, like all her ballets, could not be danced by any but a classically trained company, there is an uninhibited use in it of steps derived from court dance, folk-dance and modern expressionist dance, smoothly employed within the classical *demi-caractère* framework. Non-classical elements are often delicately injected, as in the lovely sewing solo, where the gestures recall "working" folkdances, as does the heel-toe-heel-toe extension of the foot paralleling the hand that draws out the imagined needle and thread until the body weight is moved from centre to side. Classical dance is the basis for the first two major scenes, even when it becomes free-wheeling and unfocused in the Orgy; in the gaming house and the madhouse however expressionist dance takes over except for the tragic lyricism of the Betrayed Girl's solo. She constitutes the dramatic contrast with madness which de Valois expresses by hunched shoulders, turned-in feet, small obsessive gestures, awkward steps and poses and for the man with the rope and the Rake distorted versions of arabesque and attitude coupled with clutching, beating hands.

She had the right dancers to work with in the creation of *Rake* and its subsequent early performances. Her ladies of the town were Sheila McCarthy, Gwyneth Mathews, Elizabeth Miller, Peggy Melliss and Doris (Pamela) May, all acting their parts with relish. Her ballad-singer, a special delight both then and for many years, was Joy Newton. The Dancer was Ursula Moreton, and Gordon Anthony has a telling description of her:

"A triumph of characterisation and make-up, transferring her handsome, dignified and romantic personality into a debauched Ho-garthian strumpet dancing with complete abandon, sugared with a ghastly and uncanny form of coy gentility."[8]

Anthony also defines key points in other creations:

Chappell as the Friend: "an ideal conception of an irresponsible 18th-century Macaroni ... a comical sort of preening, bibulous elegance ... The dance with the pack of cards in the madhouse—(he) gave it a

The Rake's Progress *(Vic-Wells Ballet 1935) Ursula Moreton as the Dancer*

The Rake's Progress *(Sadler's Wells Ballet 1942) Margot Fonteyn as
The Betrayed Girl*

horrible sort of vacuity, indigenous to certain types of mental cases—comic, mad and horrific at the same time."[9]

Claude Newman as the Tailor and the Sailor: "timing perfect—used needle and thread to purpose, even the sudden quick movement of his head as he bit off the thread was musically perfectly timed . . . The mad admiral—shuffling around in vague backward and sideways movements for a few bars, coping with a patched eye and a long telescope, is far more tricky than a down-to-earth solo."[10]

Joy Newton as the Ballad Singer: "a salaciously comic vignette of the sleazy and genial street singer."[11]

Walter Gore was the first Rake, brought in because Helpmann was appearing in the Hassard Short revue *Stop Press*, but in the choreographer's opinion the best Rake ever. The "balance of power" in Hogarth's paintings had been a main concern of hers in composition and she composed the ballet so that no characterisation became dominant. In Hogarth the Rake was a weak character at the mercy of the people surrounding him, and this Gore sensitively achieved.

For public taste however his performance was not quite positive enough to bring the role to life. Helpmann took it over in September and set a personal, if less accurate, stamp upon it. Although too magnetic for the true intention of the ballet, he brought it a special emotional dimension and an exciting control of light and shade.

Markova created the Betrayed Girl, and she and Fonteyn are probably the only ones who suggested, in addition to the qualities of simplicity and tenderness, of uncorrupted affection and loyalty, the conception of the character as a representation of goodness and conscience continuing to strive for the Rake's salvation and eventually mourning his fate. Harold Turner brought off a fine double as the Dancing Master and the Gentleman with a Rope.

Critical reaction to *Rake* has been varied from the beginning. For some, the shortage of formal dance sequences placed it all too firmly in that debatable category of dramatic dance works that they cannot accept as "ballets". Comparable productions debated at various times have been Fokine's *Petrushka* and Helpmann's *Hamlet*. Nowadays, although dramatic ballets are not universally appreciated, at least the breakdown of strict definition between classical and modern dance means that a wider range of choreographic movement is accepted as being valid.

The Rake's Progress *(The Royal Ballet 1958) Robert Helpmann as The Rake, Ray Powell as The Gentleman with a Rope*

Possibly because of his own early interest in the subject, Cyril Beaumont was always one of the most grudging commentators on *Rake*. He was full of quibbles.[12] He was disturbed because the Dancing Master was so clearly a *ballet* teacher instead of instructing the Rake in the steps of one of the social dances of the period. He wanted more action from the Fencing Master, and he was impervious to the delights of the Betrayed Girl's sewing dance.

Caryl Brahms found immediate pleasure in the ballet:

"Satisfactorily simple, it flows naturally from the story with no self-conscious antic ... Never has ballet been less a matter of ballerina's aria and dancing cadenza. Although Markova as the Pure Young Girl follows the Rake to his Bedlam with virtuosity, point and poignancy, she does not step inartistically from her allotted frame..."[13]

Unlike *Job, The Rake's Progress* has had a busy career in ballet theatre. Its small cast and lack of staging or orchestral complications made it a good touring ballet and it has been seen all over the British Isles and elsewhere in the world. Its firm characterisation and inbuilt dramatic dynamics mean that however much great artists may enhance it, the theatrical impact is present even with quite unexceptional performance. It recovered reasonably quickly, because it was so much needed, from the wartime losses in Holland and its revival in November 1942 at the New Theatre was a strong and rewarding one. Helpmann led the cast, judging to a nicety the comic moments and the tragic denouement. In a small theatre everyone could appreciate the intricate range of mimetic emotional expression with which he enriched the static sections of the mad scene. Fonteyn made a debut as the Girl, Alexis Rassine was an excellent Friend, Gordon Hamilton a memorable Gentleman with a Rope.

Rake was acclaimed when it was taken to Belgium and France by the Sadler's Wells Ballet in 1945. It was described as "tout simplement un chef d'oeuvre de présentation et de chorégraphie". The madhouse was

"une chose hallucinante. Des figures horribles, grimaçantes, comme on en voit dans Grünewald ou Jerome Bosch. Tout cela s'anime sous nos yeux, se trémousse. Le merveille est d'avoir tiré de ces épisodes réalistes des motifs de danse et de mimodrame. M. Robert Helpmann, qui incarne le personnage du débauché, atteint par ses seules attitudes au tragique le plus saisissant. Ce ballet est vraiment quelquechose de spécifiquement anglais ... Cela ne peut être comparé à rien. Il y a dans le peuple anglo-saxon, forte race, sous le vernis d'une civilisation raffinée et d'une réligion stricte, un fond de violence que ce ballet met admirablement en lumière."[14]

There was less appreciation from the USA when *Rake* was shown on the first American tour in 1949 but it found one adherent in John Martin. Again referring to it (as to Helpmann's *Hamlet*) as "theatre pieces rather than pure ballets" he allows it to be "wholly choreographic":

"The movement is a high stylisation of natural gesture passed through a double screening of Hogarth on the one hand and the academic ballet on the other. It is a beautifully consistent style, full of humor and comment and a high degree of subtle perception of both period and people."[15]

In 1956, when Alan Carter was Ballet Master of the Munich State Opera Ballet, he asked if he could acquire *Rake* for his company. It was the first time an English ballet was staged by a European State Theatre, and de Valois asked Peggy van Praagh to go there to set the production, which was premiered in May at the Prinz Regenten Theater. At the time there was no strong tradition of classical ballet in Germany and although ballet companies were attached to each opera house, separate repertoires were not established. The ballet master in charge was teacher and choreographer to the opera-ballet and for the few evenings when only ballets were given he was expected to create new works each season, discarding the old.

Carter revolutionised the state of affairs in Munich. He began to fight for a permanent repertoire with new productions of traditional ballets such as *Giselle* as well as modern new works or revivals. Van Praagh found the company well suited to the demands of *Rake*. The general standard of classical dancing was not high but the maturity and stage experience of the dancers came into their own in this dramatic work. She had some fine principals. Heine Hallhüber took the lead, a splendid *danseur noble* who was also an excellent actor, and Franz Baur was effective as the Dancing Master and the Man with a Rope.

The German cast had some difficulties over style, carriage and timing, as well as another interesting problem. Van Praagh writes:

"Hardest of all were the moments of complete stillness and the restraint in movement, so telling and so typical of de Valois' choreography. German dancers are used to being left to improvise by their Balletmeister-choreographers and when given nothing to do they automatically begin to 'fill in' . . . "[16]

Van Praagh took with her photographed copies of the Rex Whistler designs, coloured to match the originals, and great pains were taken locally to reproduce these and to get the lighting right. The music, owing to insufficient rehearsal time, was less than satisfactory. All the same, the ballet was an immediate success, with over thirty curtain calls.

In July 1967 *Rake* was included in the annual Royal Ballet School performance and de Valois rehearsed the revival. She considered it a chance to

"restate in detail the choreographic *form* of the original production as it was musically phrased and executed some thirty-three years ago".[17]

It was in fact a purification exercise. She was distressed—as all choreographers and stage directors must be over their creations—at the way the work had slipped from its first intentions. In the early days "there was no question of one performer outshining the others". She was specifically thinking of the Rake, created so admirably by Gore, who had gradually become a force on stage—"and theatrically this is, of course, rewarding". Two factors—apart from Helpmann's personality—had contributed to this imbalance. The replacement of most of the early dancers by younger and less experienced ones meant that any who remained from the beginning stood out as stronger; also, audiences automatically single out leaders in any performing group so that balances do subtly change. No audience really wants a weak and dominated leading character and they are rarely interested in a dramatic scene in which all the roles are equally weighted.

For this ballet school performance however de Valois got exactly what she wanted—a group of keen young character dancers (none of whom were to have exciting careers) very willing to apply themselves to her guidance and tuition. She gave them high praise for this, convinced that this "sincere, correct and unadorned re-statement of the work" had great value as a declaration to the current Royal Ballet dancers about the "pattern, phrasing, emphasis and detail" which was often missing in their own performances at the time.

De Valois was stung into making a published statement of these points by the attitude of critics writing about the school production, and she made a challenging and valid observation:

"Time and again I have heard artists praised for an interpretation that has upset the choreographer. Time and again, critics interview artists about their 'portrayal' of a role. However, it cannot be said that time and again they seek a little guidance from the choreographers..."

She advocated the idea of inviting critics to see a finished section of a new work still "strictly under the guidance of the choreographer":

"Instead, we have long articles explaining what *they* think the choreographer 'meant to express' (but apparently had utterly failed to put across at the final performance)."

Rake was staged for the Turkish State Ballet in 1961 by Claude Newman. The Turkish dancers had an excellent approach to dramatic ballet and characterisation and made a great success of it. At the beginning there was a problem. The story goes that the girls cast as the Ladies of the Town, brought up in a carefully controlled moral atmosphere, heard a disturbing rumour about their parts. One came to de Valois and said, "Oh Madam, is it true that there is a brothel in the ballet and that we are meant to be whores?" "Madam" told the girls, "Don't worry, my dears. It's just a jolly party..." and arranged to use the backcloth with the windows rather than the one with the painted bed on it.

In 1972 *Rake* was produced in Antwerp. De Valois asked Richard Glasstone to set it—he had learnt the ballet while he was artistic director of the Turkish State Ballet—before she arrived, as was her custom, for the final rehearsals. The Ballet Van Vlaanderen was directed by Jeanne Brabants, one of the regular participants in de Valois' Summer Teachers' Courses. As was also her custom, de Valois made a present of the work—she has always refused fees for her ballets and lectures or (where the lectures are concerned) taken a fee only on behalf of the Royal Ballet Benevolent Fund or the Royal Ballet School. The Antwerp company, a smallish one, was particularly strong in character dancers and the production was a great success, with a Belgian dancer born in Liverpool, Aimé de Lignière, dancing the Rake.

The Rake's Progress remained in both Royal Ballet repertoires until 1964 and since then on tour.

Rake is a particularly good ballet for television because of its positive visual impact. In 1962, when the BBC made a three-year contract with the Royal Ballet for a series of nine works to be reproduced by Margaret Dale, *Rake* was the first to be transmitted, with Donald Britton in the title role. De Valois was closely associated with the making of the films. The camera established each character in close and long shots and the impetus of the action was splendidly maintained throughout. Twenty years later a valuable set of television films showing de Valois guiding them in rehearsal was shown on Channel 4.

Chapter VII

‿‿ After *Rake*, de Valois took a holiday that included her quiet wedding, in July 1935, to Dr Arthur Connell. When the next Sadler's Wells season began on September 27 it was time to take stock. Markova and Dolin had given their farewell performance with the company in Leeds on September 7, marking the end of the first stage of the story. De Valois summarised the state of both ballet and school in an article in the October *Dancing Times*.[1]

One matter was always very much in her mind—the encouragement of choreographic talent. In November 1933 she had put before the Association of Operatic Dancing a thoroughly worked-out suggestion for a Choreographic Scholarship which was discussed at a meeting to which the principals of the most important British schools were invited, and unanimously supported. The plan was that not more than twenty students aged eighteen or over should be selected by audition to take a two-year course on dance composition. Candidates should be nominated by their school or teacher and would have to submit a solo or duet they had composed. If selected, they would attend a course of 72 classes in each of the two years on Classical Revival, Modern Production, Analysis and technique of production, and Dalcroze eurythmics applied to choreography. Markova would take the study of choreography in classical ballet, de Valois the analysis and technique of production and Ann Driver the eurythmics classes.

De Valois outlined the purpose of the course:

"Creative ability is personal to the individual; it can be trained and guided, but it cannot be made. And the creative mind can easily wear itself out if it does not receive guidance and help."

She made it clear that she was not primarily thinking about discovering great choreographers. She was interested in helping young dancers who wanted to arrange dances to make the most of their talents. She envisaged training young people who could be employed by dance schools to choreograph and produce their annual shows, not in preparing them to create ballets for professional companies. Always a realist, she stressed that young choreographers must not expect to begin at the top.

"Practice, experience and study will bear fruit eventually but it is not possible to take the world by storm with one's first effort ... The real test of ability is endurance and progress."[2]

This scheme, positive in itself, is of special interest as an example of how de Valois continually extended her influence, how much she instinctively regarded herself as having a responsibility towards the entire scene of dance and ballet in Great Britain. She was in no way limiting herself to her very onerous position as director of the Vic-Wells Ballet. The problems and policies of that company, and her own career as choreographer and dancer, were being considered by her in a country-wide context, and she looked even beyond that to the world at large. By no means a natural committee woman, she never shirked committees and administrative meetings; instead, she met them head on, full of ideas and advice put forward with disinterested vigour. When she received, in the course of time, the DBE and other honours for services to British ballet it was probably not generally realised that in countless ways she had always worked, not just for the development of the company now known as the Royal Ballet, but for the health and prosperity of the art throughout the United Kingdom and all its linked territories of the old Empire and the new Commonwealth.

Where the Vic-Wells Ballet was concerned, she produced in early 1936 a Five Year Plan in conjunction with Arnold Haskell and a committee of influential people who could help in fund-raising. The target was £25,000—enough in those days to do a great deal to improve and develop the company's work. On the academic side, she wanted money to pay for specialist guest teachers, to help special study for gifted dancers, to give scholarships to selected children. On the production side, she wanted money for staging traditional and new ballets and—an interesting point—for filming and photographing productions for the purpose of record. Additionally, she wanted money (and in 1936 this was certainly looking ahead) to help dancers on their retirement, or to "make any gift which would materially benefit the welfare and health of the members of the ballet and in consequence raise the standard of their performance". The scheme flourished, and continued to function until the Council for the Encouragement of Music and the Arts (CEMA, later the Arts Council) displaced it during World War II.

Meanwhile production went on at Sadler's Wells Theatre. *Carnaval* was given a better revival, and, although Pearl Argyle was the Columbine initially, de Valois danced it later and Michael Bayston, for one, has never forgotten the delightful and expressive mime of her performance especially in the courtship raillery between Columbine and Harlequin. An enlarged and revised production of Ashton's *Façade* (originally created for the Camargo Society) was staged, and he choreographed *Le Baiser de la fée* for Pearl Argyle, Fonteyn and Turner. In October 1935 de Valois revived *Douanes* with the Fedorovitch designs and again danced the lead; and she re-cast the choreography of *Nursery Suite* and had it re-dressed by Chappell so that the Vic-Wells Scholarship students could be displayed.

De Valois' first new ballet since *The Rake's Progress* was given in January 1936. *The Gods Go A-Begging* had been choreographed in 1928 by Balanchine for the Diaghilev Ballet to a Handel score arranged by Beecham. De Valois followed the same scenario by Boris Kochno (Sobeka) with slight alterations, and asked Hugh Stevenson to design Watteau-esque costumes and a set. Stevenson produced an extremely attractive visual whole, in autumnal colourings, and de Valois' acute sense of period was brought brilliantly into play in the choreography.

The Gods Go A-Begging has considerably more substance than may appear at first sight. Repeated viewings yield an increasing understanding and appreciation of its merits. P. W. Manchester very rightly terms it "a perfect piece of pastiche" and comments "small perfections bring their own satisfaction".[3] Much of the pleasure is derived from the variety of creative response de Valois brings to the lively and often lyrical score. The ballet begins with the arrival of servants to prepare a *fête champêtre*; the Serving Maid, two other serving girls and a neat sextet of small Black Lackeys. It is a sunny 18th century day in a French forest—Versailles? Fontainebleau? The inference of some nearby château hangs in the air. Each person on stage suggests many others of the kind—the scene is a microcosm.

Five noblemen with their ladies stroll into the glade and are joined by a young Shepherd. Their dancing is courtly, full of social asides and flirtatious glances. The Shepherd dances alone, fluently and classically, for their entertainment and joins the two serving girls in a *pas de trois*. The Serving Maid is the object of attention by two of the nobles and runs away. At last the courtiers wander off in couples into the forest and the Shepherd and Serving Maid dance a delicate and tender duet, broken into briefly by a fast *tamborino* for the little black lackeys. The noblemen and ladies return and are outraged to find Shepherd and Serving Maid embracing. They order them to leave but when they have gone the sky darkens, and the nobles are amazed by the entrance of Mercury who reveals Shepherd and Serving Maid in their proper shape as gods. All is forgiven, however, the sun returns and the ballet ends with a happy *bourrée-finale*.

Three dance styles are delightfully interwoven—court dance, eccentric character dance for the lackeys and a variety of classical and *demi-caractère* for the rest. The gods were created by Pearl Argyle and William Chappell with Richard Ellis as Mercury and a delightfully sophisticated and witty leading court partnership in Moreton and Helpmann.

The Gods Go A-Begging became a happy wartime memory for Sadler's Wells Ballet audiences. In a 1942 revival the fresh young talent of Beryl Grey particularly suited the Serving Maid while her contemporary Moira Shearer brought the role a delicate Dresden china charm. The well-balanced serenity of the work had a special appeal for people living under the threat of the blitz. Its popularity continued when it was staged by Sadler's Wells Theatre Ballet in 1946 and danced by Anne Heaton and Leo Kersley, but in June 1949 the costumes and scenery were destroyed by fire at the Theatre Royal, Hanley. It was not restored to the repertoire of either company but it has been seen again on two occasions. The Royal Ballet School included it in a week's season at Richmond Theatre in 1972 when it was danced in a selection of appropriate costumes from the Royal Opera and Royal Ballet wardrobe, and there was a briefly maintained but interesting new staging by London City Ballet in 1982.

Before de Valois' next ballet in 1936 came a triumph for Ashton, his enchanting *Apparitions* to a score from Liszt arranged by Lambert and with exquisite designs by Cecil Beaton. In it Helpmann developed and continued the mood of high Gothick romance inaugurated in *The Haunted Ballroom* and Fonteyn was everyone's dream ballerina as the Woman in Balldress.

De Valois' *Barabau* could not have been more of a contrast. Where Ashton was allowing audiences to revel in romantic melodrama de

Barabau *(Vic-Wells Ballet 1936)* NdV *as* The Peasant Woman, *Frederick Ashton as* The Sergeant

Valois was presenting an earthy satirical comedy. Again she was following Balanchine, who had choreographed the Rieti score for Diaghilev in 1925. Again, she was taking her own, very individual, way with dance and action.

There was practically no story. Barabau was an Italian peasant, featured in an Italian nursery rhyme. In translation the verse ran:

> Barabau, Barabau, why did you die?
> You'd wine in your cellar, your bread was not dry,
> And salad you grew in your garden near by:
> Barabau, Barabau, why did you die?

All that happened to him was that he entertained his friends with food and wine. A posse of Fascisti arrived and Barabau was killed.

The year 1925 had been rather too early for references to Mussolini and his regime—it was the year he took power; but by 1936 things were very different. He not only reigned supreme in Italy but had successfully invaded Ethiopia, and with Hitler ruling Germany the Nazi–Fascist bloc was a steadily growing menace. *Barabau* could not be watched without political feelings but it was comedy and not realism at which de Valois was aiming. The score was rich in Italian folk rhythms and Edward Burra, a brilliantly strong and original painter who had designed Ashton's *Rio Grande*, produced boldly coloured and characterised costumes and set. Burra was closely integrated with ballet both in France and England, a friend of William Chappell and Sophie Fedorovitch among others. All his work for the ballet stage was vigorously theatrical and artistically distinguished.

The implications of political comment and philosophical thought remained in the theme and costumes; de Valois concerned herself with burlesque, and was not entirely successful with it. Sibthorp wrote of "a sort of crazy gang riot, ingenious rather than striking" and found the treatment of the Fascisti banal. The best of the leading roles was de Valois' own, as a peasant woman who fiercely opposed the military tyranny of the Sergeant. Photographs show an unforgettable image of her in great good looks, wearing a peasant costume with a wide brimmed hat and with Chianti bottle in hand. Sibthorp, who loved her performance, fleshes it out a little:

> "For herself she created a really 'fat' part, a moonstruck moron, fantastic. Her opening dance was the very essence of crazy caution, a female Agag stepping delicately for no discoverable reason, her nose pointed in urgent pursuit of a destiny whose achievement was to involve the overthrow of tyranny in the person of the Fascist chief, and the rape of his tasselled cap and cane."[4]

Nothing else in the ballet seems to have been effective and although it was later revived it had little survival power.

In this connection it is worth considering the circumstances in which she was practising the art of choreography. She was seriously and chronically short of time, to plan, to consider, to brood about a theme, to work with her chosen artists in rehearsal. Most choreographers would complain that this applied to them as well, but the special feature of her condition was that mentally and physically she was involved in full-time, incredibly demanding work, managing, directing and developing the company and school, dealing with problems on every level, looking beyond and ahead with present and future planning. Discussions and decisions about the people and projects for which she was ultimately responsible required all her indomitable energy so that her role as a practising principal dancer and choreographer very frequently had to be given short shrift. Funds would not run to a third choreographer. Ashton was producing as much as he could reasonably be expected to do, so for the sake of variety in the repertoire she continued to stage ballets—and not all of them were the right vehicles for her unique creative gifts.

The year 1935 had inaugurated a vital activity that would be of prime importance during World War II—a provincial tour, introducing the Vic-Wells Ballet to audiences in major cities in England and Scotland. This was repeated in 1936 with a repertoire made up of four de Valois ballets, three by Ashton and single acts from *Le Lac des cygnes* and *Casse-noisette*. Out of London de Valois had to add to her duties those of Company Manager. From the first Baylis said, "Sorry, dear, we can't afford to send out a house manager with you. Go and see the theatre manager, look at the contracts, pay the orchestra, pay the theatre staff." An extra dozen chores—but in fact she was grateful. It gave her an insight into the financial side of the company as nothing else could have done.

She was thinking of students possibly coming to her from provincial schools and she was also thinking of her future public. The provinces were rich storehouses that could yield artists and audiences if properly encouraged. She already had a special connection with Liverpool and a particular ally there. Alfred Francis was a young man who trained as an architect and then turned to stage design and musical composition. As early as 1932 he was one of the group of local people who conceived and organised a dance show in aid of the Royal Southern Hospital, which they called *Southern Murmurs*. Most of the dancers were students of Liverpool dancing schools, but de Valois' ballet *The Arts of the Theatre* and her dance drama *Fedelma* were included in the programme.

In 1936 Francis founded the Liverpool Ballet Club. Provincial ballet clubs were at one time a valuable and active peripheral support to the development of British ballet. Dancing schools flourished in most towns and cities, but the performing ballet clubs filled the gap between the schools and the professional ballet world and between audiences and performers. Francis wrote of his aims:

"To obtain sufficient cooperation between aspiring dancers and choreographers on the one hand, and composers and designers on the other, to justify public performances that may be self-supporting."

He was realistic:

"At best a club production would probably fall a good deal short of firstclass entertainment; at worst it would be immeasurably better than the average dance school recital."[5]

The hope was that such local performances would encourage dancers to work harder towards professional careers, give teachers an outlet for any choreographic ideas they had, give designers and musicians a chance to gain experience of theatre productions. They would all work with guest choreographers and producers.

Not surprisingly, he came up against opposition, principally from some local dance teachers who "show stubborn, and occasionally active, resistance to any form of collective enterprise". Many of these ladies jealously guarded their territory and maintained a fierce rivalry with everyone else in the field. They wanted to have nothing to do with the theatre, in fact, but to confine themselves to the classroom and the examination syllabi. Some, fortunately, were more enlightened. Francis also felt that there was a potential large public for serious ballet. There was a pilot performance in December 1935 for which local choreographers and composers did interesting work.

This was a man and an idea worth encouraging from de Valois' point of view and she was ready to give generous help. The first opportunity came in December 1936, when she staged Act II of *Le Lac des cygnes* for the Club's performances at Crane Hall. Speakers at the meetings there included Alfred Francis and the Club's chairman, David Webster, later to be de Valois' close associate as general administrator of the Royal Opera House. In April 1937 she not only staged but danced in a two-act version of *Coppélia*, partnered by Harold Turner. This Liverpool connection continued over the years.

De Valois' choreographic contribution to the winter season of 1936/37 was *Prometheus*, set to Beethoven's *Les Créatures de Prométhée*. Lambert wrote the book, cutting and arranging the music to suit. In the first scene Prometheus returned from heaven with the gift of fire but was greeted with suspicion by the crowd and only his wife's intervention saved him from their violence. The second scene concerned Prometheus' domestic problems with his wife and six children as well as the Other Woman, who gained control of the fiery torch and used it to try and win his love. He spurned her and retained the torch, but she accused him unjustly to his wife who turned against him and called back the crowd to destroy him. He appealed to the Spirits of Fire and returned to the mountain from which he had brought fire to earth.

Comparing and considering contemporary reactions to this ballet, it seems possible that its failure to establish itself in the repertoire may have been because of the resistance of the Sadler's Wells audience of the time to a satirical and novel treatment of the legend and the music and their dislike of some of the costumes. Complaints were that the style was more *opéra bouffe* than Beethoven and that the choreography was too fussy and "busy". The critics took up totally divergent standpoints. Dyneley Hussey spoke for the opposition:

"The great old legend has been reduced to a commonplace ... This version of the Prometheus legend at Sadler's Wells has neither novelty nor point, only eccentricity and dullness."[6]

P. W. Manchester is devastating:

"The decision ... has to be made as to whether the choreography shall interpret the music or the story. Miss de Valois tried to compromise and the ballet was accordingly a hotch-potch which neither amused nor exalted ... Throughout the ballet there was a too meticulous regard for musical beats which gave an impression of that fussiness which spoils so much of Miss de Valois' choreography."[7]

There were adherents however as well as opponents. Caryl Brahms found that

"The choreography follows the classic line the music suggests. There is no straining after novelty either in the treatment of the crowds, which is vivid and effective, or in the individual dancing passages. The groupings are easily achieved and they follow naturally upon the action, punctuation marks in the choreographer's sentences..."[8]

Haskell also admired it, and the critic for *Time and Tide* called it

"one of the most finished productions that this company has given ... the ballet as pure dance form is very satisfying, thanks to Ninette de Valois' simple and unaffected choreography, faithfully interpreting the classical form of the music."

He was also delighted with John Banting's designs:

> "His skilful choice of colour, Minoan in derivation—earthy tones of brown, grey and terracotta enriched with brilliant splashes of crude purple, yellow and red—preserves a sense of unity throughout"[9]

Sibthorp writes interestingly about *Prometheus*. Although he found problems with the style—"a tongue-in-cheek twist to a legend that refused to be twisted"—he praised its choreographic invention. Prometheus (Helpmann) had a "lyrical *pas seul*, all lightness and energy" in which "an almost Petipa classicism was used to illustrate mood and character", and the ensembles were at times brilliant—a children's ball-game was full of "light, butterfly steps".[10]

The diversity of de Valois' activities at this time is underlined in any analysis of the year 1937. As planner and director for her company, she opened the year with a completely redesigned production of *Casse-noisette* by Mstislav Dobujinsky, and with the debut of her chosen young prima ballerina, Margot Fonteyn, in *Giselle*. With Helpmann as a fine Albrecht and Pamela May perfectly cast as the Queen of the Wilis, the ballet proved the excellence of her judgment over the selection of young dancers. She was very much the creator of this generation of Vic-Wells artists. Her ally in this was Ursula Moreton, but she herself was the commanding officer who decided which of her cadets were fitted by natural qualities and temperament for promotion and grooming for high office.

Each had a different contribution to make and the roles they created speak for their individuality. Fonteyn and May were products of the Vic-Wells Ballet School. They had come to it very young—May, who had been in the *corps de ballet* of the English Ballet in Copenhagen, had a slight edge where theatre experience was concerned as well as the two years' seniority that matters to teenagers. June Brae joined later but became completely identified with the Wells. The real outsider was Mary Honer, who had danced for some years in the commercial theatre after training with Legat.

The qualities of these four young ballerinas spread right across the spectrum. Honer was the virtuoso technician, a joyous allegro dancer of extrovert charm and great femininity, the embodiment of the fairy on top of the Christmas tree, especially delightful as the Sugar Plum Fairy in *Casse-noisette* or as Swanilda in *Coppélia*. Brae, never outstandingly secure technically, was an immensely talented dramatic dancer of great physical beauty and magnetism. Two created roles display her range—the seductive ruthlessness of the Black Queen in *Checkmate* and the delectably tipsy Josephine in *A Wedding Bouquet*. May, by virtue of her cool classical perfection and great elegance, was to become very much a connoisseur's prima ballerina, a fine Aurora and an outstanding Odette—she was less suited to Odile. Additionally, her creations were memorable, from the Moon in *Horoscope* to Mlle Théodore in *The Prospect Before Us*. Fonteyn is now legend. So much has been written of her that it is unnecessary to add to it, but to put her in context with this 1930s quartet it was Fonteyn who had the unawakened potential, in technique, feeling and looks, that could lead her (with an assorted amount of artistic assistance from de Valois, Lambert, Ashton and Helpmann) to outstrip the other three.

In two ballets from different periods Ashton used these artists and the principal male dancers with a perception of their abilities. *Les Patineurs* starred Turner as the cheerful, cheeky turning-top of a Blue Boy; Fonteyn and Helpmann had the smoothly lyrical white *pas de deux*, creamy and seamless when perfectly danced; May and Brae were the paired Red Girls, charmers both; Honer and Elizabeth Miller the merry virtuosos in blue. Three years later, Ashton created *Dante Sonata*, a passionate piece of sustained imaginative force, a struggle between light and darkness. Here Fonteyn with Michael Somes were the gentle lovers and May the solitary idealist among the Children of Light; Brae and Helpmann, masters of stage effect, were the tormented Children of Darkness.

De Valois' judgment over choreographers was already obvious from Ashton's *Apparitions* and *Nocturne*, the lovely Delius ballet he staged in October 1936, and it was reinforced by two of his finest productions, *Les Patineurs* and *A Wedding Bouquet*, in 1937. Lambert's outstanding contribution as musical director and conductor was an ongoing triumph and his remarkable flair for arranging ballet scores was becoming widely recognised.

In *A Wedding Bouquet* de Valois created her last role as a dancer. She was cast as Webster, the nanny-like maid, a witty key contribution to a ballet whose delicately zany charm depended on an accurate balance between the rational and the irrational, the comedy of manners and the conventions of French farce, treated with a sophisticated sense of fun. Webster introduced phases of action and linked the wedding party with the servants.

De Valois was dancing less and various causes made her decide to leave the stage at this point. It was impossible to spend enough time on class and rehearsal and there were many other things she wanted to do. Additionally, she had a physical reason. Few people knew of the polio she had had as a child, but all her life she suffered from pain right through her body when she danced. She accepted this as natural, but gradually her troubles increased and medical examination showed that, as there were dead tissues down the whole of her left side, the right side and back were taking more strain than they could bear.

Her position as a dancer, like her reputation as a choreographer, has been largely obscured by her fame as a company builder. Both she and Lambert made very real sacrifices as creative artists to serve the Sadler's Wells Ballet. With both it was deliberately done, and both gained important places in ballet history by the choice. They gave British ballet to the world, they gave the opportunity for celebrated careers to very many dancers and choreographers stretching on into the future. Without such setting aside of personal creativity, Lambert could have added substantially to his small number of compositions, with more ballets and probably operas and orchestral music. De Valois could have choreographed additional mature and considered ballets, implementing certain later projects and applying more time and consideration to some of the less successful earlier productions.

Her special dancing strength lay in *demi-caractère* and comedy. The role that extended her most was Swanilda—two acts only, but without doubt a three-act version of the ballet would merely have added to her triumph. The choreography she danced was derived from the Maryinsky production by way of Sergeyev and needed strong point-work, clean line, precise footwork and brilliant pirouettes. It is not a role that requires exceptional elevation and there was little need for elevation in any of the other roles with which she was associated, but her *ballon* was light and rhythmical. She had sufficient lyrical feeling and charm to make a satisfying Columbine in *Carnaval* as well as the scintillating speed required for Papillon. Elegant *épaulement* and flawless *port de bras* were part of her armoury. Wit was inherent in her comedy and second nature to her. Kate Neatby makes the point that tragedy (as in *Giselle*) would never have been her medium:

> "She is too crisp and practical and has the wrong sort of sense of humour. Imagination stumbles at the thought of her taking herself very seriously as the forsaken and demented heroine of this ballet."[11]

In early 1937 de Valois was occupied with writing and with choreography. Her first book, *Invitation to the Ballet*, was published by

John Lane, The Bodley Head and one of her greatest ballets, *Check-mate*, was given its premiere in Paris in June.

The literature of ballet was not extensive in 1937. It would be many years before books of all kinds—reminiscent, photographic, analytical or merely popular—would flood the market. The books that were published at the time were serious contributions to historical research or carefully considered critical works. De Valois' was a pioneer book. There is not a comparable volume, even now. Its unique character lies in the fact that after an introductory memoir—a memoir full of relevance and purpose—de Valois, a practising director, dealt with the position of repertory ballet in Great Britain as a whole and in every element with practicality and vision. Typically, she stated facts and, out of the facts as they were, offered views on what the future could be. She discussed production, dancers and choreographers; the economics and position in the theatre of ballet companies; the academic background; the audience and the critics. She was positive, stimulating, controversial and immensely amusing in a way calculated to provoke thought and discussion—and many of her points are still valid today. With perception and generosity she dedicated the book to Lilian Baylis and Marie Rambert, sponsor and rival respectively.

Paris in June 1937 was a city *en fête*, housing the great international exhibition of industry and art. Where ballet and dance were concerned, the Théâtre des Champs-Elysées was the showcase for an opulent programme of foreign visitors which included René Blum's Ballets de Monte-Carlo and Catherine Littlefield's Philadelphia Ballet. The Ballets Jooss appeared at the Salle Pleyel, a special theatre in the exhibition ground hosted folkdance companies, and various dance displays took place in the national pavilions.

The Vic-Wells Ballet followed Blum and Littlefield into the Théâtre des Champs-Elysées with a certain amount of trepidation, and immediately swept into the heart of critical Paris. They lacked advance publicity, and a brilliant first night was not backed up by public bookings, but the warm notices (particularly pleasing in a city where critics were often caustic) secured them attention. L. Franc Scheuer spoke of the season as "a revelation".

"It opened the doors on a conception of ballet which, far exceeding all expectation, surprised with its subtlety, delighted with its youthfulness, and triumphed through the unity of its ensemble ... allying tact with daring, tradition with originality, and stylisation with measure, it glorified choreography beyond them all."[12]

The repertoire that brought this praise was made up of five Ashton ballets (*Apparitions, Nocturne, Façade, Les Patineurs* and *Pomona*) and two de Valois: *The Rake's Progress* and a world premiere, *Checkmate*.

The idea of *Checkmate* had been brought to de Valois by Arthur Bliss, who composed the music. He envisaged it being done in a grand Chinese manner but de Valois was against this. It turned into a dramatic tragedy with a clear narrative line, based on the game of chess, a conflict between Love and Death who play, respectively, the red and the black to the point where the Red King is finally checkmate. It is a long work that takes time to establish the context of the struggle for supremacy and survival before entering on a brilliant series of moves and counter-moves.

A prologue shows Love and Death at the chessboard—and immediately arrests attention by the unity of music, bold and striking design and economical movement. The designer, as in all de Valois' ballets, is of the utmost importance. E. McKnight Kauffer was an American from Montana who came to England via Paris in 1914 and for twenty-five years worked as a poster designer for the London Underground and Transport company. Recent exhibitions have shown the outstanding vision and ability he brought to this, developing his personal style from the angular art of the Italian Futurists. He was commissioned to design a production of *Othello* in 1935 but did little other stage work. Kauffer was the perfect choice for *Checkmate*, producing a magnificently stylised set and costumes in scarlet, black and grey that complement and amplify the musical and choreographic statements.

The prologue begins the game, and the pieces assemble. On the red side are eight cheerful little pawns, two knights, two bishops, two castles, a frail and aged king and his tender young queen. One of the knights, the king and the queen are leading protagonists. On the black side only the queen has a principal part to play—the dominant and finally triumphant role of conqueror. There is no black king.

Checkmate exists on three levels. Primarily it is an exciting dramatic ballet. The first half is almost a romantic tragedy—the sexual conflict between the Red Knight and the Black Queen, the age-old theme of a man seduced from his duty by a woman's enchanting wiles and destroyed by her ruthlessness. The second half is another kind of

Checkmate *(Vic-Wells Ballet 1937) Harold Turner as The Red Knight*

feminine triumph, that of single-minded youthful strength over a once-powerful man's failing faculties.

On the second level, it has an appeal for chess players. This aspect has been fascinatingly researched and written about by Martin Lewis in an unpublished essay, *The Chess behind Checkmate*.[13] Arthur Bliss was a chess enthusiast, de Valois claims categorically that she "doesn't know a single thing about chess". They had many discussions however—"all," she says, "very helpful to me towards the general picture and inspiring for the 'symbolism' at work in my own mind."

Out of these discussions emerged many features that fit perfectly with the game itself. Five basic moves appear. These are the Knights' forward and then sideways jump; the Queen's freedom to move any number of squares in any direction; the Pawns' diagonal and zigzag formations for defence or offence; the Castles' commanding move but inability to use it on a crowded board. Then, when it comes to the development of the action, other fascinating parallels occur. In the chess textbook quoted by Lewis there is a Four Knights' Opening—and early in the ballet the two pairs of Knights are presented with their characteristic L-shaped leaping movement. The textbook describes this as an unadventurous beginning because it is defensive and leads to a symmetrical copycat development. It is left to Black to break the pattern and this can be done only by bringing the Black Queen into play, which is exactly what happens on stage. "A resolutely used Queen," writes Lewis, "can frighten an opponent into error," and the Black Queen immediately tests out her strength on the two Red Knights, registering the greater vulnerability of the first of them.

The special power of the Knights is that they are the only pieces that can attack a Queen undefended, and the attack of the First Red Knight on the Black Queen is a central dramatic situation of the ballet. Again, the Bishops, Knights or Queen can interpose to protect the King from check. On stage, in turn, the Bishops attempt to appeal to the Black Queen but quickly retire; the Red Queen moves forward but too timidly, and lays herself open to attack. One Queen cannot take another herself without being taken by a King or a Bishop, so the Black Queen sends in the Black Knights. The Red Queen is immobilised—"a pinned piece"—in front of the King whom she is attempting to defend, and the Black Knights violently remove her. The Red Knight is the Red King's last hope. His actions bring the Black Queen to her knees, but it is at that moment that she disarms him, feigning weakness, and then stabs him in the back. For this, there is no link with the game itself.

194

The Red King is now exposed; and here Lewis contributes some fascinating points. In a formal championship game, he reflects, with a Queen and a Knight down, the Red side would simply resign—"the players would shake hands over the board and the game would be over." On stage something very similar occurs.

"I think the resignation takes place clearly enough. The players, Love and Death, do take the stage again—Love sorrowfully leading on her rival, Death, who stalks across the board in disdainful triumph and throws his gauntlet on the body of the Red Knight. Love, dignified but defeated, makes her exit and we do not see either of them any more. She has resigned."

The dramatic narrative however has to be completed, so an End Game continues—and in an End Game the King is frequently driven about the board from check to check until there is no escape. The ballet exactly follows this pattern in its final stages, with the difference that Black mounts a full attack where in actual play a couple of simple moves could produce the same conclusion.

The third level on which *Checkmate* can be examined is for its symbolic and allegorical content. Inevitably there are many differing viewpoints on this, most of them belonging to a later period than 1937. Contemporary discussion accepted with very little comment the broad idea of a contest between Love and Death and even the denouement of a triumph for Death, as a perfectly natural dramatic subject without under- or overtones. The shaping of an effective piece of theatre was always, then, an aim in itself, and in this case it was an aim that was magnificently achieved.

The development, emanating from the American academic world, of deep analysis as applied to choreographic intention, has led to a variety of theories as to what it all means, about its "message" and significance. One rather neat school of thought takes it to relate to the pre-World War II European failure to combat aggression in the face of the rising evils of Fascism and National Socialism. Martin Lewis, hoping to find in it the philosophical and Christian belief that love can overcome death and the forces of evil, is blocked by the Red King's tragic end. He asked de Valois about her own thoughts in 1983.

She wrote that she "decided to think of it as the part played by 'fate' in man's life". She relates the pawns to "mass minds", the Knights to the chivalric ideal, the Bishops to religion, the castles to war; where she introduces a note of hope is to speak of the Red King and his queen as typifying old ways, the end of an era, and his overthrow by the Black Queen as victory for new ideas.

Her guiding symbols therefore are not, as might seem from the prologue, those of love and death, but of the old order vainly attempting to resist the forceful onrush of change and time—a fate that everyone ultimately faces:

> "I tell my dancers to move as if 'moved' by fate—to imagine being 'lifted' or pushed along the board (of life, with all its marked stops and starts). Everything that they do is an inevitable part of this fate. They must play the game of life out—the 'moves' they make are preordained."[14]

Here is a far deeper and more universal argument that any narrower emotional or political connotation.

De Valois' declaration that she is not a chess player and knows nothing about it is by no means incompatible with the evidence as to how the action of *Checkmate* reflects the game. A creative artist faced with a specific job of work gleans from other people exactly what he feels is needed for his own composition. Obviously her many sessions with Bliss, a player, yielded the kind of information necessary to her as choreographer—the kind of moves, the qualities of each piece and the possible way in which the dramatic development she and Bliss wanted to follow through could relate to the possibilities of chess itself. Once such facts were assimilated and incorporated into her choreography she would never think of them again.

Criticisms of *Checkmate* in 1937—and they were merely of minor points with a consensus of critical admiration—centred mainly on its length. Bliss had composed a long score, and there were one or two passages that might have gained by compression, but it was not de Valois' way to suggest this. It was generally agreed however that the Red Knight's mazurka lost impetus by its length and this was shortened. It is still difficult to sustain, and personally I have only seen one dancer who discovered exactly how to pace himself through its rhythms so that it never flagged. Otherwise the music, which the dancers at the time found very hard to remember and to count, provides a marvellous variety of effects, dramatic, lyrical or elegiac.

Once more, de Valois uses a range of dance styles with the utmost accuracy and flexibility. Her control of entries and exits is faultless, her groupings visually splendid. As in all her ballets, the geometrical delineation is satisfying, floor patterns are pleasing and intricate, pic-

Checkmate *(Vic-Wells Ballet 1937) June Brae as The Black Queen*

torial structure masterly. Classical dance, folkdance and social dance are fluently dovetailed. The general stylisation in no way precludes characterisation and her original cast set the example. June Brae played the Black Queen with a fine blend of dramatic strength and sensuous seductiveness. Pamela May was her gentle opposite as the Red Queen, Turner had the manly and arduous role of the Red Knight. Helpmann, increasingly establishing himself as a great dance-actor, combined subtlety with magnetism as the Red King. All the same, looking back from 1981, he felt that in 1937 he had been too young:

> "I didn't quite understand the enormity of the meaning, of the downfall of a dynasty, a kingdom. When I came back to it about three years ago I saw so much more in it..."[15]

Checkmate, which, as de Valois loves to recall, Toscanini called his favourite ballet, was not seen in London until September 1937 but it was immediately acclaimed. *The Times* praised its "seriousness", backing this up with a sweeping generality:

> "This note of seriousness is, perhaps, the characteristic English contribution to the art of ballet which has not elsewhere been endowed with so much solemnity. In this kind, *Checkmate* is a notable successor to *Job*."[16]

Richard Capell assessed it as an important work.[17] Beaumont found it "a definite contribution to British ballet, artistically conceived and presented and possessed of genuine inspiration".[18] P. W. Manchester was one of the least impressed, declaring it "one of the biggest disappointments in English ballet because it is very nearly a great work".[19] Adrian Stokes analysed excitingly the qualities he perceived in it:

> "The dancers maintain for close on fifty minutes, and even increase, a spirit of unrelaxing pressure and compulsiveness. But although idyll or elegy is absent, the characteristic poetry of ballet is affirmed by *Checkmate* in a pure and original form. Miss de Valois has entered on a grand period. *Prometheus*, first given last year, and *Checkmate* add to the life of ballet as a major art..."[20]

Checkmate had to be left in Holland in 1940. It was not restored to the repertoire until the second Covent Garden season in November 1947. McKnight Kauffer was still on hand to produce designs but these had major changes. At this point, after ten years, some of the original ideas had dated, and for the Opera House Kauffer simplified and streamlined the costumes and made slight alterations in the setting.

Beaumont compared Pamela May's Black Queen—"a vengeful, Medusa-like figure"—with Brae's "sultry voluptuous queen" and regretted Helpmann's absence from the Red King. "As now presented, the Red King is so stylised as to contribute little or nothing of dramatic value to the ballet." These comments have validity because, whether it is given in a large or a small theatre, it is most truly effective if the Queen is played as a ruthless enchantress and if the King is humanly enlarged within his proper framework rather than treated as a puppet.

Temperamentally, Beaumont was not greatly attracted to de Valois' choreography, writing of

"a sense of mathematical construction in which the music has been carefully studied and scientifically translated into choreographic terms, for, with her, music rarely engenders emotion which finds expression in movement."

He commented on the lack of "the cantilena style, which is generally the hallmark of the choreographer who composes with heart rather than brain".[21]

This reaction cannot be supported in a thorough examination of de Valois' choreography. Certainly she is an intellectual rather than an emotional choreographer but there is no lack of heart and feeling, and no lack of lyrical response, in her treatment of music. She has a special gift for creating solos (as Kenneth MacMillan for example is always at his best in *pas de deux*), offering a wide range of mood and character in them. The central situation in *Job* is summed up in the arrogant power of Satan's dance and the limpid serenity of Elihu's. In *Rake*, the Girl's two solos, in their loving tenderness and classical smoothness, are set against the disordered violence of the dances for the Rake and for the Gentleman with a Rope. In *Checkmate* the Red Knight's joyous mazurka and the Black Queen's feline baiting of the Red King are the core of the drama, together with the halting, senile solo sequence given to the Red King towards the end. In *The Prospect Before Us* there are Théodore's self-absorbed solo with her slippers and O'Reilly's uninhibited drunk dance. In *Orpheus and Eurydice*, Orpheus has an expressive dance of grief and Love a charmingly grave and tender variation. Throughout the other ballets solos emerge to charm, tantalise or make some salient point, and always they are married with complete compatibility to music.

Checkmate *(Vic-Wells Ballet on BBC TV 1938)* NdV *with Arthur Bliss and E. McKnight Kauffer*

Checkmate took time to settle in to the larger theatre. As seasons went on it looked better on the big stage, becoming eventually the only de Valois ballet to be on display at the Royal Opera House. It was taken on American and European tours, and seen in New York in 1949. As with *Rake*, John Martin proved the most enthusiastic of the critics. He found it

> "an extraordinarily engrossing work ... It is not likely ever to become a widely popular one for it is long, closely reasoned and uncompromising ... Miss de Valois is a choreographer with a mind, and if you do not object to keeping your wits about you and doing some concentrating, she will reward you copiously in this extremely complex, adult and potentially exciting work."[22]

This ballet and its original cast became part of an important pre-war television project by the BBC, who followed its presentation with a full week's season in June 1938 of performances by the Vic-Wells Ballet planned to fill in the gap for London balletgoers while the company was on its annual provincial tour. The televising of *Check-*

mate was preceded by a short discussion that involved de Valois, Bliss and McKnight Kauffer, and the whole programme was considered a success. Eric Robinson commented

> "[*Checkmate*] was perfect TV material, for the monochrome of the costumes did not matter very much and the check pattern of the chessboard was the perfect TV setting. This, like many other ballets of the time, was produced by D. H. Munro, the pioneer of intelligent camerawork in this field."[23]

In 1963 it was televised again, produced by Margaret Dale, still in black and white. As red tended to be an unpopular colour technically, and also to look black or grey on screen, the red pieces were described, and of course appeared, as white ones. In fact yellow costumes were used to get the proper black/white contrast and some stills exist looking distinctly odd as to colour values. The camerawork was again interesting and the production a good one.

Checkmate vanished from the main company repertoire in 1972. The Touring Company danced it between 1961 and 1964 and then revived it in 1975 as a tribute to Arthur Bliss who had recently died. This time the production established itself and has gained popularity with the company's audiences everywhere. In 1979 it was produced under de Valois' supervision for the Royal Ballet School performance and she also gave the public a glimpse of rehearsal work in 1980 in the programme *Steps, Notes and Squeaks*, coaching Maina Gielgud and Jonathan Kelly in the duet for the Black Queen and the Red Knight, and taking Helpmann through part of the Red King. Then, during the Royal Ballet's Golden Jubilee Year of 1981, Independent Television, looking forward to the opening of Channel 4, put in hand two excellent companion series of films simply called *Madam*. Each comprised five programmes following through rehearsals taken by de Valois with Sadler's Wells Royal Ballet of *Rake* and *Checkmate*. They included comments from Barry Wordsworth on the musical aspect and snippets of recollection from creators of roles (June Brae, Pamela May and Helpmann) but the most important feature was the sight and sound of de Valois herself coaching and producing the two ballets on which her choreographic reputation now rests.

Considered fifty years after its production, *Checkmate*'s splendour is unmistakable. It is a ballet that works well because of its solid construction and closely knit artistic unity. Like all dramatic ballets, the impact depends on the standard of performance it is given and for this two elements are essential: a strong and understanding rehearsal director who can make sure that the vital pace and dynamics are preserved, and a cast of dancers capable of characterisation who really believe in what they are being asked to do. Without these elements any dramatic ballet from *Petrushka* onwards will not only fail to grip an audience but will be diminished from its proper stature and look thin and stilted.

Checkmate however has often been fortunate in the dancers who have inherited the leading roles. Singling out names is always rather unfair, but many would agree with me in listing Pamela May and Beryl Grey as outstanding protagonists of the Black Queen. David Blair and David Ashmole have been excellent as the Red Knight. The Red King is the most intricate of the three leads, a non-dancing role that could not be taken by a non-dancer because of its need for physical control and musical timing, and Helpmann has never been equalled for poignant eloquence. It was to be the last role he would play on stage, in May 1986, four months before his death. De Valois gave the Australian Ballet permission to mount the work, asking them to dedicate it to him for his outstanding contribution to the development of British ballet, and the company, with whom he had a long association as director, choreographer and guest artist, went to great pains to do it justice. The impact of Helpmann's acting was reflected by the Australian critics. Mary Emery wrote:

"It was Sir Robert Helpmann who riveted attention with a truly definitive performance as the Red King. By simply changing the incline of his body, widening his eyes or moving a hand to throat or chair he made us feel the pathos and terrible vulnerability of his situation."[24]

For de Valois the occasion had special significance:

"I am still dazed to think that his very last appearance was in a ballet of mine and in a role that he created. The Australian public rose, with a true sense of national pride, to a wonderful and inspired performance."[25]

The production of *Checkmate* did much to put Sadler's Wells on the map. The theatre and its opera and ballet productions fell between every possible stool. It is significant, for instance, that the professional theatre weekly, *The Stage*, only began after *Checkmate* in 1937 to give it critical coverage. This reflected a change in the general attitude in London following the success of the Vic-Wells Ballet and *Checkmate*

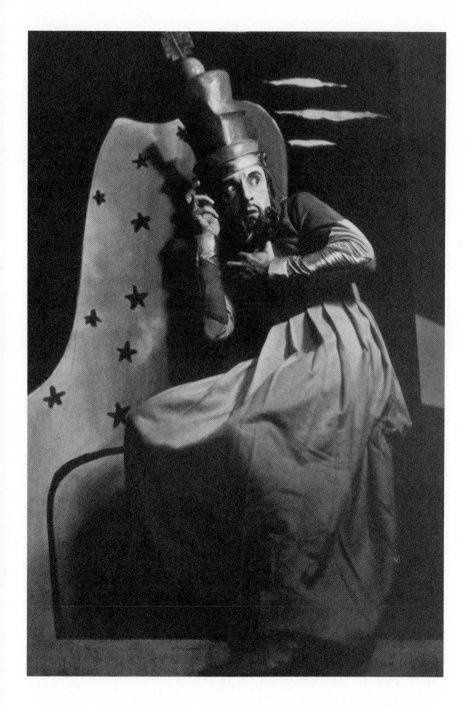

Checkmate *(Vic-Wells Ballet 1937) Robert Helpmann as The Red King*

as an important part of Britain's representation at the 1937 Paris International Exhibition. *The Stage* included an admiring notice from a local reviewer who saw *Checkmate* in Leeds in September, and from the beginning of the 1937/38 season an unnamed critic covered press nights at Sadler's Wells.

In December 1937 de Valois reverted for the last time to an old job— as arranger of dances for *A Midsummer Night's Dream* at the Old Vic. This time the director was Tyrone Guthrie, presenting a marvellous and memorable production that made theatre history. Designed by Oliver Messel and using the Mendelssohn music, it was dubbed a "Victorian" staging; but apart from a superb Bottom by Ralph Richardson its enchantment lay in the fairy scenes, with Vivien Leigh and Robert Helpmann as the essence of supernatural beauty, and choreography aptly in period from de Valois.

In a charming book, *Dramatic School*, Patricia Don Young, at that time a student actress at the Vic, looks back nostalgically to what she describes as "the loveliest thing I have ever seen, heard of or had anything to do with". She had an interesting part to play—one of the flying fairy ballet manipulated by the famous Mr Kirby.

"To fly nightly through those enchanting Messel-designed forests, to the accompanying strains of Mendelssohn's haunting midnight music, was an experience which for sheer extramundane delight surely few could match..."

De Valois was also back to the business of teaching actors how to move. Don Young remembers how, after de Valois arrived "with a full *corps de ballet* in tow", it was arranged that when she had finished rehearsing her dancers she should give the acting fairies some movement classes.

The Old Vic students had tuition in "ballet" with a variety of teachers drawn from the Vic-Wells—none of them stayed long apparently, becoming greatly discouraged over the lack of ability in their pupils. The students were also regular visitors to the audience at the Wells—they were given free passes—and devoted admirers of de Valois and the leading dancers. In *The Dream* however they were to be rather more involved. Because the stage was being opened up more dancers were needed, and more could not be spared from the Wells; so a few girls, Don Young among them, were required to work in the *corps*.

"You'll be right at the back," Guthrie explained to them, "and I'll tell you what we'll do. We don't give you any light at all so all that people will see of you will be your white skirts flitting about among the trees."

Every day they were rehearsed after the dancers had finished.

"Ninette de Valois would call a halt. 'That's enough now, girls. Are the drama students ready? Will you assemble upstage, please?' ... [she] was a model of patience with us. Never once did she allow a suggestion of the stern manner which she used with her own girls to creep into her voice when dealing with us. 'No, not quite right that time, I'm afraid. Would you mind trying it again?' ... 'No, you're not rising enough, I'm afraid. And your arms, they're still too heavy.' And as we came leaping on for the seventh or eighth time, with arms outstretched like coat hangers and faces hot and shining, we would suddenly catch sight of an amused group of ballet girls draped in Degas-like attitudes in the wings, enjoying the fun..."[26]

In de Valois' next ballet for her own company she returned to satirical comedy but failed to unify it into a successful whole. *Le Roi nu* was composed by Jean Françaix for choreography by Lifar at the Paris Opera in 1936. De Valois' use of scores created for Continental companies was beginning to be commented on. In March 1938 *The Dancing Times* questioned tartly:

"Are the possible subjects for ballet so limited that Miss de Valois must so frequently select one that has already been done by another company?"[27]

but it was the existence of the music that governed this practice. She worked often with specially composed scores by English composers but where a tight performing schedule demanded deadlines for ballets there were advantages in using an already established and theatrically tested composition. The Ballets Suédois, from which three of her ballets were acquired (*The Wise and Foolish Virgins, La Création du monde* and *The Jar*) had an extremely short life. It was a company she felt should have survived. In *Invitation to the Ballet* she commented on her decision to adopt the three works:

"A good number of the actual works embarked on by the Swedish company ... were in substance more consistent than, and musically superior to, some of Diaghilev's efforts. Some of the Swedish ballets have found their way in the past few years into the Sadler's Wells Ballet (before the English ballet could afford a greatly enlarged orchestra and company); during that difficult period it was possible to draw on the Swedish repertoire, for musically and dramatically these ballets showed merit and workmanship and had not succeeded in drastically dating themselves in the space of seven to ten years."[28]

All decisions regarding the Vic-Wells Ballet and its successors taken by de Valois in consultation with musical advisers and others were taken on the basis of completely considered facts both artistic and practical, and this question of using existing scores was a deliberate policy and not a random fancy.

Visually *Le Roi nu* was an exercise in elaborate 18th-century Chinoiserie, designed by Hedley Briggs. Choreographically it was uneven, but often ingeniously detailed and amusingly characterised. *The Stage* declared it:

"A merry piece which has its proper air of imaginative nonsense, and the music is exactly in keeping with its amusing subject".[29]

The scenario came in for criticism. Lifar, for his own ballet, removed it some way from the simplicity of Hans Andersen with the introduction of an Empress and her lover—but at least the Empress, as choreographed by de Valois, gave Pearl Argyle a superb chance of displaying her stylish classical line and personal beauty. The Emperor was the key role and a gift for Helpmann, who produced a witty study of affectation and disdain. Delightful, typically de Valois, character studies were achieved by the three Tailors—Ashton, Chappell and Claude Newman—who opened the ballet with an admirable prologue in which they hatched their plot to delude the Emperor and make their fortune. The Oriental overtones of their dances recalled for some people the operatic trio Ping, Pang and Pong in *Turandot*, and they have a place in de Valois' choreographic gallery with her other comedy threesomes: the three Comforters in *Job*, the three Lawyers in *The Prospect Before Us*, the three Gendarmes of *Douanes*.

In spite of good points however *Le Roi nu* could not be termed an unqualified success. Horace Horsnell summed it up:

"Individual dances look good but the composition as a whole lacks progressive form. The story seems to stutter and to lose control of its episodes, and one is left with the impression of a gay, amusing but somewhat shapeless performance."[30]

With this production launched, de Valois was free to apply herself to other aspects of her job. Where the building programme at Sadler's Wells was concerned, the extensive work was begun by the end of the 1938 spring season in May. De Valois' part in this was primarily in the planning stages, when decisions were taken as to the various ways in which practical improvements could be introduced. It was agreed that the stage should be enlarged, a new scene dock installed with a wardrobe room and a new ballet rehearsal room, dressing rooms and showers. The changes would greatly add to the company's comfort and efficient working, and also make it possible to implement her plan to crown the repertoire of traditional classics with a revival, the first by an English company, of Petipa's *The Sleeping Princess (Beauty)*.

This production, premiered in February 1939, was very much the result of teamwork but the various elements were pulled together and controlled by de Valois. Lambert of course was musically in charge; Sergeyev had the choreographic notes and memories; Ursula Moreton had appeared in Diaghilev's full length version in 1921 and de Valois herself knew the *Aurora's Wedding* of the twenties. The opportunity to design it was given to Nadia Benois—on a restricted budget, naturally, and this proved the least satisfactory area of the whole. The dancers had to be taught and coached in four acts of great difficulty and although the company was augmented to cope with the ballet's demands it was still far from large.

Apart from Fonteyn (Aurora), Helpmann (Prince Florimund) and June Brae (Lilac Fairy) everyone doubled or even trebled roles. In view of the fact that this ballet became such a celebrated part of the company's repertoire and that de Valois was to be closely connected with it on various occasions, it is worth while commenting on the content of the 1939 production. It followed the familiar sequence of Christening, Birthday (in the garden), the Prince's hunting party and Vision, the Awakening and the Wedding. Six fairy variations were danced in the Prologue, named Camellia, Rose, Violet, Songbirds, Breadcrumb (the Finger Variation) and Lilac. Because of the scenic limitations at Sadler's Wells the magic forest was represented by curtains rather than a fringe of trees growing upwards, and it was impossible for the Prince and the Lilac Fairy to make any part of their journey by boat.

Most of the differences came in the Wedding divertissement. Instead of Florestan and his Sisters there was the Petipa arrangement for a solo ballerina as the Diamond Fairy and three others as Gold, Sapphire and

Silver. In addition to Puss in Boots and Red Riding Hood there was a short duet for Cinderella and Prince Fortune. The Bluebird *pas de deux* (Mary Honer and Harold Turner) and the Aurora *pas de deux* were as always the classical highlights but instead of the Three Ivans the coda was danced by Aurora and Florimund. Carabosse appeared in the Apotheosis.

The publicity that surrounded this historic production, the subsequent inclusion of a "potted version" of it at a Royal Gala for the President of the French Republic at Covent Garden and a couple of live television performances ensured that the company's work became far more widely known than it had ever been before.

The Trend of the Thirties

Ninette de Valois

In the early thirties an objective was to be sighted: an effort at work for a breakthrough in the history of ballet in England.

The thirties were wonderful years; there was an influx of talent in the making and the collection of talent already established. Support came from great names in the ballet world, thanks to the belief, shown in the twenties, in English dancers by two strong branches of the Russian Ballet—namely the Diaghilev and Pavlova Companies.

In the thirties such professionals as Karsavina, Lopokova, Bedells, Markova, Dolin and Idzikovsky were all at the disposal of young English choreographers notably Frederick Ashton—who had, as an example, Markova and Idzikovsky for his first production of *Les Rendezvous*.

Briefly, the newly erected Sadler's Wells Theatre was ideal for this venture, namely, the sowing of an English State Ballet. The young students worked in close proximity with the opera company and for a time with the Old Vic drama company; they grew up within the theatre world that I had known for so long. The situation aroused in them an intelligent interest. These young artists were also in close touch with the Mercury Theatre, which housed the young dancers of the Rambert Company. Dancers from the Rambert Company such as Ashton, Argyle, Turner, Chappell and Tudor, who joined, as full-time members, the Sadler's Wells Ballet, were expected to keep up their contact with the Mercury and appear in the weekend performances.

It is not possible to forget the musical side of the Sadler's Wells venture; it was under the guidance of Constant Lambert with a certain amount of help from a great friend of his—Edwin Evans. The latter had links with the Diaghilev Company when it was performing in London; he was also musical adviser to the Camargo Society. I can recall the advice and encouragement that I received from him in the twenties. I was anxious to have, in my private school of those days, a small music library; he set it up for me with a wide range of music that was only suitable for piano or small orchestra. The result was a collection of rewarding music for choreographic works—suitable for recitals and small theatre ventures.

During this particular period the school was showing a big underground movement and had the following names as guest teachers: Legat, Idzikovsky, Craske and Sergeyev. As an example—by the out break of war it had produced Fonteyn, Brae, May, Grey, Shearer, Helpmann, Somes, Turner, Farron and others. All of them had a faithful audience who saw us into the Royal Opera House in 1946. The "Commonwealth Rush" now started. In no time we saw Grant (New Zealand), Park (Rhodesia) and Nerina, Mason and Cranko (South Africa)—many others were to follow.

How idyllic, safe and far reaching did it all seem in the early days! Then came the first signs of war; the closing of the theatre; a quickly diminishing company, due to the call-up, went on tour with piano accompaniment under the direction of Frederick Ashton and the stage manager. This venture continued for some time. I was in London with little to do but worry about the fate of the school, while carrying out some teaching and attending meetings about a possible but remote saving of the situation in general. In spite of my pleadings Tyrone Guthrie would not entertain the idea of evacuating the school because of a possible financial risk. The school stayed at the Wells throughout the war, understandably diminished as many young students could not come to London. Our staff was wonderful—we had Volkova and Ailne Phillips; Andree Howard took over choreography. But it was all a very serious setback for us, retarding any real school progress by about ten years.

The Company's early wartime problems were solved, in the end, by the late Sir Bronson Albery, a member of the Vic-Wells board. He generously gave us the then New Theatre (now the Albery) for the duration of the war. The Opera, Drama and Ballet Companies were to appear there in strict rotation. His son (Sir Donald Albery of today) was the General Manager. In no time he arranged for the ballet to have an orchestra.

The call-up went on—and that meant the loss of Frederick Ashton for over four years.

Yet the Trend of the Thirties survived. The spirit was there. The spirit was good. Wages were low; artists receiving over a certain sum could not have the full agreed salary each week until the overheads, on both Sadler's Wells and the Old Vic, had been paid off; out of profits only were such salaries completed. In other words, on all sides, survival of the two theatres came first.

The irony of it all! Today the Wells is not subsidised—and South Bank development means that it, rather than the Old Vic, is now on "The Wrong Side of the River". Bemusing for artists of yesterday to find out what poor geographical foresight they had possessed.

Does the above sound hysterical? Not really—it happens to be just historical . . .

Let us remember, for a moment, the lights of Covent Garden rising on the "Islington Dancers" (so called by a well-known music critic of the thirties) and let us reflect a little on our national style.

There was a time in the early fifties when American critics alluded to "Sadler's Wells feet". This meant that they were aware of our speedy *terre-à-terre* footwork that had been taken for granted in England. Did these feet play their part in getting us into the Guinness Book of Records? Why are we there? The answer is simple. On a certain first night in 1949 at the Metropolitan Opera House, New York, today's Royal Ballet took 47 curtain calls—the greatest number on record.

The scene is a studio in the Bolshoi School, Moscow. The writer has just witnessed a wonderful class of boy students under the direction of one of their head teachers. Gratitude and deep appreciation was passed on to the maestro through the interpreter. There followed a flow of Russian, interpreted as follows:

"Will Madam please show me some Scottish steps?"

The Russians know. They have always understood the link between classical and national dance and the significance of the latter in the development of the former. They know also that we, the English, have endeavoured to enrich our classical style with the rhythm of the Russian national folkdance; there is also the importation of the Spanish dance with its deportment and its flexible expressive hands—the latter hardly a national trait of the British!

But we are not finished with Russia. We never will be, they are too much in our past. Only a short time ago I heard that it was being said:

"The Royal Ballet School is going Russian". We are not yet 60 years old. Why not take a holiday and dip back into our past influences? I seem to remember that towards the end of the last century Russian Ballet—about 250 years old—was bowled over by the advent in their midst of Petipa (France) and Enrico Cecchetti (Italy).

This is all leading up to a question that the reader may well be asking: What about Contemporary Dance?

Contemporary Dance in its early years of structure—the days of undiluted Martha Graham schooling—had something of much value to give us. Unfortunately Contemporary Dance today seems to think in reverse. They seem to have decided that we have much more to give to them! We are showing the same tendency and are not helped by finding ourselves all stuck under the same umbrella with an ambiguous title of "Dance".

I naturally hope that all the above is a foolish phase. Purity and integrity of approach is needed on all sides. Speaking of the ballet: it is all becoming a challenge to the strength of our own foundations, and they are hardly lacking in research and development. Ruthless hasty borrowing will just lead everyone into a cul-de-sac that may, indeed, be worthy of the title "Dance". It is the task of choreographers, teachers, directors and the dancers of the classical regime to understand what is happening.

To put it simply: balletic classicism must continue to develop in its own creative world. This particular world, as we all know, has been through 300 years of development alongside classical music, architecture, painting and draughtsmanship. We are a theatre art form that covers, as other basic art forms, the *mood* of different classical time phases through the centuries. We cannot continue along this path if we are not always aware of the past, and thus make sure that we turn, with an alerted sense of discrimination, to the other sources that surround us.

After years of English Ballet development in the theatre, a little reflection· seems necessary for the sake of acquiring knowledge of certain basic facts. As an example, do we realise the position of Fokine and Ashton and what their countries owe to them? It is a fact that these two figures will historically stand out as the creators of native "style" in their respective countries. The final creative development of a national exploitation of the classical ballet in their countries.

Fokine and Ashton ballets do not die; I do not think that they will ever do so. From time to time their respective works will always be taken off their shelves and shown to all. (As a respite from what may well be happening?). In the foreseeable future, they may be considered by many as examples of "period pieces", but certain "period pieces" hold, intact, the logical side of all forms of development. In this sense, here, in these two artists, is to be traced the logical breakaway from the great Petipa impact, allowing, of course, for the maestro's inevitable influence on many countries.

I would like to give, very briefly, a few examples that are relative to these two artists' prolific national works. In Fokine we have—in his production of *Firebird*—the influence, on a classical work, of all sides of Russian folk and *demi-caractère* dancing, not to mention both the classical and the lyrical qualities that dominate the scene in general. Alongside this work (and others in the same vein) there is his *Les Sylphides*. This is surely a choreographic comment by Russia on the avalanche of *Giselles* and *Les Sylphides* given to them by Western Europe. It stands alone. A slice of Russian classicism with today's emphasis on an inherited lyrical quality.

Ashton? I would personally choose as examples: Elgar's *Enigma Variations* and Mendelssohn's *The Dream*. Last (but by no means least) the cool yet lyrical quality portrayed—with a British sense of reserve and precision—the famous Franck *Symphonic Variations*.

Do I speak of a godfather and godson? As Fokine developed, his independence came to him naturally—born and bred in a country with a then classical ballet tradition of more than 200 years. This was not the case with the younger Ashton. He had to be influenced from outside, and turned to the Petipa tradition through the examples that were the heritage of Russia. But he did not fight the natural English influence at work—an all-important event made, no doubt, without any highly conscious effort on his part.

That is as it should be.

A Wedding Bouquet *(Vic-Wells Ballet 1937)* NdV *as Webster*

Chapter VIII

When World War II broke out, on September 3 1939, the Vic-Wells Ballet were in Leeds. They were immediately disbanded.

For a few days in fact the whole country paused and caught its breath over the recognition of the coming disruption of normal life. All plans, personal and otherwise, were halted; no one knew what to do or where to go. This state of affairs was distressing in the context of family life but considerably more so where a theatrical company was concerned. London theatres were all closed for the time being and touring dates were in jeopardy. De Valois and the Vic-Wells organisation however managed to re-form the ballet at Cardiff within two weeks and began a tour with a limited repertoire and no orchestra—musical accompaniment, in those days before sophisticated recorded music, was admirably provided on two pianos by Lambert and Hilda Gaunt, the company rehearsal pianist. This tour was organised on a cooperative basis, with small basic pay and a percentage of takings where possible. It was difficult for everyone, but no one grumbled. They were drawn together into a close relationship of shared problems and solutions.

More than ever, de Valois had a matriarchal role to play and played it with strength and courage. She gave the company, both performers and backstage support, a lead throughout the whole course of the war in adaptability to changing circumstances, endurance in the face of hardship and danger and in positive response to sudden crisis. By her own example she stimulated them to produce the utmost in hard work and artistry, keeping her ballet company a tight band of thorough professionals committed to the theatre and to their ever-increasing audiences of admirers.

The war opened with months of deceptive gentleness. First precautions were relaxed and it was possible for Sadler's Wells Theatre

215

to stage a ballet season at the end of 1939, complete with orchestra. The impassioned feelings of the day were expressed in the Ashton-Liszt-Fedorovitch *Dante Sonata*, a new ballet entirely apt to its time and as such significant for all who saw it then. A second London season in April 1940 implemented a plan to produce *Coppélia* with the third, divertissement, act, staged by Sergeyev from the Maryinsky version and joyously designed in clear bright colour by Chappell, juxtaposing blues and greens or reds and purples with exquisite confidence. Another distinguished set of designs, by Rex Whistler, adorned an Ashton ballet on *The Wise Virgins*.

Two projects were occupying de Valois. She was planning a ballet of her own, *The Prospect Before Us*; and she was engaged in discussions about an important Continental tour, part of a cultural propaganda programme to strengthen Britain's relationship with neutral and allied countries, backed by the British Council (with which she would have close links over the years) and the Foreign Office.

The company travelled to Rotterdam on May 4 on a small Dutch boat and thence to The Hague by bus. The plan was that The Hague should be a base from which they would tour other Dutch centres for a ten day period. Neutral Holland seemed a return to peacetime prosperity after the rations and restrictions of wartime Britain and they opened on May 5 to a gala audience at the Royal Theatre of The Hague. For the next few days they drove radially through Holland to perform in Hengelo, Eindhoven and Arnhem, increasingly aware of military preparation and the fear of a German invasion. This came on May 19 while they were on the way back to The Hague from Arnhem.

For a long Saturday the dancers put in time while de Valois discussed with the authorities what was to happen next. In the evening they were evacuated from The Hague by bus for an uncomfortable nine hour trip to Velsen. They had to abandon sets, costumes, scores and orchestral parts for major ballets as well as everything of their personal property that could not be worn or carried, but at least their lives were saved. They travelled through a country full of soldiers and refugees and assaulted by enemy air raids. De Valois became an army commander, dividing her charges into sections under leaders: herself, Lambert, Ashton, Helpmann, Claude Newman, Joy Newton and the stage director John Sullivan—in case they were forced to split up the company group. A partial night at Velsen was followed by a grim trip to Ijmuiden. Annabel Farjeon, at that time a member of the *corps de ballet*, wrote about it vividly:

*Sadler's Wells Ballet en route for Holland 1940; (left to right) June
Brae, Mary Honer, Robert Helpmann, Margot Fonteyn, Frederick
Ashton, NdV*

"In that journey all sense of time was lost, for every now and again
there would be shots outside, the company would pile into heaps in the
gangway, the bus would pull up with a jolt and the guard would lift
his rifle and rest the barrel on the window ledge. Such moments of
terrified expectation, waiting for the bang when the guard fired and the
splintering glass seemed endless. Morning came, and we were halfway
to England in the hold of a cargo ship. The ballet, combing straws out
of its hair, shaking the creases from its clothes, wandered on deck and,
in the grey green light, girls dabbed lipstick and powder over their worn
and dirty faces ... Looking back it was possible to realise the pattern
of circumstances, and how Ninette de Valois always stood out, carrying
the weight of responsibility. Looking forward, towards England, it was
only possible to visualise a good meal and a warm bed."[1]

De Valois' own account is contained in *Come Dance With Me*, a
record that blends with great skill and imaginative power a narrative
of fact and a picture of a countryside in confusion. Sensitive to a degree
over people, places and the dramatic quality of events, she has an
enviable gift for the impressionistic use of words to conjure up per-

sonalities and moments in time. Her cameo portraits of people and the context of her experience of them suggest that a perceptive and witty novelist has been lost to literature.

In the wake of that bitter May, as German forces swept through the Low Countries, Norway and France and drove the British Expeditionary Force off the beaches of Dunkirk, de Valois had to struggle for her company's future. They could only afford to replace one or two of the lost ballets and the first to be re-dressed were *Dante Sonata* and *Façade*—good choices, as both were an emotional release for audiences, one presenting the struggle in which everyone was engaged, the other a series of marvellous jokes to provoke laughter. *Les Patineurs* was also re-staged. *Horoscope* had gone forever, a serious loss, and— typically, one feels—the last ballets to be recovered were de Valois' own *Checkmate* and *Rake*. Fortunately the staple classics were intact and all other recent Ashton ballets; and de Valois was about to inject courage and life into the company's work by a masterful new comedy.

The Prospect Before Us or Pity the Poor Dancers was a collaboration between herself and Lambert, springing out of a study of John Ebers' *Seven Years of the King's Theatre*. In 18th-century London the King's Theatre and the Pantheon Theatre, in the Haymarket and Oxford Street respectively, pursued a lively and eventful rivalry over stars of the ballet (mostly French) and productions attractive to the public. Out of this true life situation de Valois composed an economical scenario—apparently complicated, only because the personalities and events were unfamiliar—about how the theatre manager Mr O'Reilly took advantage of the destruction by fire of a rival's theatre to lure away his principal dancers; made a great success but ran into debt and ended up, after his own theatre burnt down, blissfully inebriated, cocking a snook at rivals, enemies and fate itself.

To accompany and illustrate this tale, treated entirely lightheartedly, Lambert arranged a brilliant score from a favourite composer of his, William Boyce; and Roger Furse was commissioned to do for Thomas Rowlandson what Rex Whistler had done with signal success for Hogarth in *Rake*. Furse was more than equal to the job, producing delightful sets and costumes that flawlessly conjured up the London ballet theatre of the 1780s. Only de Valois' impeccable sense of period style and ingenious wit could have breathed choreographic life into these strong musical and scenic partners but she accomplished, as she did in all her greatest ballets, a complete coordination between the artistic elements and a fine theatrical balance.

The Prospect Before Us *(Sadler's Wells Ballet 1940); (left to right)*
Margaret Dale, Pamela May, Alan Carter

The ballet opens backstage at the King's Theatre with a rehearsal
in progress involving Noverre as ballet master and the leading dancers
Vestris, Didelot and Mlle Théodore. Mr Taylor, the manager (Claude
Newman), is puffed up with self-importance. Mr O'Reilly, the manager
of the Pantheon (Helpmann) wanders in, blandly inspecting through
an eyeglass every aspect of the rival establishment. The two managers
drink together and Taylor offers O'Reilly a box for the season. A drop
curtain, joyously executed with dramatic and ribald detail, depicts the
burning of the King's Theatre, and in a front-of-curtain scene O'Reilly
lures the star dancers over to his own management. He needs money
for his theatre, however (a situation all too familiar to any director of
ballet at Sadler's Wells) and takes dancers out on the streets with a
model of the Pantheon to beg for public support. He is successful and
the next scene is his opening night. A ballet—a delicately satirical
pastiche of conventional choreography of the period—danced by
Vestris, Didelot and Théodore with a pert Cupid—is taking place,
while O'Reilly in one stage box flaunts his triumph over Taylor in the
other.

The Prospect Before Us *(Sadler's Wells Ballet 1940) Robert Helpmann as Mr O'Reilly*

O'Reilly however is deeply in debt. A typical legal muddle is represented. Although the dancers want to return to the once-more prosperous King's Theatre, the licence to stage ballet remains at the Pantheon. The solution—and it is left open whether it is a fortunate act of God or a piece of clever skulduggery by man—comes with the burning of the Pantheon (Furse's drop curtain makes a second appearance) and the ballet ends with a rehearsal on stage at the King's Theatre into which bursts a riotously drunk, coatless and wigless O'Reilly, who irreverently mimics patrons, dancers and ballet masters in a brilliantly timed solo. They all depart in high dudgeon while Taylor and O'Reilly resume drinking. This time O'Reilly refuses the offer of a box for the coming season and reels offstage.

In more than one way *Prospect* was a companion piece to *Rake*. Both opened with expository scenes of great accuracy and strong character statement. With the aid of a cast who were in sympathy with her aims and accustomed to her methods of work, de Valois sketched in a whole range of cameos—the fussy ballet master, his disdainful wife, the socialite patrons, the arrogant Vestris and self-absorbed Didelot, the elegant Théodore (May), who had a charming introductory solo in which she selected a pair of suitable dancing shoes; the chattering little groups of "ladies of the ballet" and the cunningly contrasted Taylor and O'Reilly. Taylor is the neat, fussy man of business, O'Reilly deceptively mild in appearance but in actual fact a wild and unstable theatrical gambler.

There are other resemblances between *Prospect* and *Rake*, quite apart from the use of linking scenes before a drop curtain, while both ballets end on a high note—the accumulated tension of the madhouse in *Rake* and the Rake's death, and the hilarious drunk dance of O'Reilly celebrating his freedom from debt and dancers' demands.

The "ballet within a ballet" was an apt and stylish divertissement with the gentlest of humorous touches. It contained planned pauses filled with comic byplay by O'Reilly. De Valois' cast, experienced in the creation and exposition of character, provided vastly enjoyable sketches in supporting roles. One of the most memorable was Mary Honer's dumb blonde dancer showing off her rags in the street appeal scene, while the solemn and spectacled lawyers with outsize feet invariably had everyone chuckling.

Prospect was more loosely constructed than *Rake*. It suffered from a story that did not build steadily to a final climax but sauntered along episodically without firm development. It presented characters in a number of vignettes, very much from an observer's point of view, without relating them closely to each other, and so sacrificed some substance. It was nevertheless a remarkable essay in theatre dance, full of wit and charm, and from beginning to end a tour de force for Helpmann. The endearing, ebullient and wickedly amusing Mr O'Reilly captured audiences from his first appearance and by curtain fall had totally established himself in the select gallery of great comedy ballet creations.

The production of *The Prospect Before Us* in July 1940 was a convincing testament to de Valois' indomitable spirit. To match an historic moment of national disaster, not with a rousing call to battle or a passionate statement of faith and hope but with an impudently comic account of trivial theatrical rivalries of a past century was the sign of an unquenchable, and enviable, resilience and balance.

The critics thoroughly enjoyed *Prospect*. Horace Horsnell wrote "This irresistible frolic crowns a season that has been as brilliant as adventurous",[2] and brilliant was the word that ran through the other notices. *The Dancing Times* felt it was a masterpiece:

"It contains a wealth of detail and characterisation which must be seen many times before it can be properly appreciated. It is a Rowlandson print come to life and captures the racy spirit of that age more than any words can describe."[3]

Dyneley Hussey was equally impressed by the links with Rowlandson:

"The Rowlandson element goes deeper than the mere reproduction in the terms of scenery ... the choreographer recreates the artist's sense of movement in the motions of the dancers, eliminating so far as is possible every pose or gesture that is irrelevant or contradictory to his individual style ... "[4]

Most of the audience happily accepted *Prospect* at face value as an enjoyable comedy, but one of them was puzzled by a highly specialist point. At a Morley College lecture in 1943, when de Valois spoke on "Composing a Ballet", the seventh questioner, obviously a serious student of ballet history, posed a neat little problem:

"In the ballet scene in *Prospect*, it is supposed to be Noverre in the box and the ballet itself is supposed to be his handiwork. Noverre is famed as an innovator but the ballet shown appears to be a skit on the normal type of 18th-century ballet rather than a progressive work. Why is this?"

My notes on the lecture record that

"Miss de Valois laughed. She said yes, it was Noverre. Yes, it was a skit. But Noverre, as well as doing much valuable and progressive work, had in his day composed many opera-ballets of the old sort. She thought it would add, if anything, to the complexities of *Prospect* if suddenly in that scene she began to show Noverre's ideas on ballet in a serious way. Indeed, she thought it would be quite impossible with Mr Help-mann in the box . . . "[5]

De Valois enjoyed and admired Helpmann's O'Reilly, writing

"In *The Prospect Before Us* I created in Mr O'Reilly a role that was deliberately inspired by Helpmann. He has made of this fantastic Rowlandson figure an endearing and entrancing character study of a balletic clown—culminating in the now famous inebriated dance that will have to be buried with its first and only performer."[6]

This did not quite happen. *Prospect* was revived for Sadler's Wells Theatre Ballet in February 1951, after Helpmann left the larger company in America in November 1950, and he danced the first three London performances as guest artist. The role was then taken on by Stanley Holden with a good deal of success but without the relaxed virtuosity of Helpmann's interpretation.

The war was now the dominant force in everyone's life. For the Vic-Wells Ballet it meant that its male dancers were being steadily called up, the bombing of London had begun and for a time theatres were often half empty. In September 1940 Sadler's Wells was taken over for an air raid rest centre, and in November the administration of the Vic-Wells companies—the Old Vic Drama Company and the Sadler's Wells Opera and Ballet—was transferred from the capital to the Victoria Theatre in Burnley (Lancashire).

This change of emphasis was less disturbing to de Valois than it would have been to a director whose frontiers had never been enlarged by work outside London. All her theatrical life she had been used to provincial audiences and conditions from the days of the Wonder Children to the regular tours of her ballet company. For her, and, because of her attitude, for her company also, ballet was always a part of the general theatre, and as such belonged wherever there were theatres and audiences to fill them. For the rest of the war the Sadler's Wells Ballet willingly travelled all over the United Kingdom, suffering considerable strain and hardship, and becoming welcome friends in every community they visited.

They did however acquire a London base. Bronson Albery whose son Donald became the Ballet's wartime Company Manager had been a governor of the Old Vic from 1936. He was also managing director of the Wyndham Theatres, controlling the New, Wyndham's and Criterion theatres in London's West End. Albery's work in the theatre over a very long life is a good example of how enlightened and valuable can be the contribution of a key personality in the so-called commercial area of the profession. Now, so that the three Vic-Wells companies— drama, opera and ballet—should continue to be seen by London audiences as well as the provincial audiences with which they spent most of their time, Albery made the New Theatre (now the Albery) in St Martin's Lane available. It was there that many of us spent a large part of our wartime lives, becoming closely involved as spectators and connoisseurs over repertoire and dancers.

For de Valois the administrative problems of peace were replaced by those of war—rationing and food shortages affected dancers' health and strength, clothes rationing affected costumes and practice wear, every kind of difficulty beset travel and transport quite apart from the fear and strain of air raids which everyone suffered, both in London, under constant attack from autumn 1940 until victory in Europe was assured in May 1945, and in provincial cities which experienced intermittent terror blitzes. The work load was enormously increased. The spaced-out performances that had been the norm before the war were replaced by week after week of heavy programmes involving at times three performances in one day. Adaptation and flexibility were the qualities needed for survival and these she was adept at supplying.

One hard and recurring trouble had to be faced—the calling-up of male dancers—and on this de Valois was firmly on the side of the authorities. As Mary Clarke puts it in her invaluable book *The Sadler's Wells Ballet*:

"[She] never asked for exemption although she had to watch her first vintage of male dancers leaving her one by one. She maintained that military requirements of the nation must come first, and she felt that her dancers had no greater claim than many other artists or young men at a crucial stage in their professional studies."[7]

By the end of 1942 some had already gone: William Chappell, Richard Ellis, Stanley Hall, Paul Reymond and Leo Young. Within the next few months Frederick Ashton, Leslie Edwards, Michael Somes and Alan Carter followed them. Harold Turner had left the company in March 1940 to join the Arts Theatre Ballet. Where Helpmann was concerned, he was an Australian with an Australian passport and could not be called up. This was fortunate for British ballet, as he did unsparing and arduous work as principal dancer and choreographer through the ensuing years of war. It was Helpmann's performances and personality that focused public attention on the Sadler's Wells Ballet and welded younger or less experienced artists into an inspired performing team that steadily built up a high reputation. More, as de Valois could not be with them on a day to day basis on tour, Helpmann was unnamed acting director, arranging casting and rehearsals and dealing with all the personal problems of the dancers. With Lambert, he injected a unique blend of energy, resourcefulness and undergraduate comedy into the company's daily life. De Valois recalls Lambert "spending hours with the company, playing absurd games and listening to equally absurd stories ... Helpmann's mimicry of anyone or anything left him prostrate with merriment."[8] Positive personalities like these make it possible for those around them to face up to the frustrations and insecurities of a tragic war. They were of course de Valois' people. She had found them, she had brought them into close collaboration and she could trust them to help her keep British ballet moving steadily onwards. It is sad to reflect that neither Lambert nor Helpmann prospered with the company after the war at Covent Garden. Helpmann came to a parting of the ways in 1950 and in 1951 Lambert, who had experienced bitterness and estrangement, died at the tragically early age of forty-six.

Two new ballets were premiered in London, at the New Theatre, in 1941. Ashton, in his last choreographic assignment before call-up, staged the brilliant and exciting Schubert *The Wanderer*, for which Graham Sutherland produced inventive and memorable designs; and de Valois offered a total contrast with her *Orpheus and Eurydice*.

The original intention, before Sadler's Wells had to be abandoned, was to produce Gluck's opera with the combined talents of the opera and ballet companies, and Sophie Fedorovitch's exquisitely refined sets and costumes had been created with this in mind. The project was now reduced in scale so that only certain arias were sung by a soprano and a contralto from the orchestra pit to the accompaniment of two

Orpheus and Eurydice
*(Sadler's Wells Ballet
1941); (above) NdV in
rehearsal (Robert
Helpmann as
Orpheus); (right)
working sketch by NdV
for scene of Orpheus
with the Furies*

pianos, while the dancers mimed and danced the action on stage. For some critics and audience the result was too formal, stylised and slow; for others it had an unforgettable perfection of visual and musical harmony, a clarity and limpidity in its apt union of the performing arts. Once again de Valois' sense of style and cool elegance were brought into play, and she used her cast with perception.

For the first time she created a substantial role for Fonteyn. Fonteyn was the treasured prima ballerina she had developed so carefully to follow Markova in the great classical ballets; she was also Ashton's muse, featured in roles as different as the Flower Girl in *Nocturne* and the fey and forlorn Julia in *A Wedding Bouquet*. Apart from a short *pièce d'occasion*, *Music for Ballet*, in 1936 her only appearance in a de Valois ballet had been as Young Treginnis and later as Alicia in *The Haunted Ballroom*. Now, as Love, she had fluent and delicate pointwork in slow tempi, based on the beautiful lines of arabesque and attitude, grave and serene in mood. Pamela May was a perfect Eurydice, resigned, reticent and tender. Helpmann as Orpheus sustained with great lyrical feeling andante dance *enchaînements* of meticulously controlled balances. De Valois had choreographed the scenes of the Furies and the Elysian Fields in a production of the opera many years previously; now she built up strong architectural groupings and dissolves for a small ensemble of masked Furies led by Mary Honer, created gently idyllic *corps de ballet* work for the Blessed Spirits and a joyous set of lovers' dances for the return to earth, interpreted by Julia Farron and John Hart.

Hart, John Field and Deryk Mendel were the new young men from the school, rushed into principal roles in the short months before their call-up. Other artists, mainly from the Commonwealth, were recruited, including Alexis Rassine, Gordon Hamilton and David Paltenghi. Handwritten notes by de Valois for *Orpheus and Eurydice* are lodged in the Royal Ballet School archives. They consist of a very tight precis of action, memory lines in fact, and drawings of groupings or movement—Jean Bedells, a fifteen-year-old staying at the time with de Valois and her husband at Sunningdale, remembers her sitting on the floor working on these detailed sketches.[9] There are cues that relate the words and music of arias to mime.

The ballet opened at the tomb of Eurydice, an exquisite scene of typically Fedorovitch economy: white plinth behind which Orpheus, a black mourning sash across the breast of a white sleeveless tunic, stood in grief in front of a higher pedestal on which the black-veiled figure of Love was raised. They were framed in stage-high black funereal tasselled drapes and round them mourning women appeared in poses of resignation and despair.

Love broke into Orpheus' sadness to tell him—Fonteyn and Helpmann in andante *pas de deux*—of the conditions under which he could recover his lost wife. Carrying his lyre, Orpheus danced alone before seeking out the Furies, who tested his love in menacing barefoot ensembles before softening to the sound of his music and directing him to the Elysian fields where Eurydice waited. There the spirits of the blessed surrounded Eurydice—May in ankle-length pale lime yellow draperies—before Love joined the lovers' hands while Orpheus resolutely averted his gaze from Eurydice. They returned to earth where a peasant girl and boy surrounded by young women and children in happy rural dances reminded them of human joy. Eurydice pleaded with Orpheus to look at her, weakened his resolve and was reclaimed by the Furies, leaving him desolate.

Orpheus and Eurydice was not a strikingly popular ballet but it was an acutely sensitive and visually delectable one. As Joan Lawson has pointed out, de Valois cunningly balanced narrative and descriptive passages—using musically guided mime from the dancers to accompany the words of the singers' recitatives and a variety of dancing elsewhere. As always, she blended classical ballet, folk elements, expressionist dance and *demi-caractère* dance so naturally that there was no sense of patchwork, merely of charming contrast. Joan Lawson also mentions how de Valois

> "captured not only the outer significance of the words but also their inner tenor, which she interpreted by deeply felt acting in dances which possessed the rhythm and melody of the poem".[10]

The production had the usual handsome photographic spreads in *The Tatler* and *The Sketch* and towards the end of June the BBC put out an ambitious radio programme, produced by Stephen Potter, which they called "Ballet First Night". This was a reconstruction of the production of *Orpheus*

> "in London in wartime, followed from its first conception, through the stages of discussion and rehearsal, ending with the opening bars of the overture on the first night".[11]

They recorded contributions from Lambert as musical director, de

Valois as choreographer and Helpmann as principal dancer, and reproduced one of her drawings in a back-up article in *The Listener*.[12]

De Valois now pressed for the return of the orchestra, and achieving this restored the long classics to the repertoire. Modifications were made to tailor them to the smaller stage and to the constantly altering and depleted company but no compromises of this kind affected the overall integrity of the performance. They remained true to the essential character of the ballets in a way that many full-scale, high-powered recensions staged by international companies in postwar years have failed to be.

From a viewer's point of view the comparison between then and now is full of interest. Stage spectacle and the spread of a large *corps de ballet* (in *The Sleeping Beauty* or *Le Lac des cygnes*) were of course non-existent. Certain items were cut and ensembles reduced in numbers, but the dramatic and emotional elements emerged strongly, enhanced by the quality of interpretation, the taut and sensitive conducting by Lambert and the ambience of the various theatres in which they were performed. The audience, because it contained a majority of responsive and knowledgeable balletgoers, contributed to the total impact.

The peripatetic company was shuttling backwards and forwards, up and down the map of Great Britain, pausing in weekly or two-weekly engagements at towns and cities, playing ENSA camps to "entertain the Forces", notching up escapes from air raids in Plymouth, Exeter or Bath. De Valois writes of a night in Birmingham:

> "On that very night Birmingham received one of its biggest raids. My hotel was opposite the Wren cathedral. Incendiaries hit the flat roof of the cathedral and, burning through, fell with a shower of sparks into the body of the church, while the church windows, lit by the inferno within, looked like illuminated Christmas cards. In the background (on the other side of the square) a huge warehouse, blazing its life out, silhouetted the outline of the church. Still the beautiful tower rose majestically to the skies—unscathed. Patiently, amid the rain of bombs, flashing incendiaries, fierce fires and crashing masonry, the tower clock struck each quarter, each half and each hour throughout the night ... "

Again, the company were in Bath during that city's ordeal. De Valois decided to join them:

"When we got to Bath the city looked like a cracked bowl; along the streets were queues of people, many still in their night attire, waiting for transport to take them to relief centres. Mobile breakfast vans trundled about, feeding them; there was water and smoke everywhere, and widespread damage."

Memories like these are common to all of us who lived through World War II, especially those whose homes were in London. For de Valois, the effect on her dancers mattered most. They were her children, her constant care. She recalls how they were suffering from loss of sleep, from lack of proper nourishment. "It was taking toll of everyone's reserves and even the reserves of youth were fully taxed."[13] Talking later to women's clubs in Canada, she paid special tribute to her young wartime dancers' parents:

"During the long years of war we never received one letter from a parent saying that the dangers were too great and that they would withdraw their children."[14]

For herself, she was now forty-four, and had to register for call-up. She told the woman who interviewed her that not only was she director of Sadler's Wells Ballet but married to a busy general practitioner, and that she had to stand in at weekends for work connected with his surgery. She was asked whether she had family and when she answered no, was told that she came into the category of those with no responsibilities ... However she heard no more from the authorities and "was left to continue my carefree existence".[15]

Chapter IX

೨೧ Sadler's Wells Ballet, with a rapidly growing public and reputation, was now facing problems about new repertoire. Ashton was called up in August 1941 and went into the RAF and de Valois had no time, and perhaps little inclination, to continue choreography. The decision to allow Helpmann to try his hand at a ballet was something of a gamble, but a gamble with a good deal of sound reasoning behind it. His experience of dance creation was minimal. There had been one or two short pieces in Australia and a work that he had only partly choreographed for the RAD Production Club. Inventing sparkling and virtuoso dance sequences however is only one element in the choreographer's art, especially where dramatic and literary ballet is concerned. Helpmann understood all about expressive dance movement, he had a wide and thoroughly professional grasp of theatre production and construction and he also knew the company's dancers well and could gauge their ability and potential. Added to this he had built up by his performances as dancer and actor an enthusiastic body of public support.

De Valois agreed that he should be given the chance of staging a ballet at the New Theatre in January 1942. Lambert, for whom Helpmann had a high regard as a cultural mentor, suggested arranging a Purcell score for a ballet on *Comus*. Oliver Messel, a perfect choice, was commissioned to design. The result was a ravishingly harmonious production, as appropriate in its relation to period style as could have been wished. The narrative was carried forward with clarity, the dances were delightfully contrasted and the dramatic colour was ably controlled.

Helpmann in fact proved to be a choreographer very much in de Valois' own literary school. They had always had points in common as artists. He not only shared her love of drama and character but her

231

strong appreciation and understanding of painting and sculpture. They were both very much people of the general theatre as much as of their own particular branch of it, yet both were deeply devoted to classical ballet in all its aspects. They shared a tremendous relish, and a special gift, for comedy. As performers they were elegant and sophisticated in approach and in physical movement. They were mentally quick and instantly receptive.

Comus was a success and it was followed in May by a masterpiece— *Hamlet*, to the Tchaikovsky fantasy overture, with sets and costumes by Leslie Hurry, a newcomer to theatre design. The performances Helpmann elicited from the company were of the highest interpretative order and their capacity for dance acting had of course been encouraged and honed in the de Valois' repertoire, as had his own.

By the end of the year, possibly as a result of the continued pleasure audiences had shown in *Comus* and *Hamlet*, de Valois had re-staged *The Rake's Progress*, which was greatly welcomed, and early in 1943 *Job* was also restored to the bills.

Any study of de Valois' work and influence is insufficient if it does not touch on Helpmann's choreography and make some effort to show critical justice to it. His choreographic skills have been denigrated by critics to a point where a good many minor ballet creators stand above him in the records. He has not been fairly assessed in an historical context and it is valid to recall de Valois' 1946 estimate of him as a choreographer, and to point out that she was not alone in her opinion:

> "He is not concerned with choreography for choreography's sake nor is he concerned with the development or expansion of the executant in this medium ... but along his self-imposed lines he is busy proving himself to be complete, and a modern choreographer of importance. He says all in direct terms of the theatre, a theatre seen fearlessly and aggressively through the eyes of a young man of the 20th century ... All spells vitality harnessed to controversy—yet he cannot help showing his knowledge of the very tradition that he had temporarily discarded. He fuses and drives home his production with a severe theatrical discipline ... "

In conversation and in retrospect de Valois also stresses the importance of Helpmann's wartime ballets, especially *Hamlet*, in securing respect for the art of ballet within the "straight" theatre. As she put it in 1946:

> "*Hamlet* ... is an example of a masterly and subtle control of most of the crafts of the theatre. Lewis Casson stated to me that its influence

might well be felt in every future production of *Hamlet* the play. It was the dramatic world of the theatre that upheld the importance of this dramatic ballet. The ballet world remained in the rear to bestow a guarded opinion, or to show open hostility ... but their judgment was at fault if they imagined that, by failing to qualify as a ballet in their narrow sense of the word, this work was not contributing anything to our honour in the theatre generally."[1]

There was great truth in this assessment although ballet audiences, as opposed to critics, were swift to respond to *Hamlet* and to *Miracle in the Gorbals*.

That Helpmann was deeply imbued with the same principles that had always guided de Valois was obvious, but he made a public declaration of them in a talk to the Royal Academy of Dancing in July 1942 in words that she herself might have used:

"Ballet is essentially a theatrical art; its function is in the theatre, so that its appeal must be theatrical, and therefore to me, and I am quite sure to many other choreographers, the first and foremost thing is to appeal to the theatre-going public and not to a specialised few ... and I feel quite convinced that if the ballet is to take its place in the public's heart beside the cinema and the other forms of theatre in this modern age of action, its appeal must be theatrical as well as purely technical."[2]

By the end of 1942 Sadler's Wells Ballet was almost a household word around Great Britain. Audiences had increased and press coverage everywhere publicised the repertoire and dancers. Regular references and talks on radio and excellent picture spreads in the glossy magazines made news of everything they did. They captured the imagination of a public glad to set the excitement and glamour of classical ballet against the miseries of wartime life, and their work in morale-raising was recognised by government as being valuable to the war effort. De Valois and Lambert were widely known as artistic and musical directors, Fonteyn, Pamela May and Mary Honer were all admired—the partnership of Fonteyn and Helpmann in the traditional ballets was immensely popular—and the emergence of the teenage Beryl Grey was of special interest. Helpmann was "front man" in everything concerning the company's relationship with its public—the choreographer in the news, controversial and admired in equal proportions, the performer whose magnetism brought people into performances, the personality who represented British ballet in the wider context of the theatre through his protean ability to appear successfully in all forms of dramatic entertainment while remaining a principal dancer capable of tackling classical or character roles.

May and Honer however were casualties in 1942. May fell on stage in October 1941 while dancing the Lilac Fairy and could not return for over a year. Honer had a spell of ill health (partly due to her presence in the Café de Paris when it was bombed) and then left the company in November 1942. Fonteyn had to undertake a heavy work load and seemed to thrive on it, but de Valois was forced to bring forward young talent among the girls as well as the boys. Boys was a correct word in this context, as she was very dependent on the two years from sixteen to eighteen which were all they could give ballet before being called up.

John Hart was allowed to stay until he was twenty-one and gave very creditable performances in leading roles. His going left Rassine and Paltenghi as leading dancers (with Helpmann) and partners to Beryl Grey, now the only alternative to Fonteyn in *Lac* or *Giselle*. In the modern repertoire Celia Franca, Moyra Fraser, Moira Shearer, Margaret Dale and Pauline Clayden took their chances with tremendous flair.

De Valois was always reaching out to a wider public and new opportunities. In August 1942, for instance, the company appeared for a week by arrangement with the London County Council at the Open Air Theatre in Victoria Park, Bethnal Green. This was part of a "holidays at home" campaign and coincided with the traditional August Bank Holiday. The stage of the bandstand was covered but the orchestra area was not, and once or twice performances were cancelled or delayed because of the effect rain would have on musical instruments. As the LCC handout put it:

> "The presentation of open-air ballet will involve something in the nature of a gamble with the weather but the LCC is confident that if the elements are kind Londoners will give an enthusiastic response."[3]

Londoners did. It proved a happy environment where people crowded onto hard iron chairs (over two thousand of them) or stood around the periphery of the paying enclosure to watch *Les Sylphides*, *Gods* and *Façade*. In spite of an incidence of faithful balletgoers from other areas the majority there were East End families quite unfamiliar with ballet as an art.

De Valois' responsibilities for the company were great but she also had the school to consider. It was back at Sadler's Wells with Ailne Phillips in charge and de Valois and Sergeyev teaching regularly. In addition, in 1943 she brought in Andree Howard, a choreographer from Ballet Rambert whose work she always admired, as choreographer to the School—a new appointment and an unusual one, but very much in keeping with her insistence from the earliest days of the Academy on the importance of students learning basic dance composition and with her RAD project for a Choreographic Scholarship. Andree Howard's work with the students was seen in performances presented by the RAD Production Club.

Productions for 1943 were widely varied. The previous year had been very much angled to literary-dramatic ballet, and immensely successful, with three new works by Helpmann (the third, in November, was *The Birds*, a light classical and *demi-caractère* comedy tailored to specific talents in the younger dancers) and the major revival of *The Rake's Progress*. Now Ashton was available on leave to mount a new ballet and perhaps mistakenly it was decided that this too should be literary—*The Quest*, taken from Spenser's *The Faerie Queene*, with a specially composed score by William Walton and excellent if somewhat formalised designs by John Piper. A charming revival of *A Wedding Bouquet* followed but the main efforts of de Valois and the company were devoted to a fine new production of *Le Lac des cygnes*, the first, and supreme, example of Leslie Hurry's designs for this ballet. Staged in early September, it was a brilliant and exciting event.

The production continued to be based on that of Sergeyev and for this, his last association with the company and school, the opening performance was given the ancient title of a Benefit for him. In Act III the czardas and Spanish dance were restored—the latter in an attractive arrangement for two women composed by de Valois who controlled the overall production. According to Hurry, she also "imposed a stern discipline" on his marvellously turbulent imagination. "An incredibly brilliant woman—sympathetic, understanding, marvellous to work with."[4]

She was choreographing a new ballet divertissement herself. This time a longstanding and admired friend, Edwin Evans, co-opted towards the end of 1942 as musical adviser to the company, selected what he termed "a short stroll through the works of Haydn" (symphonies and sonatas)[5] for a set of dances in a delightful First Empire setting by Hugh Stevenson. *Promenade* had an out-of-town premiere at the King's Theatre Edinburgh, in October 1943 and *The Scotsman* critic summarised it with perception:

> "[it is] marked by a vivacity and gracefulness, both in the music and in the movements, with a touch of drollery and slightly burlesque characterisation which is typically French. The Lepidopterist, the part danced by Gordon Hamilton, with its entrances and movements, forms a kind of refrain and is a link between the items. The antics of this figure, with his book of references and his net, carry also a suggestion of the gaudy butterfly-like character of the figures surrounding him and impart some degree of cohesion and unity."[6]

In *Promenade* de Valois took a number of classic ballet divertissement elements, gave them fresh and elegant life and fused them into an evocative pictorial composition. The scene was a park in Napoleonic Paris. Half a dozen very young ladies with their fussy schoolmistress composed the Entree, giggling a little at the languorous and modish quartet, three over-dressed women and a male escort, of Les Merveilleuses. A pair of lovers (Grey and Paltenghi) held a touching and romantic secret rendezvous. A thin pert girl (Clayden) careered her way through an allegro solo (Promenade), eagerly grasping at life. A charmingly feminine teaser (Shearer) with her lighthearted boy friend (Rassine) made game of an older admirer (Ray Powell). Finally, a jolly group of Breton peasants, men and women, invaded the city scene with bucolic high spirits. For this de Valois acknowledged a special collaboration with Lieut J. de Cadenet who taught her steps and figurations of Breton folkdances. Through the whole ballet the eccentric little Lepidopterist acted as a connecting thread. Her cast was ideal and she used their skills and personalities in apt choreography. The role that at one time she would have danced was the Promenade solo, with its speed, sharpness and vivacity. There were parallels in construction between the Promenade girl and Papillon, as between the *pas de trois* and that of Columbine, Harlequin and Pantalon in *Carnaval*. They were *parallels*, however, and never references or echoes. Again, as in *Gods,* a small cast was used to imply a far wider scene, the microcosm of an entire society.

Promenade was a masterly example of its genre, and it was sad that its life was so short. It was quite properly handed over to Sadler's Wells Theatre Ballet in 1946 but only survived a year with them. It would adorn the classical repertoire of any small ballet company—but it would also test their ability to deal with delicately stylish comedy and lyricism.

Promenade *(Sadler's Wells Ballet 1943) Moira Shearer, Alexis Rassine, Gordon Hamilton and Ray Powell*

Emphasising de Valois' choreographic range, *Job* was splendidly restored to the company in a moving and powerful production in December 1943. The depth, sensitivity and excitement of the performance were total. Very probably these were the peak interpretations of its existence, given by dancers so superbly tuned to the literary-dramatic style that they even built up, from evening to evening, on an already exceptional standard. Their unification as a team, their knowledge of the works, their general ability as actor-dancers, were all enhanced by the country-wide mood of living in danger, living for the moment, as life itself was constantly under threat.

The first months of 1944 were not particularly fruitful. A revival of *Le Spectre de la rose* for Fonteyn and Rassine, exquisitely designed by Rex Whistler, made little impact—although looked at in retrospect, after many unsatisfactory later productions by a variety of companies, it was a staging of distinction. A new ballet, *Le Festin de l'araignée*, was definitely unpopular. Again, hindsight helps—it was a finely unified piece, with choreography by Andree Howard, strong and sinister designs by Michael Ayrton and of course the Roussel score, a far better work than many additions to the repertoire over the years. But it was unsuited to the mood of the time, too slow, formalised and depressing for a war-tired public who were facing the new menace of V1 flying bombs.

Le Festin de l'araignée was given its premiere at the New Theatre in June, the last new ballet to be staged at that theatre. An unexpected final visit there came in the following April, but meanwhile they had a season at another, and equally attractive, West End theatre, the Prince's—now the Shaftesbury—in the autumn.

The Prince's Theatre, at which Sadler's Wells Opera had been appearing, had a larger stage and greater audience capacity than the New. The stage was fearsomely raked, but the dancers adapted well to it. It was a season of hope and pleasures—public spirit was raised by the war's turning tide and the anticipation of peace, even though London was assailed by V2 rockets. Fine revivals were staged of *Carnaval*, danced with great polish and loving care, and Ashton's *Nocturne*. The rest of the repertoire looked well, and there was a stimulating new Helpmann work, *Miracle in the Gorbals*—an admirable dramatic ballet with enough controversial content to make it a challenge and a talking point.

The opening up of Europe by the invading D-Day armies also meant that in 1945 ENSA and the British Council implemented plans to take entertainment and British cultural activities onto the Continent. Sadler's Wells Ballet, universally costumed by the authorities in ENSA uniform, were allotted a tour of Belgium and France, partly appearing to troops and partly to civilian audiences, at the end of January.

It was a grim, cold winter and everywhere shortages of heating and lighting accompanied snowy conditions. The company opened for ENSA at the Brussels Théâtre des Variétés on January 29. De Valois recorded "four inches of snow on the ground, no electric light from 7 a.m. to 6 p.m., no heating and no hot water at any time".[7] Thaw, and the arrival of some coal, helped, but a 'flu epidemic set in. They accomplished their schedules triumphantly however, appearing also for galas at the Théâtre de la Monnaie to civilian audiences. They then embarked on a fifteen-hour train journey from Brussels to Paris.

They were in Paris a month, performing at the Marigny Theatre for ENSA and the Théâtre des Champs-Elysées for civilians with a few performances at Versailles. After Paris they gave five performances in Ghent and visited Bruges and Ostend.

For de Valois, the Paris weeks were a return to the international cultural world of Europe which she had known and relished in pre-war days. The dance profession is a vast international family, forever pooling knowledge and ideas, exchanging personnel, forging contacts and human relationships without any national or racial barriers. Britain had been a beleaguered and confined territory for some years, and de Valois was eager to move outside it, to introduce her young company to new environments and to benefit herself from the stimulus of other attitudes. In Paris she had fruitful meetings with French musicians and designers, choreographers, directors, dancers and teachers, and the happiness of finding that they were enthusiastic about what she and her dancers had achieved in isolation.

Their Forces audiences were a mixture. Some had seen the company in Britain when on leave or in ENSA theatres, become staunch supporters and were renewing a fond friendship. For others it was a new experience, and de Valois began giving an explanatory talk from the stage about each ballet before it was danced—a very popular action. The press in each city provided fascinating evidence of Continental reaction to the British company.

They were impressed. In Brussels, *L'Eventail* described them:

"Independamment de leur technique, ce qui distingue ces artistes c'est leur remarquable souplesse mimique, leur art tres poussé d'expression, tant au point de vue dramatique qu'au point de vue comique, suivant les nécessités du scénario."[8]

Louis Piérard found them:

"de premier ordre, d'une homogénéité parfaite ... tous ses spectacles ont été mis au point avec intelligence, avec une rare ferveur et une patience scrupuleuse."[9]

The critic of *La Dernière Heure*, after writing of "des ballets composés avec art, habillés, décorés et éclairés avec gout" made interesting points about *Rake* and *Hamlet*—"deux remarquables ballets". In *Rake*, de Valois "fait preuve de dons d'observations inouïs, car le caractère de chaque personnage y est rendu avec une vérité hallucinante"; in *Hamlet*, Helpmann "nous montrent à quel point cet art est expressif et capable de traduire les nuances psychologiques les plus subtiles".

"De tout cela, il ne faudrait pas conclure qui'l s'agit de sortes de mimodrames. La danse n'y perd jamais des droits, et la virtuosité, le style des danseurs et des danseuses mériteraient de longs commentaires."[10]

In Paris there was also appreciation. Henri Sauguet was loyal to the high standards of the Paris Opera dancers but reflected that:

"on ne trouve pas en elle cette soumission a l'esthétique générale et cet élan collectif qui fait la vie, l'intérêt et la classe d'une compagnie de ballets dont celle de Serge de Diaghilev donna le haut exemple et que l'on trouve chez les Sadler's Wells."[11]

An ambitious plan made by the British Council to arrange a South American tour for the company in the summer of 1945 failed to be implemented. There were practical difficulties, and the particular diplomatic need for a cultural contact disappeared when first the war in Europe and later the war in the Pacific came to an end. A short, stopgap season at the New Theatre ensured that the company were able to celebrate VE day with their faithful London audience in a very merry performance of *Coppélia*, and then they returned to Sadler's Wells, old and cherished home, for a summer season from July 24.

Change was in the air and would come very rapidly. One last undertaking seemed to belong to a closing era—after the usual provincial tour they again went abroad, this time to Germany. From November 10 1945, they spent two weeks in Hamburg and two in Berlin, grim assignments in a conquered and occupied country. From the moment of their return, all energies were directed to the future.

Chapter X

∂∿ The future had been envisaged by de Valois for some years. Significantly, in April 1943 Eveleigh Leith contributed a forward-looking article, "Towards a National Ballet", to *The Dancing Times*.

The Hon. Eveleigh Leith, as well as being wartime acting press representative for the company, was honorary secretary of the Executive Committee of the Vic-Wells Ballet Fund. This started early in 1936 when de Valois worked out the Five-Year Plan with Arnold Haskell and was of immense value to the organisation. It is fair to assume that the views and suggestions Eveleigh Leith set out in 1943 reflected the thinking of the Committee of which de Valois was a member.

Eveleigh Leith began by putting the case for Sadler's Wells Ballet to become "the National Ballet". In terms of size, range and popularity it had no competitors. Ballet Rambert's unique place was as a chamber ballet company and nursery for choreographic and dancing talent. Mona Inglesby's International Ballet, a recent establishment, would not have been seriously regarded for national status in opposition to the Wells. However, the arguments Miss Leith assembled were convincing: the level of production, the nationwide public, the standards of dancing, the existing school. She then considered future possibilities. It was mistaken to think that the company as it stood could retreat to the pre-war status at Sadler's Wells Theatre. "Can the young bird which has grown its wings and flown away be made to return to the nest?" After the war (and this profession of faith in a victorious end to the war sounds particularly characteristic of de Valois' philosophy) they must continue to progress. They should be seen "in the heart of London". The Ballet School should be enlarged, with a wide curriculum, while a second homegrown company should be formed at Sadler's Wells.

Overseas audiences must be looked for—again, the sentiments sound very much the kind de Valois must have voiced at meetings: "From a world tour the company might return chastened or justifiably proud; they would certainly not bring complacency or stagnation back with them".[1]

Complacency was totally foreign to de Valois' character. Each achievement was the stepping-stone to another. Self-congratulation is an activity in which she has never indulged.

This article by Eveleigh Leith makes it very clear how far ahead de Valois and her administrative colleagues began thinking towards the status the company eventually achieved in February 1946 of being the resident ballet company at the newly reopened Royal Opera House in Covent Garden. An immense amount of work went on behind the scenes during the period between April 1943 and November 1945 when the announcement was officially made that the Wells would operate under the Covent Garden Committee from January 1 1946.[2]

The arrangement was for an initial period of four years. The School was to continue and expand, and a second company was to be based on Sadler's Wells. There had naturally been a certain amount of doubt and opposition within the ranks of the Governors of Sadler's Wells. Some wanted the ballet to stay in Islington, some wanted them to go to Covent Garden only if the Opera Company went with them. De Valois herself was hesitant, conscious of great loyalty to the Wells and wary of the possible complete dominance of opera at Covent Garden. Additionally, never publicised at the time, was the fact that the then manager of Sadler's Wells had told her that he was trying to get the company to Drury Lane. In the end, it was Ashton who persuaded her to accept the change to the Royal Opera House—and it was a major decision:

> "It meant . . . that the fundamental conception, in every direction, would necessarily be on a scale as yet never contemplated. I visualised the possibility of a sudden weakening—a position akin to that of an army, its lines stretched to a point where a breakthrough could be effected almost anywhere."

From the time of the final agreement she had less than six months to plan the enormous adventure:

> "It could be likened to a crazy nightmare, wherein I might be given Buckingham Palace, a few dusters, and told to get on with the spring cleaning."[3]

It is not every founder of a small organisation who can cope with growth, enlargement, honours and importance. It is a measure of de Valois' greatness that she adapted to, and dominated, the enlarged post-war world into which her company moved with as firm, courageous and visionary strength as she had displayed in the earlier years. She was able to relate to high level establishment circles, national and international, without ever ceasing to be first and foremost a creative artist dedicated to the theatre. At every level and in every capital city she enhanced her company's reputation by her own behaviour and ability. A natural leader who instinctively took command of every situation, she never accepted sole credit for success.

Her life must suddenly have seemed filled by committees. There had always been a good many—those of the Vic-Wells theatres and the outside ones like the Camargo Society and the various teaching organisations. Now she added the Covent Garden Opera Trust and the Arts Council. For a few months until his death these were both chaired by an old friend, Lord Keynes. He was succeeded on the Covent Garden Opera Trust by Sir John Anderson (Lord Waverley) as Chairman. David Webster, who during the war had been Chairman of the Liverpool Philharmonic Orchestra, was General Administrator.

The task of transplanting Sadler's Wells Ballet to Covent Garden and mounting the historic production of *The Sleeping Beauty* with which they reopened the great theatre on February 20 1946 was immense, and its success the result of magnificent individual contributions from many people. Their work had to be coordinated however, to be provided with a focal point and a guiding force, and this, as always, was de Valois' function.

Once, Huw Wheldon, interviewing her on BBC's Monitor programme, asked, had she always seen herself as a choreographer or producer more than as a dancer? and she replied Yes. Even when, as children, she and her family and friends had acted plays, she had tended to leave herself out of the distribution of roles because she felt that "someone must take control". She had "an ambition to be responsible for the whole".[4] It was her usual, and preferred, position . . .

Again as always, her sensitivity to human detail becomes apparent. Returning to the opera house she had known as *première danseuse* twice in the past, where she had stood, high up in the flies, with a young singer, Eva Turner, to watch performances by Melba and look over the glittering social glory of a 1919 Royal Gala performance, she was acutely aware of every element of its life as performers and even artistic directors rarely are. She was conscious of the efforts that had to be made by cleaners and decorators to restore the whole house to peacetime beauty; of the firemen hunting rats in the bowels of the building; of the machinists and the safety regulations from the London County Council that had to be adhered to; of the practical work going on in wardrobe and wigroom, in props and armoury; of the life and character of the stage door keeper . . . A topflight general, she delegated well; and once a week she met the heads of departments to deal with their problems and offer practical solutions. No smallest task confronting the theatre as well as her company was uninteresting or unimportant to her and yet she maintained the clear concept of the ultimate end, the performance which her dancers would present to their public.

She was also in charge of the new production. It was completely based on the one they had danced since 1939 but with details of difference. Ashton, returned to full strength with the company as principal choreographer and beginning the brilliant post-war career that would carry him to every conceivable height, contributed some new arrangements—the Florestan *pas de trois* to replace the Jewel Fairies in the last act and a new Garland Dance in the birthday scene. De Valois added a version of the Three Ivans.

Much as the Covent Garden company needed her, she was also essential to the new Sadler's Wells Opera (later Theatre) Ballet which made its debut at Sadler's Wells in April 1946. She was their overall artistic director too, although she appointed Ursula Moreton as her assistant director and Peggy van Praagh as ballet mistress and could trust them implicitly. Policy decisions however were hers and typically she did not make policy decisions without personal knowledge of the company, its personnel and affairs.

Overshadowed to some extent from the beginning, Sadler's Wells Theatre Ballet was in fact to prove the hidden strength of her two organisations. From this smaller group came an army of dance talent as well as two major choreographers, Kenneth MacMillan and John Cranko. Lovingly cared for by van Praagh, who became its artistic director in 1951 and to whom de Valois attributes its great success, it was the essential complement to the Covent Garden company. It was a source of directorial ability as well. It produced a splendid artistic director for its later self in Peter Wright and provided Australia with Peggy van Praagh, Canada with Celia Franca, as well as fostering an important set of South African artists who returned home to direct and teach. All this was in the future. In 1946 it was enough to launch the company, using an assortment of choreographers and a mixture of experienced and inexperienced dancers.

The isolation of wartime had made de Valois very conscious of the wide balletic world outside Britain. She followed up the 1945 tours of Belgium, France, Holland and Germany by cementing contacts between herself and directors, choreographers and dancers all over the world. Much had changed, and she was excited by news of new ideas, productions and trends. Already London had seen the fresh and imaginative work of Roland Petit's Ballets des Champs-Elysées.

In September 1946 the Wells appeared in Vienna, another British Council project. By now de Valois was used to the routines in which she played her part:

"An unrelenting Council representative presents me with a timetable that leaves not one spare minute for the next 48 hours. Lecture, broadcast, press conference and private interviews with various representatives of the theatre and musical world ... "

She was also used to the slow start in audience attendance with appreciation accelerating to enthusiasm and a demand for an extension or a return visit. But also, wherever she went, she was deeply interested in local conditions quite apart from local theatrical activity.

Vienna was a city "starved of ballet founded on the classical tradition". What they felt there, however, was that the Sadler's Wells Ballet was "a complete theatre movement" comparable in some views to an experience of the Stanislavsky Theatre. They were impressed by the company's unity and precision and also by finding that this team image did not exclude the presence of star performers. The company appeared at the Volksoper as the Opera House was still out of commission. De Valois watched local private recitals and classroom work, noting that the prevailing style was pre-war Central European rather than classical. The visit by the Wells helped greatly towards a renaissance of classical ballet.[5]

A year later a considerably more ambitious tour was arranged. They went by way of Brussels to Prague, Warsaw, Poznan, Oslo and Malmo—an itinerary that renewed and initiated contacts in her own profession and made her ever more keenly aware of the social conditions and context in which fellow artists had to work. It was a journey of dismay over ruins and destruction, and admiration over the human courage and hope that was everywhere in evidence.

In Warsaw Woizikovsky was there to greet her and recall not only memories of Diaghilev but of the Massine-Lopokova days in England. The city was devastated, and she was shocked to find seven or eight people living in one unlit and unheated room. Prague was entirely different, cheerful and more prosperous. There were Embassy parties as well as sessions with another friend, Sasha Machov, ballet master of the Prague National Theatre, who showed off his company in a divertissement of Czech and Slovak national dances—something very much to her taste. Impressive indeed to anyone totally committed to the theatre was Eastern Europe's dedication to the performing arts. Buildings were rapidly being restored and equipped so that the public should not be deprived of something that was considered vital to their mental wellbeing.

In the beginning of 1947 de Valois implemented a long-standing desire by inviting Leonide Massine to stage revivals and new ballets for her company at Covent Garden. Through the twenties and thirties Massine's reputation had been of the highest. His great *demi-caractère* ballets for Diaghilev, followed by the controversial, exciting and at the time adventurous symphonic ballets for the de Basil Ballet, combined with his total charisma as a performer, established him as an accepted leader among choreographers. In 1937 de Valois summarised her feeling about this man with whom she had worked:

> "Dynamic still in achievement and experiment, his mind has the characteristic architectural tendency of today. But to the writer this man spells the word genius, not the genius of fiction but the genius of fact; that infinite capacity for taking pains, power of analysis and concentration, and, further, imagination and judgment as opposed to originality and flair."

Her admiration was more for the older, Diaghilev, works than those of the de Basil "symphonic" era.

> "These earlier works, in relation to music and the ballet, showed, apart from composition, unquestionable knowledge of what was suitable and what was best left alone. Diaghilev was wise enough to see that his choreographers had compositions enabling them to evolve a choreography which expressed a musical understanding of both the period and mood of the work concerned."[6]

NdV with Frederick Ashton and Leonide Massine 1948

For her own company in 1947 she asked Massine to begin by reviving for them *La Boutique fantasque* and *Le Tricorne*.

Massine's career had undergone some vicissitudes during World War II. He had gone to America like so many other Russian (and non-Russian) artists of the ballet and stayed with the Ballet Russe de Monte Carlo for three years. He then choreographed for other companies. A good many of his productions were successful, but by no means all, and with the growth of American companies and a mounting tendency towards chauvinism in public response his status was definitely declining by the time he came back to Europe in 1946. A stage production in England of *A Bullet in the Ballet* did nothing to improve matters, so from his point of view the invitation from Sadler's Wells Ballet was immensely valuable.

Le Tricorne was the first production, in February 1947, and in this Fonteyn was cast, slightly against the grain, as the Miller's Wife to Massine's Miller. She had widened her range to dance Swanilda in *Coppélia* with great success, and if she could not challenge memories of great previous exponents in *Tricorne* it was still a performance of great grace and style, well worth seeing. The company responded as de Valois hoped to a challenge of a kind they had not faced before. *Boutique* followed and proved less effective. Massine's own ability to portray the Can-Can Dancer was, at fifty-one, naturally lessened and Moira Shearer, technically able to cope with the role of his partner, lacked the sparkling wit or ebullient charm of the great Russian interpreters. Three more ballets emerged from the Massine period— *Mam'zelle Angot*, in which a brilliant opening scene tailed off sadly as the action continued; *Donald of the Burthens*, a rather too serious attempt to do for Scotland what he had done for Spain in *Tricorne*; and *Clock Symphony* which was universally deplored. De Valois' hopes for Massine's influence on her company were in the main defeated but it extended their performing experience and gave new audiences some idea of two great Diaghilev ballets.

Ashton was now the dominant choreographic name at Covent Garden, a place of eminence sealed by the serene and limpid *Symphonic Variations*, the stylish and astringent *Scènes de ballet*, and the full evening *Cinderella*, the first new three-acter in the company's history. Helpmann gambled everything on the theatrically ambitious *Adam Zero*, unwisely keeping to an announced deadline in spite of an illness and operation. Not surprisingly, in these circumstances, in spite of exciting and intensely lyrical sections, this was too uneven and symbolically confused a ballet to establish itself with the critics. For the time being de Valois herself had no new choreography in prospect.

Her choreographic policy at Covent Garden over the next five years was interesting. She went back to another youthful admiration in acquiring for the company Balanchine's *Ballet Imperial*; she implemented her faith in Andree Howard by commissioning *A Mirror for Witches*; she affirmed her pleasure in the Ballets des Champs-Elysées by asking Roland Petit to choreograph *Ballabile*; and she brought John Cranko in to stage *Bonne-Bouche*. None of these were unqualified successes except for *Ballet Imperial*, but all were interesting and worth while. At Sadler's Wells new choreographers were as much a part of the picture as new dancers. It is frequently forgotten just how many choreographers were tried out there apart from Cranko and MacMillan, but numerous ballets were staged in the early years by Celia Franca, Anthony Burke, Alan Carter, and Alfred Rodrigues, among others.

Chapter XI

October 1947 saw the opening by de Valois of the new Sadler's Wells Ballet School in Colet Gardens. For the second time she was making a scholastic beginning. Just as she had closed the Academy of Choregraphic Art in 1930 to transfer and reopen at Sadler's Wells Theatre, so now a greatly enlarged, potentially comprehensive school was created to succeed the Sadler's Wells one. She knew exactly what she wanted, but as always she pursued her aim in a practical and unhurried manner. For the first year only girls were given a fully educational course (under the principalship of Arnold Haskell) and it was not until 1951 that the school was recognised by the Ministry of Education as meeting their standards for primary and secondary education. Finally in 1955 the Junior School was opened at White Lodge, Richmond—a boarding as well as day school.

Characteristically, in September 1947 de Valois started, not with a regular term for students, but with a special course for teachers and their assistants on "The Constructive Teaching of Ballet". It was the beginning of regular annual seminars for teachers which established her as an international force in the teaching of classical ballet and an influence that extended far beyond her own companies and country.

Her life now began to resemble that peripatetic period when she was commuting between London, Cambridge and Dublin. She was constantly on the move between her company at Covent Garden, her company at Sadler's Wells, the Sadler's Wells Ballet School and various sallies abroad, quite apart from her continuing home commitments to her husband's medical practice. She gained something of a reputation for occasional absent-mindedness or for forgetting people's names— hardly surprising, considering the countless people who now featured in her daily life or the concentration she had to give to so many important issues. Her comments on every situation were disregarded only by the foolish or self-important. Arnold Haskell describes her presence at the weekly grind of Saturday auditions at the Sadler's Wells Ballet School, when she might cut through a unanimous no from the judges by saying, "She's Irish, I know the type, there's something there. *I* would never have been taken at this audition": the kind of flash judgment that in her case is so often accurate but always disturbing to more cautious temperaments. Haskell goes on:

> "Disagreement with Ninette was never personal. She thoroughly enjoyed a good argument and was so quick in her reactions that she often left one breathless in sorting out the hunches from the logic, and the hunches I came to call 'Irish logic'."[1]

She could usually find good reasons to back her instinct. Like Shaw's Saint Joan, the voices came first; then she found the logic to convince other people that their advice was good.

A major step for the company now demanded her time and attention—their first transatlantic journey. Sol Hurok, the great impresario, began discussing the possibility of Sadler's Wells Ballet appearing in New York almost as soon as they went to Covent Garden in 1946 and after some false starts the negotiations were concluded for them to open at the old Metropolitan Opera House on October 9 1949.

Two accounts, by de Valois and Hurok, have been published about their first meeting at the Savoy Hotel in London in April 1946. Hurok says it was at supper, de Valois that it was at lunch. De Valois writes:

> "I do not think that we made any great impression on each other. Sol was, understandably, cautious with all ballet directors and managements, and perhaps I was even more cautious with impresarios ... he informed me that Sadler's Wells had a queer sort of idealism about it— and then left his statement unqualified. Neither the tone of his voice nor his expression suggested that he had knocked up against anything in the way of a revelation ... "[2]

Hurok saw it all rather differently. He recalls going to *The Sleeping Beauty* (as he says, earlier in the same night), and writes of his absolute enchantment:

> "Here at last was great ballet. The art of pantomime, so long dormant in ballet in America, had been restored in all its clarity and simplicity of meaning. The high quality of the dancing by the principals, soloists, and *corps de ballet*, the settings, the costumes, the lighting, all literally

The Sadler's Wells Ballet arrives at Le Guardia Airport. Sol Hurok greets NdV and David Webster

transported me to another world. I knew then, in a great revelation, that great ballet was here to stay."

and he describes the supper as "gay and charming and animated. I was filled with enthusiasm."

The intervening arrangements, both the abortive ones and the final positive ones, were undertaken by David Webster on behalf of Covent Garden and Sadler's Wells Ballet. In 1948 however, when Hurok returned to London, everyone was engaged in long conferences about repertoire, casting, touring dates, advance publicity and social relations.

Hurok was impressed by the tone of these meetings. There was none of the intrigue and suspicion to which he was accustomed when dealing with Eastern European theatre groups. Instead there was "reasonableness, logic, frankness, fundamental British honesty".[3]

Apart from everything else, this prestigious venture was looked on as a boost for British trade. Some of this was due to Hurok's friendship with Hans Juda, publisher of a British international textile journal, *Ambassador*, in collaboration with Horrocks. British fabric and fashion houses combined to outfit the company with complete wardrobes for day and evening wear, down to bowler hats and umbrellas for the men. De Valois comments:

"Gamely the girls boarded the plane clad in Scotch sweaters, woollen coats and dresses, smart macs and with even smarter tartan umbrellas ... It threatened to be a dangerously warm October ... "

The triumphant opening night in New York is firmly remembered, and frequently written about, in ballet history. It was a great event for British theatre art, for the company, and inevitably for de Valois. She did not enjoy her first visit to New York however—she was the victim of a bad virus that sent her temperature soaring—although she immediately appreciated its beauty as a city. As always, she captures its quality with her impressionistic pen:

"The sharp elegance of the skyscraper is here at home—where it belongs ... for the skyscraper, with its delicate steel structure, that appears to grow out of space itself, matches to perfection the cool brightness of its native skies. These structures edge the long, broad avenues—dying away in the distance into the unbroken line: New York has an endless vista of horizons—turning it into a fantasy city poised in space."

Anyone who has sat entranced in a 20th storey hotel room at twilight must respond to her words:

"At the close of day one watches the fading light hit these great buildings, changing the planes on them, time and again, within the space of a few minutes. Sometimes the setting sun will throw one side of the city's architecture into shadow—hitting the other with the fierce blaze of its own flame-like sunset that sparkles rather than glows ... "[4]

After the successful season at the Met there was a tour. They went to Washington where they appeared at Constitution Hall and both Fonteyn and Shearer fell on the poor surface of the stage. They continued to Richmond, Philadelphia, Pittsburgh, Chicago and East Lansing and then went on to Canada, appearing in Toronto, Ottawa and Montreal. Everywhere de Valois was involved in public relations, speaking at luncheons or receptions, telling people about British ballet and acquiring knowledge about the places she visited. The interest aroused was great and the performances proved a magnet for ballet lovers and practitioners, who travelled distances to see them. A group from Winnipeg, for instance, including Arnold Spohr and John Waks of the Winnipeg Ballet, made the 1000-mile journey to Chicago. Waks reported on a talk de Valois gave at the Chicago Library, reflecting the kind of things people wanted to know about the company—the basis of its style and discipline. Their style she defined as

> "the result of the influence of native characteristics on the form and execution of the ballet's traditional technique. The main influences on British and American dancers have been Italian and Russian. The Italian school of ballet stresses precision, geometric line and highly developed virtuosity. The Russian school emphasises dramatic intensity, sculptural quality and dynamic fire ... "[5]

She went on to say that a virtuoso dancer may not necessarily possess a perfect technique and that it is possible for a brilliant technician to have little or no outstanding virtuosity.

De Valois' last major ballet, *Don Quixote*, grew out of a musical score with an interesting history. In the early days of the war, from 1939 to 1941, the tiny Arts Theatre Club in Great Newport Street near Leicester Square provided a stage for lunchtime and teatime performances by two ballet groups. One was a combination of Ballet Rambert and the London Ballet, which had lost its founder director Antony Tudor to America. The other, established by Harold Rubin, owner of the Arts Theatre, was given the title Arts Theatre Ballet.

Shortly before the Arts Theatre Ballet had to be wound up Rubin acquired a score from Roberto Gerhard on the theme of Don Quixote, anticipating a production. Gerhard was a Spanish composer, a music-ologist attached to the Catalan National Library in Barcelona. He and his wife were stranded in Warsaw in December 1938 when Barcelona fell to General Franco and made their way to Cambridge where he was given a research studentship at King's College. In 1940 he began working out a scenario from Cervantes' four-volume masterpiece and composing a score for a ballet.

When Rubin had to abandon the project it looked as if this score would never be fully performed. Parts were broadcast, however, and in 1949 interest was expressed in it by Sadler's Wells Ballet as a choreographic project for Helpmann, scheduled for February 1950. Helpmann however was heavily committed at the time, making a debut as an opera producer at Covent Garden with *Madam Butterfly* in January 1950. There were recurring problems at this period at the Opera House over a lack of proper liaison between the opera and ballet companies and it would seem that this was a notable example where conflicting plans were laid. As Helpmann was not available, and the premiere was announced, de Valois decided to stage the ballet herself. Although it was a number of years since *Promenade* she had not abandoned the idea of choreography. The many directional activities linked with the end of the war and the move to Covent Garden had been all-demanding, but even after *Don Quixote* she considered ideas for further ballets.

Gerhard had selected about a dozen incidents from the whole Quixote saga, telescoping, simplifying, expanding as he felt necessary. He introduced an interesting final twist—Quixote, restored to sanity on his deathbed, was diminished and apathetic; while Sancho Panza, infected by the old idealism, prepared to set out as a crusading champion.

The score was enlarged to suit de Valois' choreographic plan. Her approach to the music was her usual one—as she did not read orchestral scores, she asked the composer to play her a piano reduction, explaining his intentions bar by bar. She then spent a couple of weeks listening to other pianists playing it, memorising it and envisaging dance action and characters. At last, on New Year's Day 1950, she gathered her cast together in the basement of the Kingsway Hall to teach them the choreography. Helpmann was Don Quixote, Fonteyn the double-roled Dulcinea-Aldonza, Alexander Grant Sancho Panza. It was neither quick nor easy—long periods of rehearsal resulted in quite short sequences of dance. The music was magnificent. Gerhard, a pupil of Schoenberg, was a serious and complex composer. Humphrey Searle describes it as "a brilliant and subtle score"—"one of the finest and most remarkable pieces of ballet music ever produced for the company [Sadler's Wells Ballet]".[6]

An interviewer, John Davidson, gives a pen picture of de Valois on the job:

"Watch her at rehearsal. She sits in the footlights on a bentwood chair with her back to the Covent Garden safety curtain. On the other side of the curtain the woodwind section of the opera orchestra is rehearsing bits of *The Valkyrie* Act I. On this side the rehearsal piano tinkles the Montesinos Cave music. Gerhard makes a top dressing for Wagner ... Fonteyn comes forward on her pointes displaying Aldonza's petticoat. Helpmann, wearing woollen tights and a lumber jacket, swings and leaps around her at the end of his rope. Miss de Valois makes ticks in her rehearsal book, asks for this or that bit over again, puts her book and glasses down to demonstrate a step or gesture herself, says 'Yes' or

Don Quixote *(Sadler's Wells Ballet 1950); (left to right)* Margot
Fonteyn, Robert Helpmann and Alexander Grant

'No', or 'Good' or 'That will do'. She is dry, brisk, decisive. Of creation's fury and frenzy there is not a sign. Creation in this case looks uncommonly like a job coming off the assembly line. But everybody prophesies there will be plenty of soul in the finished article.''[7]

The finished article was one of the most subtle, tantalising, difficult and elusive ballets I have seen. At first sight it looked dry to the point of aridity, totally reticent, theatrically disappointing. By the end of the second performance I was filled with admiration. In my contemporary notes I wrote of its slow and dignified movement, the half comic touches, the refined inflections of mime and reflections of the score, and the way effects were built up by sparse and economic means, using snatches of dance and movement, brief *pas de deux*, uncompleted gestures, to contrive a wonderfully moving whole.

There were five scenes, all enhanced by superb costumes, sets and drop curtains by Edward Burra in predominantly orange, red and dark coffee colours. Lighting too was deeply imaginative. An initial drop curtain of the dreaming head of Don Quixote surrounded by his visionary characters recalled in its atmospheric power the same designer's curtain of a ship in the slips of a builder's yard for *Miracle in the Gorbals*. Scene 1 saw Don Quixote armoured and the sluttish peasant girl Aldonza transformed into the Dulcinea of his dreams. Another act drop, a near view of Quixote and Sancho Panza on horse and mule, preceded Scene 2, the wayside inn. A group of peasant girls danced buoyantly and flirtatiously around and over a table with some itinerant muleteers. Quixote kept vigil and was engaged in a brief duet with Dulcinea—his lance frequently acting as her support and becoming almost a third participant in the *pas de deux*. He was then knighted by the innkeeper and set off again on his crusade.

Scene 3 brought him to the windmills—windmills painted on the backcloth but also represented on stage by giant, greyclad figures—two figures in fact, back to back, standing on five-inch platform shoes, whose arms represented sails. Quixote attacked them and was thrown to the ground. The travelling barber, a bright and humorous figure, arrived and Quixote became convinced that his cupping bowl was the legendary helmet of Mambrino. The barber handed it over, and then joined a small group of goatherds to listen to Quixote telling tales of the Golden Age of Greece. His words were embodied by a charming *pas de deux* for a youth and a girl, danced by Rassine and May. A line of chained galley slaves appeared and Quixote summoned up the goatherds to help release them. His mood changed when they refused to carry a message from him to Dulcinea, and the scene ended with a general turmoil in which Don Quixote was knocked backwards onto the great shield, under which Sancho Panza had been hiding. Very carefully Panza crawled off, like a giant tortoise, bearing the half-stunned knight on his back.

Scene 4, one of the most inventive and effective in the ballet, was set in the Cave of Montesinos. This section of Cervantes' book is unfamiliar to most people, who have only read abridgements or seen stage or film versions which concentrate on a few well-known elements. The central situation derives from the chivalrous tales which dominate Quixote's thoughts, and deals with a knight, Durandarte, whose dead body has been brought back by magic to a cave where it is watched over by his mistress, the Lady Belerma.

The plot details mattered very little in performance. Quixote, as the scene opened, was descending a rope from the top of a circular shaft down to the stage, and this introduced striking solo work for Helpmann, circling the stage sometimes in dance *enchaînements* and sometimes leaping and swinging from the rope. The Lady Belerma (Julia Farron) danced with her attendant maidens as a prelude to Quixote's view of the dead Durandarte he so much reverenced; but Durandarte abruptly sat up and dismissed him with contempt. The shock temporarily returned him to normal vision and he was horrified to see Aldonza, the girl whom he thought of as Dulcinea, appearing in a provocative, wanton dance. Catching the rope once more he began to climb it desperately as the curtain fell.

Returned home, Quixote struggled with his delusions. When the final scene began, he was caged in by symbolic prison bars of light, tormented by a triumphant dance of his adversaries and mourned by an ensemble of dark-clad figures. The bars at last dissolved and Sancho Panza helped him to his bed. Dying, he handed the barber's-basin helmet to his faithful servant and his sword to the priest—a gesture which the composer meant to represent the militancy of the Church in Spain, a touch that remained obscure to the British.

With this narrative de Valois set herself an exceedingly difficult task, and the fact that *Don Quixote* did not establish itself in the repertoire undoubtedly shows that its appreciation required too much work on the part of the audience. Most viewers were deterred by the sombre quality of the theme, the lack of comic relief or extended passages of dance. The splendid score gave them little to relax into in the way of colourful ensembles or exciting dance scenes and they became dismayed by the strong, serious development of the drama. Characters were present on stage as in all de Valois' ballets but were created in less direct terms than, say, in *Rake* or *Prospect*. Alexander Grant was a splendid Sancho Panza. Beaumont wrote of him:

> "Like the character in the novel he is in turns simple, dull-witted and shrewd, stout-hearted in every emergency and always loyal to his master."[8]

Fonteyn, surprisingly, emerged much more strongly as the earthy Aldonza than as the rather colourless dream heroine Dulcinea. Long dark hair loose, eyes and face alight with mischief, and a splendid control of the point-and-heel variations in solos that might well have been composed by de Valois for her own crisp, *demi-caractère* precision, she was a perfect contrast to the statuesque smoothness of the weaving patterns of Belerma and her women. Like all these others, the central role was inevitably governed by the character of the score. De Valois did not have the long danceable sections of music that could have involved her in the development of solos and *pas de deux* or virtuoso *enchaînements*. In Helpmann however she had a marvellous and mature mime-dancer who could make the most of every opportunity for expressive movement or stillness, and it was a performance to cherish. She could count totally on his discipline, his lack of fuss or mannerism, his theatrical subtlety. Helpmann is remembered predominantly for inventive extrovert comedy, as in Dr Coppélius or the Ugly Sister, by those who did not see the remarkable range of his restrained characterisations of which the Red King was the first.

The Times critic understood the ballet very well:

> "Every one of the five scenes contained a concentration of action in an economy of movement that gripped the attention by virtue of its visual significance..."

and of Helpmann he said:

> "Don Quixote is a character who on the stage may easily become a bore. Not, however, if he is portrayed by Mr Helpmann. The slow tempo, the strained air, the sharp decisive movements all made him into a real person capable of evoking not only Sancho Panza's devotion but our passionate concern."[9]

258

There are some interesting parallels to be drawn in this last major ballet of de Valois with her earlier works. Aldonza's predecessors were the Dancer and the Ladies of the Town in *Rake*. She flourished her petticoat as tantalisingly as one of the Ladies does her stays and the Dancer her stockings, but because of Fonteyn's ineradicable prima ballerina quality she could not be a bold and wanton tavern wench and remained a ravishing if provoking and daring child. The table from the Orgy Scene of *Rake* is also there, in the inn yard, and the rowdy dance of the peasants leads them on and off its top. The windmills, personified, relate to the Castles in *Checkmate*. Although the style of choreography was specifically for this ballet, the mood of the Golden Age *pas de deux* echoed the peasants in *Orpheus* or the Shepherd and Serving Maid in *Gods*. A pyramidal grouping in the first scene, raising Dulcinea on high, has something of the Black Queen's triumph. This is not to say that anything in *Don Quixote* was repetition. There are with all choreographers specific personal movement-words and phrases that contribute to individual style and are combined, with fresh elements, to create new works.

Reviews were divided. Scott Goddard, for instance, wrote:

"Not since Ashton's *Symphonic Variations* has a ballet so convinced one of the latent possibilities in that art. And for impressiveness in design, in dancing, decor and music combined, one's thoughts go back to Miss de Valois' *Job*. Both the idea and the treatment are different, but there is a similar cohesion and completeness."[10]

The *New Statesman* critic, while praising the music, disagreed:

"And yet such an excellent choreographer as Miss de Valois has missed her opportunity. As always, her feeling for mime is excellent, her grouping pictorially admirable; and we cannot deny that specific passages of her ballet are entirely successful. All the same, one never feels the choreography growing out of the score, the dancing never throbs or flows like the music..."[11]

Richard Buckle produced a very reasoned review based on the premise that ballet required dancing as opposed to dance movement:

"If you think, as I do, that in ballet tragic and sublime effects, the 'moment of truth', must be produced, as if by accident, in the course

259

of a series of varied dances, and suggested merely by some fine inflection of movement as they are in *Swan Lake* and *Cotillon*, then you will find *Don Quixote* unsubtle and monotonous. But if you conceive of ballet as story or drama without words, Miss de Valois' work is a fine example."[12]

So here everyone was, back in the endless debate as to what ballet should or should not be like, a debate that is sustained by personal inclination towards, or away from, "story or drama without words". There is no final resolution of the problem.

Don Quixote was included in the repertoire for the US tour of 1950/51. There is some ground for thinking that on both sides of the Atlantic it was well ahead of its time—that twenty or thirty years on, when so many varieties of ballet and dance production, often with a minimum of extended dance ensembles and brief spells of solo or duet, have been seen and admired, the climate would have been more favourable to this remarkable production. In 1950 however American critics and public disliked it. Walter Terry did not mince words:

"The report, I fear, must be ungracious, for *Don Quixote* is long, dull and relieved by few examples of choreographic imaginativeness ... It is all neat and tidy and nicely produced but the fantasy, the grandeur, the tragedy and the comedy of a great tale are rarely realised."[13]

Margaret Lloyd was devastating:

"The lighting is low-keyed, the music by Roberto Gerhard dispiriting. The scenario, also by Mr Gerhard, is over-compacted Cervantes ... which the choreography, consisting mostly of mime and tableaux, does not much expand."[14]

Two critics differed from these views, although John Martin tempered praise by declaring that "it cannot be said that the ballet is an especially effective one". He went on:

"Yet in its detail it is far more successful than in its entirety. There are some beautiful pieces of choreographic and theatrical invention and certainly the role of Dulcinea provides Margot Fonteyn with one of the most fascinating parts she has had. Quite remote from the austerities of the classic style, we find her here in extremely free and modern movement, tinged with the vulgarity of the peasant Aldonza and wonderfully conceived."[15]

Paul Affelder was the one true enthusiast:

> "One of the most arresting and effective of the modern ballets ... a tremendously interesting and moving ballet, one of the best of Miss de Valois' creations, one which we would like to see again."[16]

The failure of *Don Quixote* in America, coming after a very cool audience response in London, sealed its fate. Critical appreciation in Britain—and de Valois recalls that the BBC Critics in their weekly programme[17] were unanimously in its favour—could not counterbalance its overall unpopularity. The choreographer herself feels that it was unsuited to Covent Garden or the Metropolitan Opera House and would have looked much better at the Wells, and this is probably true. In a smaller theatre the rewarding subtleties of acting and action would have been very much more visible right through the auditorium.

De Valois produced no more choreography for her own companies. One or two ballets of which she now has no recollection were mooted in the press but she had every intention of staging "a choreographic swansong" in 1958. This was *The Lady of Shalott*, for which Bliss composed at least a major part of a score. De Valois intended to have a transparent central tower, in which the audience would be able to see the Lady, the illusion of a river and all the action contained in the poem moving across the stage in front of it: reapers, maidens, abbots and shepherds, lovers, knights and funeral processions—and at last Sir Lancelot. It was to be a vehicle for Svetlana Beriosova; but alas it never materialised...

On May 15 1950 a gala performance took place at the Wells. This was universally declared to be the ballet's twenty-first anniversary—an extraordinary mass illusion. It was certainly not twenty-one years from May 5 1931 when the first full evening of ballet was given at the Old Vic nor was it twenty-one years from the staging of *Les Petits Riens* on December 13 1928, although it may have been a belated celebration of this.

All the same it was an extremely enjoyable evening. The programme was a "party" one with some former and founder dancers returning to roles they had created. The orgy scene from *Rake* had a good many of the original cast but the most collectable item was de Valois' own performance as Webster in *A Wedding Bouquet*. She was fifty-two and had not danced for thirteen years. One change was made—she danced in heeled character shoes and not on pointe. It was a sharp, funny delightful portrait that gave those of us who had never seen her on stage a very slight taste of the elegant and exceptional artist older and more fortunate balletgoers remember so vividly. She was also the centre of the celebration—a happy, dressed-up event for the Wells, with Princess Margaret to hand de Valois an inscribed silver tray from the company and a surprising number of relaxed politicians convivially helping to pass round the champagne—Sir Stafford Cripps made head-lines for this in the *Evening Standard*.

> "It was the most glamorous night Rosebery Avenue has ever known," [wrote Cecil Wilson] "—a night of titles, tiaras, starched shirts and beautiful gowns instead of the normal sandals, sweaters and corduroys. 'We hardly ever see a boiled shirt or a bare back down here,' said a programme girl, 'but look at them tonight.' "[18]

De Valois, replying to toasts, made the point she has never failed to make on such occasions—"It takes more than one person to make a ballet." The Wells had "won through on its discipline, its comradeship and its putting its art before itself. I do assure you this is no one-man show. This is my chance to thank the artists from my heart for allowing me to help them to get there." She also thanked the audiences who had supported the company in lean times and good. Richard Buckle put it all felicitously. He wanted to

> "tell Ninette de Valois, whose evening this chiefly was and whom we are probably seeing dance on the stage for the last time, that she was brilliantly funny as Webster, and that the applause she received could only faintly suggest what a dear great woman we think she is. What an achievement hers has been! To put it mildly, she is the opposite of Josephine [in *A Wedding Bouquet*] who made no plans for the winter."[19]

Chapter XII

⟡ Life was now divided for de Valois into four main streams—her two companies and all the directorial demands associated with them; her school; her annual teaching-of-teachers courses; and ballet activity abroad. Behind them all of course lay her personal life as wife to a practising doctor, which she never neglected.

The teaching courses deserve looking at in some detail. In conversation now she stresses that the courses she devised (in consultation with Kathleen Gordon among others) were always intended as supplementary to the syllabus of the Royal Academy of Dancing, not as part of it. The syllabus could only contain so much—there was no time for anything else—and her summer schools were planned to show what more could be done to help produce and develop dancers for ballet. For the first, in 1947, she worked out, in association with Ursula Moreton, Ailne Phillips, George Gontcharov and Claude Newman, an interesting graded syllabus of exercises, *enchaînements* and dances, and a six-day course of lectures that covered every facet of the creation of a dancer: anatomy, musical approach, the teaching of classical and character dance and mime. She herself lectured on the difference between the Italian, French and Russian schools, and on the importance of differentiating between the teaching of girls and boys. She also embarked on an unusually detailed analysis of character dance.

In succeeding years the basic course was used to highlight various elements—line, *épaulement*, general expressiveness, freedom from mannerism and affectation, and work with choreographers were some of the areas analysed. Reports in *The Dancing Times*, often from Joan Lawson, help to capture the quality of de Valois' work in this sphere. In 1951 (in an issue that congratulated de Valois on the DBE she received in the New Year Honours), she was described as an inspiring teacher:

"Each step was carefully planned, appearing as one part of an *enchaîne-ment* in which the dancer had to take into account every part of her body, the relationship of the steps to each other, the music and the stage, and as an extension of his or her personal flow of movement. Such teaching must enhance the proficiency and artistry of any dancer."[1]

This was exactly the aim of the work. In 1955, during the ninth course, she related dancers to choreographers:

"She gave her audience an opportunity to see a choreographer at work on dancers, drew attention, step by step, to the highlights of *enchainements*, the breadth and lightness of the movements, the move-ment of the dancer in and through space and the varying accents by which the artist-dancer can convey the choreographer's intentions."[2]

For her demonstration she used pupils from the School, among them Antoinette Sibley, Lynn Seymour and Alfreda Thorogood. By this time teachers were attending the courses from a wide number of countries— the USA, Canada, Australia and New Zealand, Mexico, Singapore, Southern Rhodesia, Turkey, and half a dozen European countries, as well as a growing number from Great Britain.

In 1956, for the tenth course, she thoroughly revised the curriculum. Fresh subjects were introduced—a new method of character dance training, a demonstration of special exercises for boys taken from Volinin's methods, and lectures on Benesh and Laban notation. At the time she was particularly concerned with the subject of notation and put her case in a letter to *The Dancing Times*. Two years previously she had discussed the question of including dance notation studies at the Sadler's Wells Ballet School—at that point the main form available was Labanotation. "A series of circumstances made it impossible to carry the plan to its conclusion" and since that time great interest had been aroused in the new Benesh notation devised by Rudolf and Joan Benesh.[3] Because of this she had agreed that a voluntary class for studying Benesh notation should be held in the Upper School but it was not included in the general curriculum, and she felt that "time and the dancer alone will decide which of the existing notation methods will prove to be the most practical for the classical ballet to use. At the present stage I am an onlooker." Later it was decided that Benesh notation (Choreology) should be used by the (then) Royal Ballet and taught at the School.

The teachers' courses were always angled towards the preparation of dancers for a professional career in ballet and the tenth course concentrated on bridging the gap between the classroom and the stage. The differences between technician and artist were demonstrated by giving short *enchaînements* of straight classwork and then adding changes in line direction, *épaulement*, head and arm movements and so on to show even younger children the difference. De Valois' own lecture this time dealt with Alignment, and the need for dancers to understand not only their own placing of the body in space but their relationship to the stage and to other dancers around them. A culminating demonstration brought elements together: five inter-mediate students were given a set of *enchaînements* which were gradu-ally built up into expressive dances and floor patterns; then the whole was transformed into "an enchanting *pas de cinq* to a Chopin mazur-ka". In other words, de Valois was applying a choreographer's vision, developing basic techniques into a performance.

In 1957 the special study was a detailed syllabus for boys—always an area dear to de Valois' heart! It studied the differences between male and female physiology and psychology and emphasised the slower and more gradual training of turnout and footwork, the develop-ment of strong shoulders and back, to produce a clean and virile style.

A reminder about the value to students of a study of traditional folkdance and historical social dance came in 1958, the year that folkdance was firmly installed at the Royal Ballet School. By this time the summer teachers' courses were changing. Much of the work done on classical dance teaching had now been incorporated into the new RAD syllabus and in 1960 de Valois concentrated on choreography. She discussed the historical development, and the contribution made by the Diaghilev Ballet choreographers. She also lectured on criticism, describing the ideal form of criticism that might exist if editors would give their writers time and space, and treat ballet as an art in its own right. Over twenty-five years later this situation is considerably further from adjustment, at least in Great Britain, than it was then.

Even after the Constructive Teaching of Ballet courses ended, oppor-tunities arose for de Valois to give lectures or lecture demonstrations to the professional training bodies in London. In 1969 she supervised an RAD International Summer School directed by Louise Browne. In addition to all the classes and events for teachers, dancers and aspiring choreographers there were some open events, and the theme for lectures and demonstrations was the *Ballet du cour* and the *Ballet d'action*. In

1970 the theme was the Tchaikovsky ballets and in 1971 Modern Classical Ballets from 1908 to 1956.

The Constructive Teaching courses with their intensive, imaginatively conceived and executed activity towards helping teachers to realise their fullest possibilities in the training of ballet dancers were not wasted. Teachers went back to every corner of the world to put into practice lessons and ideas they had learnt in London from de Valois and her colleagues, and none of them have forgotten the value of the experience. Two who profited were Hanna Voos, who founded and directed the Royal Ballet of Wallonie in Charleroi, and Jeanne Brabants, the founder-director of the Royal Ballet of Flanders.

Lectures had always been an occasional occupation for de Valois—talks about ballet generally and her company in particular given to ballet clubs or in an educational context, or papers read to learned societies. She is a fluent, stimulating, amusing speaker who keeps her audience alert and entertained from start to finish—sometimes leaving them behind with her swift transitions of topic but always providing them with enormous food for thought and discussion. I can remember the first time I heard her lecture, as a student, at some extramural University of London course on ballet. I heard Arnold Haskell, on a platform a sombre personality with a monotonous voice but an enthusiast for his subject. I heard Rambert, physically fluttering from side to side, demonstrating the leading roles in *Firebird* like a magical sparrow; and I heard de Valois—slight, erect, controlled, authoritative and with plenty of good stories and reminiscences to colour the bare bones of fact and practicality. All her lectures were a vital part in her campaign to build up a knowledgeable public for ballet in Britain, to make anyone who was interested in the dance feel identified and concerned in the growth and development of ballet.

Now in the post-war period, as everything in her work as director of Sadler's Wells Ballet was enlarging to world scale, so her lecturing life took on new dimensions. During the North American tour in the winter of 1950/51 she undertook a two weeks lecture tour sponsored jointly by the Association of Canadian Clubs and the British Council. This began on October 5 in Ottawa. The *Ottawa Citizen* reporter went out to meet her:

> "It wasn't difficult to recognise Ninette de Valois, director of the Sadler's Wells Ballet Company, when she stepped off the plane at Uplands Airport last evening. But it was rather staggering to realise that this slender mite was the person who has built up her company to such

eminence in the past twenty years. Not much over five feet and as slender as the freshest neophyte in her company ... 'No, I don't know just what I'll be speaking about. I just ask each club what line they expect me to take, and go on from there. I never use notes,' she told reporters ... "

Some papers which belonged in her passport had been left behind in Montreal and were being sent along by the next plane.

" 'Oh, I shall lose everything,' she said cheerfully, and stepped into a car which was to whisk her off to Earnscliffe [the home of the High Commissioner for the UK]."[4]

Notes or not, she was a star lecturer. She told the story of her ballet company: "a history of struggles" that reached back twenty-one years. She described their life in World War II, she talked of their European travels, of the school, of the shortness and uncertainty of a dancer's career and—typically—of future dancers and audiences. She entirely fulfilled the British Council's belief that they could hardly have a better ambassador. The tour, for which she took no fee, only expenses, was immensely successful, immensely exhausting—especially as she was not a good traveller, frequently suffering from acute migraine after journeys. By her own account, she got a whirlwind impression of vastly differing communities, much kindness and wonderful hospitality. She has

"a swift memory of swooping down from the skies at sunset to Regina, set like a round bowl in the middle of limitless prairie"[5]

and Regina typifies the range of her influence: it was not even on the company's touring schedule and the audience that filled the ballroom of the Hotel Saskatchewan knew little about ballet from first hand viewing. Their interest had been whetted by *The Red Shoes*; now they remained "entranced" by "the vivacious, charming director and founder of Sadler's Wells Ballet" as she "reminisced over the triumphs and some of the heartaches and explored the arduous process of turning a bright little boy or girl who wants to dance into a highly specialised ballet dancer".[6]

Hurok, the impresario for the company's tour, suggested that he should send an escort with her to Canada to help with travel and accommodation. It may indeed have been some other time, but he made a good story out of it in *S. Hurok Presents*. De Valois refused. "Quite unnecessary." "She was quite able to take care of herself. She did not want anyone making a fuss over her." He then got her to agree to accept $300 for petty cash. She "stuffed the money into her capacious reticule." When she came back she returned $137—"I didn't spend it ..." [7]

De Valois rejoined her company in Los Angeles, in time for a fabulous opening at the Shrine Auditorium, when they danced *The Sleeping Beauty* to an audience of 6700 movie stars and socialites in full gala array. "The great foyer," de Valois writes, "is packed stiff with the glitter of Hollywood ... even the Garbo is not noticeably alone." She went in by the back. She quotes their stage carpenter, Horace Fox, saying "I'll always see you, madam, that night, a'picking your way calmly through them packings and saying 'Horace, it's a madhouse in front.'" [8]

According to Hurok, her arrival in LA had been unorthodox. He had planned a meeting with the press at the Ambassador Hotel on the morning of the first night, and she was due to fly in the previous evening. There was no sign of her. She turned up, "neat and calm as always", just before the conference.

> "The strangest thing, she said. When I arrived last night I looked in my bag for the piece of paper on which I had noted the name of the hotel. I couldn't find it nor could I remember it.
>   What did you do?
>   Do? I went to sleep at the airport. And this morning I tried an old law of association of ideas."

The hotel, she remembered, had something to do with diplomacy and she worked her way around from Embassy to Ambassador.

Hurok found her, as a person to work with, completely fascinating. "I have never known anyone even faintly like her." He cites all kinds of qualities that impressed him: her "magnificent sense of organisation", her brilliant handling of situations and individuals, her "art of the single withering sentence", her rapid working mind; the fact that she could be a strict disciplinarian but "a genuinely gay and amusing person"; her intolerance of sycophantic yes-men and her detestation of criticism based on personal bias. [9]

Wherever she went in the USA and Canada, although the biggest headlines shrieked about Margot Fonteyn, Robert Helpmann and "Red Shoes" Moira Shearer, de Valois made a lasting impression.

Interviewers were fascinated by her, puzzled by her, intrigued by her, and full of admiration. A typical report appeared in the *Los Angeles Times* written by Albert Goldberg, who had telephoned her for an interview to Toronto, where she was lecturing. Even with a bad transcontinental line, and the difficulty of "the clipped British accent of the interviewee and the broad American lingo of the interviewer", he decided that

> "the terse, precise, orderly manner of speech of Ninette de Valois was exactly the way one expected the dynamic director of the Sadler's Wells Ballet to sound."

He made the mistake of asking whether she was considering any movie offers.

> "The voice in the receiver seemed to chill ... 'Not at all. There are always offers. I am not interested a bit.'"

He recalled that she was reported to have turned down a Monday night television show in New York, which would have netted some $50,000, because it was the company's night off and she believed they could not be at their best if they had to give an extra performance. She then answered questions about the success of the tour, the health of the company, travelling conditions ("We are unaccustomed to the great distances but everything has gone off nicely"), whether there were any Americans in the company ("No, not at all") and when the next tour would be ("Not next year. We will be preparing for the Festival of Britain").[10]

After this arduous North American tour de Valois returned to the UK tired and ill but immediately set about staging a revival of *The Prospect Before Us* for Sadler's Wells Theatre Ballet. The circumstances were unexpected, as she and Helpmann had come to a parting of the ways, and he had left the company at the end of the San Francisco engagement. Tensions and disagreements, arising from the fact that he had been much occupied outside the company by the filming of *The Tales of Hoffmann*, were aggravated by the physical and nervous strain on them both of the cross-continent tour. It was a sad severance but in the long run their mutual admiration and affection were not impaired. Meanwhile in February 1951, Helpmann danced three performances of Mr O'Reilly as guest artist at the Wells, donating all three to the young company there.

The success of de Valois' Canadian lectures naturally resulted in other proposals and in 1956 she again took on an extended tour in the USA, hoping this time to net a sum of £4000 for the Sadler's Wells Ballet School. She was scheduled to visit twenty-two cities during the last three months of the year, but a back injury sustained some years previously gave her serious trouble. She was forced to give up halfway through the programme and return to London for treatment.

Chapter XIII

✎ One result of the successful company tours in Eastern Europe was a number of invitations to de Valois to help other countries establish or re-establish national schools of ballet. One that appealed to her particularly came from the Turkish Government, who wanted to set up a school of ballet as part of the State Conservatory of Music and Drama.

In May 1947 de Valois went to Istanbul to consider it in detail. Her brief, according to Dr L. R. Phillips, the British Council representative in Turkey, was

> "to study the possibility of setting up a school of ballet which would ultimately produce ballet dancers moulded in the British tradition, but independent, to develop, when their art was complete and their technique perfected, a Turkish national ballet of their own."

They laid on for her a series of visits to ordinary schools in and around Istanbul so that she could see children of a suitable age perform simple exercises and evaluate the potential of young Turks for classical ballet. They gave displays of their own national dances:

> "A teacher would strike up a tune, on violin or concertina, and off they'd go, singing lustily and dancing the while. The noise sometimes—and on one occasion there were two hundred children singing together in an enclosed space—baffled description but we all liked it—liked the beat of shoes on the floor and the enthusiasm of those lusty voices ... "[1]

De Valois noticed how the children often seemed to come from very poor homes—shy, and worried because they had threadbare shoes and not very clean feet. She went on to the Ankara neighbourhood, continuing the search and, to her delight, learning some Anatolian folk dances. Her report encouraged the Turkish Government to set up a ballet school at Yeşilköy in the suburbs of Istanbul, beginning with eleven boys and eighteen girls aged seven to ten, who were given a normal school education with dance training added to it. She recommended the appointment of two English ballet teachers and initially sent out Joy Newton as principal and Audrey Knight as her assistant.

For de Valois it was the beginning of a long and fruitful association, as it was for Turkey. Joy Newton feels that she

"had a real love affair with Turkey, everything there was at the beginning where ballet was concerned, in the interesting stages".[2]

She went there almost annually, advising, overseeing, coaching, producing and choreographing for the school and later the company; and as Beatrice Appleyard puts it:

"when she couldn't come herself she sent people whom she knew she could trust to represent her and carry on her work. She was quite tireless in her efforts ... "[3]

To get everyone going on the right lines, de Valois created a work for the students to dance in 1950—and gave them the chance to make local history with the first ever Turkish ballet. She based *Keloglan Masali* on a Turkish folk legend, and set it to a piano suite by a Turkish composer, Ulvi Cemal Erkin, using choreographic combinations of national dance and simple classical ballet.

Joy Newton, who had grown up as a de Valois girl in the Academy of Choreographic Art and eventually became ballet mistress of Sadler's Wells Ballet, was the perfect choice as first principal and also greatly enjoyed her work. She left in 1951, after the school moved to headquarters in the Ankara State Conservatory, and Beatrice Appleyard took over. Another pupil of the Academy and soloist from the early Vic-Wells Ballet days, Appleyard had branched out, first to the Markova-Dolin Ballet in 1935 and then to the wider world of the Windmill Theatre and the West End musical. De Valois kept in touch and in 1951 asked her to take over the Ankara school. Both Newton and Appleyard composed small ballets for the students to perform. Numbers increased, and in 1954 there were over sixty girls and boys taking classes at the school, with the first graduates scheduled to leave in 1956. In May de Valois attended the annual recital which included excerpts from *Giselle* and *Les Sylphides* and two new works by Apple-yard. She had also sent out the previous year a valued teacher, Lorna Mossford, who had been a wartime soloist with Sadler's Wells Ballet, a delicate and precise dancer all too often sharing roles with, and overshadowed by, Moira Shearer. Beatrice Appleyard married in Turkey, the director and composer Mithat Fenmen, and in 1954 the school's direction was taken over by Molly Lake and her husband Travis Kemp, who remained there for twenty years, giving continuity and sound classical tuition to more than one generation of Turkish dancers.

In May 1956 the graduate dancers began to perform in operas and to give evenings of ballet, and by 1959 they were ready to embark on a more ambitious programme. De Valois made a consultative visit to plan and advise. As a result, in December Robert Harrold went to Ankara to produce a version of *El Amor Brujo*, which shared an evening with Richard Strauss' opera *Salome*. The Old Vic pattern set by Baylis and de Valois thirty years before was being repeated.

Ailne Phillips now went to Turkey to stage *Coppélia*, an excellent ballet for dancers who had a pronounced natural bent for charac-terisation. Ailne had to adapt, as everyone did, to the distinctive Turkish/Eastern Mediterranean temperament with its charming inability to timekeep and its tendency to forget or overlook the need to turn up at classes and rehearsals. De Valois knew exactly how to deal with this, an Irishwoman with experience of the similar attitudes of her own people, and, adopting an entirely different and much less strict approach to any she used with her British dancers, managed to get the very best out of them.

• Another tried and trusted associate from early Vic-Wells days, Claude Newman, was appointed ballet master to the new company in 1961. He increased the repertoire to include *Les Patineurs* and *The Rake's Progress*, and the American dancer Todd Bolender lent variety with two works, *Création du monde* and *Still Point*. De Valois then asked Andree Howard to join them for a few months in 1962 to stage some of her ballets and choreograph a new work, *Les Barricades mystérieuses*, to music by Couperin. Newman's tenure ended in November 1963 and that month the company gave its first production of *The Sleeping Beauty*, mounted by Mossford under de Valois' super-vision. A young dancer of great potential, Meriç Sümen, was the Aurora. For two seasons Nancy Hanley was in charge of the company and de Valois' *Checkmate* was staged. Joy Newton returned in September 1964 when *Giselle* and *Les Rendezvous* were produced. The repertoire was also expanded by the addition of two Kenneth Mac-Millan ballets, *Solitaire* and *The Burrow*.

Names come thick and fast in these early years in Turkey. Contracts were short, often for one production only, and the turnover was constant. All were selected by de Valois for positive qualities which she felt were needed by the emerging company, just as the repertoire was carefully calculated to introduce the company to different choreographic demands. The constant exposure to new masters and producers also helped to keep interest and energy alive among the dancers. Analysis of the revivals and new works reveals a well-graded amount of experience for young artists. There was an emphasis on the type of ballet for which they had a natural flair—character and *demi-caractère*—giving them substantial chances of characterisation in varying styles. Classical dancing, with *demi-caractère* overtones, appeared in *Les Patineurs*, in the delicate charm of *Solitaire* with its playful comedy, and in the sparkling *Assembly Ball*. Meanwhile, the firm classical background in which they were being trained made its appearance in the showpiece sequences of *Coppélia* and eventually in the *Beauty*. This time around, *Beauty* was a standard-setting exercise, leading them on towards later productions and towards *Swan Lake*.

Swan Lake, in fact, was next on the list to be staged. It came in October 1965 and this time de Valois was assisted by Dudley Tomlinson and a Benesh notation score read by a Turkish dancer, Suna Eden. Eden had spent most of the year in London, studying at the Royal Ballet School on a British Council bursary. She had ambitions to teach, and also to work on a Turkish style of theatrical dance that would incorporate national dances and musical rhythms, and at the same time she qualified as a choreologist.

A director looking at a company, according to de Valois, sees in each member of it, from an early age, the type of potential that should be encouraged: one or two will be prima ballerina or *premier danseur* material; others will be natural soubrettes, character dancers, ballet masters, choreographers, teachers, repetiteurs. In Turkey she was on the lookout for talent which she could mould in every direction so that the company might eventually become self-sufficient, as indeed it has done.

In *Swan Lake* Meriç Sümen, emerging as the Turkish State Ballet's first prima ballerina, danced Odette-Odile with Tanju Tuzer as Siegfried. Alan Abbott, who spent eight valuable years in Turkey as musical director, was the conductor. The production also introduced Richard Glasstone to the company, as he choreographed a new *pas de six*, while de Valois created a charming dance for the six fiancées.

Glasstone, who grew up in South Africa, worked with Scapino Ballet in Holland in 1957. He then went home and got married, returning to Europe in 1963 with an introduction to de Valois from Dulcie Howes, founder of the Cape Town University Ballet. De Valois said she had nothing at that point to offer him in London; however she wondered if he would consider directing the Turkish State Ballet with opportunities for choreography. He had little hesitation in accepting.

De Valois herself composed a substantial new work for the company in 1965. It had a specific purpose—to demonstrate how elements of Turkish folkdance, theme and music could be combined in a ballet. Titled *Çeşmebaşi* (*At the Fountainhead*), it was set to Ferit Tüzün's Anatolian Suite. One remarkable feature about new productions by the Turkish company has always been the number of scores contributed by Turkish composers—a far higher ratio than in, say, Canada or Australia.

All the features de Valois had observed in Turkish villages were woven into the action of *Çeşmebaşi*. There were water-carriers, gossiping women, and a village drummer who acted as a town crier. A traditional hoop dance was included and a lively balletic representation of the ancient and popular puppet shadow show of Hacivat and Karagöz. The tales of a travelling minstrel were illustrated in dance, and he joined a dream heroine in an attractive lovers' *pas de deux*. Richard Glasstone remembers it as a delightful and popular ballet, full of charm and character.[4] Local opinion felt that although it was inevitably an outsider's impression of the scene it was a great step forward in developing indigenous Turkish ballet. Todd Bolender wrote:

"I was most impressed with what the Dame was able to do with the dancers ... Not only had she used a Turkish musical score ... but the way she used it was very effective indeed. I saw it twice and was just as interested after the second time."[5]

In spite of this the Turks' true passion was for Western classical ballet. They were eager to acquire the work of Western choreographers and devoted, both as performers and audience, to the long traditional productions.

De Valois never had any intention of continuing forever in charge of the Turkish State Ballet. It was a miniature empire-building endeavour in the highest sense of the term—a lovingly created plan always working towards the moment when local people would be able to take over.

In 1966 she went with them on their first foreign tour, to Sofia. They danced *Giselle*, to show their standard in Western classical ballet, and *Çeşmebaşi*, which delighted the many Turks residing in Bulgaria. Their greatest success however was in *Rake*, a new and illuminating choreographic experience for Sofia audiences.

That year de Valois also choreographed a new ballet for the company, *Sinfonietta*. This had a score that appealed to her greatly, composed by Nevit Kodalli, and was in a different vein from most of her previous works. It was a near-abstract dance choreography set in a rehearsal room, contrasting classical and character work, and hinting at relationships between the girls and boys but in no way presenting a dramatic narrative—in almost every way a new departure for her, and very successful. It was premiered the same evening as Glasstone's *The Lady with the Dagger*—a dramatic ballet on a Turkish theme. There was a surprise crisis between the management and the lighting designer, as his name had been left off the programme, and he refused to light the two ballets, both of which had intricately worked-out plans decided on by their choreographers. De Valois reasoned with him, and persuaded him to a compromise. "You must do the lighting for Richard's ballet. It needs the lighting particularly." He agreed to do this and not *Sinfonietta*, for which she had, as Glasstone knew, planned detailed and subtle lighting. She gave no sign that this was indeed a bad artistic blow to her as a creator. She had made a good bargain— and an unselfish one—from the directorial point of view and swallowed her grave disappointment as choreographer.

The twentieth anniversary of the company was marked by a newly choreographed version of the three-act *Sylvia* by Glasstone, now appointed director as well as choreographer. The company enjoyed dancing it and Glasstone remembers their "wonderful sense of drama, great masculinity and charming femininity". The Ankara critic, Professor Metin And, writes:

> "*Sylvia* had never been a real success in the past and had never been properly established in the international repertoire. It seemed to us that at last the spell had been broken and this new Anglo-Turkish version of the old French classic had really come to life."[6]

Çeşmebaşi *(Turkish State Ballet 1964) Dudley Tomlinson and Erhan Erguler as Hacivat and Karagöz*

The first night on January 25 1967 was followed by an official Government reception in de Valois' honour, two presentations, various other social events and wide coverage in the Turkish press and radio. The British Council was able to report that it was "a culminating point in recognition of British influence on Turkish ballet".[7]

During his years in Ankara, Glasstone created a number of ballets. *Sylvia* was followed by a successful version of *The Prince of the Pagodas*. De Valois was of immense help to him with his choreography. She is what in literary terms would be a top-rank publishers' editor— someone with a keen eye for points where slight alterations could improve a work, someone who made worthwhile suggestions without attempting to impose her will in any way. She would try and discover what Glasstone wanted in the way of a dance or theatre effect and then suggest a method of reaching this—possibly by different entries or exits, by a different deployment of dancers, increasing or decreasing the number used at certain moments, or some technical detail like the type of step or tempo which would lend more variety to an *enchaîne-ment*. "She never pushed *her* ideas; she simply tried to help me get *mine* across ... "[8]

The year 1968 was significant for the Turkish State Ballet because the first ballet by a Turkish choreographer was staged. This was *Çark (The Wheel)*, an abstract work to Ravel's String Quartet in F, choreographed by Sait Sokmen.

At the end of three years Glasstone thought of resigning. He told de Valois and she brought him a counter-proposition. If he remained one more year she would then definitely be able to offer him work at the Royal Ballet School, and to this he agreed. Together they staged *The Nutcracker* in Turkey in 1968/69, completing the tally of the Tchaikovsky ballets. It proved a smash hit in Ankara—scheduled for six performances, it ran for a year.

Towards the end of 1971 a new award, a gold medal, was instituted for distinguished services to Turkish culture, and the first recipient was de Valois. Presenting it on stage in Ankara after the premiere of Alfred Rodrigues' *Romeo and Juliet*, the Minister of Culture, Talat Halman, spoke of "the direction and shape" she had given to Turkish ballet from its inception:

"[She] has brought to our Ballet the gift of her supreme creativity and experience, imparting inspiration and excitement to Turkey's ballet achievements".[9]

She was already planning with Joy Newton a re-staging of *The Sleeping Beauty* for 1971/72 in which she also choreographed the Garland Dance. Meriç Sümen and Gülcan Tunççekic both danced Aurora with Oytun Turfanda as Florimund, and Sümen danced Giselle in a new staging by Dolin and de Valois. Sümen had just returned from the USSR where she danced leading roles as guest artist at the Kirov, the Bolshoi and in Odessa and Kiev. The British connection was not yet lost although more and more ballets were staged by Turkish choreographers. One of these, Duygu Aykal, had a government scholarship for three years at the Royal Ballet School, studying with Massine in the choreographic course de Valois had initiated and working as his assistant as well as graduating in choreology. She developed a personal choreographic style in which she united classical technique and modern dance forms.

The Turkish State Ballet was now ready to come under the direction of the Turks themselves and Nevit Kodalli became the first director. As 1973 was the 50th anniversary of the establishment of the Turkish Republic, this was appropriately timed. John Carewe took over from Alan Abbott as musical director. In the 1973/74 season de Valois arranged for Gary Sherwood and Faith Worth to stage Ashton's *La Fille mal gardée* but in 1975 a new outside influence arrived when two repetiteurs from the Bolshoi mounted Petipa's *Don Quixote*.

Ankara however owed everything to Britain and to de Valois, who had given her services generously (and freely) over so many years. There had been considerable difficulties but also great compensations, not least the enjoyment of a new territory, a new venture, to set against the increasingly established conditions of her companies in England. Moreover, by continuing beyond her Royal Ballet retirement in 1963, it constituted the kind of stimulus and interest that everyone needs at such a point in life.

Among her problems in Turkey had been the demands of an obligatory eighteen months military service for men, and the temptation for qualified male dancers to leave home for companies in Europe. There was also an ongoing condition, the exact reverse of a similar one in Britain—to persuade Turkish families that *girls* might respectably become ballet dancers ... The ballet organisation in Turkey provides career security for the dancers. They are trained for nine years, all found, and then offered jobs with pension arrangements. Turkish directors, teachers, choreographers and dancers are now drawing dividends from de Valois' very carefully planned artistic investment policy.

Her first prima ballerina, Meriç Sümen, was for a short time artistic director in Ankara before going to Istanbul also as director. Her successors at Ankara were Hüsnü Sunal and his wife Evinc.

De Valois is not forgotten by the Turks. In 1982 she was presented in London with a plaquette on behalf of the Government of Turkey on the occasion of the centenary of Atatürk's birth and in 1986 the Istanbul Turco-British Association celebrated a thirtieth anniversary with a performance by students of the ballet section of the Istanbul State Conservatoire when Joy Newton was asked to attend and receive, on de Valois' behalf, a Professorship of Istanbul University as a further token of Turkish appreciation.

Chapter XIV

⌇ This is not the context in which to examine in any detail the financial background of the Royal Ballet organisation nor the complex fabric of committee discussions and decisions, recommendations and their results. De Valois' work in the theatre however, of which this is a chronicle, cannot be properly appreciated if no mention is made of major contributions on the administrative side. Just as she had been involved in the time-and-energy absorbing business of getting her company to Covent Garden in 1946 so, when the Royal Charter was granted ten years later, it represented positive thinking and action on her part over some years. Her views were not conditioned by any ideas of grandeur or prestige but of practical security for her company. She realised that the financial grants made to Sadler's Wells Theatre and to the Royal Opera House were "for the presentation of opera and ballet but not actually for any specific company". Security for her two companies and her school had to be achieved.

In 1954 therefore she drew up a memorandum for discussion. This began by setting out clearly the relationship of the two companies of Sadler's Wells Ballet at Covent Garden and Sadler's Wells Theatre Ballet at Sadler's Wells. It emphasised the close ties between them and the fact that the smaller company had four special functions: to provide opportunities for artists specially suited in modern ballets; to develop highly talented dancers who could not be placed in the bigger company on leaving the school; to produce medium-sized ballets; to give experience to young choreographers, designers and composers. The time had come to "establish this threefold institution as a separate entity under a name which recognises the fundamental unity of the two companies and the school". One of her suggested names was The Royal Ballet.

De Valois was firm that "all drifting without a definite *protective* policy for the future should cease":

"While a change in the present system may not be urgent, it is well to have a plan for the future when the people of understanding who have watched and helped in the growth of the ballet are no longer concerned with its welfare ... I speak of a period in the history of our national ballet that may never concern me personally ... I state the case as I see it today, with the eyes of its founder and not of its present director."

High level discussions continued and at last, on October 31 1956, the Charter was ready. The Royal Ballet was constituted—

"to promote and advance the art of the ballet and in association therewith the literary, musical and graphical arts and to foster public knowledge and appreciation of the same"[1]

The Chairman of the Board of the Royal Opera House, Lord Waverley, had steered the delicate negotiations through to a highly satisfactory conclusion.

It was therefore as the The Royal Ballet that the main company made its first historic visit to the USSR, appearing at the Leningrad Kirov in 1961. This had been in the air since 1956, when de Valois first went to Moscow with David Webster, Administrator of the Royal Opera House, to work out an exchange whereby the Bolshoi Ballet would appear in London and the Royal Ballet in Moscow. This would have been the first time any foreign company had appeared on the Bolshoi stage. The Bolshoi came to London but the Royal's season in Moscow was cancelled because of the Soviet entry into Hungary.

Negotiations were reopened and in March 1957 de Valois was once more in Moscow. Her contemporary diary details her daily activities from March 24 to April 12, reflecting her interests and application on every visit she has made to other parts of the world. For the ballet performances she sees and the many classes she watches she has the keen critical eye of a woman who has worked as a dancer, teacher and choreographer through a long professional life. She sums up dancers' qualities unsparingly (Khomyakov as the Jester in *Swan Lake* "danced brilliantly and cleanly—although in years well past his prime") but often with enthusiasm. Vlassova, as Jeanne d'Arc in Bourmeister's ballet at the Stanislavsky,

> "is, for me, the greatest little actress their ballet world possesses. She reaches extraordinary heights in this performance; I find her intelligence, style and general approach shows something of Western Europe's conception of Russian ballet at its best."

Her view of Plisetskaya is a perfect appraisement:

> "She was quite lovely; a hard dancer, one might say, but compensation lay in her lightness, and scintillating technique."

She sees a rehearsal in Leningrad of *The Fisherman*:

> "a remarkable work in the making by a young choreographer—Grigorovich. The best choreography that I have seen so far; imaginative and poetic. We will hear more of him."

Yuri Grigorovitch has now been choreographer director of the Bolshoi since 1964.[2]

She gives classes as well as watching them, she discusses with teachers and doctors the technical problems of developing dancers. De Valois has always been eager to learn—not to imbibe mindlessly but to weigh up new ideas or knowledge and, if she approves, incorporate them into her work. As Joan Lawson says: "She is always willing to discuss what she doesn't understand—or even what she doesn't like—and think about it."[3] Problems of personal physique and anatomy are an absorbing interest. In Leningrad she has a meeting with a professor of anatomy that typifies this:

> "I told him of my many superficial observations—slight anatomical defects possibly in the limbs and how I noticed that they were in accord with certain points elsewhere in the body, facial bone structure, texture of hair, sloping or square shoulders etc. He kept smiling and nodding his head and at the end said 'In my capacity as a professor I have observed much about dancers but in your capacity as a teacher you seem to have observed some things that I am going to explore in theory—they are of extraordinary interest to me!'"[4]

Far beyond all this intensive professional area of her visits to Moscow and Leningrad however lies her passionate interest in the general theatre, in every branch of culture, in the history and character of the people. Her every response declares her highly civilised cultural approach, her emotional commitment—and it is unusual to find these two qualities so judiciously balanced in a personality. So often the one almost totally obscures the other. Anyone who is in equal parts academically able, imaginatively keen and humanly concerned is indeed a rare specimen of homo sapiens.

De Valois came away from the USSR convinced among other things that although the Russians badly needed "the highly concentrated one-act ballet [that] did much to embellish and widen choreography, particularly in the sphere of modern experimental work", the English needed the experience of creating three-act ballets, "the experiment in creative production of the more spacious leisured approach".

> "We need contact with that forgotten part of the theatre in modern ballet—the part I can only describe as theatre-sense; it lies at the core of these great traditional three-act ballets. The structure of the scenario alone is of immense importance, for never does it appear to be an obscure peg used to hang movement on; it becomes instead a *raison d'être* for movement itself, a return to the significance of drama in the theatre."[5]

This estimate was perhaps an unexpected one in 1957, considering the triumphant one-act literary-dramatic ballets that existed in the Royal Ballet repertoire; but just as the short story and the novel are totally different both in aim and in technique, so the one-act play (now so rarely performed but so very popular and prevalent in the twenties and thirties) differs from the three-acter and the one-act ballet from the full evening production. De Valois was therefore making an interesting and valid point—that although English ballet had an exceptional reputation (from both Sadler's Wells and Rambert) for the short literary ballet it had yet to gain facility and success at the longer length. In 1948 Ashton's *Cinderella* had been a pioneer, but it was choreographed to the existing, proved score by Prokofiev staged at the Bolshoi. The first ambitious attempt to marry choreography to a new score and top-flight designs was instigated by de Valois in 1957 when John Cranko, Benjamin Britten and John Piper collaborated over *The Prince of the Pagodas*. Its failure in the repertoire was a serious disappointment. To a viewer, the faults lay in the complicated scenario, the amount of distinctly undanceable music in the distinguished score which Cranko was at the time unable, because of his own inexperience as a choreographer, to turn to good theatrical use, and the fact that the designs never created memorable stage pictures. It is hard now to recall anything at all of the production . . .

De Valois, who thought highly of the work, gives interesting reasons for its failure:

> "If it had been produced in Russia there would have been oceans of leisurely time both in the rehearsal room and on the stage before and after the event. Time to smooth out any rough passages, to prune where necessary, and to rethink all the inevitable moments of weakness in a work of such length; time for the composer and the choreographer to get together and reconstruct certain scenes."[6]

These are the comments of a thoroughly professional woman of the theatre who knows exactly what creative artists need, ideally, to produce their best work on stage, and they apply to a great deal that is inevitably rushed and scamped because of Western haste and the exigencies of small and cramped theatres and shortage of money.

In the intervening years since 1957, no doubt largely because of de Valois' advocacy, British choreographers have produced many full evening ballets, some to specially composed scores, more to arrangements of a composer's music made by another musician. Greater ease and authority have come with practice although most of them have shown exactly the kind of weaknesses in music, choreography and scenario that de Valois' "oceans of leisurely time" might well have eradicated.

Ashton has contributed *Ondine* and the perfect example, *La Fille mal gardée*. Cranko, for his own Stuttgart company, continued with *Romeo and Juliet*, *The Taming of the Shrew* and (the most successful) *Onegin*. MacMillan has staged *Romeo and Juliet*, *Manon*, *Mayerling*, *Anastasia* and *Isadora*—three hits and two misses. David Bintley has joined forces with them, producing *The Swan of Tuonela* and the considerably better *Snow Queen*.

The Royal Ballet was now the overall name for both companies, but they remained distinct in spite of everyone's intention to thread them together. De Valois' own hopes in 1958, when Sadler's Wells Theatre gave up the second company and the Royal Opera House took it over, was that in the end there would be one company, divided from time to time according to the engagements to be fulfilled. Some ballets would be common to both repertoires, opportunities for dancing would be increased as there would be constant movement between the company in London and the company on tour, with artists alternating between the two.[7] This plan never really worked, for all kinds of reasons, most of them practical. For some time principal dancers from Covent Garden did appear fairly regularly with the touring company, either to lend cachet (as when Fonteyn appeared with them in Tokyo) or to gain experience (as when Antoinette Sibley danced her first Aurora in South Africa). Only very rarely however did a touring company principal appear at Covent Garden with the main company, and in time the policy was largely dropped.

In the fifties and sixties everyone connected with the Royal Ballet seemed to be travelling most of the time and this certainly included de Valois. While her care and concern for Turkey continued, other areas shared the benefit of her study and advice. In 1951 she went to Belgrade for the British Council as a lecturer and consultant on ballet and dance, a request emanating from the Yugoslav National Theatres. Her task was to visit the State ballet schools in Belgrade, Ljubljana and Zagreb and make "a friendly survey" of their position and prospects. The journey there was an example of how even VIP travel at the time could throw up problems for the traveller.

The outward trip involved a one-night stopover in Frankfurt, a city still under military control. De Valois was given no booking, only a green voucher entitling her to a bed somewhere in the area. This involved a very long taxi ride to the outer suburbs where she was billeted in an apartment in a half-ruined seven-storey house with a middle-aged German couple. Her tiny bedroom had a bed, a table and a heating stove, and as her hosts spoke little English and she no German, communication was by mime—in which no doubt she was more proficient than they. She was subjected to a long social evening eating and drinking with hosts and neighbours—"I looked and felt like a trapped goat"—before a 5.30 a.m. start the next morning.[8] Once in Yugoslavia she had an interpreter with her all the time, a zealous female who loved propounding Communist arguments. "Here was a human being whose mind had been subjected to imprisonment ... ... underneath it all she was just an earnest schoolmarm, serving the cause with hysterical fanaticism ... "

Wherever she went on these international journeys de Valois assessed all her contacts on this human basis, observing and considering their characters, backgrounds and the reasons they were as they were. People everywhere mattered, and always matter, to her—not merely as studies for character, as they are for most theatre artists, but for their intrinsic human worth. Their idiosyncrasies amuse her, their ability and courage in any field win her admiration, their dogmas, hypocrisy and pomp-ousness enrage her. They stay in her memory—the German landlady, the Turkish official, the Yugoslav peasant, the small-town American mother ... each one becomes as much part of her life as the famous international names in the arts and world affairs who have been colleagues and friends.

In the Yugoslav cities she made direct contact with the ballet teachers and dancers of the State schools and was able to make a positive and hopeful report—and a practical recommendation that the relevant ministry should immediately arrange for better-made ballet shoes to be available—before going on to lecture in Athens and Salonika.

Another involvement came in the fifties. This began with a visit to Turkey by the Shah of Persia, who was impressed by a ballet gala in Ankara given in his honour. Later, in 1956, Nejed Ahmadzadeh, who directed the national ballet academy in Teheran, visited London and asked de Valois if she could give her advice on the development of a ballet company. This was a cherished project of an old friend of hers, Hilda Bewicke, who had been for many years resident in Iran as the wife of General Arfa. De Valois went out in spring 1958, at the invitation of the Iran Government, on an exploratory expedition and then sent out Ann Cox, a graduate of the RAD Teachers' Training Course, to work at the Ahmadzadehs' academy. Although the situation in Teheran was not at all comparable to that in Ankara—the general theatre scene lagged far behind—progress was gradually made. Within a short time a national ballet company was established. De Valois again visited in February 1964, invited by the Iranian Fine Arts Admin-istration, and while there had a happy reunion with Hilda Bewicke. She suggested that the Iranians appoint Robert de Warren as director, and he stayed from 1965 to 1971, creating more than fifteen ballets and then spending five years studying Iranian national dance.

De Valois' dancers began to scatter around the world as directors themselves and her influence is discernible in a good many major companies. In a number of cases their appointments were the result of recommendations she made when asked.

In 1951 three ladies from Toronto (Mesdames Mulqueen, Whitehead and Woods) arrived in London to consult her about engaging an artistic director to build up a national ballet company in Canada. She suggested Celia Franca. Franca had joined Sadler's Wells Ballet during the war and became well-known as an excellent soloist with a special style of her own. She began choreographic work with Sadler's Wells Theatre Ballet on its formation in 1946 although she never established herself as a creator of ballets. She did however create a ballet *company*, accepting the challenge in Canada and remaining the National Ballet of Canada's director until 1974, building up a strong and sound organisation.

Again, the appointment of Peggy van Praagh to the then Borovansky Ballet in Melbourne on Borovansky's death, with its important consequences for the ballet scene in Australia, was made on de Valois' recommendation. She had always thought of van Praagh as directorial material and engaged her as a dancer with Sadler's Wells Ballet in 1941 on the understanding that she would gradually give up dancing and act as teacher and ballet mistress. This became her function with Sadler's Wells Theatre Ballet, and she was then upgraded to acting director in 1951 when the company toured the States. She left in 1956, but on various occasions was asked by de Valois to stage ballets abroad on her behalf. Van Praagh's long and valuable service to The Australian Ballet was comparable to Franca's in Canada.

Various companies in Europe drew on Royal (Sadler's Wells) Ballet artists as artistic directors. Alan Carter went to Munich, Claude Newman to Rome and very significant appointments were made of Kenneth MacMillan to Berlin and John Cranko to Stuttgart.

Cranko and MacMillan were both products of Sadler's Wells Theatre Ballet whose talents were fostered on de Valois' advice. It was a joy to her when they turned to choreography, and the outstanding theatre sense apparent in them both was encouraged and assisted by her. Cranko's outgoing, vital temperament, his gift for creating dance comedy, his involvement in the theatre as a whole, appealed to her greatly; but she was equally full of admiration for MacMillan's more withdrawn and enigmatic imaginativeness and his acute sense of visual drama. In some ways she was closer to Cranko because in addition to his choreographic talent he was very much a company director and teacher. He was interested in schooling and students. To him she was a guiding example. He told her, on the last occasion they met, that

"when he was in a jam about something he found himself saying 'Now what did Madam do in such a case?' He would remember and do likewise. 'But,' he added laughing, 'I was among the first to say on occasions—oh, hell, she's gone too far this time! Yet today I find myself inevitably acting the same way.'"[9]

De Valois' interest in MacMillan goes back to the audition he had with her for entry into the Sadler's Wells Ballet School in 1945. It is worth making the point that her dancers have always been known to her as individuals. She may occasionally, given the number of years and number of students, get their names mixed up but she knows their strength and weakness as well as their temperamental make-up. She is strict, she can be cross, she can make them cry over her candid remarks, but she is never lacking in sympathy and care.

Care came into the picture with MacMillan when in 1952 he ran into a severe case of stage-fright. De Valois recognised that he needed not only a rest but a respite from the pressured surroundings of Covent Garden. He joined Cranko in an interesting venture, a small ballet group that performed at Henley-on-Thames, and he began thinking about choreography and staging something for a choreographic workshop at Sadler's Wells. De Valois' encouragement was constant, as it had been with Cranko. She dropped small pieces of good advice in his way—suggesting, for example, that he should turn from jazz scores to classical music—and very soon commissioned a ballet for Sadler's Wells Theatre Ballet. This turned out to be *Danses Concertantes*, a remarkably inventive and confident treatment of the Stravinsky score which entirely confirmed her belief in him. She then asked Sir William Coldstream, Principal of the Slade School, for advice about new young designers and through him put MacMillan in touch with Nicholas Georgiadis—the beginning of a notable series of collaborations.

In the Diaghilev tradition, which she had carried on jointly with Lambert, de Valois believed in an artistic director acting as an adviser and liaison officer towards choreographers where music and design were concerned. It was a vital part of the job, she felt, to try and achieve happy and artistically satisfying partnerships in the creation of ballets. Not every suggestion would be successful but the sifting of ideas, the introduction of artists in the various fields to one another, and the general atmosphere of ongoing creativity was healthful and nourishing. In the fifties and sixties, at Covent Garden (and more remotely with the touring company) de Valois did her best to carry on into a new age the feeling of artistic networks that had prevailed in the thirties and forties.

To a surprising extent, but somehow less noticeably at the time, this was achieved in the ballets staged. The trouble was that too many of the finished productions failed to succeed on stage, for multiple complex reasons. Covent Garden, for instance, is a magnificent ambience when the stage is suited; all too often however some subtle factor, always hard to trace and define, causes a production to fail where perhaps in another theatre it might succeed.

The last dozen years of de Valois' directorship of the Royal Ballet were a particularly difficult period. The social context was in flux—in the fifties the exhaustion and malaise of postwar Britain was an important underlying condition; the sixties were suddenly 'swinging' and permissive, definitions began to crumble and the pace of change accelerated to an almost alarming degree.

Where planning was concerned, de Valois had various problems in the fifties. She needed new choreographers. Certainly Ashton was moving towards a period of great power, but he also produced two or three weaker and shortlived works on the way. She had no other seasoned regular creator of ballets on hand. She tried very hard with Andree Howard, so tremendously talented and so difficult to transplant into a larger balletic scene, but had to give up after the tenuous *Belle Dame sans merci* in 1959. She persisted doggedly with the full evening work by way of *Sylvia, The Prince of the Pagodas* and *Ondine* until it fully established itself with *La Fille mal gardée* in 1960. Two matters concerned her deeply—to give her dancers, many of them part of a new generation, a wide range of stylistic challenges to face; and at the same time to develop her two hopeful choreographers, Cranko and MacMillan.

Hindsight shows that she was successful in both aims. The dancers of the time were employed in ballets by Petipa, Fokine, Massine, Balanchine, Bournonville, Roland Petit, as well as Ashton, Howard, Cranko and MacMillan. A vast array of diverse demands were made on them, and two layers of Royal Ballet artists benefited: Beriosova, Nerina and Blair came into their own, pointing the way to an exciting vintage for the sixties.

Fate also brought her an outstanding gift that Lilian Baylis would have unhesitatingly considered a direct answer from God. Whatever the excellences, as dancers and actors, of the Covent Garden company—and these were legion—only Fonteyn, in the years following Helpmann's resignation in 1950, had the star impact in performance that could magnetise audiences and reach out beyond the close confines of the ballet world. In 1961 however Rudolf Nureyev, travelling with the Kirov Ballet to Paris and London, defected in Paris. In November, at Drury Lane Theatre, he danced at a charity gala. De Valois was there and impressed, not so much by what she saw him do on stage as by his potential. In one of her quick, clear and accurate visions of the future she looked forward towards his Albrecht in *Giselle* and immediately determined that he would dance that ballet with Fonteyn and the Royal Ballet at Covent Garden. This, in February 1962, was the beginning of one of the most famous partnerships in ballet history.

De Valois' support of Nureyev's association with the Royal Ballet was enlightened and courageous. It was by no means a universally popular decision. It introduced a catalyst into a company that was getting on, in its own and in many of its supporters' view, very comfortably without him. The Royal Ballet had moved a long way towards an "establishment" character in its years at Covent Garden— a total change from the insecurities, challenges and resulting sharpness of artistic approach of the pioneering thirties and the wartime forties. They had settled down in the fifties and, without realising it, had become much less appealing and exciting from the public's point of view. For ten years, from 1950, new works at Covent Garden had been either partially successful, totally unmemorable or distinct failures. Real pleasures or excitements had belonged to Sadler's Wells Theatre Ballet.

Before Nureyev's advent the graph had begun to change course. Ashton had given the repertoire a new look with his delectable *La Fille mal gardée*, a marvellously choreographed full evening production that gave Nadia Nerina, David Blair and Stanley Holden the roles of their careers. The impact of Nureyev's debut however was tremendous, surrounded by massive press publicity and, as always with great theatre personalities, pro and con reactions from everyone concerned, on both sides of the footlights. Arguments abounded. Changes and interpolations in traditional productions were hotly opposed or championed, male dancers who had grown up with the company and had their admiring supporters were overshadowed by the blazing talent and temperament of this cuckoo in the nest. Feelings ran high, off stage and on. Typically, de Valois held fast to her view that Nureyev would do them all good. It was a fighting point of view, the policy of an inspired general taking a calculated risk in order to improve a position. Casualties might occur, some loss might have to be faced, in order to secure the intended objective, but the objective was what mattered.

A great deal was achieved by her daring use of Nureyev as dancer and later as producer, benefits that went deeper than the initially obvious one that publicity and controversy helped the box office and introduced fresh audiences, or the fact that new life was breathed into Fonteyn's career. Longer term and of great significance, everyone connected with the company was forced to think about standards of performance, of production, of creativity. They had to reflect more, to work harder, to aim higher—and none of these things ever did anyone any harm. They are, as de Valois has said, "a shot in the arm".[10]

Nureyev and de Valois understood each other very well. She perceived, as many could not, the contradictions that made up his character between apparent arrogance and deep-seated artistic humility. She has written about him with great insight. He in turn knows what he owes her, not merely for the chances presented to him but for the generous interplay of thought and argument. They have much in common, particularly their questing minds, their perfectionist standards (even if these are different), their determination to keep ballet a living theatrical force, their onward-looking mental attitude, their universality of approach. She writes of the link between his "passionate temperament and pedagogue's mind", and this is something that has relevance to her own career. She has always been a teacher, but although some people might classify her as intellectual, practical, non-emotional, her entire life work speaks of passion—a passionate commitment to the art of ballet and to everyone who genuinely devotes himself to it.

A retirement date was set by de Valois for herself, for handing over the directorship of the Royal Ballet—the end of 1963. Inevitably, she planned ahead, as she had done at every critical juncture in the past. From January 1961 the company had three names listed as Assistant Directors (Ashton had been her "associate director" since 1952): Michael Somes' particular charge was company rehearsals; John Hart's was administration of rehearsals and the interchange of artists between the two companies as well as the arrangement of company classes; and John Field had autonomous charge of what was now generally known as the Royal Ballet touring company. In 1963 therefore she was able to advance her retirement from December so that Ashton could take over (with his three assistant directors) in September. Everyone knew what they had to do and already had experience in doing it.

De Valois was sixty-five and felt she was leaving the Royal Ballet with the kind of continuity it needed. She herself intended to devote her energies to the Royal Ballet School. Everything about her retirement was done as quietly as possible. She retired in London, privately, speaking to the company in the Covent Garden Green Room and not appearing on stage at the end of the season. Later, Ashton asked her if she would "let him do something" and reluctantly she appeared at the Benevolent Fund gala in 1964 when the entire Royal Ballet organisation took part in a traditional défilé.

The Royal Ballet Defilè for NdV, Covent Garden 1964

294

Chapter XV

～ Parties, receptions, broadcasts and journalistic celebrations marked de Valois' retirement, as they would later her 80th birthday and the company's Golden Jubilee in 1981. By now she was loaded with honorary university degrees. London had got in early (1948) with an Hon. Mus. D. Reading, Sheffield, Aberdeen, Dublin, Sussex and Smith College Massachusetts had followed on with Doctorates of Letters or Music. She was made a Chevalier of the Légion d'Honneur in 1950. In 1951 she was created a Dame of the Order of the British Empire and in 1983 was honoured by the Queen with the special accolade of Companion of Honour. Two distinctions that also meant much to her were the Albert Medal and the Erasmus Prize.

The Albert Medal was established by the Royal Society of Arts in 1863, in honour of their late President the Prince Consort, "for distinguished merit in promoting Arts, Manufactures and Commerce". Apart from royal ladies, only one woman before de Valois was selected: Marie Curie, in 1910. The annual choice is made by the Council, sifting recommendations from Fellows, and then agreed by the President, who in 1964 was HRH Prince Philip, the Duke of Edinburgh. The citation for de Valois spoke of the "great personal distinction" she had won as a dancer, teacher, choreographer and producer:

"Her over-riding achievement, based on her mastery of roles, has been in guiding the development of the English national school of ballet over a period of nearly forty years, from small beginnings to its present position of eminence and celebrity."[1]

Ten years later de Valois became the first woman to receive an Erasmus Prize. These important cultural awards had been founded by Prince Bernhard of the Netherlands and were given annually. De Valois shared the prize with Maurice Béjart, representing classical ballet and modern dance.

The presentations were in Amsterdam in June 1974 at a glittering international diplomatic occasion, and Prince Bernhard, in a long address, made many valid points. He instanced particularly the combination of two qualities which had led to their choice of de Valois: that she had, through "talent and perseverance and example profoundly influenced the development of her art", and that she had a "deep understanding for and human interest in the wellbeing, the ups and downs, of all those young people, many of whom under your guidance have grown into brilliant dancers or choreographers".

Replying, de Valois pointed out that 1974 marked the 60th year of her professional career but went on to direct attention away from herself, reflecting on the fact that "Western European ballet has gone forward since the war almost as one united effort". She spoke of shared knowledge and creativity, of the lack of a language barrier in theatre dance and of the amount of work lying ahead for the younger generation.[2]

When de Valois turned her full attention to the Royal Ballet School (Lower and Upper) on her retirement from the company in 1963 she made it clear that she felt it was on the right lines and had great admiration for the staff. The staff at the time were indeed predominantly "her people". It included Ursula Moreton, Ailne Phillips and Sara Payne (Patrick); Pamela May, Elisabeth Kennedy, Valerie Adams, Barbara Fewster and Miro Zolan had all danced with the company. Nora Roche was a colleague from the Cecchetti Society. Julia Farron was a visiting teacher as were an eminent quartet: Winifred Edwards, Joan Lawson, Kathleen Crofton and Maria Fay. Moreton was Principal of the Ballet School, Arnold Haskell its Educational Director.

Inevitably de Valois had positive plans and ambitions for the future. She hoped to implement an idea of Michael Somes for a course in the principles of choreography and to introduce some form of training for repetiteurs in the senior school as well as drama training. She had some doubts about providing modern dance training for purely classical dancers while believing in it for *demi-caractère* and character dancers— at this point in the early sixties the old artistic definitions had not been so fully broken down as they were soon to become. She intended to

The Muses *(Royal Ballet School 1962)*

give folkdance greater prominence and to create a folk group that could appear in schools and colleges.

Folkdance, as we have seen, had always been dear to her and she had brought it into the Royal Ballet School curriculum very positively in 1958 when Douglas Kennedy, Director of the English Folk Dance and Song Society, advised her on courses and teachers. "To study folkdancing," she then declared, "is to study a country's natural style in movement." She considered it an essential part of a dancer's training, to help rhythm and musicality, to promote good ensemble work, vitality and concentration. "As a choreographer, I feel the call of these dances very deeply."[3]

In an address to The Royal Society of Arts in 1957, she went more deeply into her views on this. Making the point that although many people believed in the "inherent artificiality" of ballet,

"nothing could be further from the truth; it is a fact that all the ballet's fundamental dance steps are derived from the folk dances of Western Europe ... there can be traced, from the Basque country to the Highlands of Scotland, not only the steps but the very style of the classical dance. I know of no pastime that gives me more delight than to witness the annual display of folk dancing at the Albert Hall; I am able to recognise and name, according to the academic terminology of the classical ballet, every step that I see executed. Here I see these steps unadorned, yet neatly executed in their original simple form ... Western European dance masters lifted many of the actual dances wholesale into the theatre, the steps were heightened in their execution; in the end they were developed into their present state of perfection ..."[4]

Although it was not until 1971 that the School's annual performance began to contain the now familiar and tremendously popular section of folkdances from England, Scotland and Ireland, a group of boys presenting Morris and other traditional dances were featured in a Folk Dance Festival as early as January 1959. The operative name in the solid development of this group was that of Ronald Smedley. With his colleagues Bob Parker and, for Scottish and Highland Dancing, Colin Robertson, his strong influence over twelve years' association with the Royal Ballet School brought a wide range of dances into play and fostered in many of his pupils a keen and lasting enthusiasm. One of them, Jonathan Burrows, took over from him as teacher in 1979.

Burrows has been a key figure in an interesting development, the Bow Street Rappers. This Royal Ballet Morris group had its first big success when the company toured China in 1983. They were able to respond to demonstrations of Chinese folkdance with a display of English traditional dance—something quite unexpected from the Chinese point of view. Later, on a ballet tour to Eastern Europe, the British Council asked the Hungarian Police Department to allow the Rappers to dance through the streets of Budapest. Crowds turned out to see them and praise flooded in from people of all ages. In Barcelona they shared an open air performance with the local folklore group who danced their dignified Sardana, and in Moscow gathered on admiring crowd in the new shopping precinct Arbat.

The Rappers—the name comes from Covent Garden's siting in Bow Street and from the Tyneside Rapper Sword Dance—are run on Morris cooperative lines, meeting annually to elect a Squire who makes programme decisions and a Bagman to act as treasurer. About ten dancers, drawn from the Royal Ballet (Covent Garden) company, a fiddler and an accordion player, plus Ron Smedley and Bob Parker, make up the number involved in this offshoot of de Valois' mainstream work—one very close to her heart.

Over the years it has been excellent for both pupils and public to be able to relate traditional dances of Great Britain to ballets in which they have been featured as, for example, *La Fille mal gardée* with its stick, clog and maypole dances, and to discern traces of steps and figures in other choreographic works. Through de Valois' infectious interest in folk and social dance all the choreographers of the Royal Ballet have been either directly or indirectly influenced—time and again sequences or patterns, even in pure dance ballets, reveal on analysis a spicing of English or Scottish traditions. The most overt result of folkdance training was in *The Winter Play*, which Burrows staged for Sadler's Wells Royal Ballet in April 1983. This very positive attempt to bring into the ballet theatre the ancient tradition of the Mummers' Play of the winter solstice was by no means unsuccessful, but as an inexperienced choreographer Burrows failed to free it from his deep researches and specialised excitement and give it true balletic life. It was a bold and interesting statement in the cause of English folkdance but only reaffirmed that ballet, as a highly refined and complex art of the theatre, has to process the multiple and widely varied strands of dance forms into its own resplendent fabric. The choreographer has to work freely (and de Valois is a brilliant example of this), culling what he or she needs from the entire range of classical, modern, folk or ethnic dance and weaving it cunningly into a new and personal pattern.

A two-year Craftsman's Course was begun at the School by de Valois in 1964, with the interest and cooperation of Kathleen Gordon of the Royal Academy of Dancing. The intention was to help dancers who would eventually find their real vocation in the class and rehearsal room. The course was planned to avoid conflicting with existing RAD or other teacher training courses and was more closely related to the theatre scene. Students were shown how to teach classical and character dance, folkdance, the examination syllabi of various institutions, and excerpts from ballets. They learned stage management, make-up and Benesh notation. They were taught how to work with pianists for their classes, they had lectures on ballet history, they studied films of Royal Ballet rehearsals. The coordination with choreology was forward-looking—to suggested music, students wrote solos, duets and small ensembles in notation.

About this time one of the principal folk and character dance teachers from the Hungarian State Ballet, Agnes Roboz, visited London and the Royal Ballet School and watched de Valois giving class:

"Her personality is fascinating. The graduate class of girls are training with immense intensity. The teacher notices and mentions each mistake.

At the end of the lesson the students are practising variations from *The Sleeping Beauty*. Ninette de Valois perfects each of them. The students listen eagerly to each word of the great master. Her lesson was a wonderful experience."[5]

These classes were in preparation for the 1964 Royal Ballet School performance at Drury Lane when they presented *The Sleeping Beauty*, the first time the school had tackled such a demanding production. This ballet had become an ongoing specialisation in de Valois' life. It was the subject of the first pantomime she ever saw, in Ireland; she watched the Diaghilev *Sleeping Princess* from the audience, she danced in *Aurora's Wedding* with his company, she worked with Sergeyev and Lopokova in staging *The Sleeping Princess* for the Vic-Wells Ballet in 1939. Then, with the historic success of the 1946 revival she had produced as *The Sleeping Beauty* at Covent Garden and its later triumph in New York she became established as its expert director. In 1956 she accepted an invitation from the Royal Danish Ballet to stage a production in Copenhagen the following year, and went there to watch company classes and discuss casting. It was decided that Margrethe Schanne should be the first Aurora but de Valois also chose a second partnership of Kirsten Simone and Henning Kronstam.

This production inaugurated the pattern she followed frequently in later years—she would ask a specific dance teacher who knew a work intimately to set the production on the foreign company and then go over herself for an intensive period of final rehearsal to supervise the whole and to coach leading roles. For the Danish *Beauty* she asked Peggy van Praagh to teach the work and went to Copenhagen herself in February 1957.

It was a special occasion for the Danes—the first time a full length Petipa ballet had been performed by the company. Success was not unqualified. The smaller stage, and designs by André Delfau that failed to make the most of the dancing area, meant severe cuts in ensembles and "extras". However, the performance had important merits. Allan Fridericia, the distinguished Danish critic, particularly praised de Valois' coaching of Simone and Kronstam:

"Simone really develops from the young gay girl through the lyric unearthly dream to the proud brilliant bride. Kronstam is in every way noble . . ."[6]

How often one looks in vain for an Aurora to achieve that important development! Not unexpectedly, given the Danes' special aptitude for

NdV demonstrating hand movements in 'Job' (Royal Ballet 1970)

mime, there were notable cameos from Niels-Bjørn Larsen as the Tutor and Lizzie Rode as the Countess.

De Valois staged the *Beauty* twice in Turkey and then in 1977 came back to it for the Royal Ballet at Covent Garden. Two of their productions had for different reasons misfired and the Linbury Trust and the Friends of Covent Garden made it possible to have a third try towards recapturing the charm and excitement of the 1946 revival. This did not quite happen, but the production stripped away some unnecessary coats of varnish and restored vital points of dance and mime. De Valois was not entirely happy and was determined to go on working at it—"we must get it *right*".[7]

De Valois retired from the directorship of the Royal Ballet School in 1972. Haskell and Moreton had already retired—Michael Wood had been appointed in Haskell's place—and from now on, inevitably, there were constant tributes to be written or spoken about the retiring and the dead. *The Dancing Times*, month by month, reproduced appreciations from her, generous, perceptive estimates of lives and work, as colleagues of widely varying ages were the subjects of citations or obituaries. She appeared on television programmes, contributing recollections of Diaghilev, Rambert and others. She adjudicated awards, she made presentations. Presentations were made to her.

Many other matters preoccupied her. She wrote prose and poetry, she gave lectures and took part in seminars, she kept constantly in touch with the ballet and dance world. There was work still to be done. She remained on the Board of Governors of the Royal Ballet, set up at the time of the Royal Charter to safeguard the company's interests, and on the Board of the Royal Ballet School. She frequently watched performances by both companies and continued to participate in the affairs of the teaching organisations. She had pertinent things to say about any issue that concerned dancers and ballet, for example the Arts Council's Resettlement Scheme for dancers which aimed at helping those whose careers came to an end in their early forties to make a new start. In 1973 she collaborated with Ashton to produce a work for Ballet for All—the title for this educational group founded by Peter Brinson in 1964 was an original idea of Kathleen Gordon's. For *The Wedding of Harlequin or Harlequin Revived* Ashton composed the dances while de Valois staged the character work and mime, with a Harlequinade based on the one she had known at the Lyceum pantomimes.

Ashton retired as director of The Royal Ballet in 1970 and Kenneth MacMillan succeeded him as artistic director and resident choreographer. The dual responsibility did not work out, so he resigned as director in 1977 and was followed by Norman Morrice. In 1986 Morrice was replaced by Anthony Dowell, who had been associate director for a year. This was an appointment full of hope for the future, and Dowell, who grew up in de Valois' time and graduated from the school to the company in 1960, made it plain at his first press conference that he had not only discussed his appointment with her but had been encouraged by her to accept it.

*   *   *

"A dancer of distinction, a splendid administrator, a gifted choreographer, an expert producer and an inspiring teacher all combined in one person..."[8]

This was Cyril Beaumont's tribute to de Valois in 1964 when she was made an Hon. Fellow of the Imperial Society of Teachers of Dancing. Any great and positive personality however attracts as much antagonism and disapproval as admiration. Fierce criticism is the measure of outstanding ability and inevitably there are people in de Valois' profession who have disliked her methods or her policies. Like every strong ballet company director she is accused of favouritism or neglect, the promotion of some careers and the blight of others. The partisan of a dancing talent necessarily simplifies every situation into black and white elements, positing a powerful and prejudiced person in command who is responsible for any setback, any disappointment, any failure. Their natural reaction is to say "She never gave him/her a chance," "She pushed so-and-so who had far less talent," "She didn't understand his/her problems," "She wasn't sympathetic," "She refused him/her roles, or extra tuition, or an opportunity to do choreography" ... the list of accusations is as endless as personal love and loyalty can work out. Within her companies dancers have felt there was sometimes favouritism. Moira Shearer talks of what she terms "phases" of popularity that some dancers had where de Valois was concerned, admitting that it happens:

" ... in all companies probably ... too much would be given to the dancer of the moment and nobody could ever fulfil all that was expected, whereupon they would be dropped ... To my great good luck she never had a phase on me at all, which I found a very good thing."[9]

Whatever the rights or wrongs of individual cases, one thing is certain—no one who cannot take difficult and unpopular decisions and stick to them, no one who cannot ride out criticism and opposition, is suited to the artistic direction of a ballet company. "The ballet director" de Valois has written "commences his career by growing several extra skins."[10]

De Valois is a woman of strength and courage, decisive but never hard or unimaginative. To talk to her is to be convinced that whatever she has decided, whether it has been right or wrong, has been considered in its current context. She does not act on whims or fancies. She has sound reasons to back up her views. She may turn out to have been mistaken—that is an inevitable human risk—but she will have definite grounds for what she has done.

It can be argued that positive decisions, even if they are not proved to be right, even if they are hurtful to some people, are in the long run better for any organisation than shilly-shallying. De Valois is impatient with indecisiveness, with inaction, with uncertainty, with waffle, with sitting on fences and waiting to see which way winds will blow. She may love an argument, like any of the Irish, but she has to end it on a definite note by taking action. She is always a couple of steps ahead of her interlocutors, forward rather than backward looking, baffling them by relying on the intuition and instinct that has so often served her well rather than on the in-depth documentation that they have so lovingly prepared. Her intuition however is closely allied to common sense. She can at one and the same time contemplate the whole and the part, a woman who can see both the wood and the trees.

While she is analytical and observant, she spends little time looking back. If something has gone wrong, she is less interested in a post-mortem to discover reasons or affix guilt than in finding a way to put it right so that one can move on towards the future. The future has always been more important to her than the past. She has always looked ahead, planned ahead, and like all active rather than passive people she cares about what she or anyone else is going to do rather than what they have done.

Dowell, speaking of his intentions on taking up the directorship of the Royal Ballet in 1986, emphasised that he meant to get the company back to the discipline he had known under de Valois in the early sixties. Unconsciously, he was echoing a speech Helpmann made to a dinner in her honour at Claridges in June 1947 when he said:

"She has imparted such style and discipline to the company that I for one would never work with any other; though I might occasionally run away to act, I would always come home to the Wells if they would have me, because I could not be happy associated with any company that had less discipline or less style."[11]

In class and in rehearsal she scared her dancers. The more talented they were the more furious she got, trying with perfectionist dedication to draw from them qualities she perceived but they were unaware they possessed. Fonteyn recalls her as "a marvellous and unpredictable woman". Looking back, she realises the work load that made de Valois, in the thirties, short tempered: directing rehearsals and giving classes, attending to office business, and then perhaps dancing Swanilda in the evening, "doing *brisés* which seemed faster than the speed of light". In class and rehearsal she gave no quarter, shouting at them, banging the floor with her stick, terrorising them—and then, because of her "enormous sense of fun" altering at a moment's notice into better humour. With these quick-change moods she kept her dancers keyed up and striving to do their best to satisfy her very stringent standards, and this continued through all her years as a director. Again in retrospect, Fonteyn declares:

"Intelligent to a degree, and far-seeing, she made decisions that often appeared completely wrong at the time and yet turned out to be completely right in the long run."[12]

Although she is generally highly thought of as a teacher, there are of course dissentient voices. No subject could be more complex, more endlessly debatable or more coloured by personal convictions than the merits of dance teachers. Spend a day listening to divergent views on systems and syllabi, on the best primary, intermediate and advanced tuition, and you will have a faint glimmering of how hotly and individually dogmatic are professional opinions. So it is not surprising to find de Valois at one and the same time admired or deplored for her teaching methods. Like all top-line teachers, she suited some dancers completely and others not at all. Where the Royal Ballet School was concerned, however, the curriculum she adopted and the teachers she employed, balancing one against another, resulted in a glorious crop of artists who came to prominence in the sixties. The attainments of dancers like Antoinette Sibley, Merle Park, Lynn Seymour, Christopher Gable, Anthony Dowell and David Wall testify to the success of her system better than any amount of literary analysis. They appreciated her.

"Madam gave me the opportunity to succeed. Without her trust I might have wilted away. She let the teachers and choreographers know that she liked me. There were times when I must have annoyed her greatly but she never reproached me for the way I managed or mis-managed my life. Without Ninette de Valois there would be no Lynn Seymour."[13]

So Seymour wrote in tribute. Sibley's glowing memories of care and attention throughout her years at the School, vividly recorded in Barbara Newman's book about her, conjure up another fascinating and fruitful director/pupil relationship.[14]

Three areas in which de Valois, again like most founding directors of companies, comes in for criticism from many people are the appointment of teachers, coaching and the use or non-use of guest artists. Where teachers are concerned, she engaged many over the years from very different sources, chosen always because she felt they could contribute some special qualities she felt essential for her dancers. As Joan Lawson says, she was "determined to establish a company style"[15] and for that reason, although very willing to bring in a variety of tutors, she was reluctant for dancers to go outside for private tuition. Although a ballerina might find that a private teacher could help her to strengthen certain areas in her technique, this could also introduce stylistic differences that disturbed the company's overall character. The earliest company teachers, apart from de Valois herself, were Ursula Moreton, Margaret Craske and Anna Pruzina. Sergeyev taught, and also Idzikovsky. Later, during the forties, two Russian teachers who came to England via Shanghai were important influences—Vera Volkova, who had been trained by Agrippina Vaganova, and George Gontcharov. Once the company were at Covent Garden Joy Newton was ballet mistress for the first season with Jean Bedells taking over later in the year. Harjis Plucis, an eminent Latvian teacher, became ballet master in June 1948 and was soon joined by Mary Skeaping. They shared a strongly defined regime until Skeaping left to direct the Royal Swedish Ballet. Plucis remained as professor of dance and repetiteur until 1956 and then John Hart took over until de Valois' retirement in 1963.

For better or worse, coaching has never been treated outside Russia in the intensive, one-to-one relationship that they favour. With de Valois' companies it has been a matter for the choreographer, producer or repetiteur to help dancers with interpretation, and the disadvantage of this is that whereas first casts are generally excellently prepared their successors often suffer from lack of coaching and rehearsal time. Where specific revivals have been concerned there was a good record in de Valois' time. Serge Grigoriev and his wife Lubov Tchernicheva, who were with Diaghilev and later de Basil, staged three ballets, *The Firebird*, *Petrushka* and *The Good-humoured Ladies*. Karsavina's store of knowledge was probably insufficiently used over the years, but she eventually coached Fonteyn in *The Firebird* and was consulted by Ashton over the mime scene in the last act of *La Fille mal gardée* and over the 1960 production of *Giselle*.

Guest artists have always been chosen from a wide background. The earliest of course were the Diaghilev artists Lopokova, Dolin and Idzikovsky and, from the Empire Theatre days, Phyllis Bedells. The conditions of the war years accustomed people to thinking that guest artists were unnecessary but immediately the company reached peace and Covent Garden de Valois initiated a steady stream of them as well as engaging Violetta Elvin (Prokhorova) as a regular member of the ballet. Massine, Markova and Dolin, Danilova and Frederic Franklin, Yvette Chauviré, Melissa Hayden, Sonia Arova, Caj Selling, Carla Fracci, Lydia Sokolova, Eric Bruhn and Nureyev, all brought particular challenges of style and presentation to de Valois' own dancers.

De Valois' belief in ballet's close kinship to the other dramatic arts, its place in the theatrical scene, has remained unshaken and is reflected in many ways. Unlike many artistic directors, she has maintained a complete balance between the two aspects of ballet—dance and drama—from the earliest days, but the fact that both she and Ashton were so much part of the theatre in the thirties has been reflected in the repertoire and the dancers of the Royal Ballet.

Ashton, master of dance invention, has often chosen to work to a theme or story and created brilliant and subtle characterisations. MacMillan and Cranko continued this dual interest and it has moved into another generation with David Bintley. Equally each new batch of dancers has included artists capable of memorable acting—as for example Stephen Jefferies, who is as much at home with the comedy of Petruchio as with the tragedy of *Mayerling*.

De Valois' views of ballet in the late 1980s were as positive and personal as in the 1930s. She opened a talk to the London Ballet Circle in 1985 by taking a firm stand on her conviction that "the ballet world and the contemporary dance world are getting too mixed up".[16] Now this is a considered opinion from someone who has always, as a choreographer, moved easily and fluently through a wide spectrum of dance forms and believed, with Fokine, that it is important to marry the right kind of dance to the subject or theme of a choreographic

NdV with Dame Alicia Markova, Alexandra Danilova and Dame Eva Turner 1983

work. De Valois is not, in this statement, putting up fences between the various techniques of theatre dance. She is talking of the conservation of artistic identity, of the need for recognising and preserving different traditions and the fact that at present it is not so much a question of one tradition drawing on another for a special purpose as of a general confusion of styles, often practised by people who have not thoroughly studied any of them. Those of us who see a good deal of novice or poor class choreography know that there is these days considerable work of a completely amorphous kind, where all edges have run into each other like water spilt over dabs of paint.

In her talk to the London Ballet Circle de Valois began by quoting a letter she had received from Fonteyn that happened to chime with her own current thoughts:

"I have been thinking about the state of ballet now and in the future ... I find it all so confusing that I am very glad I am not in it any more. It seems to me like Paris fashions. One used to know what style of dress, what type of waist, what length of skirts were right for that year but now there is no more right or wrong..."[17]

Two honourable traditions, classical ballet and modern dance—the first going back three hundred years, the second belonging predominantly to the 20th century (Martha Graham's "two bibles of the dance world")[18] should not, in de Valois' view, lose their specific character in some faceless merger. "I do not believe that when you mix the actual forms choreographically you get the best out of either."[19] Classical ballet, because of its long history, has much in common with opera and drama—"time travellers", de Valois calls them, moving from the classicism of the 18th century through the romanticism of the 19th to the neo-classicism of today. Its privilege is to be able to present works from many different periods and in a variety of styles, meeting a range of challenges from Petipa to the present time, all within the framework of classical ballet. Ballet dancers can adapt to the demands of a great diversity of dance creators. Classicism, as she says, "is a tough world—and what a lovely world it is!"[20]

The interaction of influences and ideas is something she has always accepted and welcomed. What she deplores is "the indiscriminate mixing of the classical and contemporary in movement"[21] and the emphasis she places on maintaining identity between the traditions is echoed in what she feels about dancers themselves. She believes in recognising the strong points and the limitations of any particular artist, the differences between "the contralto and the soprano", between the classical dancer, the *demi-caractère* and character dancer within ballet, as well as the difference between classical and modern. She believes in accepting ethnic and racial characteristics of physique and temperament and not attempting to mould one into the other. Dancers should be helped to discover their individual talent and take pride in it rather than force themselves into wrong channels. Often physique is the key. She recalls

"seeing an excellent contemporary company give a wonderful evening's entertainment, but at the end of their performance they stood in a row—and to my surprise I realised I could not have trained any of them as classical dancers because of their lack of certain physical requirements."[22]

Equally, this must be applied territorially. "Every race and every nation must aim at its own perfection and realise that its particular perfection cannot be imitated by some other country." She went into more detail about this in her talk:

"I was invited somewhere up north to a state school to watch some dancing by a girl from Asia. She danced as they danced in the forest where she came from and it was beautiful to see ... She was not a bit like any of our people, she didn't seem to have a bone in her body but she moved beautifully ... [then] this entire school rose to its feet ... and they copied her ... They were doing things they didn't understand with their stiff bodies ... When they sat on the ground the little girls were turning their feet—now the oriental foot turns quite naturally inside but ours don't and are not meant to. If they did, you could not do classical ballet."[23]

Study other forms, observe them and eventually draw from them what is right for your own cultural tradition and personal make-up—this is the method on which she based her own teaching and choreography, distilling from Espinosa, Cecchetti, Legat, Preobrajenska and the Diaghilev Ballet what she believed to be proper for herself as dancer and choreographer and for the development of her company's special English style.

What is this special style that because of the company's rise to pre-eminence has come to be considered "the English style"? It is salutory to look back to some observations de Valois made when she was writing her first book, *Invitation to the Ballet*.[24] She analysed the English temperament with the outside view of the Irishwoman who has nevertheless matured in English society. She listed problems: sentimentality, the "negative refinement"; modesty, "a forced and simpering mannerism"; a lack of rhythm; a "neglect of salient emphasis, which is noticeable even in their speech", a lack of dynamic shading. She aimed at countering the sentimentality by developing an acute sense of characterisation, of replacing modesty by artistic humility; she recommended the kind of wide curriculum of training in the arts which she had inaugurated at the Academy of Choregraphic Art and continued into the Royal Ballet School, stressing especially music and languages "to quicken the ear to an important degree" and draughtsmanship to develop "a sensitive reaction to line, pattern and composition". She did not feel the lack of rhythm was basic, considering the strong rhythms of Morris and country dance but she had found that the English dancer's sense of metre was more highly developed than his sense of rhythm. English dancers however were musical,

NdV teaching at The Royal Ballet School 1987

graceful, flexible with no natural disadvantages where strength and physique were concerned.

Some of this remains apparent. The dance style developed by the training and repertoire of the Royal Ballet (and Ashton's choreography has been as strong an influence as de Valois' teaching policies) is, at its best, remarkable for purity of line, fluency, musical feeling, speed and precision. "Salient emphasis" and technical virtuosity are often lacking, as are outstanding elevation and ballon. The Royal Ballet style—and this is a better description than the English style, for it includes the various radical elements of the British Isles and its overseas territories—has had its perfect examples in Margot Fonteyn and Anthony Dowell, as well as less celebrated names. De Valois' understanding of their capacity and perception in training have been superbly justified by their performances.

She has also consciously encouraged and developed, quite apart from her classicists, her *demi-caractère* dancers, on every level from great central roles to tiny cameos and in both dramatic and comic contexts. Because of her, because of her devotion to the theatre and her conviction that ballet has an important contribution to make to it, the Royal Ballet and its predecessor companies have an unequalled record of great dramatic ballets and great actor-dancers, both male and female, the best of whom are historically and internationally on the very highest level. Through her creation, our national ballet, she has written a vital chapter in the story of British theatre.

❊   ❊   ❊

"And Ninette de Valois, the person? What is she? 'A beast but a just beast? A despot, benevolent or otherwise? A visionary? A mad Irishwoman? A very kindhearted human person? All of these, and some simultaneously . . .'"[25]

Leo Kersley, a former principal dancer with both companies, wrote this on the fiftieth anniversary of the staging of *Les Petits Riens* at the Old Vic. In his view she "could be absolutely ruthless in the furthering of her ideals but was never ruthless for herself". This selflessness is indeed the key to her complex life and character. Although she had enough of the performer's self-assurance and belief in her own ability to make a great reputation as a *première danseuse* and pursue an intensive and effective career as a choreographer, de Valois completely lacks the self-absorption and desire for personal success usual in a

312

stage artist. The word ruthless was also used, and in much the same context, by Brian Masters in 1983:

> "She has been ruthless (and wise) in her pursuit of glory and excellence for her dancers, totally indifferent to whether she should receive the credit for having done so; Ninette de Valois has pride; she has no vanity."[26]

This is not a pose. She does not turn aside compliments in order to have people insist on repeating them. She does not spread the credit for achievement to others (from the famous down to the hard worker in the background) to gain merit with them. She does not ask people to admire her or to love her, she does not expect them to understand her motives, to give her the benefit of any doubt. She has no affectation or artificiality. She does not want to manipulate lives and careers, to destroy other ventures, to engage in the machinations of art politics. She has never desired financial gain, and power only to create what she felt compelled to create—dancers, ballets, and above all a company. All her life she has worked, and made others work, for an ideal, sure of her destiny but considering herself its instrument rather than its director. "I am convinced that we shape no event as forcibly as events shape us."[27] She has been impelled by her vision as completely as any Don Quixote—but her magnificent sanity, her tremendous sense of humour and unfailing practicality, her deep concern for other people, have supplied the perfect balance to her missionary dream. The measure of her unique personality is exactly as a graphologist, puzzled by her handwriting, once declared: "She is an idealist with absolutely no illusions."

Ninette de Valois Reflects

You say I am repeating
Something I have said before. I shall say it again.
Shall I say it again? In order to arrive there,
To arrive where you are, to get from where you are not,
    You must go by a way wherein there is no ecstasy.
In order to arrive at what you do not know
    You must go by a way which is the way of ignorance.
In order to possess what you do not possess
    You must go by the way of dispossession.
In order to arrive at what you are not
    You must go through the way in which you are not.
And what you do not know is the only thing you know
And what you own is what you do not own
And where you are is where you are not.

T. S. Eliot "East Coker III"
from *Four Quartets*

NdV with Lord Drogheda

"The Green Table"
Portrait of a Board Room

Ninette de Valois

~ Do they differ at all? Opulence characterises the older boardroom. The chairs are heavier and upholstered, the table longer and more heavily polished. There will no doubt be double-glazed windows, and walls adorned with portraits of "Past Chairmen". On the table, at each place, is a trim long pencil and a file of minutes. Minutes—hours might be more appropriate.

The chairman's assistant, or secretary as the case might be, recalls an official discreetly speeding up the line-up of horses for a race. Each member of the committee enters their respective little box (in the shape of a chair) as a restless or subdued steed, all a little apprehensive. Then they are off to the chairman's start and an escape from secretarial manœuvring.

No boardroom likes too long a sit-in. The actual function of a governing board is to be godparents to innumerable births elsewhere, sub-dividing itself into sub-committees with sub-chairmen.

Nevertheless, "The Board says" or "The Board is looking into it" has a comforting, omnipotent ring about it. "The Board" can be lovable, exasperating, weak, strong, wrong or right, but it is a necessary part of any establishment, and it will always bear the full burden of accusations with hardly enough time being allowed to change from one epithet to another.

The English boardroom of any national theatre venture wears the air of a long-sighted, benign institution. To see some national theatre boardrooms as run elsewhere makes one accept the characterisations already listed, discovering that they are capable of a degree of compromise that is comforting and a display of final decision that amounts to a state of fair dealing not to be experienced elsewhere.

As you get older, vision and memory form a partnership that reproduces conflicting impressions—remote yet personal, true yet possibly

315

too often not true. Nevertheless they are there—the work of some form of indelible pencil of the past.

As a habituee of the Boardroom, I have writhed under a formidable list of names. From the very beginning I decided to treat one and all as studies in a form of dedication to the objective point of view, clinical in its approach, awaiting the outcome of a diagnosis. Then, and then only, the surgical knife of experience would be inserted with such unobtrusive skill that the content of the whole operation was laid bare. One was tempted to ask for at least the surgical gloves as a souvenir.

The Earl of Lytton was my first experience. Aristocratic, remote, extremely gentle and rather embarrassingly deaf. A 19th-century figure, representing the end of an era, who served the arts as a good vicar serves his parish. He quite simply wanted the best for everyone. He served Lilian Baylis and the Old Vic until after World War II with a spirit of nobility of both birth and mind. I once witnessed him facing a raging theatre manager. Through an arrangement that had been clumsily made with the Home Office, a foreign company was not allowed to appear within a short distance of the then Vic-Wells Ballet when the latter was on tour. I got the worst of the manager's indignation—and noted with amusement that he was a bit flustered and overcome with the Earl although certainly not with the girl. Throughout, Lord Lytton remained calm, cool and courteous. In the end all was well and a plan set up that appeased everyone.

The last story I heard of him was about his gentle guidance over the release (not relished by all of the Sadler's Wells Board) of the Sadler's Wells Ballet so that it could move on to Covent Garden. The story—I cannot absolutely vouch for its authenticity, but I heard it from a very reliable source—concerns the finale. It was thrashed out in a rarefied state of calm by two peers, my Lords Lytton and Keynes, sitting in full regalia in the House of Lords during some state occasion that did not in any way concern the fate of the Sadler's Wells Ballet.

Lord Keynes, as Chairman of the Camargo Society and first Chairman of the Royal Opera House, could well be regarded as the Chairman who seemed to have all the answers as far as the ballet was concerned. Married to Lopokova, he was a dedicated follower of ballet. An awesome chairman, a man of sudden dramatic decision, yet possessed of an unblushingly warm heart where it concerned artists—artists in any form. He understood them, their problems, their value to society, their correct position in the world. He would sum up their talents with interest and insight, and their shortcomings with a tolerance that smacked of an uncomplimentary attitude towards the possible existence of any grey matter.

We had a game we used to play together. When the Arts Theatre was first opened in Cambridge, we would sit in a box before the performance started and guess how much money there was going to be in the house. I used to get nearer the figure than England's great economist. He was curious to fathom the reason. I explained that a "good" house came in with a degree of equality—the side seats would be filled with the same equality of numbers as the middle seats. A "bad" house always filled up in the middle first—because these were the obvious seats to give away for the sake of appearance. He was delighted and very intrigued.

His direction of the Camargo Society was quite masterly and, when necessary, equally ruthless. CEMA (The Council for the Encouragement of Music and the Arts) under him became the Arts Council of Great Britain. Covent Garden reopened under his chairmanship and the Sadler's Wells Ballet moved in after Islington consultations, finalised by those two distinguished peers in the House of Lords when other matters were on the agenda.

Keynes' death from a heart attack in 1946 was followed by a new Chairman of Covent Garden's Board of Governors. Entered the Viscount Waverley, known to all in those days as Sir John Anderson, the founder of the famous wartime "Anderson Shelter" that decorated back gardens as necessary blemishes for those grim, bomb haunted years. My first personal memories of him were some doubts expressed about the propriety of staging *Job*. He was a Scotsman and a devoted adherent to the Church of Scotland. It reached my ears that ecclesiastical research work was being launched and some ecclesiastics of not very liberal views were ordered to see the ballet. My slate remained clean...

Lord Waverley was a distinguished and respected figure, an ex-Chancellor of the Exchequer, a civil servant of the hierarchy and a Chairman of the Port of London. Each Oxford and Cambridge Boat Race was followed by the City's Port of London launch resplendent at that time with Lord Waverley and his guests. He was invaluable to Covent Garden because he had certain powers over our demands for increased financial aid, and it was "not done" to say no to Lord Waverley.

He was so right for us at this time. Not having a personal interest in the Arts, he was only dedicated to ensuring some form of financial stability. As a true Scotsman, though, he did privately uphold the talented Moira Shearer. He insisted on Lord Montgomery, who was devoted to the art of Margot Fonteyn, coming to see her fellow artist. Montgomery, very much an Anglo-Irishman with a leprechaun's Celtic nimbleness, watched Moira with her beauty and her dancing as aflame as her red hair. He turned to Waverley with an assumed innocence and said, "Couldn't she wear a wig?" I don't believe that even Waverley was ready with the appropriate answer.

Lord Waverley was a superb Chairman of tradition. I used to be mesmerised, fascinated. A problem came up at one meeting concerning an individual. Lord Waverley listened with his stoical Scottish withdrawal and then, after a pause, "But there is no problem"—and forthwith told us in a matter of seconds why there was no problem, and suddenly it was true, just a cold bald fact. The Board table relaxed and deflated like a balloon ... I found myself mentally reciting "Everybody's blowing bubbles" ... Lord Waverley did more, though; he pricked them all in sequence, rhythmically, practically and effectively.

How well I recall, and with gratitude, his objectivity when I put forth my reasons for us not yet having a third theatre name—"The Royal Opera Ballet". He took nobody's side, but just listened and eventually embarked on the Royal Charter for the Ballet, that "intriguing little document" as he chose to allude to its difficulties. I will always recall his quizzical but very kind smile when, while saying goodbye to the Board, I said "You see, sir, I really do not think that we exist—and I want the ballet to do just that."

I had the honour to visit him, at his request, during his last two weeks of life at St Thomas's Hospital. The hospital was still in its battered postwar condition, and I was deeply worried by the shabby gloom of his room. It would hardly be the fate of a distinguished civil servant of today to die in such cheerless surroundings—something that he and his medical doctors had to accept at that time. He had announced his retirement as Chairman and was relaxed, yet curiously excited and hopeful about Covent Garden's future. "Lord Moore will be the new Chairman. He's the right man, is he not? I have every faith in young Moore ... " Even at the end he saw things with astonishing clarity.

Enter the Viscount Moore, soon to be the Earl of Drogheda. Enter indeed; it was to present an Anglo-Irish challenge and naturally proved to be a stimulating and sometimes argumentative experience, but a true sense of friendship and generosity of spirit always saw things through. This vibrant Irishman swept away a great deal of boardroom red tape and aloofness under the flush carpeting of the Royal Box. Notes, to be known as "Droghedagrams", arrived from the Box via the prompt corner entrance onto the stage to those concerned with the contents.

Lord Drogheda belonged to the style of Chairman who had never worried about the dignity of his position. He did not accept "no" or "yes" in the spirit of the hereditary Chairman. He did not bide time by being either shrewd, over-discreet or patient. Commonsense showed him with a tinge of that Irish devastating impatience of "things" observed, "things" standing still and "things" sliding—and the "things" that were right that could be left alone. This resulted in some people finding his sense of appreciation "shortsighted". Yes, perhaps someone like Drogheda did appear occasionally to have a form of shortsighted sense of appreciation. But the other side of the penny holds the answer: no amount of graciously expressed approval is of any good to the engine-driver for his smooth, steady, well-conducted driving if an unobserved inebriated express is bearing down on him, swaying in a state of alarmingly destructive speed. Drogheda saw such off-balance terrors long before anyone else. His staff victims (not excluding the writer) sometimes went a little crazy. But commonsense suggested a careful study of the Drogheda notes and further commonsense hinted that sleeping pills were not the answer, nor would there be any acceptable form of pigeon-holing.

He was the first of the Garden's Chairmen to love equally both the opera and the ballet, and he did his best to balance this wellworn theatrical IRA situation ... ("Do you have in London, between opera and ballet, as we do here in Russia, a case of the Montagues and the Capulets?"—a question once asked of me by a Moscow ballet director.)

Lord Drogheda was, in spite of his many duties elsewhere, an extremely wanted man for this particular chairmanship. He regarded with horror the lack of any form of staff pensions. (I was scolded for not noticing the omission in my own case.) Needless to say he set about it all and, no doubt, in a way that far exceeded in length any of the Droghedagrams. We knew him to be as generous as he was far-seeing.

Perhaps his very true enjoyment of both opera and ballet made some of his criticisms rather more personal than we would want to have heard. But no company can expect all the answers all the way from their Chairman. The Anglo-Irish are noted for using language that would be considered here "too strong for the situation under discussion" and anticipation of the inevitable "bloody" as a form of appendage to the expression of a strong point of view was a part of the Boardroom scene. But the forceful statement looked forward to somewhere during the meeting was always a thoughtful one—it generally represented his keen frustration over one of the inevitable cul-de-sacs, or it could be levelled at an adverse criticism in the press regarded as having gone too far rather than to have concerned themselves with being strategically fair.

He was a great champion of our cause, and it was up to us to accept his rockets from time to time. Humour, understanding and kindness were always present. Where Lord Waverley said there was "no problem" and unobtrusively smoothed out the crease, Lord Drogheda decided there *was* a problem and that something should be "done about it". A question of a different approach; but seeing the inevitably more complicated scene of the late 1960s and early 1970s, I think we needed by that time the Drogheda recipe. It was no soufflé—there was more of a T-bone steak touch, but all for our ultimate good. He did not know the meaning of lethargy or of wasting too much time on an over-analysis of any situation—yet any junior member of the Company had the right to a Board hearing. A lovely Hibernian highlight was his last party for members of the Royal Ballet in his London house, complete with impromptu piano concert from his gifted wife. We had just the right Celtic speech from the outgoing Chairman.

Closely connected with work at the Garden was the Chairman of the Arts Council, Lord Goodman. I always regarded him as a Master in charge of a Perfection Class. His approach concerned essentials, you were presented with intricate steps and movements that hinted at an assumption of your collaboration, understanding and knowledge. A brilliant Chairman with an equally brilliant and persuasive technique... You could receive in the course of an hour a wisely-worded rebuff; a sympathetically accepted request; a general and economical summing-up of some larger issue; and a feeling that you were embarking on a valuable course in the study of chairmanship strategy. Always, though, there was present a true humanitarianism.

I once asked to see him privately. "Of course," he said, "come to breakfast...." So to a 10.0 a.m. breakfast I came and was aware that I was made to feel at ease. Lord Goodman with tact equally distributed his interest between my remarks and his two poached eggs on toast.

He always showed a thoughtfully expressed humour. Its quietness could contain a touch of the ironic as when someone said to him that "Margot Fonteyn was worth her weight in gold." "*My* weight you mean," he was heard to murmur...

His weight in all senses was capable of upholding the huge, heavy, overloaded Arts Council boardroom table. Massive slabs of mahogany, endless minutes and memorandums; the distribution of grants accompanied by groans that greeted all lists of expenditure.

We come back to the question of the boardroom to acknowledge that there is no other answer. In the end the Board prove themselves to be the most objective body, the only real redress between Company and direct administrative direction. "The Board does not know anything about anything"—how often do we all make this remark! Yet in the end we know that in between the boardroom meetings some wise and helpful thinking has been embarked on. This, of course, we accept—for who knows during the presentation of a more than adequate dish of food whether you may be in for a bout of indigestion afterwards...

It is thus "the Board" sits, serves and also listens.

EPILOGUE

Ninette de Valois

I hope that the following will not prove to be a too demanding readjustment on the part of the reader. For the writer it records a lively but lasting memory concerning the all-important experience of "directorship".

It is Lilian Baylis' office. A tense morning followed an even more tense night when I, and many others, had witnessed chaos, injury, panic and the quick and untimely descent of the curtain at the end of a Shakespearian production where a fight between several actors—with their swords at random–actually ended in an unintentional injury to one actor.

I had visited Miss Baylis early the next morning, just before a line of shame-faced young actors were due for single interviews. She bid me stay and "*listen*". The ensuing scene needs a better pen than mine to portray its full value...

In came the actors, sheepish or defensive, dazed or defiant; all they got as they appeared was "Sit down, young man" (bang went the notebook on the table) "sit down and give me *facts*, just *facts—for I want nothing but facts, facts* ... " One of the many who came in and sat down was polite, nervous, but nevertheless quietly determined to state his case. He was listened to with a slightly lower, more rumbling demand for "*facts*: stick to 'em, remember just *facts* ..." she murmured, in this case with a sign of encouragement. The handsome, polite, patient young man was the young Laurence Olivier. It is my favourite portrait of him.

She obtained all her "*facts*", cleared the atmosphere with a severity equally distributed over everyone, a philosophical removal of severe blame for anyone, a terrible 'don't do it again" refrain covering everyone on and off the stage—and finish. The day's work must now be tackled. Her last words to me: "You see, dear? Always stick to *facts*, you get at the truth that way—and you can stop the trouble happening again ..."

I must say that I have, since then, made many a cautious note of "*facts*" and found them very illuminating.

Notes and References

I

[1] York Dance Review, Spring 1977: "Dame Ninette at York" by Diana Theodores Taplin
[2] *Come Dance With Me*, Ninette de Valois, Hamish Hamilton, 1957 (subsequently CDWM)
[3] The Dancing Times, March 1916 (subsequently DT); Interview with Mlle Rosa
[4] DT March 1915
[5] DT, Feb 1913
[6] DT, June 1913
[7] Eastbourne Chronicle, 18 July 1914
[8] CDWM
[9] CDWM
[10] Portsmouth Evening News, 24 Jan 1914
[11] CDWM
[12] The Stage, 31 July 1913
[13] DT, Apr 1914
[14] DT, March 1915
[15] The Era, 30 June 1915
[16] *Step by Step*, Ninette de Valois, W. H. Allen, 1977 (subsequently SBS)
[17] DT, Jan 1916
[18] DT, Jan 1917
[19] *And then he danced*, Edouard Espinosa, Samson Low Marston, 1946
[20] DT, Feb 1918
[21] The Era, 5 June 1918
[22] DT, July 1918
[23] The Stage, 19 Sep 1918
[24] SBS
[25] DT, April 1919
[26] The Stage, 8 May 1919 and 6 Feb 1919 (combined)
[27] The Tatler, 6 Aug 1919
[28] The Graphic, 7 June 1919
[29] The Era, 2 Jan 1918
[30] The Era, 30 Jan 1918
[31] The Era, 30 Apr 1919
[32] The Era, 21 May 1919
[33] DT, Aug 1919
[34] DT, Aug 1920
[35] Dance News (USA), Nov 1982
[36] The Stage, 27 Oct 1921
[37] *Jan Caryll: a Dancer's Memories*, Caxton Press, New Zealand, 1981/82
[38] Illustrated London News, 15 Apr 1922
[39] CDWM
[40] The Era, 30 Nov 1922

[41] Programme, London Coliseum, 23 Oct 1922
[42] The Graphic, 3 Feb 1923
[43] CDWM
[44] *Dancing with Diaghilev*, Lydia Sokolova, Murray 1960
[45] CDWM
[46] SBS

II

[1] *Invitation to the Ballet*, Ninette de Valois, John Lane The Bodley Head, 1937 (subsequently Invit.)
[2] *Early Memoirs*, Bronislava Nijinska, trans. and ed. by Irina Nijinska and Jean Rawlinson, Holt Rinehart & Winston, 1981
[3] *The Choreographic Art*, Peggy van Praagh and Peter Brinson, A. & C. Black, 1963
[4] The Times (London), 6 July 1914, letter to the Editor from Michel Fokine
[5] Invit.
[6] Invit.
[7] Invit.
[8] *The Diaghilev Ballet in London*, Cyril W. Beaumont, Putnam, 1940
[9] DT, Feb 1934
[10] *The Diaghilev Ballet in London*
[11] Interview with Dame Alicia Markova DBE
[12] Invit.
[13] *The Diaghilev Ballet in London*
[14] CDWM
[15] *Constant Lambert*, Richard Shead, Simon Publications, 1973 (letter from CL to his mother, 24 May 1926)
[16] CDWM
[17] Interview with Gordon Anthony

III

[1] Letter from Sheila McCarthy, 8 Sept 1983 (to the author)
[2] DT, Feb 1926
[3] *Quicksilver*, Dame Marie Rambert DBE, Macmillan, 1972
[4] Academy of Choregraphic Art prospectus lodged at Royal Ballet School Archives
[5,6] Notes by Beatrice Appleyard, lodged at Royal Ballet School Archives
[7] Notes by Nadina Newhouse, lodged at Royal Ballet School Archives
[8] Notes by Joy Newton, lodged at Royal Ballet School Archives
[9] Interview with Joy Newton
[10] The Stage, 31 May 1927
[11] DT, July 1950
[12] SBS
[13] DT, July 1950
[14] Granta, Cambridge, 20 May 1927
[15] *The Other Theatre*, Norman Marshall, John Lehmann, 1947
[16] Cambridge Daily News, 23 Nov 1926
[17] Cambridge Review, 26 Nov 1926
[18] *The Other Theatre*
[19] CDWM
[20] The Stage, 11 Nov 1926
[21] Programme, Festival Theatre Cambridge, 31 Jan 1927
[22] *In the Days of my Youth*, Grace Lovat Fraser, Cassell, 1970
[23] Interview with Joy Newton
[24] DT, Feb 1928

[25] Cambridge Daily News, 1 Feb 1927
[26] Cambridge Review, 4 Feb 1927
[27] *The Other Theatre*
[28] Granta, 4 Feb 1927
[29] DT, March 1927
[30] Interview with Ailne Phillips
[31] Interview with Joy Newton
[32] Programme, Festival Theatre Cambridge, 2 Feb 1929
[33] Granta, 19 May 1928
[34] CDWM
[35] *Collected Letters, W. B. Yeats*, ed. Allan Wade, Rupert Hart-Davis, 1954
[36] *Dance-Drama: Experiments in the Art of the Theatre*, Terence Gray, W. Heffer & Sons, 1926
[37] Cambridge Review, 7 Oct 1927
[38] SBS
[39] CDWM
[40] Irish Independent, 31 Jan 1928
[41] *Theatre in Focus: Terence Gray and the Cambridge Festival Theatre*, Richard Cave, Chadwyck-Healey, 1980
[42] *The Other Theatre*
[43] *The Other Theatre*
[44] Cambridge Daily News, 13 Nov 1928
[45] Interview with William Chappell
[46] Irish Statesman, 25 Sep 1928
[47] DT, Jan 1929
[48] *Dance-Drama* etc.
[49] DT, Jan 1929
[50] BBC Radio, broadcast by Francis Toye, "Music in the Theatre" 5 Dec 1928
[51] *Adam's Opera*, Clemence Dane, Wm Heinemann, 1928
[52] Cambridge Daily News, 21 May 1929
[53] Irish Independent, 28 Apr 1929
[54] *Pageant of the Dance and Ballet*, M. E. Perugini, Jarrolds, 1946
[55] Cambridge Review, 21 May 1929
[56] *Collected Letters, W. B. Yeats*
[57] *Bad Boy of Music*, George Antheil, Hurst & Blackett, undated
[58] *Joseph Holloway's Irish Theatre*, ed. Robert Hogan and Michael J. O'Neill, Dixon Calif. Proscenium Press, 1968
[59] The Spectator, 24 Aug 1929 (A. de B.)
[60] Irish Independent, 17 Apr 1928
[61] *Collected Letters, W. B. Yeats*
[62] Irish Independent, 17 Apr 1928
[62] CDWM

IV

[1] CDWM
[2] *The Vic-Wells Ballet 1931-40*, H. S. Sibthorp, unpublished Ms in Theatre Museum, London (subsequently Sibthorp)
[3] Bournemouth Echo, 30 Dec 1930
[4] DT, March 1942
[5] *Frederick Ashton and his Ballets*, David Vaughan, A. & C. Black, 1977
[6] Sibthorp
[7] The Era, 11 Nov 1931 (Leslie Rees)
[8] The Era, 25 Nov 1931 (Leslie Rees)
[9] Cambridge Daily News, 9 Jan 1931
[10] Theatre Arts Monthly, New York, Nov 1931, "The Cambridge Festival Theatre" by Alistair Cooke

[11] *The Vic-Wells Ballet*, Cyril W. Beaumont, C. W. Beaumont, 1935
[12] The Spectator, 7 May 1931 (Richard Jennings)
[13] Sibthorp
[14] The Stage, 7 May 1931
[15] The Stage, 4 June 1931
[16] The Spectator, 6 June 1931 (Richard Jennings)
[17] Letter from Dr Geoffrey Keynes to Diaghilev, 29 June 1927, in Dance Collection, New York
[18] *Blake's Vision of the Book of Job*, Joseph Wicksteed, London, 1910
[19] *Job and The Rake's Progress: Sadler's Wells Ballet Books*, The Bodley Head, 1949
[20] *Job and The Rake's Progress*
[21] The Times (London), 9 July 1931
[22] DT, March 1933
[23] The Spectator, 11 July 1931 (Richard Jennings)
[24] Daily Telegraph (London), 7 Nov 1934 (Richard Capell)
[25] Ballet (magazine), June 1948 (Richard Buckle)
[26] *The Vic-Wells Ballet*, C. W. Beaumont
[27] Interview with Nesta Brooking
[28] Programme, Abbey Theatre Dublin, 6 Dec 1931
[29] Irish Times, 7 Dec 1931
[30] *Joseph Holloway's Irish Theatre*
[31] Interview with Dame Alicia Markova, DBE
[32] DT, Apr 1984
[33] *The Ballet in England*, Arnold L. Haskell, New English Weekly, 1932
[34] *Vic-Wells: A Ballet Progress*, P. W. Manchester, Gollancz, 1942
[35] The Era, 23 March 1932
[36] The Times (London), 21 March 1932
[37] Programme, Camargo Society, Savoy Theatre, 13 June 1932
[38] Dagens Nyheder
[39] Politiken   Copenhagen journals, Sep 1932, reported in DT, Oct 1932
[40] Dagens Nyheder
[41] The Era, 26 Oct 1932 (Leslie Rees)
[42] Programme, Sadler's Wells Theatre, 11 Oct 1932
[43] Sibthorp
[44] DT, March 1953
[45] *Vic-Wells: A Ballet Progress*
[46] DT, March 1933
[47] DT, Apr 1929
[48] Association of Operatic Dancing Gazette, Aug 1932
[49] DT, Jan, Feb, March, April 1933, four articles by Ninette de Valois on "Modern Choreography"

V

[1] Morning Post, 5 Dec 1934
[2] The Era, 12 Dec 1934
[3] *A Camera at the Ballet: Pioneers of the Royal Ballet*, Gordon Anthony, David and Charles, 1975
[4] DT, Nov 1976
[5] *The Dramatic Imagination of W. B. Yeats*, Andrew Parkin, Gill & Macmillan, Dublin, 1978
[6] Irish Independent, 26 July 1933
[7] The Era, 4 Oct 1933
[8] Sibthorp
[9] *Robert Helpmann*, Gordon Anthony, Home and van Thal, 1946 (Foreword by Ninette de Valois)
[10] Daily Telegraph (London), 1 March 1934 (W. A. Darlington)
[11] The Times (London), 1 March 1934
[12] The Era, 7 March 1934 (Leslie Rees)

[13] Daily Mail, 1 March 1934 (Edwin Evans)
[14] *A Camera at the Ballet*
[15] DT, Apr, 1965 (G. B. L. Wilson)
[16] South Wales Evening Argus, 21 March 1965 (Jon Holliday)
[17] Daily Telegraph (London), 2 Apr 1965 (A. V. Coton)
[18] South Wales Evening Argus, 2 Apr 1965 (Clive Barnes)
[19] DT, May 1965 (Oleg Kerensky)
[20] SBS
[21] Notes for *Bar aux Folies-bergère* by Ninette de Valois, 1934, Ballet Rambert Archives
[22] Morning Post, 9 Feb 1935 (F.T.)
[23] *Markova, her Life and Art,* Anton Dolin, W. H. Allen, 1953
[24] Letter from Ninette de Valois to Nesta Brooking, undated 1934
[25] CDWM
[26] *Collected Letters, W. B. Yeats*
[27] Copy of book of *The King of the Great Clock Tower* by W. B. Yeats in Ninette de Valois' possession
[28] SBS
[29] Irish Independent, 4 Oct 1934
[30] CDWM
[31] SBS
[32] Interview with Joan Lawson
[33] SBS
[34] SBS

VI

[1] *Vic-Wells: A Ballet Progress*
[2] Sibthorp
[3] SBS
[4] Interview with Sir Frederick Ashton, OM, CH, CBE
[5] SBS
[6] *Hogarth*, David Bindman, Thames & Hudson, 1981
[7] *Notebooks of George Vertue*
[8] *A Camera at the Ballet*
[9] *A Camera at the Ballet*
[10] *A Camera at the Ballet*
[11] *A Camera at the Ballet*
[12] *The Sadler's Wells Ballet*, Cyril W. Beaumont, C. W. Beaumont, 1946
[13] Time and Tide, 25 May 1935 (C. B./Caryl Brahms)
[14] Le Peuple (Brussels), 13 Feb 1945 (Louis Piérard)
[15] New York Times, 13 Oct 1949 (John Martin)
[16] DT, July 1956 ("The Rake in Munich" by Peggy van Praagh)
[17] About the House, Christmas 1947

VII

[1] DT Oct 1935 ("The Vic-Wells Ballet" by Ninette de Valois)
[2] Association of Operatic Dancing Gazette, Aug 1934
[3] *Vic-Wells: A Ballet Progress*
[4] Sibthorp
[5] DT, June 1936 ("Liverpool Ballet Club" by Alfred Francis)
[6] The Spectator, 30 Oct 1936 (Dyneley Hussey)
[7] *Vic-Wells: A Ballet Progress*
[8] Daily Telegraph (London), 14 Oct 1936 (Caryl Brahms)
[9] Time and Tide, 17 Oct 1936 (A.G.)
[10] Sibthorp
[11] *Ninette de Valois & the Vic-Wells Ballet*, Kate Neatby, British-Continental Press, 1934

[12] DT, Aug 1937 (L. Franc Scheuer)
[13] *The Chess behind Checkmate*, Martin Lewis, unpublished MS in its author's possession
[14] Letter from Ninette de Valois to Martin Lewis, 3 June 1983
[15] Television programme, Channel 4, 2 Jan 1984, Interview with Sir Robert Helpmann, KBE
[16] The Times (London), 6 Oct 1937
[17] Daily Telegraph (London), 21 June 1937 (Richard Capell)
[18] *The Sadler's Wells Ballet*, Cyril W. Beaumont
[19] *Vic-Wells: A Ballet Progress*
[20] The Spectator, 15 Oct 1937 (Adrian Stokes)
[21] Ballet (magazine), June 1948 (Cyril Beaumont)
[22] New York Times, 3 Nov 1949 (John Martin)
[23] *Conducted Personally*, Eric Robinson, London, 1955
[24] The Australian, 8 May 1986 (Mary Emery)
[25] Tribute from Ninette de Valois at the Thanksgiving Service for Sir Robert Helpmann, KBE, St Paul's Church, Covent Garden, 25 Nov 1986
[26] *Dramatic School*, Patricia Don Young, Peter Davies, 1954
[27] DT, March 1938
[28] Invit.
[29] The Stage, 14 Apr 1938
[30] The Observer, 10 Apr 1938 (Horace Horsnell)

VIII

[1] *The English Ballet*, W. J. Turner, Collins, 1944 (contribution from Annabel Farjeon)
[2] The Observer, 8 July 1940 (Horace Horsnell)
[3] DT, Aug 1940
[4] The Spectator, 12 July 1940 (Dyneley Hussey)
[5] Author's notes on Morley College Lecture by Ninette de Valois, "Composing a Ballet", 28 Sep 1943
[6] *Robert Helpmann*, Gordon Anthony
[7] *The Sadler's Wells Ballet*, Mary Clarke, A. & C. Black, 1955
[8] CDWM
[9] Interview with Jean Bedells
[10] DT, March 1942 ("Literary Ballet" by Joan Lawson)
[11] Radio Times, June 1941
[12] The Listener, June 1941
[13] CDWM
[14] Toronto Globe & Mail, 7 Oct 1950 (Herbert Whittaker)
[15] CDWM

IX

[1] *Robert Helpmann*, Gordon Anthony
[2] DT, Aug 1942
[3] London County Council handout, summer 1942
[4] Evening News, 6 Sep 1943 (Leslie Hurry)
[5] DT, Feb 1944 (Edwin Evans)
[6] The Scotsman, 26 Oct 1943
[7] DT, May 1945
[8] L'Eventail (Brussels), 13 Feb 1945
[9] Le Peuple (Brussels), 13 Feb 1945 (Louis Piérard)
[10] La Dernière Heure (Brussels), 16 Feb 1945
[11] La Bataille (Paris), 15 March 1945 (Henri Sauguet)

X

[1] DT, Apr 1943
[2] SBS
[3] CDWM
[4] The Sunday Times, 29 Oct 1961 (report by Richard Buckle)
[5] DT, Dec 1946
[6] Invit.

XI

[1] *Balletomane at Large*, Arnold L. Haskell, Heinemann, 1972
[2] CDWM
[3] *Sol Hurok Presents*, Invincible Press, Australia, 1955
[4] CDWM
[5] Ninette de Valois, talk at Chicago Library, 1949
[6] *Ballet Music*, Humphrey Searle, Cassell, 1958
[7] Leader (magazine), 25 Feb 1950 (John Davidson)
[8] Ballet (magazine), Apr 1950 (Cyril Beaumont)
[9] The Times (London), 21 Feb 1950
[10] News Chronicle, 21 Feb 1950 (Scott Goddard)
[11] New Statesman, 25 Feb 1950
[12] The Observer, 26 Feb 1950 (Richard Buckle)
[13] New York Herald Tribune, 30 Sep 1950 (Walter Terry)
[14] Christian Science Monitor, 7 Oct 1950 (Margaret Lloyd)
[15] New York Times, 30 Sep 1950 (John Martin)
[16] Brooklyn Eagle, 30 Sep 1950 (Paul Affelder)
[17] BBC radio programme, The Critics, 26 March 1950. The critics were Malcolm Muggeridge, Frank Tilsley, Stephen Bone, Edgar Anstey and Philip Carr.
[18] Daily Mail,16 May 1950 (Cecil Wilson)
[19] The Sunday Times, 21 May 1950 (Richard Buckle)

XII

[1] DT, Feb 1951
[2] DT, Sep 1955
[3] DT, Aug 1956
[4] Ottawa Citizen, 4 Oct 1950
[5] CDWM
[6] Regina Leader & Post, 11 Oct 1950
[7] *Sol Hurok Presents*
[8] CDWM
[9] *Sol Hurok Presents*
[10] Los Angeles Times, 15 Oct 1950

XIII

[1] DT, Dec 1947
[2] Interview with Joy Newton
[3] Letter from Beatrice Appleyard, 3 Dec 1986 (to the author)
[4] Interview with Richard Glasstone
[5] DT, Nov 1967
[6] *Turkish Dancing*, Metin And, Dost Yayinlari, Ankara, 1976
[7] Report by Head of Drama, British Council, London, 2 March 1967
[8] Interview with Richard Glasstone
[9] *Turkish Dancing*

XIV

[1] SBS

[2] SBS

[3] Interview with Joan Lawson

[4] SBS

[5] Paper read by Ninette de Valois to Royal Society of Arts, 24 May 1957 ("The English Ballet"), reprinted in SBS

[6] SBS

[7] DT, Jan 1958

[8] SBS

[9] SBS

[10] SBS

XV

[1] Journal of the Royal Society of Arts, July 1964

[2] DT, Aug 1974

[3] DT, May 1960

[4] Paper read by Ninette de Valois to Royal Society of Arts, 24 May 1957

[5] DT, Oct 1964 (interview with Agnes Toboz)

[6] DT, June 1957 (Allan Fridericia)

[7] DT, Dec 1977

[8] DT, Sept 1964 (Cyril Beaumont)

[9] *Striking a Balance*, Barbara Newman, Elm Tree Books, 1982 (interview with Moira Shearer)

[10] Invit.

[11] Author's note of speech given by Sir Robert Helpmann KBE at dinner for Dame Ninette de Valois DBE at Claridge's, 15 June 1947

[12] *Margot Fonteyn* by herself, W. H. Allen, 1975

[13] *Lynn*, Lynn Seymour, Granada Publishing, 1985

[14] *Antoinette Sibley*, Barbara Newman, Hutchinson, 1986

[15] Interview with Joan Lawson

[16] Talk by Ninette de Valois to the London Ballet Circle, 23 April 1985 (notes by the author and Sue Merrett)

[17] Letter from Margot Fonteyn to Ninette de Valois, 1985, referred to in 16

[18] Quote from Martha Graham mentioned by Ninette de Valois in 16

[19] The Stage, 21 Oct 1982 ("The aim of a dancer should be perfection" by Ninette de Valois)

[20] Talk by Ninette de Valois, 23 April 1985

[21] do.

[22] do.

[23] do.

[24] Invit.

[25] The Stage, 29 Dec 1978 ("The Royal Ballet 1928–78" by Leo Kersley)

[26] The Times (London), 16 June 1983 ("Why Madam is a winner on points" by Brian Masters)

[27] *Antoinette Sibley*

Appendix 1

Ninette de Valois as dancer

This list includes engagements and appearances as a dancer and first occasions on which a role is danced.

Abbreviations:

p.d.	*première danseuse*	Abbey	Abbey Theatre, Dublin
cr.	created role	ROHCG	Royal Opera House, Covent Garden
divt	divertissement		
pdd	*pas de deux*	Col.	London Coliseum
pdt	*pas de trois*	( )	role
pdq	*pas de quatre*	[ ]	composer
chor.	choreography	V/SW	Vic-Sadler's Wells Opera Ballet
DBR	Diaghilev Ballets Russes	Op Blt	
OV	Old Vic	All theatres named are in London unless
SW	Sadler's Wells	otherwise stated
FC	Festival Theatre Cambridge		

1913	Jan	*The Children's Dream* (p.d.) Lila Field Co. (solos and adage with Doris Murray)
	Apr 7	*Roses Red* (p.d.) Lila Field Co. Kilburn Empire

1913/14 On tour with Lila Field's "Wonder Children"

Russian Ballet—Woodland Ballet (The Poppy Queen, The Moonlight, Bird Dance)
 Butterfly Ballet (Pas de deux, Bacchanale, with Eileen Dennis)

Here We Are! (revue)—The Great Pavlova (solo, The Swan Dance)
Russian Dance solo and lead in character divt

1914	c. March	Private recital at home (23 Earl's Court Square)

Programme of solos, no choreography cited:

The Invocation [Chopin Waltz No. 7]
Valse Caprice [Rubinstein]
La Nuit [Rubinstein Romance]
Valse Coquette, the Mi-carême [Osborne Roberts]
Le Papillon [Gillet, Loin du Bal]
Pipes of Pan [Chopin Waltz No. 9]
Oiseau de feu [Chopin Waltz No. 6]
Aases Tod [Grieg, Peer Gynt]
La Mort du cygne [Saint-Saëns]
Russian Dance [Brahms]

1914	July 14	*Cupid & Co. in Pierrot Land* (p.d.) Lila Field Co. Ambassador's Theatre

1914	Dec 24	(into 1915) *Jack and the Beanstalk* (p.d. with Robert Roberty) Lyceum Theatre. Grand Fairyland Ballet
1915	c. June 30	Dance Scena (p.d. with Robert Roberty) Oxford Music Hall, London. *La Sylphe* (solo), Adage and finale.
	July 19	Dance Scena transferred to London Palladium for two weeks.
1915	Aug 11	*Romance in E flat* [Rubinstein] (solo), Devonshire Park Winter Garden Pavilion, Eastbourne. This dance is possibly *La Nuit*— see 1914 c. March
1915	Dec 27	(into 1916) *Robinson Crusoe* (p.d.), Lyceum Theatre
1916	Dec 23	(into 1917) *Mother Goose* (p.d.), Lyceum Theatre (The Fairy of the Golden Valley)
1917	Apr 16	*Music, Dancing and Pictures* (p.d.), Devonshire Park, Eastbourne (solos)
1918	Jan 4	Charity Matinee, Sisters of Mercy (p.d.) Vaudeville Theatre. *Valse Arabesque* [Lack] (solo, chor.) also Adage with Violet Curtis
	June 2	Programme by Lady Constance Stewart-Richardson, (p.d.) Royal Court Theatre (three solos)
	June 7	Charity Matinee, Stick Crutch Fund, The Dancers' Tribute. (p.d.) Criterion Theatre. Programme as 1918, Jan 4

Beecham Opera and Ballet, London Palladium, in music-hall bill

	Sep 16	Scenes from *Faust* (p.d.)
	Sep 23	Scenes from *Phoebus and Pan* (p.d.) (solo, chor.)
	Sep 30	Scenes from *Carmen* (p.d.)
	Dec 26	(into 1919) *Cinderella* (p.d. with Alexander Goudin) Lyceum Theatre. (Sunray)
1919	Mar 31	*Laughing Eyes* (revue) (p.d. with Fred A. Leslie) Theatre Royal, Newcastle. *The Dope Fiend* (The Stranger) [Howard Carr]
		(May 1, Kennington Theatre. June 17, Strand Theatre)

Grand Opera Season, ROHCG (p.d.)

	May 13	*La Traviata* (also May 19, 24 mat)
	14	*Thaïs* (also May 20, 31 mat, June 13, July 3)
	28	*Aida* (also June 7, 20, 24, July 5 mat, 11)
	June 6	*Louise* (La Danseuse) (also June 16, 25, July 1 mat, July 31 gala excerpt)
	July 18	*Naïl* (also July 22, 31 gala excerpt)
	Nov 25	Sunshine Matinee (p.d.) Queen's Theatre. *Danse fantasque* [Chaminade] (solo)
1920	July 14	*Oh! Julie!* (musical) (p.d. with Fred A. Leslie) Shaftesbury Theatre. [Herman Darewski and H. Sullivan-Brooke]
	Nov 26	Sunshine Matinee (p.d.) Queen's Theatre. *Pas seul* [Tchaikovsky]
1921	Oct 26	Programme with own group of eight girls (p.d.) Partner Serge Morosoff, later replaced by Jan Caryll. Own choreography. In music-hall bills on Gulliver Circuit for non-consecutive six weeks. Opened Camberwell Palace *Valse Arabesque* [Lack] (solo) *Valse* [J. Strauss] (pdd) *Hungarian Dance* (pdd) *Adage*

1921	Nov 29	Sunshine Matinee (p.d.) Palace Theatre
		Extract from above own group programme
1922	March	On tour in England and Scotland with Massine-Lopokova Russian
	to May	Ballet group (p.d.)

Massine-Lopokova Russian Ballet group (p.d.), ROHCG, in bill with films

	Apr 3	Week I. NdV danced *Cupidon* [Gounod] (solo)
		Fanatics of Pleasure [J. Strauss] (suite) (*Valse pdq, Polka, Galop*)
	10	Week II. NdV danced *Pass-pied* [Delibes] (pdd) With Errol Addison
		Gopak [Moussorgsky]
		Three Graces [Ponchielli]
	17	Week III. NdV danced in *The Cockatoo's Holiday* (divt) (*Valse* [Gounod]; *Gavotte* [Czibulka] (pdd) with Errol Addison; *Finale* [Gounod])
	24	Week IV. No new items
	June 19	Same programme at London Coliseum in music-hall bill, new item *Czardas* [Brahms] (pdt)

Lopokova Russian Ballet group (p.d.) London Coliseum, in music-hall bill

	Oct 9	*The Masquerade* (p.d.) (cr. a masker) [Mozart, Serenade in G] chor. prob. Lopokova, prod. Vera Bowen
	23	*Les Elegantes* (p.d.) [Chopin]
		Pavane [Fauré]
	Nov 20	Programmes as Oct
	28	Sunshine Matinee (p.d.) Winter Garden Theatre
		Variation [Cimarosa] (chor. Massine) (solo)
1923	Jan 27	*You'd be Surprised* (revue–jazzaganza) ROHCG (p.d.) (with Massine group)
		Ballet later called *Togo or The Noble Savage* contained in scene "Wild Cat, Arizona" chor. Massine (cr. Negress Servant) [Milhaud] *Record Girl of Mine* (cr. The Dancer)
	Feb 24	*You'd be Surprised*, change of programme. *Togo* replaced by *Lezginka* (ensemble) [Rubinstein]
	May 14	*You'd be Surprised*, new dance in item, *Chicken à la King* (p.d., chor.)
		You'd be Surprised transferred to Alhambra Theatre without Russian dancers. NdV continued to dance the two numbers, *Record Girl of Mine* and *Chicken à la King*.

Lopokova Russian Ballet group (p.d.) London Coliseum, in music-hall bill

July 23 and Aug 6	No new roles danced
Sep to Oct	NdV joined Diaghilev Ballets Russes in Paris. On tour in Switzerland and Holland
Nov 25	Opening of season, Théâtre de Monte-Carlo
	Prince Igor (a Polovtsian maiden)
	Cléopâtre (an Egyptian)
27	*Le Tricorne* (cdb)
28	*Petrushka* (cdb)
Dec 4	*Aurora's Wedding* ("Finger" Variation; Red Riding Hood)
6	*Schéhérazade* (cdb)
11	*Narcisse* (a nymph)
18	*Le Lac des cygnes* Acts II and III (a swan; czardas)

1924	Jan 1	{ *Daphnis et Chloe* (a Greek) { *La Colombe* (opera), (cdb)
	3	*Schéhérazade* (1st Harem)
	5	*Le Medecin malgré lui* (opera) (an apothecary)
	6	*Les Biches* (cr. Rondeau—ensemble)
	8	*L'Après-midi d'un faune* (a nymph)
	10	*Philémon et Baucis* (opera) (cdb)
1924	Jan 17	*Une éducation manquée* (opera) (cdb)
	19	*Les Fâcheux* (cr. un joueur de volant)
	22	*Les Sylphides* (a sylph)
	28	*Daphnis et Chloe* (Lisinion)

Mixed opera/ballet season ended Jan 30. Opera only opened Feb 2

Dancers appeared at Cannes (Jan 31) and Nice (March 6)

	Feb 2	*Carmen* (opera) (seguidille, pdq)
	26	*Manon* (opera) (cdb)
	Mar 4	*Roméo et Juliette* (opera) [Gounod] (cdb)
	13	*Samson et Dalila* (opera) (divt)
	18	*Faust* (Gounod] (cdb)
	22	*Mefistofele* (cdb)
	Apr 4	*Thamar* (a friend)
	6	mat. *Faust* (opera) [Schumann] (a fisherwoman) eve. *Nuit sur le mont chauve* (un esprit des tenébres)
	8	*Midnight Sun* (a peasant woman)
	14	*Chout* (cdb)
	19	Ballet opened at Gran Teatro del Liceo, Barcelona
	23	*Children's Tales* (a sister)

On tour, The Hague (May 5), Amsterdam (May 7), Rotterdam (May 10)

	May 26	Ballet opened at Théâtre des Champs-Elysées, Paris
	26	*Les Noces* (cdb)
	June 13	*Le Sacre du printemps* (a young woman)
	20	*Le Train bleu* (cr. une poule—ensemble)

On tour, Munich (Sept 15), Leipzig (Oct 1)

	Oct 2	*Aurora's Wedding* (cr. Florestan pdt, chor. Nijinska)

On tour, Chemnitz (Oct 4), Berlin (Oct 9)

	Oct 11	*Cimarosiana* (cr. pdq, chor. Nijinska)
	15	*The Good-humoured Ladies* (Pasquina)

On tour, Breslau (Oct 27), Hamburg (Nov 4), Frankfurt (Nov 10) Cologne (Nov 13), Hanover (Nov 21)

1924	Nov 24	Ballet opened at London Coliseum. NdV programmed as Nina Devalois
	Dec 1	*Les Tentations de la bergère* (cr. a Baroness)
	18	*La Boutique fantasque* (a friend)
1925	Jan 5	*Le Tricorne* (a neighbour)
	17	Ballet/opera season opened at Theâtre de Monte-Carlo

1925	Jan 27	*Thais* (opera) (cdb and Act I divt, cr. vision solo)
	Feb 3	*Samson et Dalila* (opera) (cdb and divt)
	18	*Le Festin* (grand pas hongrois)
	21	mat. *Carnaval* (Papillon)
	26	*Fay-yen-fah* (opera) (un lys; un parot)
	Mar 4	*The Good-humoured Ladies* (Dorotea)
	6	mat. *L'Assemblé* (danse des amoureux)
	7	*Hérodiade* (opera) (cdb)
	21	*Papillons* (cdb)
	24	*L'Enfant et les sortilèges* (opera) (cdb)

Dancers appeared Nice (Jan 29), Cannes (March 27), Marseille (Apr 2)

	Apr 21	*Les Fâcheux* (Gossip)
	28	*Zéphyr et Flore* (a muse)
	May 2	Ballet opened at Gran Teatro del Liceo, Barcelona
	5	*Cléopâtre* (The Favourite Slave) (female)
	11	*Le Lac des cygnes* Act III (pdt)
	May 18	Ballet opened at London Coliseum
	June 5	Ballet opened at Gaîté-Lyrique Théâtre, Paris
	17	*Le Chant du rossignol* (cr. a lady of the court)
	July 1	Ballet resumed at London Coliseum
	Aug 1	end of London Coliseum season. NdV left DBR.
	Dec 8	Sunshine Matinee (p.d.) Queen's Theatre. *The Art of the Theatre* (own chor.) (cr. Painting)

| 1926 | Feb 5 | Ballet, title unknown, by Rupert Doone (p.d.) Playhouse Theatre |
| | March | Opening of Academy of Choregraphic Art |

DBR (p.d., guest artist) Théâtre Sarah-Bernhardt, Paris, from May 18

	May 28	*La Pastorale* (cr. a villager–ensemble)
	June 10	*Roméo et Juliette* (The Nurse)
		His Majesty's Theatre from July 1
	21	*The Good-humoured Ladies* (Felicia)
	Aug 2	Music-hall tour with Anton Dolin (taking over from Phyllis Bedells). First performance Manchester
	18	Programme with Dolin opened London Coliseum, in music-hall bill. *Lacquer* (pdd) *Little Boy Blue* (pdd) [Elgar, Chanson de matin and Chanson de nuit] *Jack and Jill* (pdd) [Gerrard Williams] *Variation* (solo) *Exercises* (group) [Percy Grainger]

DBR (p.d., guest artist), Lyceum Theatre, from Dec 1

| | Dec 4 | *Cimarosiana* (pdt) |
| | | Teatro di Torina (Turin) from Dec 24 *Les Biches* (The Hostess) (also 25 and 28 Dec) |

1927	Jan 31	FC (p.d. and chor.) *Dance Cameos* *Rout* (cr. leading role) *A Daughter of Eve* (solo) (cr.)
	Apr 26	Charity Show, *Pretty Prattle* (p.d.) New Theatre (unnamed dances)
	May 31	*White Birds* (revue) (p.d. with Anton Dolin) His Majesty's Theatre in *Traffic in Souls*
	Oct 31	FC (p.d. and chor.) *Three Dances* *Pride* (solo) (cr.) *Russian Peasant* (solo) (cr.) Third solo unknown
1928	Jan 30	Abbey (p.d. and chor.) *Venetian Suite* (cr. The Romantic Lady)
	Apr 16	Abbey (p.d. and chor.) *Rituelle de feu* (cr. The Maiden) *Serenade* (solo) (cr.)

1928   Grand Opera Season (p.d.) ROHCG

	May 1	*Armide* (also May 3, 9)
	22	*Samson et Dalila* (also May 25, 30)
	24	*Louise* (La Danseuse) (also May 28)
	29	*Carmen* (also June 1, 4)
	June 15	*Aida* (also June 20, 25, July 3, 10)

DBR (p.d., guest artist) His Majesty's Theatre

	July 2–28	No new dancing roles
	July 10	Sunshine Matinee (p.d.) Apollo Theatre. No new dancing role
	Aug 15	Recital (p.d. with Anton Dolin), Harrogate. No particulars of programme
	Sept 24	Abbey (p.d. and chor.) *The Faun* (cr. The Shade)
	Nov 26	Ballets for the Repertory Theatre (p.d. and chor.) Academy of Choreographic Art, Royal Court Theatre. Beauty and the Beast (Beauty)
	Dec 13	OV (p.d. and chor.) *Les Petits Riens* (cr. Rosalind)
1929	Feb 4	FC (p.d. and chor.) *Danse Profane* (pdd) (cr.) *Polka* [J. Strauss] (pdd) (cr.)
	Apr 22	Abbey (p.d. and chor.) No new dancing role
	May 14	Abbey (p.d. and chor.) *Fighting the Waves* (cr. Fand)
	July 4	Association of Operatic Dancing (p.d.) Gaiety Theatre *Hommage aux belles viennoises* (cr. pdd)
	Aug 13	Abbey (p.d. and chor.) Tyrolese pdt from *Hommage aux belles viennoises*
	Nov 5	Nellie Chaplin Matinee (p.d. and chor.) Rudolf Steiner Hall No new dancing role

1929	Nov 19	Abbey (p.d. and chor.) Movement perpetuel (leading dancer)
	Dec 19	OV (p.d. and chor.) No new dancing role
1930	Feb 17	FC (p.d. and chor.) The Tryst (solo)
	Mar 28	Academy of Choregraphic Art, FC and Abbey (p.d. and chor.) Lyric Theatre Hammersmith. No new dancing role
	July 8	Sunshine Matinee, (p.d. and chor.) New Scala Theatre. No new dancing role
	Oct 19	Camargo Society (p.d. and chor.) Cambridge Theatre, London Variations and Coda [Glinka] (chor. Legat) (leading dancer)
	Dec 1	Maddermarket Theatre, Norwich (p.d. and chor.) Prélude orientale Fugue No. 5 Mexican Dance (trad.) (solo)
	18	OV (p.d. and chor.) Suite of Dances [Bach] (cr. Bourrée solo, Sarabande pdd, and Gigue)
	29	V/SW Op Blt (p.d. and chor.) Bournemouth Pavilion No new dancing role
1931	Jan 5	OV (p.d. and chor.) Carmen (opera) (cr. leading dancer)
	25	Camargo Society (p.d. and chor.) Apollo Theatre No new dancing role
	Feb 9	Abbey (p.d. and chor.) Russian Court Dance (solo)
	14	Abbey (p.d. and chor.) No new dancing role
	Mar 2	OV (p.d. and chor.) Aida (opera) (cr. leading dancer)
	9	OV (p.d. and chor.) Faust (opera) (cr. leading dancer in full ballet)
	May 5	OV (p.d. and chor.) The Jackdaw and the Pigeons (cr. The Jackdaw)
	21	SW (p.d. and chor.) Cephalus and Procris (Aurora)
	Sept 14	OV (p.d. and chor.) Samson and Delilah (opera) (cr. leading dancer)
	22	OV (p.d.) Regatta (chor. Ashton) (cr. A Foreign Visitor)
	Oct 12	OV (p.d. and chor.) La Traviata (opera) (cr. leading dancer)
	23	Association of Operatic Dancing recital, (p.d.) Crane Hall, Liverpool. No new dancing role
	Dec 15	Camargo Society Midnight Ballet Party (p.d. and chor.) Carlton Theatre The Dancer's Reward (cr. leading dancer)
1932	Mar 4	OV (p.d. and chor.) Italian Suite (chor. with Dolin) (cr. pdd and variation)

1932	Mar 8	SW (p.d.) *Le Spectre de la rose* (The Young Girl)
	11	SW (p.d.) *The Enchanted Grove* (chor. R. Doone) (cr. The Courtesan)
	Apr 10	Abbey, (p.d. and chor.) *Nursery Suite* (Bo-Peep)
	July 2	Camargo Society (p.d.) Savoy Theatre *Giselle* (Berthe)
	Sep	The English Ballet Company visit to Royal Theatre, Copenhagen (p.d. and chor. Also directed company) No new dancing role
	Oct 5	SW (p.d. and chor.) *Fête Polonaise* (leading role)
	11	SW (p.d. and chor.) *Douanes* (cr. The Tight-Rope Dancer)
	Nov 1	SW (p.d. and chor.) *The Origin of Design* (Dibutade)
	Dec 8	SW (p.d. and chor.) *Nursery Suite* (The Princess)
	13	SW (p.d.) *The Lord of Burleigh* (chor. Ashton) (Katie Willows)
1933	Jan 3	SW (p.d. and chor.) *Cephalus and Procris* (Procris)
	Mar 21	SW (p.d.) *Coppélia* (two acts) (Chief Village Dancer)
	Apr 3	SW (p.d.) *Coppélia* (two acts) (Swanilda)
	July 5	Abbey (p.d. and chor.) *Bluebeard* (cr. Ilina, the Seventh Wife) *At the Hawk's Well* (cr. The Guardian of the Well)
	Nov 29	SW (p.d. and chor.) *Orpheus* (opera) (cr. leading dancer)
	Dec 5	OV (p.d.) *Les Rendezvous* (chor. Ashton) (cr. pdt) *Le Lac des cygnes pdt* (divt)
1934	Jan 1	SW (p.d.) *Giselle* (peasant pdd)
	June 25	Open Air Theatre, Regents Park (p.d. and chor.) *The Wise and Foolish Virgins* (The Bride)
	July 30	Abbey (p.d. and chor.) *The King of the Great Clock Tower* (cr. The Queen)
1935	Jan 7	SW (p.d.) *Carnaval* (Columbine)
	Oct 8	SW (p.d. and chor.) *Douanes* (revised chor. and prod.) (The Tight-Rope Walker)
1936	Apr 7	SW (p.d. and chor.) *Barabau* (cr. The Peasant Woman)
1937	Apr 27	SW (p.d.) *A Wedding Bouquet* (chor. Ashton) (cr. Webster)

1937   Apr 30   Liverpool Ballet Club (p.d.)
                             Coppélia (two acts) (Swanilda)

(NB. This is included as a matter of interest because the role was no longer in her regular repertoire)

During World War II, date unknown, Arts Theatre, Cambridge
                             Les Patineurs (White pdd)

Appendix 2

Choreography: ballets, ballet-plays and divertissements

Abbreviations:

M.	Music	ACA	Academy of Chore-
S.	Scenery		graphic Art
C.	Costumes	Abbey	Abbey Theatre Dublin
D.	Dancers	V/SW ⎱	Vic/Sadler's Wells Opera
All theatres named are in London unless		Op Blt ⎰	Ballet
otherwise stated		divt.	divertissement
ROHCG	Royal Opera House Covent	cdb	*corps de ballet*
	Garden	m.	male dancers
OV	Old Vic	f.	female dancers
SW	Sadler's Wells	Pdd	*pas de deux*
FC	Festival Theatre	pdt	*pas de trois*
	Cambridge	pdq	*pas de quatre*

De Valois composed dances from an early age but has kept no record of them. The most important items before 1925 are included in this list.

1918	Solo in *Scenes from Phoebus and Pan* M. Bach D. NdV	London Palladium, Beecham Opera and Ballet, 23 Sep
1921	*Albumblatt No. 7 (The Letter)* M. Grieg D. poss. 3 f.	Camberwell Palace, 26 Oct
	Hungarian Dance M. Brahms D. NdV and Serge Morosoff	do.
	Pas de deux (Adage) M. not known D. NdV and Serge Morosoff	do.
	Pas de trois M. Dorothy Foster D. 3 f.	do.
	Valse M. J. Strauss (Blue Danube) D. NdV, Morosoff and group, f. (poss. the Waltz given at the Abbey Theatre, 13 Aug 1929)	do.

| 1921 | *Valse Arabesque* (solo) | Camberwell Palace, 26 |
| | M. Theodore Lack | Oct |

1921   *Valse Arabesque* (solo)   Camberwell Palace, 26
         M. Theodore Lack   Oct
         D. NdV
         staged V/SW Op Blt, Bournemouth Pavilion, 29 Dec 1930
         (NdV danced a Valse Arabesque [Lack] at the Charity
         Matinee at the Vaudeville Theatre, 4 Jan 1918. This is
         probably the same dance.

1923   *Chicken à la King*   ROHCG, "You'd be
         M. not known   Surprised" (revue) 14
         D. NdV and six f.   May

1925   *The Art* (sometimes *Arts*) *of the Theatre*   Sunshine Matinee
         M. Ravel (from *La Valse*)   Queen's Theatre
         Decorations & costumes. Kathleen Dillon   8 Dec
         D. Dorothy Coxon (Music); NdV (Painting); Molly Lake
         (Dancing); Margaret Craske (Comedy); Ursula Moreton
         (Tragedy)
         staged FC 31 Jan 1927 (practice dress)
         Abbey 10 Apr 1932
         Royal Court Theatre Liverpool, in *Southern Murmurs*,
         Nov 1932

1927   *Beauty and the Beast*   FC 31 Jan
         M. Ravel
         C. Kathleen Dillon
         D. Ursula Moreton (Beauty); Mary Tree (The Beast)
         staged Abbey 30 Jan 1928
         Royal Court Theatre London, ACA 26 Nov 1928

         A Daughter of Eve (solo)   FC 31 Jan
         M. Arensky
         C. Kathleen Dillon
         D. NdV
         staged Abbey 30 Jan 1928
         Sunshine Matinee, Apollo Theatre, 10 July 1928
         OV 19 Dec 1929
         Maddermarket Norwich, 1 Dec 1930
         Association of Operatic Dancing, Crane Hall Liverpool
         23 Oct 1931

         Mouvement Perpetuel   FC 31 Jan
         M. Poulenc
         D. Ursula Moreton
         given as pdt 4 Feb
         D. Vivienne Bennet, Joy Newton, Anne Coventry
         staged Abbey, 19 Nov 1929

         Prélude orientale (solo)   FC 31 Jan
         M. Glière
         D. Frances James
         staged Abbey, 16 Apr 1928
         Maddermarket Norwich, 1 Dec 1930

         Rout   FC 31 Jan
         M. Bliss
         Bk. (based on poem by Ernst Toller, trans. Ashley Dukes)
         D. NdV and group of 5 f.
         Vivienne Bennett (speaker)
         staged ACA studio, 22 Jan 1928 (7 f.)
         Royal Court Theatre, ACA 26 Nov 1928
         Abbey, 22 Apr 1929

1927	Association of Operatic Dancing, Crane Hall Liverpool 23 Oct 1931 Royal Theatre, Copenhagen (The English Ballet Company), 24 Sep 1932 SW 3 Jan 1933 Gala, Cambridge Theatre, 4 May 1936	FC 31 Oct

Russian Peasant (Dance of the Peasant) (solo)   FC 31 Oct
M. Trad. (also credited Liadov)
D. NdV
staged Abbey 30 Jan 1928
Royal Court Theatre ACA, 26 Nov 1928

1928	*Pastoral* M. Schubert D. Cepta Cullen, Doreen Cuthbert (This is possibly the same as *Idyll*, 24 Sep 1928)	Abbey 30 Jan

Venetian Suite (*Scène Vénitienne*)   Abbey 30 Jan
M. Respighi
C. (1) Rosalind Patrick
    (2) Kathleen Dillon
D. NdV (The Romantic Lady), Vivienne Bennett (The
Sophisticated Lady), Marie Nielson, Freda Bamford (Two
Unsophisticated Ladies), Eileen Murray (The Minstrel)
staged at Sunshine Matinee, Apollo Theatre, 10 July 1928
revised version staged Royal Court Theatre, ACA, 26 Nov
1928, addition of Nadina Newhouse, (A Black Page)

The Awakening (solo)   Abbey 16 Apr
M. Ravel
D. Marie Nielson

Les Bouffons   Abbey 16 Apr
M. Liadov
C. Freda Bamford
D. Sara Patrick and group of 5 f.
(leading solo sometimes given on its own)
staged Sunshine Matinee, Apollo Theatre 10 July 1928
Royal Court Theatre, ACA 26 Nov 1928
FC, 4 Feb 1929

Rituelle de feu   Abbey 16 Apr
M. Falla
D. NdV (The Maiden), 6f.

Serenade (solo)   Abbey 16 Apr
M. Boccherini
D. NdV
staged Maddermarket Norwich, 1 Dec 1930 V/SW Op Blt,
Bournemouth Pavilion, 29 Dec 1930
OV 14 Jan 1931

Silhouette   Abbey 16 Apr
M. Grieg
D. Cepta Cullen, Doreen Cuthbert, Toni Repetto-Butler

Thème Classique   Abbey 16 Apr
M. Chopin
D. NdV (leader) and 6 f.
(This is probably the same as *Les Sylphides* given at the
Abbey Theatre, 14 May 1929)

1928   *The Faun*   Abbey 24 Sep
        M. Harold R. White (on 3 Irish airs)
        C. Rosalind Patrick
        D. NdV (Leading Shade), Arthur Hamilton (The Faun),
        Elves (5 f. 1 m.) Shades (6 f.)
        (This ballet is not to be confused with *The Faun/The
        Picnic/The Satyr* with music by R. Vaughan Williams)

        Idyll   Abbey 24 Sep
        M. Schubert
        D. Doreen Cuthbert, Cepta Cullen
        (This is possibly the same as *Pastoral*, 30 Jan 1928)

        Nobodye's Jigg (solo)   Royal Court Theatre
        M. Richard Farnaby (from Fitzwilliam Virginal Book)   (ACA) 26 Nov
        C. Hedley Briggs
        D. Hedley Briggs

        Peter Pan Suite   Royal Court Theatre
        (pantomime scene)   (ACA) 26 Nov
        M. William Alwyn
        C. Joyce Peters
        D. Marley Bell (Peter), Pamela Twells (Wendy), Grania
        Guinness (Tinker Bell), Peggy Mellis (Captain Hook)

        Scène de ballet   Royal Court Theatre
        M. Gluck   (ACA) 26 Nov
        C. Kathleen Dillon
        D. NdV, Stanley Judson (pdd), Ursula Moreton, Molly
        Lake, Stanley Judson (pdt), NdV and 3 f. (pdq)
        Pdd only staged V/SW Op Blt, Bournemouth Pavilion 29
        Dec 1930

        The Scorpions of Ysit   Royal Court Theatre
        (from a dance drama by Terence Gray)   (ACA) 26 Nov
        M. (1) Elsie Hamilton (with chanting)
        (2) Gavin Gordon
        C. (1) Kathleen Dillon
        SC. (2) Sophie Fedorovitch
        D. (1) Letty Littlewood (Ysit), Ursula Moreton (1st Marsh
        Woman), Hedley Briggs (Tefen), Anne Coventry (2nd
        Marsh Woman), Scorpions 5 f.
        Jessie McDonagh (harp)
        revised version staged SW 15 Nov 1932
        D. Beatrice Appleyard (Ysit), Ursula Moreton (1st Marsh
        Woman), Freda Bamford (Tefen), Phyllis Worthington
        (2nd Marsh Woman), Scorpions 6 f.

        Les Trois Graces   Royal Court Theatre
        M. Stravinsky   (ACA) 26 Nov
        C. NdV
        D. NdV, Molly Lake, Ursula Moreton

        Les Petits Riens   OV 13 Dec
        M. Mozart arr. Lambert
        S. Doria Paston
        C. O. P. Smyth
        D. NdV (Rosalind), Stanley Judson (Corydon), Ursula
        Moreton (Clymene) Hedley Briggs (Tircis) Cupids 2 f.
        Shepherdesses 8
        staged FC 20 May 1929
        Charity matinee Kingston 1929
        Lyric Hammersmith, 28 March 1930

                                    344

1929	*Danse Profane*
	M. Debussy
	C. and masks. Hedley Briggs
	D. NdV, Hedley Briggs
	(This may have been a study for the later ballet *Danse*
	Sacrée et Danse Profane 19 Oct 1930

1929   *Danse Profane*   FC 4 Feb
M. Debussy
C. and masks. Hedley Briggs
D. NdV, Hedley Briggs
(This may have been a study for the later ballet *Danse Sacrée et Danse Profane* 19 Oct 1930

Polka   FC 4 Feb
M. J. Strauss
C. Hedley Briggs
D. NdV, Hedley Briggs
staged Abbey, 13 Aug 1929
V/SW Op Blt, Bournemouth Pavilion, 29 Dec 1930

Jack and Jill   Abbey 22 April
M. none cited
D. Eileen Kane, Toni Repetto-Butler
(This may have been revised for inclusion in *Nursery Suite*, 19 March 1932)

Turkish Ballet Suite   Abbey 22 April
M. none cited
D. group of f.

The Picnic   OV 9 May
M. R. Vaughan Williams (*Charterhouse Suite*)
SC. Hedley Briggs
D. Ursula Moreton (a Nymph), Harold Turner (a Satyr),
Molly Lake (Phoebe), Stanley Judson (Colin) Dryads 4 f.,
Phoebe's friends 6 f.
staged FC, 17 Feb 1930
Lyric Theatre Hammersmith, 28 March 1930
Sunshine Matinee, New Scala Theatre, 8 July 1930
V/SW Op Blt, Bournemouth Pavilion, 29 Dec 1930
(Alternative titles were *The Satyr* (17 Feb 1930) and *The Faun* (29 Dec 1930). The versions differed in choreographic detail as well as nomenclature)

Les Sylphides   Abbey 14 May
M. Chopin
D. 6 f.
(This is probably the same as *Thème Classique*, Abbey, 16 April 1928)

Hommage aux belles viennoises   Gaiety Theatre,
M. Schubert arr. Norman Franklin   Association of Operatic
SC. (1) O. P. Smyth   Dancing,
       (2) Nancy Allen   4 July
D. NdV, Stanley Judson (mazurka pdd), Eileen Baker,
Sheila McCarthy, Walter Gore (Tyrolese), pdq f. Pas de 8, f.
staged OV, 19 Dec 1929
Royal Theatre, Copenhagen (The English Ballet Company) 24 Sep 1932
revived with new designs SW 5 Oct 1932
Liverpool Ballet Club, 13 May 1938
(The Tyrolese was given separately in divt programmes)

Fighting the Waves
(ballet play by W. B. Yeats)
M. George Anthiel
C. and curtain. D. Travers-Smith

345

| 1929 | Masks. Hildo Krop | Abbey 13 Aug |

1929   Masks. Hildo Krop   Abbey 13 Aug
D. and actors. Michael J. Dolan (Cuchulain), Meriel
Moore (Emer), Shelah Richards (Eithne Inguba), NdV
(Fand), J. Stevenson (Singer), Hedley Briggs (Ghost of
Cuchulain), Waves 6 f.
staged Lyric Theatre Hammersmith, 28 March 1930

Pavane   Abbey 13 Aug
M. not cited
D. Margaret Horgan, Doreen Cuthbert, Mariequita
Langton
(This may be the dance to music by Fauré included in the
Lopokova group prog. 23 Oct 1922 at the London
Coliseum)

Tambourine   Abbey 13 Aug
M. Manlio de Veroli
D. Chris Sheehan, May Kiernan
staged Maddermarket Norwich, 1 Dec 1930 FC, 17 Feb
1930
V/SW Op Blt, Bournemouth Pavilion, 29 Dec 1930
OV, 14 Jan 1931

Waltz   Abbey 13 Aug
M. J. Strauss
D. group of 3/4 f.
staged FC 17 Feb 1930
(This was possibly included in 1921 programme)

Etude   OV 19 Dec
M. Debussy
D. Ursula Moreton, Joy Newton, Beatrice Appleyard
staged FC, 17 Feb 1930
Maddermarket Norwich, 1 Dec 1930
(This is probably the same as *En Bateau* (29 Dec 1930)
and *Pas de trois* (25 Sep 1932))

1930   *Fugue*   Faculty of Arts Gallery,
M. Bach (Fugue No. 5 in D major from The Well-tempered   ACA 22 Jan
Clavier)
D. Iris James, Joy Newton, Anne Coventry, Nadina
Newhouse
staged FC, 17 Feb 1930
Maddermarket Norwich, 1 Dec 1930

The Tryst (The Broken Tryst) (solo)   FC 17 Feb
M. William Alwyn
D. NdV
Staged Maddermarket, Norwich, 1 Dec 1930

Jeunes Paysannes   FC 17 Feb
M. Dunhill
D. Sheila McCarthy, Freda Bamford, Nadina Newhouse
staged V/SW Op Blt, Bournemouth Pavilion, 29 Dec 1930
OV, 14 Jan 1931
(This is probably the same as *Dance of the Three Peasants*
(10 Apr 1932). These are credited to NdV. However a trio
called *Jeunes Paysannes* was given at the Abbey 9 Feb 1931
and a solo *Jeune Paysanne* (Dunhill) on 19 Nov 1929,
both credited to Sara Patrick)

346

1930   *The Rake's Progress*   FC 17 Feb
        M. Poulenc
        D. Sheila McCarthy, Freda Bamford, Stanley Judson
        (This has no connection with the later ballet of the same
        title)

        Danse sacrée et danse profane   Cambridge Theatre,
        M. Debussy   Camargo Society 19 Oct
        C. and masks. Hedley Briggs
        D. Ursula Moreton and 4 f. (Danse sacrée) Sheila
        McCarthy and 4 f. (Danse profane) John Cockerill
        (harpist)
        staged OV 5 May 1931

        Fantasie Espagnole   Maddermarket,
        M. Moskovski   Norwich, 1 Dec
        D. Ursula Moreton, Iris James, Joy Newton
        staged V/SW Op Blt, Bournemouth Pavilion 29 Dec 1930

        Sunday Afternoon   Maddermarket,
        M. A. Somerville   Norwich, 1 Dec
        D. Sheila McCarthy, Freda Bamford
        staged V/SW Op Blt, Bournemouth Pavilion, 29 Dec 1930
        OV 14 Jan 1931

        Suite de danses (Suite of Dances)   OV 18 Dec
        M. Bach arr. E. Goossens
        SC. O. P. Smyth
        D. NdV (Bourrée, sarabande and gigue), Harold Turner
        (Gavotte, sarabande and gigue), Sheila McCarthy, Freda
        Bamford (Menuet and gigue) Iris James, Joy Newton,
        Beatrice Appleyard (Air on G String and gigue) Ursula
        Moreton, Harold Chapin (leaders of gigue) and 4 f.
        staged V/SW Op Blt, Bournemouth Pavilion, 29 Dec 1930
        (cut version) Abbey, 14 Feb 1931
        Air on G String and Sarabande staged separately in divts
        at the Abbey

        En Bateau   Bournemouth Pavilion
        M. Debussy   V/SW Op Blt 29 Dec
        D. Ursula Moreton, Joy Newton, Beatrice Appleyard
        (see *Etude*, 19 Dec 1929)

1931   *Cephalus and Procris*   Apollo Theatre,
        M. Grétry arr. Edwin Evans   Camargo Society 25 Jan
        Bk. NdV and E. Evans after Marmontel
        C. William Chappell
        S. black curtains
        D. Alicia Markova (Procris), Harold Turner (Cephalus),
        Prudence Hyman (Aurora). Attendants on Diana, 4 f.
        Attendants on Cephalus 4 m. Attendants on Aurora, 4 f.
        staged OV 21 May 1931

        Solitude (solo)   OV 4 Feb
        M. Debussy
        D. Ursula Moreton
        staged Abbey, 6 Dec 1931, when
        M. credited to Grieg

        Pas de trois classique   Abbey 9 Feb
        M. Tchaikovsky
        D. Jill Gregory, Eileen Kane, Toni Repetto-Butler

1931 *Russian Court Dance* (solo)   Abbey 9 Feb
    M. Zverkov
    D. NdV

    Carmen Ballet Suite   Abbey 14 Feb
    M. Bizet
    D. NdV and group of 6 f.
    (First given in prod. of opera, OV 5 Jan 1931)

    Fedelma   Abbey 14 Feb
    (mime ballet in 1 scene)
    M. William Alwyn
    C. D. Travers-Smith
    D. Doreen Cuthbert (Fedelma), Victor Wynburne (The
    Son of the King of Ireland), Nesta Brooking (The Hag),
    Doves 4 f. Ravens 3 m.
    staged Royal Court Theatre, Liverpool, Nov 1932 in
    Southern Murmurs

    The New Hat (solo)   Abbey 14 Feb
    M. Grieg
    D. Geraldine Byrne

    Once Upon A Time   Abbey 14 Feb
    M. none cited
    D. Jill Gregory (The Princess), Toni Repetto-Butler (The
    Prince), plus 1 f. 1 m.

    La Création du monde   Apollo Theatre,
    M. Milhaud   Camargo Society 26 Apr
    Bk. after Blaise Cendrars
    SC. and masks. Edward Wolfe
    D. Ursula Moreton (The Woman) Leslie French (The
    Man) Ivor Beddoes, Stanley Judson, Peter Fine, (The
    Gods) Animals 4 f., Trees 2 f., Plants 6 f.
    staged Royal Theatre, Copenhagen, (The English Ballet
    Company) 26 Sep 1932
    OV 30 Oct 1933
    revived without black make-up, SW 12 March 1935

    Faust scène de ballet   OV 5 May
    M. Gounod
    C. O. P. Smyth
    D. NdV, Stanley Judson (pdd), Marie Nielson, Sheila
    McCarthy, Freda Bamford (pdt) plus 8 f.
    (first given in prod. of opera, OV 9 March 1931)
    f. variation given Abbey, 10 Apr 1932

    The Jackdaw and the Pigeons   OV 5 May
    M. Hugh Bradford
    Bk NdV after Aesop
    SC. William Chappell
    D. NdV (The Jackdaw), Joy Newton, Beatrice Appleyard,
    Joan Day (Jackdaws), Pigeons 5 f.
    staged Camargo Society, Cambridge Theatre, 5 July 1931

Job
(a masque for dancing)
M. R. Vaughan Williams
Bk. devised by Geoffrey Keynes   Cambridge Theatre,
SC. (1) Gwen Raverat after William Blake   Camargo Society
Masks and wigs by Hedley Briggs   5 July
(2) John Piper after William Blake
D. Anton Dolin (Satan), Stanley Judson (Elihu). Job, His
Wife, Job's Spiritual Self, Daughters 3, Sons 7, Messengers
3 m. Comforters 3 m., War Pestilence & Famine 3 m.
Children of God 8 f., Sons of the Morning 4 f. added
1935, Wives 7
staged New Theatre, Oxford, for International Society for
Contemporary Music Festival 24 July 1931
OV 22 Sep 1931
Royal Theatre, Copenhagen (The English Ballet
Company) 25 Sep 1932
revived with Piper designs and lighting by Michael
Benthall, ROHCG, 20 May 1948
BBC televised a condensed version 11 Nov 1936

Fête Polonaise   SW 23 Nov
M. Glinka
SC. (1) O. P. Smyth
(2) Edmund Dulac
D. Phyllis Bedells, Stanley Judson (Adagio pdd and
variations), Pas de 6, f. (two soloists), Mazurka, 4 couples
arr. Judson
staged Camargo Society, Savoy Theatre, 29 Nov 1931 with
designs by Dulac. These were used by Vic-Wells Ballet
from 12 Feb 1935. From 17 April 1941 given with scenery
by William Chappell from 1940 prod. of *Coppélia* by SW
Ballet
staged Royal Theatre, Copenhagen (The English Ballet
Company) 28 Sep 1932

The Dreaming of the Bones   Abbey 6 Dec
(ballet play by W. B. Yeats)
M. J. F. Larchet
SC. none cited, poss. D. Travers-Smith
D. and actors. W. O'Gorman (The Young Man), J.
Stevenson (The Stranger), Nesta Brooking (The Girl),
Joseph O'Neill (The Singer), D. Browne (Flautist), Julia
Gray (Zither), Doreen Cuthbert (Drum)

He Loves Me, He Loves Me Not (solo)   Abbey 6 Dec
M. MacDowell
D. Eileen Kane
staged with M. by Gordon Jacob, Royal Theatre,
Copenhagen (The English Ballet Company), 25 Sep 1932

The Water Lily (solo)   Abbey 6 Dec
M. MacDowell
D. Muriel Kelly

351

1933   Bridegroom), Claude Newman (The Musician), Wise   SW 26 Sep
Virgins 6, Foolish Virgins 6, Angels 2 f.

1934   *The Haunted Ballroom*
M. Geoffrey Toye (and book)
SC. Motley
D. Robert Helpmann (The Master of Treginnis), Alicia
Markova (Alicia), Ursula Moreton (Ursula), Beatrice
Appleyard (Beatrice), William Chappell (The Stranger
Player), Freda Bamford (Young Treginnis), Butler,
Footmen 2, Shapes 11 f. 3 m.   SW 3 April
staged Liverpool Ballet Club, 21 Apr 1939
SW Theatre Ballet, 7 Jan 1947
London Festival Ballet, 1 Apr 1965 at New Theatre, Cardiff
Univ. of Cape Town Ballet, 1949
BBC TV 24 Feb 1958, prod. Christian Simpson

Bar aux Folies-bergère   Mercury Th. 15 May
M. Chabrier (Dix pièces pittoresques) arr. Lambert
SC. William Chappell (after Manet)
D. Alicia Markova (La Goulue), Frederick Ashton
(Valentin, garçon), Pearl Argyle (La fille au bar), Diana
Gould (Grille d'Egout), Mary Skeaping (Nini Patte en
l'air), Tamara Svetlova (Hirondelle), Mona Kimberley
(La Mome fromage), Oliver Reynolds (Le vieux
marcheur), William Chappell (Adolphe), Walter Gore
(Gustave), Susette Morfield (Servante)

The King of the Great Clock Tower   Abbey 30 July
(ballet play by W. B. Yeats)
M. Arthur Duff
C. D. Travers-Smith
Masks George Atkinson
D. and actors. F. J. McCormick (The King), NdV (The
Queen), Denis O'Dea (The Stranger), Robert Irwin (1st
musician), Joseph O'Neill (2nd musician)

The Jar   SW 9 Oct
M. Alfredo Casella
Bk. based on Pirandello
SC. William Chappell
D. Walter Gore (Zi Dima Lucasi), Robert Helpmann (Don
Lollo Zirafa), Beatrice Appleyard (Nela), Hermione
Darnborough (Village Beauty) William Chappell (Young
Man with Guitar) Claude Newman (Peasant), Young
peasants 4 f., H. Tree (Singer)

1935   *The Rake's Progress*   SW 20 May
M. Gavin Gordon
SC. Rex Whistler after Hogarth
(1946, false proscenium by Oliver Messel)
D. Walter Gore (The Rake), Alicia Markova (The
Betrayed Girl), Harold Turner (The Dancing Master and
The Gentleman with a Rope), Ursula Moreton (The
Dancer), William Chappell (The Friend). The Mother,
The Serving Girl, The Jockey, The Bravo, The
Hornblower, The Tailor, The Sailor, The Violinist, The
Card-player, The King, The Bishop, Ladies of the Town
5, Visitors 3 f.
revived after loss in Holland, New Theatre 27 Oct 1942
staged Royal Ballet touring co. 18 June 1952

Munich State Theatre of Opera and Ballet, 17 March 1956
Turkish State Ballet, 1961
Vienna State Opera Ballet, Apr 1964
Rome Opera Ballet, 1964
Royal Ballet School, 17 July 1967
CAPAB, Cape Town, 1971
Ballet van Vlaanderen, Antwerp, 1972
Zürich Opera Ballet, 1976
BBC TV, prod. Margaret Dale, Aug 1962
Channel 4 TV rehearsal & perf. beg. 27 Dec 1982

1936   *The Gods Go A-Begging*   SW 10 Jan
M. Handel arr. Beecham
SC. Hugh Stevenson
D. Pearl Argyle (A Serving Maid), William Chappell (A
Shepherd), Richard Ellis (Mercury), Ursula Moreton,
Robert Helpmann (Leading Nobles), Ailne Phillips, Mary
Honer (two serving maids), nobles, 4 f., 4 m. black lackeys
6 f.
staged Sadler's Wells Theatre Ballet, 10 June 1946
Royal Ballet School, 3 July 1972
London City Ballet, 7 Dec 1982
BBC TV 8 June 1938, prod. D. H. Munro

Barabau   SW 17 Apr
M. and text. V. Rieti
SC. Edward Burra
D. Harold Turner (Barabau), NdV (The Peasant Woman),
Frederick Ashton (Sergeant), Barabau's Servants 12 f.,
Soldiers 6 m. Chorus of singers
revised SW 22 Aug 1940

Music for Ballet   Cambridge Theatre Gala
M. Malcolm Sargent   4 May
D. Margot Fonteyn, Robert Helpmann and cdb

Prometheus   SW 13 Oct
M. Beethoven arr. Lambert
SC. John Banting
D. Robert Helpmann (Prometheus), Mary Honer (His
Wife), June Brae (The Other Woman), Harold Turner,
William Chappell (Friends), Children 7, Spirits of Fire,
Citizens 6 f. 7 m.

1937   *Checkmate (Echec et mat)*   Th. des Champs-Elysées,
M. Bliss   Paris 15 June
SC. E. McKnight Kauffer
(revised 1947)
D. June Brae (The Black Queen), Harold Turner (The
Red Knight), Robert Helpmann (The Red King), Pamela
May (The Red Queen), William Chappell (2nd Red
Knight), Alan Carter, Michael Somes (Black Knights),
Frederick Ashton, Alan Carter (The Two Players, later
called Love and Death). Bishops 2, Castles 4 m. Red
Pawns 8 f. Black Pawns 4 f. (later 8 f.)
staged first in UK at Theatre Royal, Newcastle 2 Sep 1937
SW 5 Oct 1937
revived after loss in Holland, ROHCG 18 Nov 1947
staged Royal Ballet touring company, Tokyo Festival Hall,
18 Apr 1961

1937	Vienna State Opera Ballet April 1964 Turkish State Ballet, 1964 Rome Opera Ballet, 1964 revived Sadler's Wells Royal Ballet, 1975 staged Royal Ballet School, 11 July 1979 The Australian Ballet, Sydney Opera House, 6 May 1986 BBC TV 8 May 1938, prod. D. H. Munro BBC TV 31 July 1963, prod. Margaret Dale Channel 4 TV rehearsals and perf. beg. 2 Jan 1984	Th. des Champs-Elysées, Paris 15 June
	Dance for Four Girls M. Elfentanz, Grieg, Bk. 1 op. 2 taught to RAD scholars and printed in RAD Gazette Aug 1937	Royal Academy of Dancing c. July
1938	*Le Roi nu (The Emperor's New Clothes)* M. Jean Françaix Bk. Serge Lifar after H. C. Andersen SC. Hedley Briggs D. Robert Helpmann (The Emperor), Pearl Argyle (The Empress), Harold Turner (her Lover), Claude Newman, Frederick Ashton, William Chappell (The Tailors), Margaret Bolam (The Child). Ministers 3, Serving Maids 3, Peasants 1 f. 1 m., Guards, Peasants, Pages	SW 7 Apr
1939	*Grande Fête de Ballet* M. various SC. Roger Furse D. Ruth French (Camargo), Molly Radcliffe (Guimard), Audrae Swayn (Allard), Travis Kemp (Dauberval), Wendy Toye (Fanny Elssler), Florence Read (Grisi), Patricia Sharpe (Cerito), Moyra Fraser (Grahn), Joan Burnett (Taglioni) NdV directed the whole programme. This *Grande Fête de Ballet* was repeated on 18 July 1939 at the Westminster Theatre in a programme by the RAD Production Club, when Alicia Markova, as Camargo, danced a new solo specially composed for her by de Valois	Royal Academy of Dancing Ball, Grosvenor House 8 June
1940	*The Prospect Before Us or Pity the Poor Dancers* M. William Boyce arr. Lambert Bk. An incident in the life of 18th century dancers as recorded in Eber's *History of the King's Theatre* SC. Roger Furse after Rowlandson D. Robert Helpmann (Mr O'Reilly), Claude Newman (Mr Taylor), Pamela May (Mlle Théodore), Frederick Ashton (Noverre), Alan Carter (Didelot), John Hart (Vestris), Margaret Dale (Cupid), Mary Honer (A Dancer). Mme Noverre Patrons, Ladies of the Ballet, Lawyers 3, Street Urchins Vestris and Didelot were combined for the 1941/42 season staged Sadler's Wells Theatre Ballet, 13 Feb 1951	SW 4 July
1941	*Orpheus and Eurydice* M. Gluck SC. Sophie Fedorovitch D. Robert Helpmann (Orpheus), Pamela May (Eurydice), Margot Fonteyn (Love), Mary Honer (Leader of the Furies), Julia Farron, John Hart (Peasants), Margaret Dale	New Theatre 28 May

354

1943	(leading child), Mourners, Furies, Blessed Spirits, Peasants, Singers 2 f.	New Theatre 28 May

| | *Le Lac des cygnes, Spanish Dance* | New Theatre Sep 7 |

M. Tchaikovsky
C. Leslie Hurry
D. Celia Franca, Palma Nye (in Act III of full production)

1943   *Promenade*   King's Theatre
M. Haydn arr. Edwin Evans (nos. 2 and 5 orch. Gordon   Edinburgh 25 Oct
Jacob)
SC. Hugh Stevenson
D. Gordon Hamilton (The Lepidopterist), Pauline
Clayden (Promenade), Beryl Grey, David Paltenghi
(Rendezvous pdd), Moira Shearer, Alexis Rassine, Ray
Powell (pdt), Merveilleuses 3 f. 1 m., Schoolmistress,
Schoolgirls 6, Peasants 6 and 2 leaders
staged Sadler's Wells Theatre Ballet 8 Apr 1946
(help acknowledged over Breton folk dances from Lieut
de Cadenet of the Fighting French Air Force and member
of the Association des Bretons de la France combattante)

1946   *The Sleeping Beauty, The Three Ivans*   ROHCG 20 Feb
M. Tchaikovsky
C. Oliver Messel
D. Harold Turner, Gordon Hamilton, Franklin White (in
Act III Scene III of full production

Dance of the Tumblers   SW 16 Dec
M. Rimsky-Korsakov
SC. Barbara Heseltine
D. 5 f., 5 m.
(This is from *The Snow Maiden*, given as a divt by SW
Theatre Ballet)

1950   *Don Quixote*   ROHCG 20 Feb
M. Roberto Gerhard
SC and curtains. Edward Burra
D. Robert Helpmann (Don Quixote), Margot Fonteyn
(Dulcinea/Aldonza), Alexander Grant (Sancho Panza),
Harold Turner (The Travelling Barber), Julia Farron (The
Lady Belerma), Pamela May (The Shepherdess), Alexis
Rassine (The Shepherd)
Housekeeper, Niece, Priest, Barber, Innkeeper, Oriana,
Angelica, Urganda, Amadis of Gaul, Orlando Furioso,
Palmeris of England, Durandarte, Montresinos, Wenches,
Muleteers, Mourning women, galley slaves, giants,
goatherds, cuadrilleros, attendants on Belerma

Keloglan Masali   Turkish State Ballet
M. Ulvi Cemal Erin (Bes Damla)   School Oct
D. Students of the School

1958   *Variation* (solo)   ROHCG Gala 27 March
M. Schumann arr. Robert Irving
D. Nadia Nerina

1962   *The Muses*   Royal Ballet School,
M. Arensky   opening of Waverley
D. group of 9 senior f. students of the Royal Ballet School   Studio 6 June
staged Coventry Cathedral 8 June 1962

1964   *Çeşmebaşi* (*At the Fountainhead*)   Turkish State Ballet
M. Ferit Tüzün (Anatolian Suite)

1966	*Sinfonietta* M. Nevit Kodalli D. Gülcan Tunccekic, Hüsnü Sunal	Turkish State Ballet 13 April
1966	*Swan Lake, Dance of the Fiancées* M. Tchaikovsky D. 6 f. (in Act III of full production)	Turkish State Ballet
1971	*Swan Lake, peasant dance in Act I* M. Tchaikovsky C. Leslie Hurry D. This dance was credited to NdV on programme but no dancer was named and the dance seems to have been omitted from the production. The first time a dancer was named (Suzanne Raymond) was on 27 Oct 1972	ROHCG 17 Feb
	The Sleeping Beauty, Garland Dance M. Tchaikovsky SC. O. Sengezer D. cdb (in Act I of full production)	Turkish State Ballet
1973	*The Wedding of Harlequin or Harlequin Revived* (with Ashton) NdV choreographed the mime scenes, character dances and Harlequinade	Felixstowe (Ballet for All) Oct

Appendix 3

Choreography in plays etc. and operas

Abbreviations

dances	arranged dances	pdd	pas de deux
chor.	choreography	cdb	corps de ballet
mvt	movement	divt	divertissement
OV	Old Vic	(P)	play
SW	Sadler's Wells	(O)	opera
FC	Festival Theatre Cambridge	M.	Music
Abbey	Abbey Theatre Dublin	D.	Dancers
All theatres are in London unless otherwise		m.	male dancers
stated		f.	female dancers
p.	production		

1926	Sep 27	*A Midsummer Night's Dream* (P) D. 11 f.	OV	Fairy Dances
	Nov 8	*The Tempest* (P)	OV	Dances in banquet and masque
	Nov 22	*The Oresteia of Aeschylus* (P) M. Donald Tovey and Gordon Jacob SC and masks. Terence Gray, Doria Paston & Michael Hampton D. Hedley Briggs and 6 f.	FC	Chorus mvt
	Dec 20	*Christmas Eve* (P) M. Dorothy Howell SC. John Garside	OV	Dances
1927	Jan 31	*On Baile's Strand* (p)	FC	Mvt
	Feb 28	*Love for Love* (P) M. Patrick Hughes	FC	Dances
	Apr 4	*The Dybbuk* (P) M. Hassidic by F. Staub	Royalty Theatre	Dance of the Beggars
	Sep 12	*The Taming of the Shrew* (P)	OV at Lyric Th. Hammersmith	Dances
	Oct 10	*The Oedipus Tyrannus of Sophocles* (P)	FC	Mvt
	Nov 7	*The Comedian* (P)	FC	Chorus mvt
	Nov 21	*Much Ado About Nothing* (P)	OV at Lyric Th. Hammersmith	Dances
	Nov 28	*A Florentine Irony* (P) D. Molly Lake	FC	Dance

1928	Feb 14	*Romeo and Juliet* (P)	OV	Dances
	Feb 20	*Richard III* (P)	FC	Mvt
	Mar 5	*The Knight of the Burning Pestle* (P)	FC	Dances
		M. arr. E. J. Dent and Bernard Ord		
		D. Anne Harker		
	Mar 12	*The Two Noble Kinsmen* (P)	OV	Wedding Masque
		D. 6 f. 6 m		
	May 7	*The Riding to Lithend* (P)	FC	Mvt
	June 4	*The Birds of Aristophanes* (P)	FC	Mvt
		M. Auric		
	Sep 8	*Love's Labour's Lost* (P)	OV	Dances
	Nov 12	*As You Like It* (P)	FC	Mvt
	Dec 3	*Adam's Opera* (P)	OV	Dances
		M. Richard Addinsell		
	Dec 3	*Marriage à la Mode* (P)	FC	Dances
1929	Feb 4	*The Prometheus of Aeschylus* (P)	FC	Chorus mvt
		M. Philip Cathie		
		D. Vivienne Bennett and 6 f.		
	Apr 8	*Henry VIII* (P)	OV	Dances
		D. 6 f. 6 m		
	Apr 19	*Beggar on Horseback* (P)	FC	Ballet
		M., SC. Hedley Briggs		
	June 3	*The Shoemaker's Holiday* (P)	FC	Dances
		D. Hedley Briggs		
	June 9	*Salome* (P)	FC	Dance of the
		D. Vivienne Bennett		seven veils
	Dec 24	*The Sleeping Beauty* (pantomime)	Drury Lane	Poss. dance for Marie Nielson
1930	Mar 28	*So Fair a Satrap* (P)	FC at Lyric Th. Hammersmith	mvt
1931	Jan 5	*Carmen* (O)	OV	ballet
		D. NdV and 6 f.		
		(see also Appendix 2)		
	Jan 7	*Faust* (O)	OV	dances
		D. 6 f.		
	Jan 8	*Aladdin* (pantomime)	FC	ballets and mvt
		M. Walter Leigh		Fairy Ballet and
		D. Prudence Hyman and cdb		Ballet of the Jewels
	Jan 9	*The Magic Flute* (O)	OV	dances
		D. 6 f.		
	Jan 14	*Il Trovatore* (O)	OV	dances
		D. 6 f.		
	Feb 9	*Henry VIII* (P)	FC	Mvt
	Feb 11	*Maritana* (O)	OV	dances
		D. 8 f.		
	Mar 2	*The Insect Play* (P)	FC	chor.

1931	Mar 2	*Aida* (O)	OV	ballet
		D. NdV (principal), Priestesses 8, Negro Boys 4 f.		
	Mar 9	*Faust* (O)	OV	scène de ballet
		D. NdV, Frederick Ashton (pdd), pas de trois, cdb 8 f.		
		(see also Appendix 2)		
	Mar 14	*The Lily of Killarney* (O)	OV	dances
		D. 4 f.		
	Apr 1	*The Marriage of Figaro* (O)	OV	dances
		D. 4 f.		
	Apr 9	*Tannhaüser* (O)	OV	dances
		D. 8 f.		
	Apr 20	*The Festival Revue* (revue)	FC	dances
	May 26	*The Antigone of Sophocles* (P)	FC	chorus mvt
		D. 5 f.		
	May 27	*Salome* (P)	Gate	dance of 7 veils
		M. Lambert		
		SC. John Armstrong		
		D. Margaret Rawlings		
	Sep 14	*Samson and Delilah* (O)	OV	dances
		D. NdV, Stanley Judson (pdd) Ursula Moreton, Marie Nielson, 8 Rose Maidens		
	Sep 19	*The Bohemian Girl* (O)	OV	dances
		D. 5 f.		
	Sep 21	*Rigoletto* (O)	OV	dances
		D. 4 f. 2 m.		
	Nov 6	*Dido and Aeneas* (O)	OV	dances & chorus mvt
		D. 6 f. 4 m.		
	Nov 16	*The Tales of Hoffmann* (O)	OV	dances
		D. 4 f.		
	Nov 19	*La Traviata* (O)	OV	dances
		D. NdV, Stanley Judson, Travis Kemp, 6 f.		
	Nov 23	*Salome* (P)	FC	dance of 7 veils
		M. Lambert		
		D. Beatrix Lehmann		
1932	Jan 4	*Bow Bells* (revue)	London Hippodrome	ballet
		Scene 3 Rainy Weather— "Love keeps out the rain"		
		M. Henry Sullivan		
		SC. Herman Rosse		
		D. Ruth Mackand, Harold Turner and cdb		
	Jan 27	*A Masked Ball* (O)	SW	dances
		D. 6 f.		
	Feb 25	*Mignon* (O)	SW	dances
		D. 6 f. 2 m.		
	Apr 2	*Don Giovanni* (O)	SW	dances
		D. 4 m. 4 f.		

1933	Feb 10	*The Force of Destiny* (O)	SW	dances
	Apr 12	*The Snow Maiden* (O) Stanley Judson and 4 m., 5 f. (Tumblers) Flowers 9 f. soloists, Trees 11 f., Birds 7 f. soloists	SW	dances
	June 21	*The Fantasticks* (P) D. Beatrice Appleyard, Peggy Melliss, Freda Bamford, Robert Helpmann, Travis Kemp, Guy Massey	Lyric Theatre Hammersmith repeated at Open Air, Regents Park	ballet
	Oct 11	*Tsar Saltan* (O) D. Robert Helpmann, Travis Kemp and 4 f.	SW	dances
	Nov 29	*Orpheus* (O) D. NdV, mourning women 4, Furies 4 m. 10 f. Blessed Spirits 10 f. Peasants	SW	dances
1934	Feb 28	*The Golden Toy* (musical play) M. Schumann SC. Rudolph Bamberger, Friedrich Winckler, René Hubert D. Wendy Toye and cdb	London Coliseum	dances and mvt
	June 14	*La Cenerentola* (O) D. Alicia Markova, Robert Helpmann and cdb	ROHCG	ballet
	Dec 12	*Eugene Onegin* (O)	SW	dances
1937	Dec 27	*A Midsummer Night's Dream* (P) (repeated Dec 26 1938)	OV	dances
1946		*The Snow Maiden* (O) Tumblers' Dance only D. Donald Britton and cdb (See also Appendix 2)	SW	dance
1948	Sep 29	*Aida* (O) D. Moyra Fraser and cdb	ROHCG	dances

Note on Sources

Books consulted in addition to those mentioned in Notes and References

Barker, Felix, *The House that Stoll Built*, Muller, 1957
Beaumont, C. W., *The Complete Book of Ballets*, Putnam, 1937
Bell, Anne Olivier (ed.), *The Diaries of Virginia Woolf,* Vol. III 1925–30, Hogarth, 1980
Bevan, Ian, *Top of the Bill*, Muller, 1952
Bland, Alexander, *The Royal Ballet 1931 to 1981*, Threshold Books, 1981
Bliss, Sir Arthur, *As I Remember*, Faber and Faber, 1970
Buckle, Richard, *Diaghilev*, Hamish Hamilton (paperback), 1986
Carpenter, Humphrey, *W. H. Auden*, George Allen & Unwin, 1981
Dolin, Sir Anton, *Divertissement; Ballet Go Round: Autobiography*, 1930, 1938, 1960
Dominic, Zoe, and John Selwyn Gilbert, *Frederick Ashton*, Harrap, 1971
Dorn, Karen, *Players and Painted Stage; the Theatre of W. B. Yeats*, Harvester Press, Sussex, and Barnes and Noble, 1984
Findlater, Richard, *Lilian Baylis*, Allen Lane, 1975
Goossens, Eugene, *Overture and Beginners*, Methuen, 1951
Haltrecht, Montague, *The Quiet Showman—Sir David Webster and The Royal Opera House*, Collins, 1975
Harewood, Lord, *The Tongs and the Bones*, Weidenfeld and Nicolson, 1981
Hones, Joseph, *W. B. Yeats 1865–1939*, Macmillan, 1967
Howard, Diana, *London Theatres and Music Halls 1850 to 1950*, Library Association, 1970
Hunt, Hugh, *The Abbey*, Gill and Macmillan, 1979
Jeffares, A. Norman, and A. S. Knowland, *A Commentary on the Collected Plays of W. B. Yeats*, Macmillan, 1975
Jefferson, Alan, *Sir Thomas Beecham*, Macdonald and Janes, 1979
Kennedy, Douglas, *English Folk Dancing*, G. Bell, 1964
Keynes, Milo (ed.) *Lydia Lopokova*, Weidenfeld and Nicolson, 1986
Knight, Freda, *Cambridge Music*, The Oleander Press, 1980
Macdonald, Malcolm, *John Foulds: His Life in Music*, Triad Press, 1975
Mackintosh, Iain, "The Festival Theatre Cambridge" in *Granta*, Nov 1968
MacLiámmoir, Michéal, *All for Hecuba*, Progress House, Dublin, 1961
Markova, Dame Alicia, DBE, *Markova Remembers*, Hamish Hamilton, 1986
Massine, Leonide (ed. Phyllis Hartnoll and Robert Rubens), *My Life in Ballet*, St Martin's Press, Macmillan, 1968
Medley, Robert, *Drawn from Life*, Faber and Faber, 1983
Moorehead, Caroline, *Sidney Bernstein*, Jonathan Cape, 1984
Morley, Sheridan, *A Talent to Amuse*, Pavilion, 1985
Morris, Margaret, *My Life in Movement*, Peter Owen, 1969
Motion, Andrew, *The Lamberts*, Chatto and Windus, 1986
Newton, H. Chance, *Idols of the "Halls"*, Heach Cranton, 1928
Percival, John, *Theatre in my Blood: A Biography of John Cranko*, The Herbert Press, 1983
Powell, Anthony, *Messengers of Day* (Vol. 2 of *To Keep the Ball Rolling*), Heinemann, 1978
Ridge, C. H., *Stage Lighting*, 1928

Robinson, Lennox, *Ireland's Abbey Theatre*, Sidgwick & Jackson, 1951

Rosenfeld, Sybil, *A Short History of Scene Design in Great Britain*, Blackwell, 1973

Rosenthal, Harold, *Two Centuries of Opera at Covent Garden*, Putnam, 1958

Scott, Harold, *The Early Doors*, E. P. Publishing, 1977

Seed, R. Alec, *The Sheffield Repertory Theatre*, published by the company, 1959

Shead, Richard, *Constant Lambert*, Simon Publications, 1973

Sidnell, Michael, *Dances of Death: The Group Theatre of London in the Thirties*, Faber and Faber, 1984

Spalding, Frances, *Vanessa Bell*, Weidenfeld and Nicolson, 1983

Taylor, Richard, *The Drama of W. B. Yeats: Irish Myth and Japanese No*, Yale University Press, 1976

Thorpe, Edward, *Kenneth MacMillan: The Man and the Ballets*, Hamish Hamilton, 1986

Trewin, J. C., *Shakespeare on the English Stage 1900–1964*, Barrie & Rockliff, 1964

Wheatcroft, Andrew (compiled by), *Dolin, Friends and Memories*, Routledge and Kegan Paul, 1982

White, Colin, *Edmund Dulac*, Studio Vista, 1976

Wilson, A. E., *Pantomime Pageant*, Stanley Paul, 1946

Index

Numerals in **bold** refer to illustrations